GREY MAIDEN

THE STORY OF A SWORD
THROUGH THE AGES,
THE COMPLETE SAGA

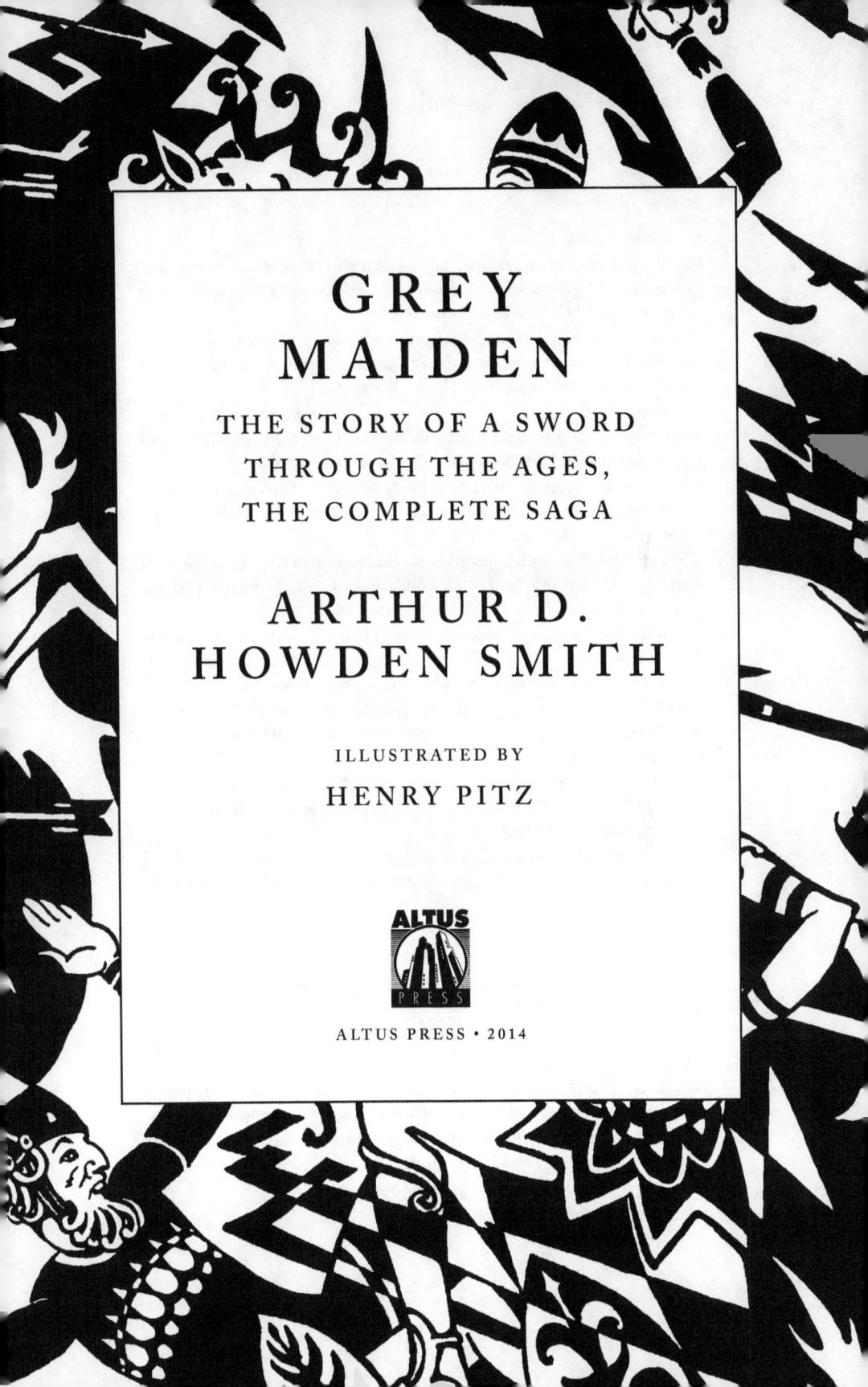

GREY MAIDEN

THE STORY OF A SWORD THROUGH THE AGES, THE COMPLETE SAGA

ARTHUR D. HOWDEN SMITH

ILLUSTRATED BY

HENRY PITZ

ALTUS PRESS • 2014

© 2014 Altus Press • First Edition—2014

EDITED AND DESIGNED BY

Matthew Moring

PUBLISHING HISTORY

"The Forging" originally appeared in the June 23, 1926 issue of *Adventure* magazine. Copyright 1926 by The Ridgway Company. Copyright renewed 1953 and assigned to Adventure Pulp LLC. All Rights Reserved.

"The Slave of Marathon" originally appeared in the July 23, 1926 issue of *Adventure* magazine. Copyright 1926 by The Ridgway Company. Copyright renewed 1953 and assigned to Adventure Pulp LLC. All Rights Reserved.

"A Trooper of the Thessalonians" originally appeared in the August 23, 1926 issue of *Adventure* magazine. Copyright 1926 by The Ridgway Company. Copyright renewed 1953 and assigned to Adventure Pulp LLC. All Rights Reserved.

"Hanno's Sword" originally appeared in the November 8, 1926 issue of *Adventure* magazine. Copyright 1926 by The Ridgway Company. Copyright renewed 1953 and assigned to Adventure Pulp LLC. All Rights Reserved.

"The Last Legion" originally appeared in the December 31, 1926 issue of *Adventure* magazine. Copyright 1926 by The Ridgway Company. Copyright renewed 1953 and assigned to Adventure Pulp LLC. All Rights Reserved.

"The Rider from the Desert" originally appeared in the February 15, 1927 issue of *Adventure* magazine. Copyright 1927 by The Ridgway Company. Copyright renewed 1954 and assigned to Adventure Pulp LLC. All Rights Reserved.

"Thord's Wooing" originally appeared in the April 15, 1927 issue of *Adventure* magazine. Copyright 1927 by The Ridgway Company. Copyright renewed 1954 and assigned to Adventure Pulp LLC. All Rights Reserved.

"The Gritti Luck" originally appeared in the June 15, 1927 issue of *Adventure* magazine. Copyright 1927 by The Ridgway Company. Copyright renewed 1954 and assigned to Adventure Pulp LLC. All Rights Reserved.

"A Statement for the Queenes Majestie" originally appeared in the hardcover edition of *Grey Maiden: The Story of a Sword Through the Ages.* Copyright 1929 by Arthur D. Howden Smith.

THANKS TO

Doug Ellis, Joel Frieman, Everard P. Digges LaTouche, Gerd Pircher, Rob Preston, Sai Shankar and Jonathan Sweet

THIS IS the story of the sword, Grey Maiden, and of a few of the mighty deeds wrought with it in the passage of the centuries. Forged in the dim beginnings of time, when men first discovered the resiliency of iron tempered with carbon, and made of the knowledge a magic and a mystery, it saw the rise of Greece, and the crowning of Alexander's fortunes; it was witness to the majesty and the decay of Rome; it led the rush of Islam. It knew the glories and the agonies of the Old World and the birth-pangs of the New. For generations it lay hidden in tomb or burial mound or hung in grim quietude upon the walls of armories. Yet often when men turned to war eager hands reached out for it, and its shining blade was bright in the van of battle. As some mediaeval owner scratched in the hard, grey steel:

> *Grey Maide men hail Mee*
> *Deathe doth Notte fail Mee*

The Arab scrambled to his feet and
struck again at the Roman.

TABLE OF CONTENTS

THE FORGING

"The King, himself, he led the way of his army, mighty at its head like a flame of fire, the King who wrought with his sword."
—inscription of Thutmose III, B. C. 1479.

I T WA S quiet as death in the lofty chamber. The sculptured friezes on the walls were not more motionless than the lean figure of the Pharaoh on his lonely throne and the slave girl who crouched against his knees. From afar came a mournful chanting of priests, and closer at hand the apartments of the palace gave forth a subdued, murmurous hum, like the buzzing of a beehive about to swarm. But in the throne room was only silence—a silence that smote the eardrums.

The Pharaoh's chin rested on one clinched fist; his thin lips were pressed tight; his eyes stared unseeingly at the carven scenes of his father's triumphs. The girl at his feet stole an upward glance from under the masses of her hair, and moved closer to him. And that lithe, rippling sway of her torso broke the spell that had bound the two. His free hand sought her cheek, and his voice echoed under the painted roof.

"You gave the message, Asta?"

"Yes, Lord."

"Yet he does not come! You spoke with the captain of the guard?"

Her almond eyes studied his stern features a second time.

"Yes, Lord," she murmured.

"Except you, whom can I trust?" he exclaimed fiercely. "But I shall find a way to tame these priests. By the splendor of Ra—"

The heavy curtains at the opposite end of the hall were thrust apart, and a tall man in priestly raiment entered, his stave of office ringing on the stone floor.

"The favor of Amon upon you, Lord of the Two Lands," he boomed. "Your servant comes—"

The Pharaoh's lips tightened; his body snapped erect.

"'Twas not you I sent for, Hapuseneb," he interrupted. "The guards were bidden to admit the General Thutiy."

"I ventured to counsel them to admit me, Lord, knowing the Pharaoh would never keep waiting the high priest of the god." Hapuseneb's square-jowled features were impassive, but his small eyes glittered with an angry light, as he strode toward the throne.

Thick-set, imperious in manner, resonant of voice, he moved as one accustomed to obedience.

"I am come to inform you of the ceremonies planned to achieve the honor of the sister-wife, whose death has burdened you with the task of fulfilling the requirements of the god. You, who have dwelt so long amongst priests, need not be instructed in the opportunities Amon has conferred upon you—"

The volcanic passion in the Pharaoh's face stemmed the tide of the high priest's eloquence.

"Stay!" The command rang out like a trumpet-blast. "The priests no longer rule in Thebes, Asta!"

The girl cowered away from the, throne, almost as if she expected to be struck.

"Bid the captain of the guard come in to me—and with him the General Thutiy."

She fled, and her master turned again upon Hapuseneb, whose haughty mien was still unwilted.

"In my father's time he ruled," the Pharaoh stormed on. "He ruled the Two Lands, and the priests served the temples. After, when my sister Habshepsut succeeded him, because she of his children only was of the untainted blood, you priests were swift to seize the chance to bend a woman to your purpose."

"It was we priests, Lord Thutmose, who advanced you to rule with your sister," interposed Hapuseneb.

"For your own ends," snarled the Pharaoh, "For a time you thought it would be easier to have a man puppet, instead of a woman. But when you learned I was loath to become a mere mouthpiece of the god—"

"Blasphemy!" cried the high priest, covering his ears.

"—you had me shorn of all power," Thutmose swept on, "You made me of no more account than the slave girl, Asta. For you knew, priest, that if I had a voice in the palace there would be an end to the flow of wealth that you sucked up out of every corner of the land. Yes, you sought to make Egypt a desert of temples and tombs—"

"Oh, blasphemy!" lamented the high priest again.

"—and the people you would have become builders and repairers of temples and tombs or servers of them. And this when the frontiers were crumbling, and the stranger peoples overrunning the countries my father conquered—my father and Pharaohs before him! I say you have much to answer for, Hapuseneb, and not the least is your insolence in countermanding my orders to my own guards."

Hapuseneb was purple with wrath and outraged pride.

"Lord Thutmose, you overstep the god's mercy," he stammered, "You—you speak wildly, without reason. Pharaoh though you are, you may not assail the righteousness of Amon, nor dare you deny the god his due of reverence and fitting service."

"Dare not!" The Pharaoh's bony height reared above the high priest as he bounded to his feet. "Beware, priest, you and I may come to a trial of strength, if you do not watch your tongue. But I will teach you what I intend. You shall learn through another's doom that when I say come, he I command must come, as when I say go, that man shall go promptly."

The high priest turned hastily on his heel at sound of a clank of metal behind him. Two men were following the slave girl Asta up the long room. One, Hapuseneb recognized as the captain of the king's guard in the anteroom without, the other was of sinewy middle-age, his skin tanned by the desert sun, his hands calloused by the reins of the war-chariots, his eyes peering hardily from between puckered lids. Both wore armor, but the guardsman's gear was spotless and shiny, as his skin was soft and smooth; the equipment of the second man was dinted and worn. The captain of the guard, too, had a look of concern on his face; the stranger swaggered after the slave girl as if he feared nobody.

The pair tramped up to the steps of the throne and sank to their knees with a final clash and stir, the guardsman shooting a glance of appeal at Hapuseneb, who, by now, had regained his ordinary impassivity.

"You are the General Thutiy?" Thutmose addressed the stranger.

"Yes, Lord."

"Stand, Thutiy. I have a task for you."

"I am accustomed to tasks, Lord," Thutiy answered bluntly. 'But I hope you will give me more means to accomplish it than we have had in recent campaigns."

For the first time the Pharaoh's lips twitched slightly.

"You need not fear," he reassured his general. "This task you may accomplish unaided."

"You are captain of my guard?" he challenged the other.

"Yes, Lord."

The man's voice quivered.

"I sent you an order that the General Thutiy, being fresh come from the land of Zahi, was to be admitted to me at once?"

"Yes, Lord."

"And the high priest, Hapuseneb, bade you disregard that order?"

"Lord, he said that there were matters of great moment you must be told before—"

"Said he so! And you disregarded my orders?"

The guardsman hesitated.

"Lord, I—the high priest—he—"

The Pharaoh stepped down from his throne.

"The Pharaoh rules the soldiers, not the priests," he said harshly. "I shall prove it to both—that there may be no mistake in future. Thutiy, your sword!"

The general drew the bronze blade, and offered it hilt first. Hapuseneb took a step forward.

"Lord Thutmose!" he protested. "The man but did as I—"

"And for that must he perish," rasped the Pharaoh.

He lifted the greenish blade above his head, and slashed downward at the base of the guardsman's neck. The man dropped without a cry, his spine broken, his head hanging by a shred; but the sword was bent and twisted on the upper edge of his corselet.

Thutmose cast the battered weapon on the floor.

"You shall have a new sword, Thutiy. But it is not a strong blade for a man to put his trust in."

The general shrugged his shoulders.

"Why, Lord Thutmose, it answered my needs. Any sword will bend under a shrewd blow."

"Not the sword I wield," said the Pharaoh.

"Asta!"

She wavered toward him.

"Bid in the slaves to carry out this carrion."

Hapuseneb hammered his stave upon the floor as he pushed himself in front of the frightened girl.

"This is an ill deed you have done, Lord," he said grimly.

"Do you think so?" questioned Thutmose. "I did it as Pharaoh, not as priest."

"Priest or Pharaoh, any man does ill who slays a servant who has not intended to offend him," persisted Hapuseneb. "It was I—"

"Yes, priest, and look well to it that you do not so offend me again," rebuked the Pharaoh. "I wish to be alone."

The high priest clutched his stave fast.

"This—this—Lord, in my temple did you serve for twenty-eight Niles! In all that time you showed no symptom of blasphemous intent or unwillingness to heed the god's commands. In all that time the god was honorably served. His temples waxed prosperous. His servants—"

"Waxed rich," concluded the Pharaoh, "But tell me this, Hapuseneb; what has it profited the god to have the lands overrun by stranger races?"

"Pay the god honor, and the lands shall be protected."

"Honor the god has had! By your own contention, Amon has been placated with out stint for twenty-eight Niles. With what result? The strangers are in Naharin, and the black people assail our garrisons in the south!"

"It may be that thereby Amon gives warning of greater afflictions if his service be reduced," fumed the high priest.

"It is a sorry warning," Thutmose seemed to grow as he stood there, frowning down on the high priest.

The long face became longer, the lean body lengthened out.

"Who will serve the god, who will build him temples, who will build new tombs for the dead, if the land is ravaged by the strangers? But enough! I must bid you be gone: I will talk privately with Thutiy."

The heavy jowls pendant on either side of Hapuseneb's jaw became a fiery red.

"I go, Lord Thutmose. You bid me, and I go. But going, I say to you, I, who am versed in the high mysteries, I, who am the mouthpiece of the god, I, whom the sister-wife delighted to honor, I, Hapuseneb, high priest of Amon, I say you set your feet upon a stony path. You would veil your eyes to make your blindness blinder. You would put your trust in a sword—"

"Ha, you have said it," exclaimed the Pharaoh. "Yes, I would put my trust in a sword. Too long have we put our trust in temple-building. I think a wise god will have his people strive for themselves betimes."

"A wise god!" The high priest tossed his arms aloft. "O Amon, heed him not. But I must go. I, Hapuseneb, am thrust forth from the Pharaoh's presence like a tax-collector who has shortened his accounts!"

And he whirled about, and stamped from the chamber.

"I gave you an errand, Asta," the Pharaoh reminded the slave girl in the gentle tone he reserved for her.

She started, a crimson glow spreading across her Semitic features, and sped after the high priest.

Thutmose turned to Thutiy.

"Everywhere around me are spies." There was a note of weariness in the Pharaoh's voice. "I can learn naught of what goes on in the land, save by chance, and what I have learned causes me great distress. It was for that reason I summoned you when I heard you were sending word to certain men in Thebes that the frontier must break before the strangers in another Nile."

"I sent such word also to you, Lord," replied the soldier.

"Hapuseneb must have kept it from me. Here in the Two Lands the high priest is become mightier than the Pharaoh. See what comes of having a woman Pharaoh. Always the priests have striven for power, but never have they possessed so much as under Habshepsut."

Thutiy nodded.

"That is what the people say. The Pharaoh and the sister-wife have given all to the temples."

"Blame me not, Thutiy! In the beginning there were three of us, for I had a brother, besides Habshepsut. The priests persuaded my father to name Habshepsut to succeed him, then they married us. I was cautious, and when she fell ill they put forward my brother and me. For five Niles we ruled jointly; but Habshepsut was always in the palace, and I dared not try to break free. It was well I did not, for she cast off the illness which had weakened her and resumed her rule. My brother died.

I—there were times I wished myself dead. I am an old man, Thutiy. See, there is gray in my hair. Twenty-eight Niles have I waited!"

"That is a long time, Lord," said the soldier uncomfortably. "I cry to Amon it be not too long."

The Pharaoh regarded him sharply.

"That is to be seen. Now, do you tell me your troubles."

"They are soon told, I have few men, and no money to pay those few. From all sides the strangers are hammering at us— the Shesu-Beduins—on their horses from the desert, myriads as dense as the sands; the Zahi Phoenicians—in their galleys, and on the land; the Khita-Hittites—and the Mittani— unnamed people from east of Euphrates—who come from beyond the sky and are powerful men of war. Everywhere the word has been carried that the Pharaoh weakens. All the Fe-buku-Asiatics—are mustering against us."

"Have you prayed to Amon?" demanded Thutmose sarcastically. "Have you offered fitting gifts?"

Thutiy rubbed his chin thoughtfully.

"We have made prayers, Lord. As for the gifts, there has been scant plunder on the frontier."

"So the god has abandoned you?" sneered the Pharaoh.

The soldier became articulate again.

"I am no priest to say why the god shows favor or disfavor. But I know that men who should be on the frontiers are building for the priests, and funds we should have to keep back the Fehuku and the black folk are spent the same way."

The Pharaoh eyed him with a certain cold respect.

"I have never had much to do with soldiers," he said. "Are they all like you?"

"I do not know, Lord," rejoined Thutiy. "Those in Thebes like that—" he jerked a thumb at the corpse of the guardsman, which still bloodied the steps of the throne —"are of a piece with the priests. They are not real soldiers. Curtain-holders I call them. The men on the frontier are a different breed. They eat little, and labor hard, and die soon. Their clothes are dirty, and their skins are black. They grumble when they are not fighting, and they grumble more when they are."

He grinned.

"But they do not talk as that priest did about leaving the god to defend the land. They go out and fight with such swords as you bent her, and some of the strangers, the Zahi and the Khita, have better weapons than we make, Lord. Ah, they are master smiths!"

"Can we defeat these strangers, with their better weapons?" asked Thutmose eagerly.

"Why not, Lord Thutmose? All that is required is a man and a sharp sword. Let such a man curb the priests until they adjust their demands to what the land can afford, and there will be soldiers to follow his sword to conquest. But he must be a man of men, Lord, one to wield a sword as you did on this dog who lies dead beside us."

The Pharaoh's hand clinched until the knuckles showed white.

"I like the feel of a sword," he said hungrily, "Yes, we must find a way to make the land safe. So do you bide in Thebes, Thutiy. I have much to accomplish, who can reckon upon the loyalty of one soldier and a slave girl—I, who hold in my hands the shadow of the scepter Hapuseneb holds! But perhaps we shall find a god with open ears to our needs, if we pray loud enough. Or perhaps we may hew ourselves a path."

He snatched up the crooked blade at his feet.

"Ah, gods of the underworld—Amon or Aten or Baal or Ashtoreth or Yahoveh, whichever will aid me—grant me a sword that will not bend in my hand! No more I ask of you."

II

THE HIGH priest dropped the papyrus he had been scanning,

"If this continues there will not be one stone capping another in any temple of the Two Lands," he exclaimed bitterly. "Everywhere the Pharaoh drains our workmen from us. All the funds he took to the weapon-makers. Ah, I should have bidden one with a sure hand make away with Thutiy when first he came to Thebes. But perhaps it is not yet too late to quench this fire of heresy in the palace. Tell me, Asta, what does Thutmose talk of these days?"

"Always the same thing," she answered sullenly. "When he is with Thutiy it is of men and chariots and horses and weapons and of how the desert shall be passed and the strength of towns."

"Naught else?"

She considered.

"Yes, he is forever asking Thutiy to bring him a sword which will not bend. He has a block of cedar, and on it he tries each blade."

Hapuseneb's eyes kindled with a light of inspiration.

"And they all bend to the stroke?"

"All, O Hapuseneb. The bronze is not forged in Thebes can support the vigor of the Pharaoh's arm and the thickness of the cedar."

The high priest rose from his chair, and strode up and down the room, immersed in thought.

"Yes, that is the way," he decided at last. "If I can not shortly convict him of heresy against the god he will become greater than I, the lands will be plunged in war and the temples will be empty of offerings."

He came to an abrupt halt.

"Look you, girl, men say that some of your wise men are at once wizards of great power and smiths who handle a metal which can shear through bronze as bronze hews flesh."

"It is so," she conceded.

"Is there one such in Thebes?"

Her heavy-lidded gaze surveyed him inscrutably.

"None is mightier in the sight of Baal than Sutekh, who dwells in the street of the goldsmiths."

"And can he work in this hard metal?" pressed Hapuseneb.

"He has the secret of the gray strength, which comes from beyond the country of the Mittani, from beyond the rising-place of the sun."

"Oh, Amon, be thine the glory!" The high priest's voice rang with exultation. "Go to the Pharaoh, Asta, put in his thought the plan to sample Sutekh's sorcery. And I will catch him in the act of his heresy. Yes, I will come upon him as he blasphemes, and I will make his name a shame and a mockery throughout the Two Lands. He shall be denied the rites of sepulcher. He shall be consigned to the outer darkness. The farther world shall be barred to him. He shall never tarry in the west where dwell the folk who have received the god's favor. He shall be no more than a handful of dust scattered in the winds that blow out of the red land."

But Asta tarried as if she had not heard him.

"And what reward shall I reap?" she asked.

He waved her away.

"Do as I have bidden you, and you shall have what you will."

She left him softly, her sandals whispering over the stone floor. Her long, black hair hung down to the kilt which was her only garment, and under the veil of her locks her face was convulsed with passion.

"Fat pig!" she muttered. "You, too, shall die on Baal's altar. Out of the land of Zahi shall blow a flame which will devour you, and the courts of Amon shall be buried under the sacrifice. Yes, high priest and Pharaoh together!"

She walked swiftly through the long corridors and hallways, crossed a courtyard and entered the section of the palace reserved for the Pharaoh's accommodation. None of the guards or chamberlains ventured to halt her, for she had access where no other might pass. Men might whisper behind cupped palms, as her slender figure flitted betwixt the pylons.

"Asta, the Pharaoh's slave girl! She has come from the high priest." But he who was addressed would answer curtly:

"Psst, you fool! What she does is of no concern to us. Would you have Pharaoh or priest lusting for your death?"

When she came to the great, bare throne room, where Thutmose sat in lonely state, frowning gloomily at a twisted sword that lay across his knees, she tossed back her hair and ran forward with short, quick steps, as if, having been long gone, she could not regain his company too soon.

"My lord is unhappy again," she murmured, dropping at his feet, her warm body nestling lithely against his knees.

"I can not find a sword which will serve me as I wish, Asta," he said. "This one Thutiy had forged for me—yet behold it! Flesh it will cut, I doubt not, but a bone might turn it. I do not wonder our soldiers slay more with the point than with the edge—and that the spear is a mightier weapon than the sword."

She drew closer to him, and locked fingers around the wrist of his sword-hand.

"Would you be happy with a sword which did not bend to your stroke, Lord?"

Her voice was shy, gentle as a child's.

"Not otherwise shall I ever find happiness," he groaned. "For I have a feeling that one who is temple-bred requires a sharp sword to master his foemen. And how shall a man fight confidently, knowing his blade will twist in his hand?"

"I know of one could forge you a blade of the gray strength," she offered, lifting to him eyes that glowed mistily. "It is a secret of my people, known only to the mightiest of our wizards, but—"

"Do you mean the blades that the Khita and the Mittani carry?" he interrupted eagerly. "Those of which Thutiy has told me?"

"Yes, Lord. There are not many even in the stranger lands, but—"

"You know of one who could make me such a sword?" he cried, more impatient than ever. "Where is he, Asta? In Thebes?"

She lowered her head to conceal the triumph that flared up in her face.

"Yes, Lord. Sutekh the smith, who dwells in the street of the goldsmiths, is a wizard who holds the old powers."

The Pharaoh shuddered involuntarily.

"What god serves he?"

"Baal, Lord," she sighed. "If the priests came to know that you had used him, they would cry out that you had betrayed Amon, and—"

"Let them," Thutmose rasped hoarsely. "What has Amon done for me that I should hesitate to employ a wizard of Baal? Go, Asta, and bring Sutekh to me. See that he has whatever tools he requires, at once! Do you hear, girl? At once!"

She appeared to hesitate.

"But—but what of Thutiy, Lord Thutmose?"

"I have dispatched him on an errand without the city. But Thutiy is no craven priest. He is willing to accept a keen blade if he can find it, whether it was tempered in Baal's name or Amon's. You need have no fear of him! Nor of me. Amon is become greedy, and I am of a mind to make trial of Baal. If I can have of him the sword I seek— But go, Asta! Fetch me the smith."

III

"STAND, SUTEKH," commanded the Pharaoh. The smith straightened his sinewy body, and Thutmose was conscious of an instinctive revulsion against the cruel eyes and wide mouth as merciless as a crocodile's.

"I have been told you are a wizard," continued the Pharaoh.

"Men—and women—say that which comes into their minds, Lord," replied Sutekh.

"You have not answered me!"

"Who am I to boast, Lord Pharaoh?" rejoined Sutekh. "If you employ me, it maybe you will know better of your own knowledge how I am gifted than if I claimed what you were ill-disposed to credit."

Thutmose nodded.

"There is reason in what you say. I am told, too, that you are a smith, acquainted with the secret of the metal your people call the gray strength."

"That is true, Lord," Sutekh admitted composedly.

The Pharaoh curbed his anxiety. No ordinary man, this Baal-worshipper, who could meet the Pharaoh of the Two Lands face to face, and contrive to show independence without evidence of disrespect. Thutmose surveyed the thick, furry limbs, the matted barrel-chest, the big face and predatory nose and the spreading black beard that mingled with the curly body hair. Not a tall man, Sutekh yet gave an effect of towering stature. There radiated from him a sinister authority more impressive than Hapuseneb could achieve.

"I require a sword such as you can forge me," said the Pharaoh slowly: "No ordinary sword, Sutekh, but a sword of conquest, a sword which will not break in my hand, a sharp sword before which all peoples shall bow down and bend the knee."

The smith smiled evilly.

"A sharp sword I can forge you, Lord Pharaoh," he assented. "But if it is to possess greater powers than the metal contains I must have help from you."

"What help?"

"Two bodies—of man or woman—one you love and one you hate. A blade tempered in their bloods will triumph over any enemy."

Thutmose smiled wryly.

"One I love, and one I hate," he reflected. "Concerning one I hate, that would be easy, but I am poorly supplied with people I love, Smith. No, I will not ask of you this measure of wizardry. Forge me a sure sword of the gray strength, and I will be content"

He clapped his hands, and Asta glided through the outer

curtains of the chamber, peering covertly from Pharaoh to smith.

"You have your tools? Then it is my will that you begin your work. A place has been prepared for you, and this slave who guided you hither will fill whatever wants you make known to her."

IV

THE LAMPS made pools of light in the shadows; one by the throne and two by the portal which communicated with the anteroom.

The Pharaoh's tense figure appeared and disappeared with rhythmical precision as be strode from the folds of the door curtains to the steps of the throne and back again. Hands clasped behind him, now and then he inclined an ear toward the low doorway in the vast chambers rear wall through which came the monotonous rumor of the smith's efforts.

Cling—clang! Cling—clang! Sssss—ssss, sswooooish! as the bellows blew upon the flaming charcoal. Hissss—ssssissтst! as the molten metal was plunged in the tempering trough. Cling—clang! Cling—clang! again.

"He should soon be finished," Thutmose murmured abstractedly. "But I must be patient."

He laughed sardonically.

"Who can be more patient than I, who have waited twenty-eight Niles to be my own master!"

An echo of laughter, biting in its mockery, rolled from the curtains at his back. He spun upon his heel, startled, almost unmanned by the suddenness of it.

"Your pardon, Lord Pharaoh, but how comes it that you have not been your own master, you who can afford to flout the god in his temple and deal in the foul sorceries of stranger lands? Surely, one who is greater than Amon is master wherever he stands!"

Hapuseneb stepped from the curtains' folds, big-bodied,

proud and intolerant of face, radiating contempt, assured of himself. And beneath the bare white arm that held the high priest's ivory staff of office Thutmose had a glimpse of heavy lidded eyes that shone with a snaky malignance. Involuntarily the Pharaoh stooped forward.

"Asta!" he gasped. "You!"

She writhed out from the curtains, and fronted him silently, hatred vibrant in every muscle; and sick with revulsion he gave ground before her. He was appalled, his manhood tottering. Asta an enemy! Asta betraying him to the high priest! Asta, whom he had regarded as the one living soul who loved him, the one soul he had loved!

When she spoke it was to the high priest.

"Do you hear, O Hapuseneb?"

She raised her hand, and the Cling—clang! Cling—clang! of the smith beat upon the Pharaoh's brain.

"So!" exclaimed Hapuseneb. "The Pharaoh deserts Amon! It will not be Amon who suffers."

"Who shall say?" answered Asta in a voice Thutmose had never heard before. "A priest of Baal celebrates in the palace of the Pharaoh! Will Amon retain any honor henceforth?"

The high priest's heavy features became suffused with blood; he swung up his ivory staff as though he would strike the Pharaoh.

"Desecration," he gritted angrily. "Oh, what punishment shall suffice to atone for this!"

Cling—clang! Cling—clang! The hammer strokes resounded under the lofty roof, and Thutmose made as if to retreat from the high priest's wrath.

"There is no harm done," he expostulated. "I am having a sword forged, that is all."

"O tool of wickedness," boomed Hapuseneb, "of what use is it to add falsehood to your sins? I know what you would do! I know that within there you are harboring Sutekh, who is a priest of Baal, and who, by his unholy rites, propitiates the god he serves, to the despite of Amon. You forge a sword for the benefit of the stranger peoples, a sword to be put to our necks."

"It is the truth, O Hapuseneb," cried Asta with an irony the Pharaoh did not miss. "Loud shall the Fehuku acclaim that sword!"

Thutmose retreated behind his throne.

"I have done no wrong," he pleaded. "Come, Hapuseneb, you shall see. With your own eyes you shall see."

The high priest swept forward impulsively.

"By the splendor of Ra, that will I," he retorted. "And I will blast this Sutekh with a curse which will condemn him to the outermost darkness."

He caught from the Pharaoh's hand the curtain veiling the low door in the rear wall of the chamber, and followed Thutmose across a shallow anteroom. A reek of soot gagged him as they passed a second curtain into the chamber which was Sutekh's smithy. The high priest's ear ached from the clangor, his eyes smarted as he strove to peer through the swirling smoke and steam to where the smith labored, incredibly gigantic in the eerie light.

Beside Hapuseneb the Pharaoh rapidly surveyed the room. Midway was a stone trough heaped high with ruddy coals; a huge block of stone served for anvil, whereon the smith was pounding a hissing bar of metal; beyond the anvil was a second trough, into which Sutekh plunged the metal as Thutmose watched. The cloud of steam that responded was like a fog in which a man could scarcely see his hand in front of his face.

The Pharaoh leaped sidewise, and fastened one hand on Hapuseneb's fat neck; with the other he clutched a knot of the high priest's robe.

"O fool," he snarled. "You, who so dread sorcery, shall be the occasion of it. I am of a mind to see if Baal is not potent over so sorry a wretch as you."

Hapuseneb struggled feebly, and a choking cry escaped his

lips. The smith whirled around as he was about to pluck the cooling bar from the water trough.

"Who comes?" growled Sutekh.

"I, smith," replied the Pharaoh. "I am of a mind, after all, to try your sorcery. Therefore I bring you one I hate that the gray strength may be tempered in his blood."

A yell of laughter came from Sutekh.

"Baal calls you, Pharaoh? But what of one you love?"

"Be patient," answered Thutmose grimly: "I deliver one at a time."

"That is just," endorsed Sutekh, and staring closer through the smoke-clouds, "Will you have help?"

"No, if you will make ready for him."

The smith lifted the metal bar and buried it in the coals. From his leathern apron he drew a curved knife such as Thutmose had never seen—a gray, hollowed blade that was marked by innumerable bluish whorls.

"I am ready," he said. "Drag him here."

The high priest kicked and twisted, but Thutmose inexorably forced him across the blackened floor and pressed him to his knees, with his head over the edge of the trough on the right of the anvil.

"Ho, it was time," commented Sutekh. "I was running short of water. Lift his chin a little, Lord Pharaoh. So! You are new at this, but—"

The gray knife flashed, one bubbling cry—and the red blood foamed from the sagging corpse.

Sutekh propped his victim in place and reached for the glowing bar of metal which was to be the Pharaoh's sword.

"Now, you to your work, and I to mine," he exclaimed. "With the blood of hate, remember, I can achieve naught, unless it be followed by the blood of love."

He turned from the Pharaoh, and fell to pounding the bar so that the sparks flew up from the tortured metal. Cling—

clang! Cling—clang! He paused, laid down his hammer and seized the bar in a pair of pliers. Thutmose, watching fascinated, saw it flash, then drop into the red heart of the trough.

The metal sizzled, and an acrid, meaty odor permeated the humid air.

"Pour in your might, O hate," prayed Sutekh as he lifted the bar again.

Cling—clang! Cling—clang! went his hammer, and accompanying its beat his voice snarled out:

"Make the blade keen and terrible, O hate that was relentless unto death.

"Let the edge be without mercy, and the point as cruel as your purpose. Gift this sword with a rage which shall never know fear. Be ever hungry of life, O gray strength. May the flame of your wrath bear down all who oppose you. Temper the metal with—"

The Pharaoh remembered he had performed but half his vengeance. He tore his eyes from the savage spectacle, and brushed through the curtains into the anteroom. The far curtain over the door to his throne-room was stirring as he entered, and he ran to it, suspecting Asta's intent. Yes, he had been right. She must have spied upon him close enough to suspect the high priest's doom, for she was hurrying toward the stiff folds of the curtain which shut off the Pharaoh's apartments from the rest of the palace.

"Asta," he called.

She looked over one shoulder, ashen faced and trembling, then tried to run again; but he caught her short of the pylons of the portal.

"So you loved me, girl!"

She cowered before the cold cruelty of his tone.

"Yes, yes—always—suffer me—"

The torrent of his wrath swept on, unheeding.

"You loved me that you might tell my thoughts to the high

priest. Yes, and I believe you would have betrayed him, too, in time. False? You are all falsehood."

She fumbled with, groping hands at his fingers that were sunk deep in the flesh of her arms.

"You do not understand!" she gasped frantically, "Hapusen-eb—I—I—"

"Do you know now you shall repay me?" he went on as if she had not spoken. "This smith of yours will temper my sword in the blood of you whom I loved—and you, who would have betrayed me, shall guard my life in the gray strength's fabric!"

"No, no, no. I cannot die."

"Die?" His mirthless laugh echoed hollow in the vastness of the throne-room. "It is more than death I shall take from you. So long as I live you shall serve me, dead and forgotten though you be. Oh, I owe you much, Asta! You have taught me that only a fool would love. You have shown me how to obtain a sword which will triumph over all others—and you shall give me the blood of your veins to make the sword resistless!"

She sobbed and pleaded brokenly as he dragged her by the shadow of the throne.

"Sit with me, Lord—it was there I—my head against your knees—"

But he said no more to her. It was as if he did not hear her, and presently she ceased to struggle. With one hand clamped over her mouth, he carried her into the reeking smithy, where Sutekh hammered at the sword that glimmered on the anvil.

"Is this the one you love?" called the smith, craning his bull-neck as be tried to piece the eddying smoke. "A woman? That's well, Lord. My knife is by the other there. If you will slit her throat, I'll soon make an end of things. Careful! Don't waste a drop."

Thutmose flung his burden beside the high priest's body, and snatched the knife from the floor. She lay supine, eyes closed. For a moment his resolution weakened. He shuddered as he had when she told him of Sutekh's powers. That neck he had often caressed. Those eyes had lighted answering fires in his heart. And the recollection of her treachery nerved his shaking hand. The knife-blade crimsoned. Her muscles tautened, and went limp. He wiped the knife on a fold of the high priest's robe, and thrust it carefully into his belt. Sutekh had set the fire to roaring again, and the hammer beat its resonant accompaniment to the smith's prayer as the terrible odor of cooking blood mingled with the stench of the charcoal.

"Pour your vigor into this metal, O blood of the loved one! Let the sword thrill with affection. Nerve the blade with the valor of forgetfulness. Toughen the gray strength with the sacrifice that has been offered. Sharpen the point against all enemies. Speed the edge when it strikes. Let no weapon resist it. Let no brain outwit it. Be a staunch guard for him who holds the sword. Resistless is Baal, O love, and in Baal's name, I conjure you, fight always for the sword's master. O Baal! Great is Baal! Over all other gods is Baal."

The anvil-music died away, and the roaring of the fire became a crackling buzz. The smokeclouds eddied roof ward, and Sutekh's swart figure assumed its true proportions. The smith's face wore a derisive leer. In one gnarled fist he clutched the slim, gray shape of the new-forged sword.

"It is finished, Lord Pharaoh," he said tauntingly, "this wizard's sword that you would have wrought for you—all save the sharpening, which any hand can achieve."

Thutmose took a step toward him.

"Give it to me, Sutekh!"

But the smith put the sword behind him, and cast an inquiring glance at the door..

"Not so, Lord, "he denied. "There are other matters to be settled. My price, for one."

"Name your price," snapped Thutmose.

"As for those you await, they lie dead at your feet."

He stooped and turned the two ghastly faces so that the dim

light revealed them, and a hoarse scream was wrenched from the depths of the smith's chest.

"Asta! By the anger of Baal, you have slain her! Your head, Pharaoh, I will have your head!"

The smith heaved up the gray sword to strike, but Thutmose scooped a handful of the clotted blood in the tempering-trough, and dashed it in his eyes. He staggered, and in the instant of his hesitation the Pharaoh covered the narrow space between them and tore the rough blade from his hand.

"Your price!" mocked Thutmose, "Since you conspired with these others, smith, your price shall be their price—death!"

He plucked the curved knife from his belt and buried it to the hilt in Sutekh's side—and as the smith sank to his knees, the Pharaoh wound his fingers in the black mat of beard and hacked at the extended neck with the blunt edge of the sword.

"Cut, sword," he gasped. "Prove to me you can bite this wizard who made you. Cut! Cut!"

Slowly, the wavery edge bit into muscle and tissue, the spine cracked apart, the last shred of skin yielded. The dreadful trophy came free in the Pharaoh's hand.

Thutmose lifted it above his own head, and stared triumphantly at the starting eyeballs of the smith, then buried it with a gesture of contempt into the dying fire, which seethed up in a last gust of tempestuous life.

"So shall I conquer," cried Thutmose, "Hear me, gods, whatever men call you! By this sword shall I conquer—and no prayers shall stay me!"

The echoes answered him.

"Conquer! I! I! I! Conquer!"

V

THUTIY LOOKED doubtful
"But to divide the army, Lord Pharaoh!" he objected.

"If the Fehuku should come upon you with the mountains between us—"

"They will not come upon me," returned Thutmose. "It will be I who come upon them. They will be surprised, not I."

He leaned across the apron of his chariot, and pointed his long, gray sword—that blade which the Egyptians already called "the Pharaoh's handmaiden"—at the craggy summits of the Carmel range.

"Continue, Thutiy, by this road until the enemy know that you act upon it. They will be certain that you march on Taanach, and will draw their forces south from Megiddo. But so soon as your scouts report the Fehuku are coming into touch with them retreat and march after me. For I shall swing north and follow the direct road across the hills to Megiddo. The Fehuku will then be out of position, their men scattered all along the line of the hills, and they will come to battle with me weary and uneasy. I shall beat them, and when I have beaten them I shall take Megiddo—and once the fortress falls the Fehuku must flee beyond the Orontes."

"But, Lord, how if they overwhelm you before I arrive?"

"They can not overwhelm me. Now, go! Or I must find another general to execute my orders."

Thutiy bowed low in obedience.

"If another than you fathered this plan, Lord Pharaoh," he said sturdily, "I should believe the god had deserted him, but you—"

"No god can desert me," said Thutmose, smiling bleakly, "for no god aids me. I am sufficient to myself."

And the Pharaoh sat impassively in his chariot while his favorite commander led off nigh half his troops. Later, when the way was clear, he too, drew out of the road at the head of a second column, which included dense blocks of heavy-armed spearmen, hordes of light-footed archers and the naked black slingers of the deserts and sea isles, and hundreds of rattling, bumping war-chariots.

A day's march to the north, the Pharaoh's troops entered the road which wound across the hills to Megiddo, where his spies had discovered the final concentration of the Asiatic hosts that had rebounded from his initial blows. Secure behind the Carmel wall, they awaited his coming, intending to strike swiftly as he issued from whichever pass he followed and crumple his army by divisions; and it was to frustrate this plan of his enemies that he had devised the strategy of feinting against Taanach to mask his intended drive at the fortress of Megiddo. He would dislocate his opponents, draw them away from the mouth of the Megiddo pass and so gain time to lead forth his entire array before they could attack.

The second night the Pharaoh's army camped in the hills, lighting no fires lest they attract the attention of outlying detachments of the Fehuku; and the third day, late in the afternoon, they defiled from the pass Thutmose had chosen into the Plain of Esdraelon, taking up their battle position in a slope within clear view of the walls of Megiddo. Southward there was a great turmoil and din of marching men; the dust clouds obscured the sky, and all night long the Egyptians, lying in their ranks, could hear the noise of the army that was panting back from Taanach like a wearied beast.

Morning showed the plain black with the myriads of the Fehuku, and still the southern sky was dingy with the dust of the rearward columns, toiling up to be in time for the battle. The captains of thousands who clustered around the Pharaoh's chariot for their orders had frowns of foreboding on their faces, for they were greatly outnumbered, and a messenger had just brought word that Thutiy was a day's march distant in the pass. But there was no misgiving in the Pharaoh's face. His eyes shone with the zest of battle that men never ceased to wonder at, after his life of priestly tutoring; his lean body was tense with unleashed energy; his gray sword seemed a living flame; his voice was gruff and menacing.

"There is but the one order for all," be said. "We go forward—to victory."

An old officer of the heavy-armed spear men coughed apologetically.

"It would be safer to stand fast, Lord Pharaoh," he suggested. "This hillock would protect the right wing, and on the left—"

"Forward!" snarled Thutmose. By tomorrow Thutiy—"

The Pharaoh drove his sword deep in the man's chest.

"Forward!" he snarled. "That man who fears, I, myself shall slay."

And the captains of thousands hastened to their posts ready to dare all odds.

The battle opened with a rushing hiss of stones and arrows. The Egyptian spearmen, compact, rested, well drilled, bore down upon the disordered masses of the Fehuku and crashed deep into their array. When the foot were engaged, Thutmose led his chariots in a diagonal charge across the surface of the plain, slashing into the left flank of his enemies like a sickle leveling the ripe wheat. He cut a swathe to the front of his spearmen, easing the pressure of the superior numbers surrounding them, then dashed on and tore a gap through the mass of the Fehuku's right.

Tired, discouraged troops were unable to stand up to the thrust of that spearhead of disciplined horses, men and vehicles. Such chariots as the Asiatics mustered were incapacitated by the condition of the horses. Their light troops were already in flight; their heavy infantry were disintegrating—and the third charge of the Egyptian chariots rent them apart. The Plain of Esdraelon was swept by a torrent of fugitives, and weaving in and out of the frantic stream Thutmose laced the turf with heaps and windrows of corpses. Reddened sword in hand, his eyes roaming the fray for any lingering sign of opposition, the Pharaoh slew as long as an enemy remained in arms between the Carmel ridge and the flanks of Mount Gilboa.

There was plunder and booty for the humblest Egyptian soldier; there were long strings of captives to be herded to this building of the frontier stations by which Thutmose was making safe the Two Lands. Afterward, when Thutiy came up with his troops, footsore, dusty and disgusted to have missed the battle, they erected an earthen wall around Megiddo and starved it into submission. And then the Pharaoh marched on to the line of the Orontes, harrying the fragments of the Fehuku before him. That winter Egypt was again safe; her dominions and subject state were cleansed of foes; and the Pharaoh who had been a priest won the fearful admiration of his people as "the Pharaoh who wrought with his sword."

Men said it was strange that he would never suffer himself to be separated from his sword

The priests grumbled because he would spare so little attention for their ceremonies and was niggardly in his allowances for temple buildings; but few ever remonstrated with him, and those few died. And so he lived and reigned for a very long time—he was more than eighty when he was laid in his mummy-case—cruel, lonely, cynical of the regard of men and women; rather scornful toward all gods, a staunch defender of his country, the greatest of the Pharaohs and one of the first of the great conquerors.

The sword, which was called "Soft," was buried with him in his rock-tomb at Thebes, and he placed a stark and dreadful curse on whoever stole it from that place; but not even Thutmose could influence the destiny of the gray blade that Sutekh forged and Hapuseneb the high priest and Asta, the slave girl died to temper. It served him while he lived and was to serve others who came after him down through the stingy centuries of recorded time. Epochs were to come and pass before the secret of the gray strength became common to men, but nowhere did master smiths ever forge a sword more potent for good and ill.

THE SLAVE OF MARATHON

UPWARD WHITE tentacles of sea mist fluttered out from the dense bank that overlay the plain, spiralling up ward through the darkness along the mountain slopes. A charred glow in the east, beyond the invisible rim of the Ægean, was the first indication of the dawn. Closer at hand, in copse and grove and thicket, fires were crimson blobs against the green background of the foliage, and the men who crowded each circle of warmth were dim spectres, dwarfed and distorted by the tossing shadows and the twining ribbons of mist. It was very cold, a damp cold that pierced to the bone.

Glaucus squatted as close to his fire as he could come in the press of slaves, and gnawed diligently at the handful of raw onions and hunch of black bread which were the slaves ration. The slow grinding of their jaws sounded through the crackle of the flames and the sullen murmur of comment.

"By Hercules, this onion is rotten"— "Be content, Zike, the bread is also sour"— "Yes, yes, any food is good enough for slaves to fight on"— "Do you see the hoplites eating the dust from Antigonus bins!"

Glaucus scowled at the last speaker.

"Go to the War-ruler, and demand us a sheep," he sneered.

"No, no, it is you Callimachus consults," retorted the other.

Hoarse laughter applauded thrust and counter-thrust. It was interrupted by a hail from the lower hillside.

"Ho, Glaucus! The slave of Æschylus! Say to Glaucus that Giton summons him."

Glaucus stumbled to his feet, cramming the last crumb of bread and sliver of onion into his mouth, trampling his fellows right and left. He was a man of gigantic build, with a sour, resentful expression, and the slaves made way for him unprotesting.

"May the Furies tear his liver," he growled. "It seems I am to have two masters, Giton as well as Æschylus. A poet is no easy task-setter, but a freeman who cannot afford slaves of his own is worse."

The hail came again.

"Glaucus! Ho, Glaucus!"

"When the slave eats the master calls," quoted a wit.

Glaucus replied with a curse, and crashed down the slope, forcing his way between the cedars and pines that rose above the lower shrubbery. Steel glimmered ahead of him, a broad belt of cuirasses, and he halted on the flank of a detachment of hoplites leaning patiently on their spears.

"Ho, Giton!" he called softly.

"Is it you, Glaucus? Where is Æschylus?"

"How do I know?" the slave answered sulkily, as the thin figure of the freeman approached through the mist. "What madness is he up to now?"

"No madness," returned Giton, slinging shield to back. "We are to prepare for the battle."

"We shall all go to our deaths," exclaimed Glaucus. "Eleven thousand hoplites, and it may be thirteen thousand of us slingers and javelin-men—and against us more Persians than there are folk in Athens!"

"If all felt as you do, it might be so," rejoined the free man; "but the Persians can never stand against the hoplites."

"The hoplites!" echoed Glaucus. "It is all very well for them, with armor to protect them, but what of men like me, who must go naked?"

"I have no armor," said Giton.

"You have a shield and a helmet—and a sword. That is something. I have my sling and a knife."

The voice of Æschylus drawled quietly almost at the slave's elbow.

"Now, who would have thought you a coward, Glaucus, with that great body of yours?"

"I am not a coward," snapped the slave. "But I say it is nothing for men to go into battle armed as you are, while we slaves—"

"Can outrun us in retreat," derided his master. "But I did not come to listen to your woes. We are going down into the plain, a few of us, to determine if the Persians have cavalry in their camp and to make sure that the marshes on our right can not be crossed. Giton, you will see that Glaucus does not—ah—lose us in the mist."

"Lose you!" rumbled Glaucus as he fell in with the free man's little detachment of light-armed slaves. "It would serve you right if I was killed, and you had to buy a Libyan to replace me. I have a good mind to complain of you to the Archons. You never had a slave who could work as hard as I, and instead of appreciating me you must throw my life away!"

He turned to Giton.

"You are as crazy as any citizen of them all," he went on. "You were doing well at your carpentering until you came here to Marathon. I don't see what you expect to make out of it."

"I would have preferred to stay at my carpentering, but when the Persians landed what was a man to do?" countered Giton.

"Let the citizens fight," retorted Glaucus. "It is they who profit by wars."

"Are you sure? If the Persians conquer Athens my carpentering must suffer."

Glaucus snorted contemptuously.

"Yes, for you are a freeman. I suppose they might make a slave of you. But it would be no disadvantage to us, who already are slaves, to change masters."

"Are you sure?" the freeman challenged again. "Did you ever know one who had been a Persian slave?"

Glaucus became thoughtful.

"Yes, that is so," he acknowledged. "That fellow, Zike, was bought from a Tyrian, and he said he would rather be a slave in Athens than a freeman in Tyre. But he is always trying to say smart things!"

"A Persian slave who grumbled as you do would be slain." said Giton. "And as for beatings, you would live on them."

"Humph," grunted Glaucus. "Perhaps, but I still don't see what advantage you or I obtain by being killed to keep the Persians out of Athens."

Giton was silent for a while. The eastern sky was one vast sea of fire from the mountain tops, but the column down in the plain of Marathon moved in a shadow-world of mist. The clanking of the hoplites armor, the shuffling of feet, a few low-voiced orders, were as distinct as thunder claps in the quiet dimness.

"What is one man's life?" asked the freeman suddenly. "What are many men's lives—compared with the State?"

The slave regarded him, puzzled.

"Why, a man's life is—is—his life. It's the only one he can have."

"But how many men must die to make a city great!" persisted Giton. "Think, Glaucus! There is Æschylus, ahead of us. He writes poems that sweep all the people in the theatre out of themselves. He is a greater man than I. But he ventures his life without thinking that the city may be preserved."

"Yes, and he has a fine cuirass to preserve himself, and a helm and greaves," grumbled Glaucus, returning to his original complaint.

"He is a citizen, many men have lived and died to make him."

"True, and there were those who came before me did not sleep in the slaves quarters, but a slave I am."

"That is the fate the Gods send us. What the Gods offer,

man must accept. Yet it must be pleasing to them to see men live and die, thinking of others than themselves."

"If you do not think of yourself, who will?" demanded Glaucus.

"True," admitted Giton. "And if the City be not greater than any man, it is less than any man."

"What care I if it be less than man or greater?" parried the slave. "It means nothing to me."

"But does it?" argued Giton. "Without it, you might not be sure of food and clothing and a kind master and laws to make a slave's life easy."

"You may call my life easy," growled Glaucus, "but you are not a slave. As for what the City does for me, it sends me out here in a wool tunic, with a bag of stones, a sling and a knife, and if the Persians—"

A long-drawn, wailing cry came from the mist ahead of them, and the ranks of the hoplites clanked to a halt. Presently an order was whispered down the column:

"Giton's slaves are wanted up forward. Æschylus bids them hasten."

The score or two of slingers and javelin-men trotted along the brazen line to where Æschylus crouched behind a myrtle-bush, staring into the mist.

"Ho, is it you, Giton?" he murmured. "Have you that big slave of mine? Then heed me. The Persians have a heavy outlying force in front of their camp. That cry came from one of their sentries. It is my wish that your fellows should steal forward on the right, and take one of those sentries as soon as you have tested the morass under the foothills. Let Glaucus conduct your prisoner, but be sure to await taking him until you have tested the morass. Lose no time, for the sun will soon burn this mist away, and we dare not tarry in the plain, unsupported."

Giton's spare, bony figure straightened.

"It shall be done," he promised.

Æschylus rose, and gripped his hand.

"I would go with you, if I might; but you must be free to run, unhampered by armored men. It is for the City, Giton!"

The freeman's answer rang like a muted trumpet-blast.

"For the City!"

Glaucus smothered an exclamation of contempt. Citizen and freeman were equally foolish. Why, they spoke of the City as if stone walls were sacred as the very Gods!

II

THE WAILING cries of the Persian sentries sounded faint behind them as the little band crept through the mist that was beginning to turn ruddy overhead where the sun's rays smote level across the distant sea floor. The course they followed trended to the right, and soon brought them to the edge of the morass which ran inland from the shore to the base of the mountains, a mucky slough, impassable for men even as unencumbered as themselves. Satisfied of this, Giton ordered the detachment to swing back into the middle of the plain to undertake its second task.

The freeman prowled in advance, with Glaucus attending him. A javelin's cast behind these two shambled the rest of the slaves, as ardent as a herd of sheep. They crossed the shallow brook which bisected the valley's floor, and were creeping forward cautiously, when a vagrant wind-puff tore a lane in the mist-blanket, and there, in front of them, plainly visible, appeared the Persian camp, a narrow huddle of booths and tents, swarming with men and backed by hundreds of galleys and transports, some beached and more at anchor. Six miles it stretched from horn to horn of the curving bay. Nearer, indeed, a scant bowshot from them, was the outlying camp, which Datis, the Persian commander, had formed to guard against a surprise attack on his main force. One of its sentries stood leaning on his spear, so close that the watching Greeks could distinguish the pattern of his conical hat and long, quilted coat.

Glaucus wiggled excitedly.

*A giant officer in brazen mail, upholding
stiffly a lean, straight sword of grey steel.*

"I can take *him* for you, Giton! I'll knock him on the head with this stone. See!"

He lifted his sling.

"No, you would slay him," objected the freeman. "It is a live prisoner Æschylus must have. The *strategoi* would question him."

"I won't kill him," urged Glaucus. "That hat of his is padded like his coat. I'll strike him on it, and—"

He broke off, amazed at an extraordinary spectacle disclosed by another eddy in the mist. The outlying Persian camp projected past them, parallel with the course of the brook. The open area in the mist had widened abruptly, and revealed a considerable body of the long-skirted infantry arrayed in line, midway of them, facing the Greek position, a giant officer in brazen mail, upholding stiffly a lean, straight sword of grey steel. He was not brandishing the blade. Rather he appeared to be addressing it, and whatever he said, the soldiers at his back shouted a response.

"He prays to the sword," murmured Glaucus. "Gods, what a blade! Look to the sheen of it."

"I am more interested in that sentry you said you could stun for me," answered the freeman. "Show me your skill, and— Wait! Wait! What will you do?"

For the slave had risen to the straddled position of the slinger, and already was whirling his leathern weapon around his head.

"I am going to slay that Persian. He is a great man, Giton. Better to bring him down than a poor—"

"Hold," remonstrated the freeman, jumping up in dismay. "No, no, we can never take that man. He is a *strategos*, at least."

It was too late. The stone whirred away into the air, and the huge officer dropped with a crash of mail as it rapped his helm.

Giton wrung his hands.

"You fool!" he cried. "Now, we shall be discovered. Quick! At the sentry. No, wait—he sees us— Oh, go on, go on! Loose, fool, loose!"

The Persian officer was on his feet again, shaking his head

like an angry bull, grey sword flashing as he peered this way and that to discover his antagonist. The sentry, too, was staring up the brook, and shouted a shrill warning at sight of the two Greeks. But Glaucus, to do him justice, had a second stone in his sling, and launched it even as he grumbled at Giton's unreasonableness.

"You are never satisfied. I was of a mind to have that sword. It has the look of a stout blade. Not that a sword means anything to you, who have one. Well, there goes your sentry. Shall I take him?"

"Who else?" snapped Giton. "Be swift, and I will cover you."

For the collapse of the sentry had drawn the attention of the Persians in the outlying camp to the Greeks who lurked by the brook, and as the mists swirled together again a confused shouting echoed over the plain, and the dull thudding of sandalled feet.

III

GLAUCUS FOUND his victim without difficulty, ascertained the man's heart was beating and slung him lightly over one broad shoulder, then trotted back up the brook until a hail from Giton summoned him to the left side of the watercourse.

"We shall be lucky to get off," the freeman said unhappily. "The Persians have been as far as this, but something distracted them. I think they have been fighting the rest of our party; I heard men calling to one another in Greek."

"Oh, we shall get off," replied Glaucus, "If the Persians catch us you can carry this fellow I have on my shoulder, and I will teach them a lesson. Bah, you are fortunate to have me, Giton. I do not know what you would do elsewise."

"You do not!" observed Giton. "Suffer me to remind you that you require your wind to carry that sentry to Æschylus. I will make good your retreat."

The slave chuckled goodnaturedly.

"That is to be seen," he said. "Up to this point it is I who have pushed the fighting. Ho, Giton, two Persians have I struck down!"

"It would have been better had you struck down the one I bade you to," rasped Giton.

One of the vagrant breezes that blew out of the mountain heights snatched at the dissolving mists, robbing the Greeks of all protection. The surviving slaves of the detachment were safe under the spears of the clump of hoplites, and the horde of Persians who had pursued them turned with exultant howls and splashed into the brook to head off the pair with the prisoner, in advance of all the giant officer of the grey sword.

"Can you run faster?" panted Giton.

"Easily," boasted Glaucus. "But instead, do you take this fellow as I suggested, and I will have another try at Grey Sword over there."

The slave halted in his stride, fumbling for his sling with one hand while he balanced his captive with the other.

"Hurry," he urged petulantly. "I can't do everything."

But Giton faced him with eyes blazing.

"Slave," the freeman's voice was so cold that Glaucus involuntarily shivered, "what I bid you to do, that shall you do. Put up your sling, and run."

"But I can kill him this time."

"Run or I slay you as you stand!"

There was no uncertainty in Giton's grey eyes, and Glaucus ran; but the slave still had breath to spare for grumbling.

"Talking of slaying me, eh? You couldn't get someone else to slay me, so you might as well do it yourself. This is fine treatment for an honest slave! Yes, yes, we shall see what the Archons have to say of it."

"If you lose your prisoner, do not try to reach Æschylus," Giton answered grimly. "You would die as surely at his hand as at the hand of a Persian."

The freeman glanced back over his shoulder with a worried frown, for the Persians were gaining upon them; the officer of the grey sword was only a few spear lengths behind, his black bush of beard bristling savagely, his face convulsed with fury.

Giton measured the distance which was yet to be traversed to reach the protection of Æschylus's spears, and shook his head.

"It is too much," he said.

"Eh?" grunted the slave.

"I must stop and hold back that Persian," explained Giton. "You can never reach Æschylus before he overtakes us."

"Why does not Æschylus come out to aid us?" snapped Glaucus.

"His men are too few. Go on, Glaucus. Run like Pheidip-pides."

Glaucus looked back in his turn, and exclaimed in dismay.

"You can never stand up to that fellow! He is as big as I am—and mailed, besides."

A faint smile showed in Giton's face.

"That is probably true, but this is one of those times when the City is greater than a man's life."

He slackened pace, but the slave reached out a knotted arm and dragged him on.

"What? What's this?" growled Glaucus. "You are no fool, Giton. Hurry on with me. If he catches up, we'll turn on him together."

"And lose the prisoner." Giton twitched free of the other's grasp. "On what that fellow has to say depends whether the *strategoi* will decide for battle—and it may be that on their decision rests the fate of Athens."

The slave slackened his pace to match the freeman's.

"You'll be killed," he babbled. "That sword— Here, you take the prisoner."

"I am not strong enough to carry him. It is your part to run and live today, mine to die. We both fight for the City. The Gods speed you safe, Glaucus. Run!"

Glaucus bent his head dumbly, and ran. A moment later he heard the clatter of meeting blades, and Giton's voice, vibrant now with a triumph beyond victory:

"For the City! Back, Persian, back!"

The slave peered over his shoulder again. Giton was dripping blood, and his shield was split in two, but he hewed recklessly at the Persian, careless of his own body if he might only force his enemy to yield ground. Glaucus choked a sob. A sudden gift of vision oppressed him, and he saw, so clearly that it hurt him, the carpenter's tiny shop as it had looked when he visited it with errands from the house hold of Æschylus; the clean smell of the cedar planks, fresh hewn and stacked against the wall, mingled in his nostrils with the odor of the grease on the tools and the resinous perfume of the sawdust on the floor that was soft to his bare feet. Somewhere behind the shop he knew there was a wife, and he had heard a babe's plaint.

A roar from the Persian sped him on. He fled through the gap the waiting hoplites opened to him, and cast his burden at the feet of Æschylus.

"It was not right," he stammered hoarsely. "The Persian had a sword—they prayed to it—Giton was not big enough—I could have saved him."

His master's shrewd, satirical face, lofty with a loftiness Glaucus had never understood, was grooved with bitter lines.

"A man has but the one death to die," answered Æschylus. "Is it not well that he should be glad of an ending such as must rouse the applause of the Gods? One who dies like Giton is never forgotten."

"All for one prisoner," protested Glaucus.

"Who knows what may come of this prisoner?" returned his master. "Perhaps Hellas may be saved. Perhaps a slave's soul may be awakened. And I say again, Glaucus, a man who dies bravely never dies in vain."

The slave lifted a clenched fist.

"Then the Gods grant I may find that Persian, and slay him as Giton would not let me."

Æschylus eyed him curiously.

"When it is your task to slay him, I hope the Gods will show you their favor. Pick up this captive, and complete the task set you. Close ranks, hoplites. Quick march!"

I V

YESTERDAY GLAUCUS would have glared sulkily at the haughty bearing of the group of chiefs crowded about the prisoner and the interpreter who questioned him; he would have envied covertly their graven armor and splendid weapons. Now he gave them no thought. His mind was occupied with the shattered heap on the plain that had been Giton, and the Persian who had hacked the freeman to pieces with his terrible grey sword. He hungered for the order to battle. He would show Æschylus what a slave could do, unarmed, unarmored.

Then he heard the sword mentioned, and directed his attention to the interpreter's report.

"—they have no doubt of victory, for their principal leader possesses a magical sword, one forged in the beginning of time of a metal they call the Grey Strength, which has a peculiar virtue insuring its bearer against death by another blade. All mail is like a woollen cloak before its edge."

"If the Gods favor us, our enemies will require more than a magical sword," commented Miltiades, who had been chosen to command that day. "What of the morass?"

"The prisoner confirms the statement of this slave that it is impassable."

"Did you, yourself, try it, slave?" interrupted Miltiades.

"Yes," Glaucus answered gruffly. "Seeing I was the heaviest of those with him, Giton sent me in until I was mired above the knees."

"Good tidings!" exclaimed Miltiades. "But what of their horsemen?"

"The prisoner says the horses have all been sent to Euboea for pasturage," translated the interpreter.

"What of that, slave?" interposed Callimachus the Polemarch or War-ruler, who represented the Archons in the counsel of the *strategoi*. "Did you approach sufficiently close to see into the camp?"

"There are no horses in the camp," said Glaucus.

"But how can you be sure?" demanded one of the *strategoi* who were of the party opposed to giving battle, a man named Lysimachus. "They might be concealed."

"When a score of men come out from a tent, that is only large enough to house a score of men, there are no horses concealed in it," returned the slave contemptuously.

The *strategos* flushed.

"Your slave is free-spoken, Æschylus," he complained.

"He answered a question that was put to him, and with sense," spoke up Miltiades. "Thus it appears that we have not to fear the attack of the Persian horse if we bring on a battle. Also, that the plain is constricted in width by the morasses on either side—for I have already determined that the swamp on the left cannot be crossed. The sacrificial omens are propitious, and therefore I urge upon you all, as I have urged before, that we seize this last opportunity to strike for freedom."

"But if we wait until the full of the moon the Spartans will come to our aid," objected the *strategos* who had complained of Glaucus.

"And it is equally likely that the Persians may be reinforced," retorted Miltiades. "They may bring back their cavalry from Euboea. They may call in other forces. There are those in Athens who may be persuaded to make use of factional differences, and surrender the city by treachery."

No man answered him, but after an interval the War-ruler spoke.

"We have a serious decision to make. Let us vote upon it. Those of the *strategoi* who favor the advice of Miltiades stand with him; those who oppose him stand back."

There were ten of the *strategoi*, one for each of the tribes into which the Athenians were divided, and they separated five and five.

"Yours is the casting vote, Callimachus," said Miltiades.

The War-ruler assented gravely.

"It is a great responsibility you lay upon my shoulders, Athenians. If harm comes of what I say my name shall be accurst."

"And if you vote wisely, oh, Callimachus," cried Miltiades, "you will win for yourself an immortality of fame. For it rests with you either to enslave Athens or to assure her freedom. Never, since they were a people, have the Athenians been in such danger as they are at this moment. If they bow the knee to the Persians they will have set over them for masters the outcasts they have expelled from their midst. But if we fight, and are victorious, as I believe we can be, Athens has it in her to become the first city of Greece."

"Not so! No, no!" cried several of the chiefs opposing him.

And Lysimachus called to Miltiades direct:

"How can you advise us to fight when we number at the most eleven thousand hoplites? As for the light-armed troops, you are not so foolish as to reckon them. Nearly all are slaves like this fellow here."

He pointed to Glaucus, who stood with arms folded over his powerful chest a pace behind Æschylus.

"I struck down two Persians out there," growled the slave.

The *strategoi* regarded him in amazement, and Lysimachus reached for his sword, then shrugged his shoulders, and said curtly to Æschylus:

"After all, he is your slave. Slay him, yourself."

"Why should I?" inquired Æschylus. "He spoke the truth."

Even Miltiades looked aghast, and the War-ruler protested:

"The fate of Hellas hangs upon what we do today. Shall we linger to discuss the boast of a slave?"

Æschylus pursed his lips in a whimsical grimace.

"Nevertheless, Callimachus, the Gods have many ways of making manifest their will. It is possible they speak through the mouth of a slave."

"You are pleased to talk as a poet rather than a warrior," answered the War-ruler coldly. "It is true that the Persians have no heavy infantry to match the hoplites, as Miltiades contends, but of light troops they have many more than we, chosen archers, freemen— But it is a purposeless discussion. They can sweep our slingers and javelin-men from the field."

"But how if we contrived that in doing so they should cause their own defeat?" proposed Miltiades. "You smile, Callimachus! But I say it can be done. Mass our strength on the wings, leaving the centre weak—five thousand hoplites on the right, five thousand on the left, in the centre a thousand hoplites backed by all the light-armed troops."

"We should be split apart," derided Lysimachus.

"Yes, the centre would break at the first shock," agreed the War-ruler.

But Miltiades pointed down into the plain, which was spread out at their feet.

"The mountains bend inward to the centre," he said. "See! Below us here the distance to be covered is twice that to right and left. So the wings would meet the enemy first. They would be fighting before the centre engaged; the Persians would be fleeing from the wings by the time the centre came up. Is that plain?"

Strategoi of both factions nodded eagerly. The face of Æschylus was lit with high resolve.

"The Persians will break the centre, as Callimachus has said," continued Miltiades. "They will pursue it, and the wings can close in upon them in the midst of the plain and destroy them."

"If they do not turn right and left upon the wings after defeating the centre," suggested Callimachus.

"That will be for the centre to check," answered Miltiades. "The centre may be defeated and broken, but it must die to a man sooner than leave the Persians free to turn upon the wings. And surely, the Gods have veiled their faces from us if we can not find enough Athenians, freeborn and slaves, who will dare all for the City!"

"Here is one slave," growled Glaucus.

"And the slave's master," added Æschylus.

Several of the *strategoi* who supported Miltiades called that they would fight in the centre, but the War-ruler raised his hand for attention.

"Who is this slave who is so glib of tongue amongst his betters?" he asked fiercely.

"One of two men who have struck for the City today," replied Æschylus. "If we ask his kind to die for us, and find them willing, we can do worse than permit them a free tongue—which is the least dangerous of all liberties."

"It is a good sign," cried Miltiades. "If a slave is fearless, can we be less so?"

Callimachus plucked at his beard, uncertain, pondering.

"Tell me, slave," he asked suddenly, "why are you anxious for battle?"

Glaucus answered hesitantly, like a boy conning a lesson:

"I—seek—vengeance—and—a sword."

"But why, slave? Why are you willing to risk death?"

"Giton showed me," said Glaucus simply. "A man must be willing to fight for what he has. He owes it—to the City."

"To the City!" repeated Æschylus. "Did I not say the Gods might speak through a slave?"

"I am content," said Callimachus. "My vote is for battle. Miltiades, bid the trumpets sound."

V

A CONFUSED CLAMOR rippled from end to end of the Persian camp as the Greeks burst from the shelter of the trees, and solid columns of well-drilled Medes filed out to meet the attack, attended by throngs of bowmen and javelin-men, representatives of half the nations of hither Asia and Egypt and Ethiopia, careless of order, confident of victory.

Across the plain the hoplites moved in compact masses of thousands, bristling with spears, except in the centre where a bare handful were strung in loose formation to cover the un-armored freemen and slaves. Because of the longer distance the centre had to cover, as Miltiades had predicted, the two wings were in action with the enemy before the centre had established contact; but what Miltiades had not foreseen was that the re-morseless pressure exerted by the wings tended to force the Persians in upon themselves, so that when the centre finally came to the shock it was opposed by an impenetrable array that increased from moment to moment.

Two columns, one of Medes and one of Sacians, converged upon the tenuous line which was captained by the *strategoi* Themistocles and Aristides—Themistocles, who was to be the victor of Salamis; Aristides, who was to lead the hoplites twelve years later in the final overthrow of Persia on the glorious field of Platxa. The air was black with buzzing arrows almost before the Greek slingers realized that death was in their midst, and discharged their answering hail of stones.

Glaucus saw the slingers on each side of him pierced by the hard-driven arrows of Phrygian bow-men, saw hoplites col-lapsing in the ranks with shafts feathered in neck and armpit, groin and thigh. He whirled his sling as fast as he could unpouch stones, seldom attempting to aim. But he had time only for half-a-dozen shots. Then the Medes and Sacians had lapped the flanks of the dwindling line of hoplites, and repeated on a small scale the treatment their comrades to right and left were receiving from the Greek wings. But the centre refused to be crushed. It gave ground to gain room for the hoplites spears—and the attackers were beaten back.

The battle was still undecided when Giton's slayer appeared. Glaucus, panting beside his master, in an interval of the combat, saw three fresh columns of the long-coated Persian infantry of the Immortals, tall men, with braided beards and high, peaked helmets and oblong, wicker shields, tramping through the ruck to renew the assault. At their head strode the warrior of the grey sword, his brazen helm and mail agleam in the afternoon sunlight, his lean blade flashing above the chased brass of his shield.

As he came on he tossed the sword high in air, and caught it again, brandishing it as though in invocation, and the men who followed him responded with a deep-throated roar.

"See," whispered Glaucus. "They pray to it."

Æschylus sighed, and stepped into his position in the diminished ranks of the hoplites.

"Perhaps," answered the poet. "Any man is to be excused for praying to any Gods this day. Stand to it, Glaucus. Remember Giton."

But the slave never heard him. Already Glaucus had his stone in the sling and was whirling it around his head.

"Ah!" he gasped with his effort, and released it; but it dinted into the brazen warrior's breastplate. The Persian scarcely felt it.

Grinding his teeth, Glaucus cast again, and struck his enemy's helm a glancing blow, no such outright rap as had knocked him sprawling that morning. The Persian shook his head like a bull that has been bitten by a fly, and strode on. He was singing now, his voice resounding above the clamor of the fray. Glaucus sought a third stone, placed it carefully in the lip of the sling and marked the range.

"Ah!" He let it go, and could have knifed himself to see it shattered on the polished surface of the brass shield.

"The Gods have deserted you, it seems," commented Æschylus, dressing the heavy spear that was the hoplite's chief weapon. "Keep my back, for there are only enough of us for the one rank."

"Yes, the Gods will have none of my sling," said Glaucus furiously, and he threw it from him. "Sling, I am done with you. Henceforth I fight with what weapons I can come by."

"Try for the grey sword," advised Æschylus.

"I will," snarled the slave.

The three columns of the Immortals crashed into the slender line of hoplites, pushed it back and ground it up in a broken mass of light-armed troops, slaves and freemen, Persians and Greeks, inextricably mingled. The centre had caved in. Slingers and javelin-men broke and fled. The hoplites were running together in groups of a score or a dozen and standing back to back, prepared to die if necessary, determined to hold what was left of their position. Glaucus, a dead Persian's sword in his hand and a riven hoplite's shield on his arm, ran forward in the press to meet the giant of the grey sword, who was battering down all opposition that was offered him. The lean, straight blade sheared helm and breastplate, made nothing of tempered bronze and steel. Whenever it struck it maimed or slew, and its owner talked to it, sang to it, besought it, and the troops who followed him thundered their response.

Afterwards a slave who understood Persian translated invocation and response for Glaucus:

> *Drink deep, oh, Grey Handmaid of Death!*
> *Be a steep wall to protect thy wielder,*
> *Lead thy servants to the slaughter,*
> *Feed us who feed thee!*
> *We will not flinch from thee,*
> *We will come after thee,*
> *Handmaid of Death!*

The grey sword had just lopped a man's arm as Glaucus came within reach of its owner, and the slave struck quickly, thinking to take the Persian by surprise. But with one of his bull roars, the brazen warrior spun upon his heel, and caught the blow on ruddied blade. The slave's sword shivered to atoms, and Glaucus saved himself from the return blow by plunging headforemost over the ground. His hand clutched at the first weapon available, a hoplite's spear, and scrambling to his feet again, he ran back at the Persian, the spear leveled breast high. But the grey sword's master laughed at this menace, caught the spearpoint on his shield, and as it glanced, hewed off the head and two handsbreadths of the shaft.

"No weapon touches me," gibed the Persian in mongrel Greek. "That is the virtue of this sword—and the name of it is Death."

He struck again, and as he struck, Glaucus hurled the battered shield at his face. The Persian checked his sword-arm in air, raising his own shield to ward the clumsy missile—and Glaucus leaped like an angry snake, flinging his body low and hard, wrapping his arms around the brazen greaves, and tossing his enemy, clanging, to the ground.

A startled bellow from the stricken giant became a snarling mumble of protest, a babble, a whine, a groan. To and fro they tussled in the dust, but the Greek, half-naked, was always atop of the Persian, weighted by his mail. Twice the brazen giant tore his sword-arm free, and slashing wildly at his nimble foe; each time Glaucus twisted to avoid the cut. And after the last effort the slave succeeded in pinning his enemy's arms with sinewy knees, stabbed his thumbs into the hairy throat, and with a sharp wrench, broke the Persian's neck.

Glaucus snatched the grey sword from the stiffening fingers, and tottered erect.

"So, Giton," he murmured, "rest at peace. Ha, I always craved a sword. By Hercules, what a blade!"

A tingle ran up the slave's arm from the wire-wrapped hilt, and that tingle became a fire, a flame, a gust of energy and emotion.

He circled the blade around his head, exhaustion forgotten, his whole being exalted by the deadly purr of the keen edge, and he shouted hoarse phrases novel to his slave's tongue:

"Forward, Athenians! For the City! For the honor of your temples! For your fathers graves! Hellas conquers! For the City! Forward!"

The weary hoplites took up the cry, the Immortals wavered, dismayed by the death of their leader, superstitions aroused by the glint of the grey sword in their faces. The freemen and slaves, who had thought only of flight, commenced to retrace their steps, and Themistocles succeeded in reforming a fragmentary line, which slowly advanced again. On the wings Callimachus and Miltiades wheeled their victorious hoplites against the flanks of the inchoate multitude of the Persian centre. In the snap of a finger the invaders dissolved into a herd of fugitives, each man intent on gaining a place in the galleys which were already pushing off from the beach.

V I

THE *STRATEGOI* were gathered before the tent of Datis, the Persian commander, when Æschylus fetched Glaucus from the scene of the last struggle on the shore.

"This is he who made good the centre when the rest of us had failed," said the poet.

Callimachus offered Glaucus a hand nearly as bloodstained as his own.

"You have deserved well of the City, slave—"

Glaucus cast the hand of the War-ruler from his, and Æschylus explained quickly:

"No more a slave, Callimachus. I have freed him. Shall an Athenian hold for slave a man who has saved Athens?"

A murmur of approval answered the poet, and he dropped a friendly palm on the ragged shoulder of the man beside him.

"What said I when the sun was overhead, Athenians? That the Gods might speak for us through a slave! And but for a slave I think we should be dead or disgraced who gather here, and Athens would be a city in mourning by the morrow."

"No, no," denied Glaucus in his rude slave's voice that had acquired a ghostly timbre of warrior's pride. "Give the credit where it is due. Giton made me—Giton and this sword."

Miltiades bowed his noble head in the twilight.

"What man shall estimate the sum of his deeds?" he exclaimed solemnly. "We chiefs planned and wrought as best we could. But we must have failed, except that a poor freeman inspired a slave with the greatness of loyalty!"

"Any man may be a slave," said Æschylus, "and any slave may be a king."

"But not every king has a sword like mine," boasted Glaucus.

Miltiades, the far-travelled, Prince of the Chersonese, bent over the whorley surface of the long blade, and pointed a finger to a series of tiny symbols etched in the grey steel.

"Yet has it been a king's sword, Glaucus," he said, "for there is the Egyptian 'seft' for sword, and some Pharaoh's emblem."

The worn features of Glaucus were suffused with a dim light like the light of the rising sun burning through a seamist heavy with the night dews.

"Henceforth it shall be an Athenian's sword," he exclaimed.

And in truth, the Archons honored him with citizenship, and in after years a statue of him in his brown woollen tunic, sword in hand, was reared on the very spot where he turned at bay. But that statue long since became slaked lime in the wall of a Greek peasant's hut, and Glaucus was forgotten more completely than Æschylus—only the sword of the one and the plays of the other lived after them.

A TROOPER OF THE THESSALIANS

YOU ARE a stranger, eh? I thought so! I always talk with the strangers who come to Antioch; some of them are from the countries I helped to conquer in my day. A long time since—a long, long time! But I can still sit a horse with any youngster, and handle a drungos on the citadel parade or in battle. Messala they call me. I command the garrison for Seleucus…. Ho, varlet! Another cup for this stranger, and a jar of your Cyprian—a mellow wine that, as good as we used to get from Tempe's vineyards before I marched from Macedonia, little thinking—emptyhead that I was!—that I should never see the sunset fade on the Troad's peaks again.

Well, well, it is all by and done with…. Where did you say you were from? Rome? Humph! Rome! Ha, I remember! A city in Italy, midway of the peninsula. It grows in power, men say. No, I never saw it. Alexander turned east, not west, or I doubt not I should have tried the height of your walls…. I? Why, yes, I rode with him from the beginning. The crossing of the Granicus, Issus, Tyre, Egypt, Arbela and afterward, I was through all. Up and down the world we marched, and back and across, and everywhere we conquered. Men said there was magic in it, and worshipped Alexander as a God, but I know better. It was discipline and valor and consummate strategy. But mostly discipline.

Ha, this wine is good after a hot day in saddle. By your leave, I'll slip off my armor. What said the poet? "A cuirass to an old man's back is like a peasant's heaping sack." Ha, ha, ha! There was a time I recked no more of my mail than that varlet does of his tunic.…This sword? You like it? I see you have a soldier's eye, Roman. Yes, it is not as other swords. There is a saying—and that I am alive to repeat it may go for proof of it—that he who wields it can not be slain by any other blade. And there is this further proof: that he who owned it last was not slain as I have ever seen a man slain in the four score and seven fights and sieges I have known, as also, that the man who owned it before *him* died of an arrow. Before that I have only legend to go by. You may see the marks upon the blade. Those at the top are Egyptian; below it is Greek. He who died of the arrow was my shieldmate, a true friend, Roman, one in ten thousand. May the Gods remember him! Agathocles was his name—he used to tell us that the sword had been in his family since Marathon, when an ancestor of his who was a slave, took it from a Persian and won great renown.

You think it strange that a slave should fight for his city? Well, so do I, Roman. But we Greeks ordered it so in the old days, and if the histories go for anything the slaves fought better than many freemen. At Marathon they beat the Persians, four to one against them. After all, a Greek slave is a better man than any Persian or— Humph! Hrrrrrrumph! Yes, as I was saying, it is a strange sword Those who use it without fear it will protect, but let a coward touch it!… The story? Yes, there is one, if you can tolerate an old soldier's rambling tongue; but we shall have to leap far over the past, back to Arbela, where we Greeks crushed the Persians once and for all, and made Asia a satrapy for Macedon. Ha, lad, that was a fight!

I'll pass over all that came first. For two years we had been tramping about from the shores of the Euxine to the Nile, besieging cities and beating armies. We beat King Darius, himself, at Issus, but he got away, and Alexander was too busy consolidating our conquests to pursue the Persians then. But after we had taken Tyre, Gaza, Pelusium, and Memphis and made Egypt safe, we turned eastward again, and collected an army the like of which no man has ever seen. Forty-seven thousand Greeks, Roman; forty-seven thousand veterans. Gods, what men! There was the Phalanx, six drungoi, each of three thousand men, eighteen thousand altogether, the pick of Macedon, who dug a way with their sarissas through every enemy that dared to meet them. There were the shield-bearers, heavy infantry that could stand against anything short of the Phalanx. There were archers and javelin-troops and slingers, who were not afraid to face the Persian elephants. There were light horse used to charging without thought the Persian *cataphracti*. And last, there were us of the cuirassiers, *cataphracti* who—but of what use are words?

Roman, did you ever see two drungoi of armored men on armored horses, sheathed in mail like metal statues, thundering to the attack? The Gods, themselves, never witnessed a more sublime spectacle. A gigantic lance-head forged out of three thousand men, striking with the impact of a Hercules! And in truth, we were the lance-head of Alexander's army, as he, himself, would say: "The Phalanx to thrust with, and the *Cataphracti* to hew the way for them." But I am wandering from my story.

My shieldmate Agathocles and I were hekatonarchs in the first regiment of the Thessalian drungos…. No, I never served with the Macedonians. They were the King's Guard, but for that very reason we of the Thessalians made it a point of honor to outride and outfight them. It was well known in the army. Alexander had one of his sayings about it: "My Macedonians at my back, and the Thessalians to make the flank good." And it is true that we were always put to it to resist the mass of the enemy the while the Macedonians over-rode the line elsewhere. Our replacements were twice theirs…. Indeed, it was by reason of our constant drain of replacements that my story had its origin.

The *strategos* of the Thessalians was a Pharsalian named Philip, a good soldier, but a courtier—I say no more of him, since he was my general. He had a son, Dion, for whom he secured the appointment of chiliarch of our regiment soon after Issus, where Tigranes, our first chiliarch, was slain; and I will not deny that this left a bad taste in the mouths of all of us squadron commanders. We had thought Agathocles should have it, for you must know that Dion had served his father on the staff and never ridden in the charge with the drungos. But we swallowed twice and kept our mouths shut, thankful when Philip sent Dion home to Macedonia to recruit for the drungos, leaving it to the hekatonarchs to command the regiment by turns.

We went on after Issus, and stood by aiding the infantry as best we could at the sieges which followed. The next year found us in Egypt, with more work to do, and Dion still lingered in Macedon, sending us recruits and stores—horses we obtained from Asia, where the finest were ours for the seizing. When we turned back at last, with Egypt a Greek province, and the word trickled through the ranks, as it will in any army, that the King was determined to force conclusions with Darius, and either break the Persian power or else wreck his own army in final defeat, we of the Thessalians were overjoyed, and we hoped, too, that Philip would give our regiment a new chiliarch in recognition of all that we had accomplished in his son's absence.

But our hopes were disappointed. At Damascus Dion rejoined us with a draft of recruits, and took over the regiment. Did I say that he was as vain as he was cowardly? For coward he was. Such are to be found amongst all races, Roman, although I thank Hercules that we Greeks have fewer than most.... Yes, he was as vain as a Mede, who will tell you how great his people once were, forgetting that he is now little better than a slave. His first thought was to muster the regiment for inspection outside Damascus, and try to find fault with the discipline and equipment. But his father, who was no fool, put a quick stop to that, and smoothed over the ill-feeling that was aroused by complimenting us officers on the efficiency we had shown and serving out an extra wine ration to the men. I made no doubt that he dropped a word of advice in Dion's ear, too,

He was sitting his horse close by where we were grouped above the river crossing.

as that was the last we heard of inspection. But the fool's vanity was incurable, and when he was denied the opportunity of exploiting it by humiliating those who were better men than he and who had done his work for him, he must needs vent it in peacock parading and thrusting the regiment into all manner of additional service, in which he never took part, but for which he always claimed credit.

It was this cursed vanity of his which brought about my shieldmate's death. From Damascus we marched north by Hamath to the Euphrates, which we crossed at Thapsacus toward the end of summer. There was a small force of Persian horse watching the crossing, and they would have retired without any pressure in face of such an array as ours; but Dion must rush to his father and Alexander and offer to send a squadron of ours to teach the Persians what was in store for them. Alexander said nothing, and Philip gave the boy leave—I think, because he was always hoping that Dion, himself, would lead one of these dashes and quickly win honor thereby. The result was that Agathocles squadron was ordered out to brush back the Persians. And mark you, Roman, it was foolish to waste armored horsemen on a venture which could have been performed by light horse. So said many of the generals afterward, although none of us could find fault with Alexander for not checking Dion, for we loved the young King because he would never refuse a man who desired to attempt some dashing exploit.

I can see him now—he was sitting his horse close by where we were grouped above the river crossing—watching Agathocles lead his men down against the Persians. Only a boy like the rest of us, with a boy's eager, restless manners, forever twitching at his weapons or rubbing his beardless chin, but with a brain that never slept and as keen an eye for battle strategy as old Parmenio, who was his right hand and the one man who dared to talk to him like a father. Fever-hot he was in all he did, fierce in battle, tireless in carouse, unbounded in imagination. Who but he would have thought of invading India and dreamed of conquering the yellow men beyond? He lived in a day an ordinary man's life, and to prove that he was no god the Gods smote him while his boyhood was unblemished. If he had lived! Give thanks that he did not, Roman, for your turn would have come had he been spared us a few years more. And then, instead of a score of kingdoms and principalities carved out of the wreckage of what he won we should have had one land, all Greek, from the Pillars of Hercules to the east where the world ends.

Be sure, though, that no such thoughts as these were in my head as I sat behind Alexander on the Euphrates bank and watched Dion in his silvered mail, pompously erect and trying to achieve the look of the eagle that Alexander assumed by nature…. You know the eagle, Roman? He is your emblem? That is well for your people. The eagle is a conqueror; a people who take him for emblem should carry their arms far, yes, as far as the eagle flies—and wherever I have travelled, there the eagle has assailed his prey… But Dion was no eagle. Not he! He looked like a plump partridge hoisted into saddle and hung about with a housewife's pans from the kitchen.

The Persians had already commenced to retire when they saw Agathocles coming down to the ford, and because they were brave men and were five times the number of his squadron they turned back and attacked him savagely as he rode up from the water, smiting his ranks with the arrow-hail of their Scythian archers and flinging other companies in headlong charges upon the lances of his troopers. But Agathocles rode right through them, split his squadron in halves, and then stormed from two sides upon the wreckage he had made. The Persians were beaten, and fled, raining arrows behind them, with Agathocles pelting at their heels, his sword flickering like a blown flame. "We on the opposite bank set up the shout of victory, and Alexander waved the light troops forward to the crossing. And it was that moment, Roman, that Agathocles fell from his horse. An arrow from a wounded Scythian on the ground had pierced his cheek and driven upward into the brain.

Gods! What an ill hour. He was— But of what use words now? A man has but one shieldmate of his youth. Other friends, perhaps. Others to share his shield. But none like the shieldmate of youth…. I pour this libation to him, Roman. Ha, you do well! The Gods will look favorably upon one who honors the dead, even a barbarian….

I was first to reach his side, and it was I who stripped off his armor and loosened his fingers from the hilt of his sword. My thought was to make the sword my own. I knew that would have been his wish. But that fop Dion must ride up as we were burying Agathocles and cry out in his squeaky voice:

"Where are the hekatonarch's equipments? They must be sold according to camp law."

I pointed to the little heap of armor and weapons beside Agathocles horse that a trooper held by the bridle.

"But the sword?" persisted Dion. "Is the sword there? I have heard much of that sword. Men say he who carried it cannot be slain by another blade—and all of us saw that Agathocles died by the arrow."

"I have taken the sword," I answered briefly. "Mine can be sold in its place."

"No, no," squeaked Dion. "Camp law is camp law."

At this several of my brother officers spoke up and exclaimed that Agathocles had been my shieldmate, and that they were willing for me to have the sword to remember him by. But the chiliarch shook his head stubbornly.

"Let Messala buy it in, then," he said. "It is camp law that a dead man's effects be sold at auction."

And off he rode without another look at the man he had sent to his death.

He was chiliarch. There was nothing to do but obey him. And I had this reassurance in doing so: that I knew no other man in the regiment, yes, no other in the drungos, would bid against me for the sword, whatever magical qualities it possessed. What is camp law to soldiers in face of the love betwixt shieldmates?

That night the camp marshal offered Agathocles equipment at auction before the headquarters of the chiliarch. The horse was bought in for the reserve of the drungos; the horse-armor went with it. A man in another regiment bought the body-armor; a dekarch of ours bought the shield and lance. Last, the sword was offered. There was a dead silence while the circle of officers looked at me in sign that none would compete with me, and my sadness began to lift with this evidence of their affection.

"Ten staters," I called. For I did not wish to set a cheap price upon what had been my shieldmate's or to take advantage of the consideration my brother officers showed me. But the words were scarce out of my lips when Dion's mincing voice squeaked from the shadows by his tent.

"Eleven staters, marshal."

Roman, I could have slain the swine where he sat. My heart boiled with rage.

"Fifteen staters," I shouted.

The marshal looked uncomfortable. He would have liked to declare the bidding ended, for no sword—as a sword—was worth fifteen staters. But he dared not, and there was a grating edge to Dion's squeal as the chiliarch called:

"Sixteen staters."

I had no more money, but men behind me in the circle thrust upon me whatever was in their pouches, and so I was able to carry on my bidding to twenty-two staters.

"Twenty-three staters," shrilled Dion.

The marshal looked toward me inquiringly.

"Your bid, Messala?"

"I have offered my last bid," I growled.

An answering growl echoed from the circle of officers. The marshal hesitated a moment, and Dion stepped out and lifted the sword from the cloak on which the equipment had been spread.

"If there is no more bidding the sword is mine," he declared with the abrupt insolence we hated.

After all, as I have said, he was chiliarch. What could the marshal do?

Dion drew the long grey blade and flashed it in the firelight. And as I sit here, Roman, it hissed as a man does in derision—or better still, as a woman does, vibrant with the contempt that scorches and sears. Not one of us stirred or breathed, for that note we had never heard before. Not so had the sword sung when Agathocles wrought with it in battle! Then it had whistled and purred. This—this was unspeakable, horrible—like a chained beast that waits to strike—or perhaps a snake—yes, perhaps a snake.

Men who were closest to Dion moved away from him, uneasy for the sword's evil voice. But there was no misgiving in his face, only puzzlement, as he held the blade before him—thus—lengthwise, and studied the clean sweep of edge and point.

"Man's voice or woman's voice," he squeaked, "it has a woman's shape."

And therein he was right, Roman, as I have ever maintained. Look closely, and you will perceive that it suggests the gracious slimness and strength of some green maid, most wildly perfect and thirsty of life. Yes, very thirsty!…

"It seems to cry out against you," returned the marshal. "There is no luck for you in that sword, Dion."

But Dion frowned upon him reprovingly, striving for the expression with which Alexander received a captive satrap.

"Not lucky!" he squealed. "You babble. The sword hisses at the enemies it will guard me against. It serves notice that the Gods have given me into its protection. Yes, yes, it is a good servant, this sword. I have heard Agathocles tell how it guarded all who possessed it."

"Yet Agathocles is dead," I said, the wrath throbbing in my voice.

"Slain by his own foolishness," he twittered. "Rash one that he was! And he should have had his shield up to guard his cheek below the helmet-rim. So much the Gods do for us—no more!"

No more! Two men caught me by the arms and dragged me back from the fireside lest I should smite him. And that would have meant one thing in any army Alexander led—death! Right, too. Discipline overrides personal hatred. Remember that, Roman. Yes, yes, discipline before all....

Where was I? Ah, yes! They dragged me away from the fireside, and I lay out under the stars that night and prayed and cursed by turns until exhaustion drugged me. But I was up with the trumpets at dawn, and my squadron was first standing to horse. Sleep is a great chastener, and an hour dulls bitter memories—dulls where it does not erase....

We left the Euphrates behind us, and plunged boldly into the heart of the Persian dominions, marching east toward the Tigris. South of us was the rich plain which lies betwixt the two rivers, full of fat, prosperous cities and all manner of wealth. Mark, Roman, how our King's craft prevented him from falling into the trap which would have caught most invaders. Southward was loot to repay ten campaigns; eastward was the broad Tigris—and we already had the broad Euphrates at our backs. Men snarled and grumbled as we continued eastward. "Why put our necks in the noose?" "Why run headlong into space?" "Why pass two rivers when we have only to turn right, and find all the plunder we can handle?"

Ah, but Alexander thought farther than they! He knew that if we had turned southward between the rivers Darius would have fallen upon our rear and straddled his mighty army across the plain from river bank to river bank, and we should have been sealed up there with no chance to exploit the strategy and discipline which were our only means of overcoming the myriads of our enemies. He knew, too, that booty and plunder did not spell empire, any more than the victories we had been winning for three years. What he must have was the defeat and humiliation of Darius, the dispersal of the Persian armies. It was that he sought—or destruction for himself.

So we crossed the Tigris as we had the Euphrates, forty-seven thousand men, with an immense column of transport, a column that stretched for parasang after parasang, two days march from van to rearguard. Four days we marched south after we passed the Tigris, and then our scouts reported the enemy in force ahead; and Alexander, himself, rode forward with some of his Macedonians, and shattered a considerable body of Persian horse, who fled away across the low, rolling hills that clutter this country. There was no sign that more of the enemy were within striking distance, but from prisoners we learned that the whole bulk of their army, with Darius in command, was lying a few parasangs south, awaiting us in a prepared position.

We had been marching steadily for many weeks, and were become footsore and weary, besides which we had several thousand sick and wounded men who were unfit for duty; and Alexander decided to halt where we were for four days to rest the army and fortify a camp to contain the invalids and our train of military stores and engines. A drungos of Thracians was appointed to garrison it, and in the darkness of the early morning of the fifth day we resumed our advance, planning to attack the Persians at sunrise. But the Gods decreed otherwise.

We climbed several ridges of hills, maintaining the battle order at every step, and as we were ascending the last we heard the trumpeting of the Persian war-elephants and the clamor of their cymbals, growing louder and louder, then fainter and fainter as the alarm spread to the distant wings. When we reached the summit the sun was just rising, and in the crimson light we could see the hosts of Darius spread out before us like a forest, a great, thick hedge of men and horses, war-chariots and elephants. Their shouting as they sighted us—was like—was like Roman, did you ever hear the sea pounding the Euxine's beach? It was like that.

It was plain now that we had failed to surprise the enemy, yet we still thought to be sent forward, and were disgruntled at the command to halt in our tracks. But officers of the staff soon brought us an explanation of Alexander's caution. In the growing light we had observed a wide area of fresh-turned earth in front of the Persian centre, and suspected that Darius had constructed a system of pitfalls to disorder our cavalry. And while the rest of us squatted on the grass and studied the far-off Persian lines, the young King rode close up to it and determined the strength of its several parts, as likewise, that what he had believed pitfalls were no more than a leveling of the ground to improve the speed of the Persian war-chariots.

All day the two armies faced each other, without exchanging a blow. We of the Thessalians simply sat beside our horses or gathered in groups to talk over the latest bit of gossip that had come down the line; Dion stood apart by himself, nursing Agathocles sword. I watched him whenever I could, and I knew his coward's soul was shrivelling inside him. I could tell by the way his throat contracted and expanded, and the feverishness with which he clasped and unclasped the sword's hilt. And once when his father rode up to inspect us I heard Dion ask if there was to be a night-attack in a tone that convinced me he hoped to make use of the darkness to conceal himself out of harm's way. But old Philip gave him no encouragement. Any one could have told the fool that it was not Alexander's way to risk the disorder that fighting in darkness brings.

On the verge of dusk the *strategoi* drew up the drungoi in ranks and announced to us that the attack was postponed to the morrow. In the meantime we were to eat heartily and sleep in confidence of the result. Later Alexander rode through the ranks and shouted encouragement to every regiment, singling out officers and men he knew. How we cheered him! It was the first cheer that had come from us since we topped the hill, and you should have seen the Persians running this way and that, tightening their formations and preparing to meet an immediate attack. It put us in a good humor, the men forgot the tension of the day and we slept on our arms as easily as though we had been in winter-barracks.

Morning brought another story. Gods! My blood quickens with the memory, Roman. Remember, we were in open country, with no natural flank defenses, and the enemy were five times our number. His horse alone were equal to our entire strength. It was a certainty that he would lap around us, flank us at the least, probably come at us from the rear as well as the front. So we marched in a great hollow square, arranged so that each part could be supported by the other parts. But our principal strength was massed in the front line, and mainly in the right wing of that line, which Alexander led. Do you see his plan? It was simple. He could not beat the Persians all at once with the army he had, but what he could do was to beat them so badly at one point, holding them in check elsewhere with inferior numbers, that their resistance would crumble away.

And it was the old story: Alexander and the Macedonians were to deliver the whirlwind attack, while we of the Thessalians resisted the better part of the Persians to give them their opportunity. Not that we minded, any of us. No, no! It was a point of pride with us to do the heavy thrusting. And we knew that the King knew what we did.

We were on the far left of the front line, and old Parmenio, who commanded the left wing, rode with us in the midst of Philip's staff. Our regiment was first in the column, and Dion led, his cheeks tallowy, his hands moist with sweat. Next to us was a drungos of light cavalry of the Greek allies. Then two drungoi of heavy Greek infantry. Then the Phalanx in an oblong bristle of pikes. Beyond them the shield-bearing infantry, two drungoi. And on the right Alexander and the Macedonian *cataphracti*. In advance of the right wing was a swarm of light troops.

The second line was one drungos of the Phalanx and three or four bodies of Greek and Macedonian infantry, mostly light-armed troops. It was linked with the first line at either extremity by regiments of light-armed infantry and horse; they were the sides of the square. And it was for the two drungoi of the *cataphracti*, we of the Thessalians and the Macedonians, to make sure that those sides were not burst in. By Hercules, every face of the square, except only the right of the front line, was slender enough. Our whole front was no longer than the Persian centre, and to avoid driving full into the midst of the Persians Alexander gave the word as we descended the hillside to incline to the right, with the result that the Phalanx and the Macedonians were directed at the juncture of the Persian centre and left wing.

This did not suit King Darius, who had hoped to engage us with his centre and then fold his two wings around us, and he launched two attacks to herd us back. First, he loosed a cloud of Scythian and Bactrian horse to strike our right flank. Alexander stopped them with the light troops of the right side of the square. And while this fight was going on, the Persians sent their scythe-armed chariots at our front. They came rattling and bumping across the plain in a cloud of dust, and Dion turned chalk-white as the sunlight was reflected from the long blades that projected from their sides. But they never even reached us. Our light troops met them in the open, and slew horse and driver with arrows and javelins.

So far, you see, we of the left wing had not lifted a weapon. We marched along quietly, keeping our alignment with the front of the square, and watched the cavalry combats that swirled in and out of the dust-clouds away over on the right. But our turn was coming. I saw a gap open between the Persian left and centre as a huge column of Susian horse abandoned their position to go to the assistance of the Scythians and Bactrians who were waging a losing fight with our light horse on Alexander's right. And quick as a flash Alexander struck. The Macedonians darted out from our line like a spear-head of galloping horses and men, and flung themselves into the gap, shearing deep into the unguarded flank of the Persian centre. After them charged the shield-bearing infantry and the Phalanx.

There was a roar of exultation all along our front, but the Persians answered it; and their right wing and half of their centre charged us of the left at a run. One moment we had a clear view of the battlefield from end to end. The next we were swallowed up in a sea of enemies. They engulfed our front; they boiled around the left side of the square and smote the second line in the rear; they even started to wedge in between our two drungoi of heavy infantry and the Phalanx, who were striding forward like a machine, crushing all the opposition before them. But Simmias, who commanded the left drungos of the Phalanx saw what the Persians were up to, and he wheeled his men out of position and dropped back to make good our right. Thanks to the Gods for that! But for him, I think, we should have been torn apart in that first mad rush of half the races of Asia. Wave after wave of men beat upon our spears, and the clashing of weapons and armor, the neighing and screaming of horses, the shouts and the thudding of feet were deafening. The elephants lumbered at us, waving their trunks and bellowing with rage, and it seemed as though nothing might stay them from crushing a bloody path through our ranks. But, Roman, know this: disciplined troops need never fear those beasts. A few well-directed arrows, and they turned about despite their drivers prodding and wreaked amongst the rearmost Persians the very havoc their masters had sought to accomplish against us.

And what of the Thessalians you ask? Well you may! For if Simmias and his drungos of the Phalanx made good the right of our half of the front it was we of the *cataphracti* who must resist the greater assault upon the far left. We were like a shield a warrior interposes between his body and an enemy's blows— yes, and at times we ceased to be a shield, and became a weapon, a lance, a sword. Ah, yes, a sword! And that reminds me of what happened at the beginning, when the Persians stormed down upon us, and old Parmenio shouted to Philip to hurl Dion's regiment forward to break the force of their rush.

My squadron was leading the column, Dion was not two

spear-lengths from me and I heard every word that passed as Philip trotted up to give the order.

"Honor to you, boy," said the *strategos*. "Yours shall be the first charge."

Dion fumbled with the hilt of the sword that he held naked in his hand, and his voice quavered in reply.

"Only one regiment to—"

"One is enough," Philip cut him short. "Be off! Time presses."

I have often wondered whether Philip knew his son was a coward. Some suspicion he must have had, but I think he hoped the boy would gradually accustom himself to danger; many men do.

"Do not go too far," he added. "Swing around and cut your way back to our rear. The second regiment will fall to as soon as you have driven home your blow. We must check the enemy before they reach us, else they will overrun the foot."

"It is foolish not to strike with the whole drungos," whined Dion, gathering his bridle shakily. "One regiment! We shall be devoured—"

His father gave him a frown.

"I hear you have a new sword," said Philip. "Prove it!"

Dion snarled the order to the trumpeter, and Philip rode aside as we urged our horses to a gallop. For myself, I admit I paid little attention to the enemy. My thought was for Dion, and I made up my mind that he should stand the shock if I had to hold him in his saddle.

We crashed into the Persian line where Babylonian and Uxian infantry were formed a hundred men deep. They yielded to us, and receded; but troops flocked to their aid and no matter how deeply we penetrated the mass there were always ranks in front of us. Very brave men, these, who tried to grapple our spears when we pierced them or to leap up and drag us from our saddles. Sometimes they succeeded.

Through all this turmoil Dion rode without raising his sword, and presently I understood that he was dazed by fear. Persians struck at him in passing, their blades scraping on his armor. But he ignored both friend and enemy, galloping on like a man in a dream.

I judged now that we had thrust as far as was safe into the Persian array, and so I called to him.

"Back, chiliarch!"

He did not even hear me, and I ordered the trumpeter to sound the call. The brazen notes rang clear above the uproar, but Dion would have continued to ride forward if I had not seized his bridle-rein. His eyes were glassy with terror.

I was of two minds what to do. First, of course, my duty was to extricate the regiment; but I hungered to lesson Dion as he deserved, and as we turned I peered across the field in search of an opportunity. The Gods favored me.

The Babylonians and Uxians had fled, and a column of Persian cavalry rode out to intercept us, led by a very tall warrior in a high, gold headdress. I bade the trumpeter sound the charge again, and contrived our course so that Dion should come face to face with the Persian, dropping my hold on his bridle-rein a moment before they met.

The Persian hewed at him, and Dion squatted low in the saddle, ducking his head, as though that would save him. He was no weakling, that Persian, and sparks flew from his sword as it clattered on Dion's helm. Yet the stout mail turned the blade, and Dion involuntarily raised his own sword. I thought he was going to strike back. But no. His bemused face stared right and left, stark with the agony of utter fear. Armed men hemmed him in. He could not fly.

The Persian struck again. Gods, the marvel of it! His blade fell upon Agathocles' sword, wavering over Dion's helm, and the grey steel that my shieldmate had loved bit through the crest of the helm and deep into the coward's skull. No hostile blade had smitten him, Roman. The sword, itself, had turned upon him. The marvel of it! And some men deny that the Gods deal justly!

I wrenched the sword free as he slipped from his saddle, and cut the Persian to the lungs with it. An ill-requital for a good deed. But in battle a man may not choose his course. Smite your enemies or they will smite you…. The rest? We broke through the enemy, and regained the rear of the drungos, where Philip and Parmenio received us.

"Well done, Thessalians!" cried old Parmenio, his beard standing out from his face as it always did in the excitement of battle.

Philip's mouth was set in a straight line.

"You will take the chiliarch's place, Messala," he said.

Not a question. Not a comment. Perhaps he knew it was better to say nothing. I don't know. I have often wondered….

The battle? Yes, I was forgetting it. The sword meant more to me than any battle, just as Dion's death meant more than all the Persians I slew with the blade that had come to me in so strange a manner. For I wielded it diligently. That first charge was one of many, at first by regiments, but as the Persians heaped more men around us we used the drungos as a whole, hammering away wherever our infantry were most sorely tried.

By afternoon we decided the battle was lost. An immense column of Indian horse from the Persian centre had slashed through the square—not on our side of it, of course—and ridden back over the hills to the camp and captured that. We were too busy with our own troubles to observe what Alexander was doing, so we were as surprised as the Persians when the cry started in their ranks:

"Darius flees! Run, brothers, run!"

They commenced to scatter, and we headed our tired horses into their midst again, lest they should regain self-confidence—our infantry were worn out, finished—when what should we see but a brazen streak of armor, and Alexander galloped up to meet us with his Macedonians. Lucky fellows! *They* had been chasing beaten Persians ever since their first charge, with the Phalanx at their backs to keep the Persians beaten. But we were glad to see them, for all that, and we croaked an answer to their cheers. I remember I waved my sword around my head thus! Do you hear it? As if a man spoke low to a friend. It is always so; I have never heard the hiss since Dion held it. Many times it has kept my head for me. Men say I shall die in my bed, but I do not like to think of that. If the years carry me to feebleness I will divorce the Grey Maid—so I call it—and give her to some youth of promise—Eh? Well, it might be, Roman. Prove your worth, and I'll take thought of it. Why not? She has drunk the blood of every race in the East. Let her try the West. But first prove your worth. Agathocles' sword is not for any chance passer-by. Remember Dion, Roman. If there is luck in the blade there is peril, too.

HANNO'S SWORD

SHRILL THROUGH the clamor of embarkation pierced the squealing of the elephants. Hamilcar, picking his way over the trireme's cluttered deck, grinned sardonically at the indignant note of protest.

"The beasts have more sense than we," he grunted to himself.

A great glare of torches beat upon the quay, and the masts and hulls of the ships appeared and disappeared in the flickering light like living things. Ashore the streets were dotted with fires that wove a patchwork pattern across the starless mantle of the night. Men's voices, rattling hoofs, the din and crash of shifted cargo were fused in one thunderous cacophony.

"They should hear us in Rome," mused Hamilcar.

He crossed the grating above the larboard oar-banks, and wrinkled his beaked nose at the fetid stench of the close-packed slaves.

"Phaugh, it is long since I smelt that smell! Sea, there was a time when you meant much to me, but I think Carthage and I are no longer in your debt. Better mould in dry earth than rot in water!"

Forward he came to the ladder ascending to the forecastle, and climbed this to secure a better view of the spectacle; but as he reached the top a dark figure stepped from the shelter of the catapult that cumbered most of the deck-space.

"Back, soldier," snapped the newcomer. "Your quarters are below."

"And who are you?" returned Hamilcar coolly.

"My name is Norgon. I command this trireme."

Hamilcar peered closer as a cresset of pine-knots on the quay alongside flared up in a sudden burst of yellow light.

"Norgon! Cast back, Norgon. Once, when you were a youth, there was a lad named Hamilcar, who rode with you in the armored horse. But that was before Hannibal marched from Spain—or before you captained a trireme. Is it too far gone in the years for memory?"

The other bent forward in his turn, and the two fierce, hawk-nosed faces frowned from under the helmets rims.

"I remember Hamilcar," answered the sailor slowly. "But he was young—and beardless."

"Look," bade the other. "That was a youth's age ago. By Astarte, friend, there is frost on your head as well as mine."

Norgon nodded almost wearily.

"It is true, Hamilcar. We have not grown younger, either of us. So you rode with Hannibal into Italy?"

"I led my troop of horse out of Spain," answered Hamilcar moodily. "That was fifteen winters ago—a youth's age, as I said. And now I sail back to Carthage, captain of some four hundred Gaulish infantry, I, who was to be general over armies and Hannibal's right hand!"

The sailor's teeth showed in a wolfish grin of appreciation.

"Youth's ambitions! Who realizes them? There was a day I saw myself leading squadrons in a battle that should sweep Rome from the sea. And what happens? I sail a trireme to Crotona in the fleet that fetches home the wreckage of Hannibal's army to stand betwixt Carthage and Scipio. The gods will have none of us, old friend."

"They will have none of Carthage, either," exclaimed Hamilcar. "Even Hannibal has lost their favor. By the Ram, Norgon, this is a strange experience for some of us, who rode in the rout at Lake Trasimene and Cannae, red to the bridles with Roman blood! It is a great night for the Legions."

"Rome triumphs," assented Norgon. "There will be fighting yet, but not even Hannibal can avert the wreck—for Carthage is rotten, old friend, the Senate think first of their own fortune, last of the public good. There is jealousy of Hannibal. Watch what happens after the fleet returns. If Scipio does not take the city the Senate will fall upon you of the Italian party and cast you by companies in the Byrsa cells."

Hamilcar rapped his sword-hilt on the rail.

"Let them try it! Do they think we will go to the furnaces like Nubian captives?"

"Ah, but they will set the city against you! They will divide you against each other. They will tell some of your generals that Hannibal has taken over-much credit, and so— But you know the tricks. Soldiers and sailors are of no use at politics, Hamilcar."

"I will have nothing to do with such tricks," fumed Hamilcar. "Sooner than be gulled by a set of fat-bellied merchants—"

He broke off as the continued squealing of elephants was dominated by an angry trumpeting. Up the quay, where a giant quinquereme was berthed, arose a frantic babble of voices.

"There is trouble with the elephants," he said, leaning over the rail to peer into the darkness.

Norgon shrugged his shoulders.

"We have scant room for men. It is foolish to embark elephants when there are plenty at home."

"No, no. Hannibal is right," said Hamilcar. "Leave anything that is strange to them for the Romans to study, and they soon learn how to use it or counter it. We cannot abandon the elephants."

He called down to an officer who was hurrying along the quay.

"What is wrong? Are men needed to handle the elephants?"

"No more men are needed," replied the officer. "One elephant will not follow its mates aboard the quinquereme, and Baraka, the Captain of the Elephants, is taking it back to the stables."

"Is any one hurt?" asked Norgon.

"The General Hanno. I go for the physicians."

"Hanno!" exclaimed Hamilcar. "That is strange."

"Is this the Hanno who is called 'of the Sword'?" asked the sailor.

"Yes, he was in charge of embarking all troops. Gods, if he should meet his end through a sullen beast, he whom no steel could touch!"

Norgon signed himself with the crescent.

"I have heard of him. He has a wizard sword."

"I know not if it be a wizard sword," said Hamilcar; "but it is a sure blade, and a true. And of all of us who followed Hannibal from Spain Hanno has been foremost in every battle and never a scratch to show for it. Still, I would rather die under steel than be smashed by an elephant."

They fell silent as a little procession of men passed up the quay.

"I should like to learn more of this," said Norgon. "How if we followed them? There is ample time."

Hamilcar tugged thoughtfully at his beard.

"Yes, there is no man in the army like Hanno—and no sword to compare with his. My Gauls are safely stowed below. So lead on, Norgon. How shall we go?"

The sailor raised a coil of rope from the base of the catapult and tossed it over the ship's side.

"A sailor can land this way," he replied. "And if a soldier cannot, there is a gangplank in the waist."

Hamilcar slung his big shield on his back with a resounding clang.

"A soldier can follow anywhere a sailor he has ridden with of old," he growled.

A moment afterward they were striding together up the quay, threading a path between parties of soldiers, slaves loading stores and troops of frightened horses. They had almost caught up with the group surrounding the injured officer when a tall figure in gilded mail stepped directly in front of the litter-bearers.

"Hannibal," murmured Hamilcar.

The Iberian slingers who carried Hanno halted, and their officer, a dissipated-looking Greek, came to the salute. But Hannibal paid no heed to them. He had eyes only for the limp body the Iberians carried shoulder-high, and at a word from him they lowered their burden gently to the stones, while he stooped over it. A mutter of voices came faintly to Hamilcar and Norgon, then Hannibal rose quickly and delivered a curt order to the Greek mercenary.

"To the Temple of Juno," he said. "In all things do as Hanno bids you."

The next moment he was gone, his face very sad and white in the torchlight, his broad shoulders braced back as though with the physical exertion of supporting his responsibilities.

"So that is Hannibal!" commented Norgon as the Iberians lifted the litter and continued on their way. "Gods! He has aged no less than we. Well, what next?"

Hamilcar was staring after the litter.

"Some one must fall heir to that sword," the soldier reflected aloud.

"And why not you?" gibed Norgon. "O me, eh?"

"Why not?" echoed Hamilcar. "I—we are old, but with the Gods favor—and that sword— Come, it is worth trying!"

"Anything is worth trial in defeat," endorsed the sailor. "But why carry a dying man to the Temple of Juno?"

The soldier knit his brows, puzzled.

"I do not know, unless— Ha, yes, Hannibal has reared there tablets of bronze inscribed with the names of his victories, the towns he has taken, the provinces he has ravaged and subdued, the Consuls he has humbled. And Hanno, like the old lion he is, will die in the shadow of the great deeds he helped to perform."

Norgon's features twisted as if with pain.

"Great deeds," he repeated. "And for what purpose? Rome triumphs, despite them."

"Yet it is not we who have fought with Hannibal who must own shame," cried Hamilcar. "The Legions have never seen *our* backs."

"That is the shame of it," answered Norgon. "Fourteen campaigns has Hannibal waged, undefeated. And now he must leave Italy because Carthage is too weak to stand without him. Carthage defeats him, I say, not Rome!"

"I would I might never see Carthage again," scowled the soldier.

"Moloch hear me, but I feel as you! But what next?"

"The sword!"

"Jackals work, but jackals we are, old men who have failed. Come, then!" A note of hopefulness rang in his voice. "Perhaps we shall have to fight the Iberians."

"Those fellows!" snorted Hamilcar. "I know Colchus, that Greek who commands them. Leave them to me! We are not mercenaries."

II

ON THE steps of the temple they met Colchus and his Iberians descending, and the Greek hailed Hamilcar with an amused leer.

"So the sword draws you, too, old wolf!"

"Have you a better right to it?" growled the Carthaginian.

"There are two of us, Greek," added Norgon.

"Two or twenty, I care not," answered Colchus coolly. "Hannibal bade me see that Hanno passed as he wished—and he wishes to pass, undisturbed, here in the temple."

The Carthaginians stepped back, crestfallen.

"Oh, if Hannibal will have the sword it is not for us to push forward," grumbled Hamilcar.

"Not he," denied the Greek. "But the plain truth is that Hanno is of no mind to yield it up so long as he has strength to hold it. He would have us set him down under those tablets Hannibal placed above the altar, and there he lies, pulp from the thighs down, the sword in his hand. 'I am finished,' he said. 'Send away the physicians. But perhaps I can last until the Romans come, and if the Gods will *that* I would face them armed.' Yes, Hamilcar, to Hannibal he said: Grieve not. I would rather end so. And it is fitting I should hold the army's rear. It will seem like old days when we lured Sempronious to the shambles at the Trebia. He—Hannibal—could have wept, I think."

"A man to share deckroom with, this Hanno," remarked Norgon.

"Honor to him," rumbled Hamilcar. "He is luckier than we, who may live to wear Roman chains."

"He who lives, lives," said Colchus cynically. "Better be a horseboy alive than a King and dead. But as to this sword—"

"No, no," protested Hamilcar, "I will be first to defend Hanno's right to it. Tanit send me a like death!"

The Greek shuddered.

"A poor prayer, my friend. Death comes, in any case. But you mistook me. What I would say is that Hanno's life ebbs fast. By morning he will have no more need for his sword, and then—"

"Why, then," rasped Norgon, "the best man who claims it will have it."

"Something like that," agreed the Greek. "But by Hercules, three claimants are enough. We shall do nobody a service if we spread the news. Now, I suggest that we tarry patiently against the morning's coming, and when the Gods have accepted Hanno's spirit we poor mortals, betwixt us, one way or another, can arrange who shall inherit Hanno's sword."

Hamilcar looked questioningly at Norgon.

"My ship can do without me," said the sailor slowly.

"And so can my Gauls," affirmed Hamilcar. "We shall soon be bound fast to your decks, eh? And there should be luck in this sword."

"Luck?" grumbled Norgon. "Humph, if to be crushed by an elephant is luck! But I own to a wish to see so strange a blade. And at the least, a man may say with truth that he would be honored to possess the sword of Hanno."

"Honor is often luck, and luck is usually honorable," said Colchus, chuckling. "Shall we pour a libation to the Gods in Hanno's behalf and perhaps each man for himself? I know a wineshop behind here in the Street of the Rhodians where they had some sound Carian this noon. There may be a skin or two left."

Norgon ran his tongue over sun-dried lips.

"Now, that is a suggestion surpassing all else you have said, Greek," proclaimed the sailor. "Wine? By the Ram, let us seek it out!"

"A man never knows when he may drink again," agreed Hamilcar. "Lead, Colchus. We must take all we can with us. Bah! What else is left to us but to drink?"

"You are not happy," answered Colchus, with a shrug. "He who is unhappy should drink deep. But let me post my Iberians. They will keep the sword safe for us— And afterwards we can decide who shall have it. He must be a deep drinker, for the sword has drunk deep. It is always thirsty—like a young maid for love, Hanno said. He is a droll fellow, Hanno, lying there with his crushed legs and the grey sword he can scarcely lift. He says he is thinking of the lives it has taken. 'I accustom myself to the company of ghosts as I wait to hail Charon's bark.' He has as pleasant thoughts as Hamilcar."

"He knows a man's death is not worth considering when a whole nation drifts toward death," replied Hamilcar.

"He knows death is the surest of messengers," said Norgon. "Yes, yes, he would be a good shipmate, this Hanno. Why fear the unescapable? If the sword could not protect him—"

"Yet the three of us seek the sword," jeered Colchus. "For myself, comrades, I hold that no man welcomes death before he must. Until the shadow falls life savors sweet on the tongue, and if a certain sword will win me one more kiss or another cup of wine I'll slay my shieldmate to have it."

"Humph," growled Hamilcar, "we are warned in time."

And the sailor menaced the Greek:

"Remember, there are two of us!"

"It would seem the advantage is on your side," grinned Colchus.

III

CHOKING AND sputtering as the water sluiced through his beard, Hamilcar pulled himself up on the bench.

"Brrr! Squolsh! Has that Greek— May the furies—"

"Yes, all drunk as Greeks," answered a voice like the edge of a saw. "Ha, it is good for you Hannibal is not here! An empty town—except for a handful of neighing Iberians—and an elephant and drunkards! Ill work, I say. Phaugh! Drunk as Greeks, and the three of you officers!"

Blinking the water from his bleary eyes, Hamilcar peered unsteadily across the table at a little, bow-legged man in the light brass breastplate and helmet of the Numidian Horse, whose flatness of nose and kinky locks betrayed the half-breed.

"Hold your tongue," snarled Hamilcar. "Are you always free with your betters?"

"If you are my better, you will have to prove it," said the little, bow-legged man composedly. "Who are you?"

"I am Hamilcar, of the Gaulish Infantry."

"And I am Mago of the Numidians. Why did you not send to warn me when the fleet sailed?"

Hamilcar staggered to his feet, amazed, and for the first time perceived his two companions huddled amongst the floor-rushes. The sailor was snoring audibly.

"The fleet sailed!" he repeated dumbly. "When?"

The little, bow-legged man lifted his eyebrows.

"When? The Iberians say it was on the verge of dawn. It seems there was a sudden alarm—a trireme came in with word the Roman fleet was off Tagentum—and our people were away as swiftly as they could fend oars." Indignation grated in the thin voice. "Ba'al's wrath, it was not like Hannibal to flee without giving the outposts time to draw in! Here am I left with close to three hundred men, and not a ship for the lot of us."

Hamilcar propped his aching brow on one hand, and tried to think.

"It must have been sudden," he groaned. "Last night there was no intent to sail before dawn. We—the three of us stopped for a drink—to pour a libation—"

"To guzzle a vintage!" rapped the little Numidian. "What am I to do with my men? The Romans are fond of us Numidians! Well, what do you say? Don't sit there like an offering on the altar!"

The word "altar" reminded Hamilcar of Hanno—and the sword.

"What of Hanno?" he asked eagerly. "The General Hanno, fool! He lies in the Temple of Juno—"

The Numidian whistled softly.

"So that was why the Iberians were posted there! They would not let me in without their officer's permission, sent me here to find him. So Hanno was left to command us? That's not so bad. He—"

"No, no," exclaimed Hamilcar impatiently. "He is dying—or dead. An elephant crushed him, and Hannibal ordered him left in the Temple. It was his wish."

"Was that why Baraka, the Captain of the Elephants, was left, too?" demanded Mago. "He waxed sullen when I called to him as we passed the barracks, said something about one of his beasts being mad."

"How should I know?" answered Hamilcar. "Gods, what a mad business! Is it to be wondered that an elephant should go *must?*"

He dragged himself to a window whence he had a view of the bay, sapphire-blue against the green of the shore slopes—and empty! Not a ship, not a sail, near at hand or within the scope of the horizon's band. A few people moved in the sunny streets, a troop of Numidians was picketed at the next corner. In rear of the temple stood a brace of the Iberian sentries Colchus had posted before they began their carouse.

"The wreck of the wreck of an army," he muttered.

"What?" snapped Mago.

But Hamilcar ignored the question.

"Is there more water? Help me with these others. Make haste, man! We have scant time. If the Romans learn of this our lives will not be worth a broken javelin."

The Numidian picked up a big, brown amphora from the floor and sprayed a stream of water on Norgon's head. Hamilcar fell to work on the Greek. The sailor came to first, groaning and belching windily, presently cursing and complaining; but Colchus must be pummeled as well as soaked before his sodden wits threw off the effects of the wine.

"Drunk as Greeks," complained the little, bow-legged horseman as he labored over Norgon. "A woman could have slain the three of you as you lay here."

"Only one Greek," said Norgon with drunken gravity. "Two Carthaginians, one Greek, all three drunk—drunk as—drunk as Romans."

"Where's sword?" asked Colchus abruptly.

He swayed to his feet.

"You get sword, Hamilcar?" he pressed.

"Hanno still has the sword," replied the Carthaginian, "and

your Iberians mount their guard. Come, friends, let us go to him, and ask his advice. If he lives, that is."

"Why—ask—advice?" challenged the Greek. "Take sword—that's all."

Hamilcar explained their plight, and Colchus sobered as though a keen wind had blown through his brain and cleansed it of the night's vapors.

"Great Hector, this is bad! The fleet gone—and the Romans beyond those hills. How close, Mago?"

"No legions nearer than Venosa," said the Numidian; "but horse—" he waved a hand vaguely—"who can say? Any where out there."

"Perhaps we can find a ship," spoke up Norgon hopefully. "I am a sailor, my friends, I can sail a ship for you—"

"There may be a fishing-boat or two on the beach," said the Numidian brusquely; "but everything that would keep afloat sailed with Hannibal. All the townsfolk went who might be accused of friendliness with us. Forget the sea. We can not take to it, if we wish."

There was an interval of silence, and in the midst of it the stamping hoofs of the horses at the corner beat like distant drums. A bee buzzed in and out the window.

Colchus reached under the table and dragged out a flabby wine-skin.

"Here's a drop to settle your stomachs, friends," he said casually. "Well, why be cast down? All Italy is in front of us."

"If we can ever wriggle out of Bruttium," returned Hamilcar.

The Numidian nodded approval.

"Yes, yes, we are in the heel of the sack here. If we are to break free we must have elbow-room."

Norgon stared at the three of them aghast.

"You are out of your minds! What hope for us is there in Italy? Gods, it stretches away for hundreds and hundreds of stadia, long and lean like an Iberian. We are down in his foot. Will the Romans let us escape clear up his leg?"

"Who can say what the Romans will do?" retorted Colchus. "But we can say this, comrades: they are not so well-loved in Italy, are they?"

"My Numidians know the hills like their own deserts," added Mago. "We have raided in every province for fourteen summers, now. But he was right who said we should seek Hanno's advice. Hanno of the Sword is the general for me—after Hannibal. Ha, many is the time I have followed him in the slaughter, him and his Grey Maid!"

"So you know the sword, too!" commented Colchus.

"Who does not? The best blade ever forged, men say. Wizards wrought it. He who wields it need never fear steel."

"But it is of no avail against an elephant afraid of a gang-plank," amended the Greek. "And now there are four of us to heir Hanno!"

The Numidian looked puzzled.

"I have no claim to it." He shook his head. "The spirits protect me! The sword is not my weapon. I fight with bow and javelin."

"So be it," said Hamilcar. "Well, have we talked enough? Here, give me that skin, Colchus! The man might have thirst-ed a week. Will you drink, Mago? No? Then one draught to cleanse my mouth. The rest is yours, Norgon. A monster, this one, he could drain the sea! I am full of wine-courage, friends. Let us see what the wreck of a wrecked army can accomplish. If Hanno yet lives, he is the man to relish such an undertaking. Come, Colchus, and pass us through your Iberians."

I V

THE IBERIAN sentries stood aside from the temple door with a dry rattle of missile-pouches as the four of-ficers tramped across the pillared porch.

"A gloomy place to die," grunted Mago, then corrected himself at sight of the interior, lofty and spacious, the altar opposite the door bathed in sunlight that flooded down from an opening in the roof: "But a soldier could find a worse tomb."

"A tomb it is become," said Hamilcar, pointing to the still figure that lay on a heap of cloaks and hangings at the foot of the altar-steps.

The words echoed back from the marble walls, and a hand fluttered amongst the tumbled cloths. Eyes gleamed vividly in the leaden face. But the voice that answered Hamilcar seemed to come from a great distance.

"You, Colchus? And who else?"

The Greek stepped forward, suavely deferential, contriving a certain martial dignity, for all his wine-spotted cuirass and dingy helm and the floor-rushes in the folds of his kilt.

"Three of our Captains, Hanno. We come to you for advice. The fleet is gone, and we left behind with a handful of men."

The eyes blazed brighter, the timbre of the far-off voice was more definite.

"Left! How chanced it? That is not like Hannibal."

"Why, Mago and his Numidians held the outposts, and there was no time to call them in." Colchus hesitated. "These others—bided with me."

The four had advanced closer to the altar's foot, and Hanno's eyes surveyed the two Carthaginians with a kind of satirical humor.

"They bided with you!" An uncanny touch of mockery in the feeble tones. "Did they drink with you?"

"Some while, yes," Colchus answered unwillingly.

"I thought so." The mockery was more pronounced. "By the Sword, I could wager Hannibal sent to withdraw you, Colchus, and you were not to be found. So your men were left—and these others. How are you called?" He addressed Hamilcar abruptly. "I have seen you, but your name—"

"I am Hamilcar. I hold a command in the Gaulish infantry. My friend Norgon is a captain in the triremes. He—came with me. We were curious about your accident."

"My accident!" The eyes twinkled with raillery. "It was not—my sword? I marked Colchus hungering for it—last night."

Hamilcar swallowed hard.

"Any man would wish to have Hanno's sword," he said stiffly.

"Humph! An honest man. But there are four of you."

"Mago says the sword is no weapon of his," replied Hamilcar. "We others— Well, when three men desire the same thing there is always a way to settle it."

Hanno's head shook ever so gently; his bloodless lips quirked into a smile.

"No man gains anything by fighting for this sword; it goes where it will. It is a wanderer."

His right hand fumbled in his cloak, and raised a long grey blade a few inches from the folds. The steel was marked with little whorls and wavy lines, and in it were etched letters and symbols in many tongues. It hovered in air for a breath or two, then sank again as his hand wavered beneath the weight. Tiny beads of sweat on his brow told of the effort he had made.

"I—weaken," he said irrelevantly.

There was silence while the four officers grouped around him stared down at his grizzled face and the shattered remnant of what had been a giant's frame.

"Heed me," he said at last. "If Hannibal is gone, I command here. When I am dead— Humph, let the sword command. You hear? He who has the sword commands. I know you Captains, always jealous, always disputing with one another. So let the sword be arbiter. But never fight for it. Remember, it goes where it will."

The perspiration covered his whole face. Norgon stooped quickly, and offered him a little amphora of wine which rested on the altar-step. The dying man sipped a swallow, then motioned it away.

"There is no luck in the sword unless it comes to you of its own accord," he resumed. "So my father said, and he had it of a Roman in the sea-fight of the Ægates Isles; and the Roman had it of a Cretan pirate, and the pirate had it of a drowned man. But he—the Cretan—had known of it before, or so he said. It has a long history, old as human life, I think. Men have slain each other with it for ages. What tales it could tell!"

He took another swallow of the wine.

"They say it is a lucky sword. Well, of that you must judge. True, it kept me safe from steel's edge, as it kept my father, and the Roman, and the Cretan and the man who was drowned. But all of us came by death in the ordinary course. Still, every man has his own idea of luck. But the sword's luck goes only to him who comes by it naturally. Fight for it, if you will. One of you will win, but the sword will not stay with him for that reason. No, no! Gamble for it, rather—and if it will have none of the winner, if by any mischance it goes to another, leave it with him, unless it seeks a new master."

The four who stood over him eyed one another uncertainly.

"But if we fight, Hanno," said Colchus, "it will be as much of a gamble for the sword as if we pitched knuckle-bones."

"You cannot afford to sacrifice your lives in that fashion." The faint voice became stern. "It is for you four to carry your men safe out of Italy. And that will require the wits and craft and weapon-skill of every one of you."

"But how?" queried Hamilcar.

"Take to the mountains—the Numidians know every byway. Ride like the wind—and always north and west. Fight when you must, but flee when you can. In Apulia and Etruria the people are friendly to us, hostile to Rome. You can find friends elsewhere. When you reach the northern mountains cross into Gaul."

Hanno's voice was so low that they had all to bend down to hear it.

"But then?" asked Colchus.

"No, I can say no more. From Gaul you may reach Spain. Or, if Carthage is beaten, you might do better to take to yourselves wives in some far country of the North beyond reach of the Roman eagles. The sword will see you safe."

"Safe?" queried the Greek eagerly. "Did you say it would see us safe?"

Hanno's eyes lighted up once more with a gust of vitality.

"Not all. No, no, my Colchus, be reasonable. Men must die to carry some of you safe, but safe some of you will be—if you follow the sword."

Hamilcar bent closer to the general.

"Give it to one of us," he urged. "Give the sword to one of us for a sign."

The grizzled head rolled in negation.

"The sword goes where it will. That is how to make sure of its luck. Gamble for it. Follow whoever wins it. And if it leaves you altogether, forget it. You cannot compel it. Remember that. It comes to a man, and fights for him. Sometimes it will fight for his son, and his son's sons. But it stays with no man longer than it lists."

"But if it goes to a Roman?" cried Norgon.

"It came from a Roman. If it wishes to, it will return to a Roman."

The sweat was heavy as dew all over Hanno's face. His voice choked.

"Lift me," he ordered abruptly. "Yes, by the arms, two of you. Face me— Where are those tablets Hannibal set up for the Romans? My eyes are dim. Show me."

Colchus and Norgon raised him; Hamilcar turned his lolling head toward the angular lines of Punic lettering erected on the altar. The little bow-legged Numidian was crying.

"Is my sword in my hand?" asked Hanno. "Leave it to me— while I live—or I will set a curse upon you all. Ha, the light grows better! I see the tablets, now. The Trebia, 40,000 Romans slain—Trasimene, the Consul Flaminius killed, 15,000 Romans slain, 20,000 taken—Cannæ, 72,000 Romans slain or taken of 87,000—' The light grows dim again— Who said Hannibal

was beaten?— No, no, Carthage is beaten—Rome is beaten—
never Hannibal— Ho, Keepers of the Underworld, a place for
Hanno! I am weary of victory."

V

MAGO BRANDISHED a javelin at the statue of
the goddess behind the altar, brooding and aloof.

"How could a man live in the shadow of that stone witch?"
shrilled the half breed. "Let us destroy it!"

But Colchus waved him back.

"You err, friend. It was an elephant, not a statue, destroyed
Hanno. And this temple he would have for tomb, even as
Hannibal left it. What we came for was the sword."

The Greek's hand hovered toward the plain hilt of the weapon
that Hanno's fingers clutched in a grip that impressed the
silver-wire binding upon the stiffening flesh. But Hamilcar
thrust him aside.

"You are hasty," rebuked the Carthaginian. "Have you forgotten so soon the injunction Hanno laid upon us?"

"Yes, yes," assented Norgon. "Not so fast, Greek, not so fast.
Gamble for it, said Hanno."

"What harm to try its balance?" scowled Colchus. "But have
your way. How will you gamble for it?"

"So," answered Hamilcar, and he plucked a handful of floor-
rushes from the folds of the Greek's kilt. "Here, Mago, you will
have none of the sword, you say?"

"The sword is not my weapon," returned Mago doggedly.
"And whatever you say or Hanno thought, I think there is bad
luck in this sword."

"What you think is of no account," Colchus snapped ill-
temperedly. "This affair lies between us three. We—we are white
men."

"White or black, all men must die," said the Numidian se-
renely; "and I think, too, that he who keeps away from that
sword will live longer than those who are tempted to it."

"Very possibly," interposed Hamilcar; "but death owes none of us anything; we have played with it too long. As for Mago, if he is good enough to command Numidians he is good enough to fight beside me. So I suggest that we give him these rushes to hold. Each of us three shall draw one from his hand, and he who has the longest shall have the sword."

"A fair device," approved Norgon.

Colchus gulped down a curse.

"There is no skill in drawing a rush by chance," he objected.

"No, it is an honest gamble such as Hanno had in mind," Hamilcar agreed smoothly. "But if you wish, Colchus, you may have the first draw."

"Yes, let him have the first draw," grumbled Norgon.

The Greek hesitated, then snatched at the three rushes projecting from Mago's clenched fist.

"It is not very long," he said dazedly.

"Not so long as this, by Tanit's help," said Norgon, drawing his rush in obedience to a gesture from Hamilcar.

"But longer than the third," said Mago, opening his hand to reveal Hamilcar's.

Colchus cursed openly, but Hamilcar clapped Norgon on the back.

"You win. Ha, a sailor, you shall command soldiers! The hills shall be your sea, old friend. Take up the sword. Go on! Hanno would have wished it so."

Mago nodded approval of this.

"Luck won him the sword, whether it be good-luck or bad-luck. But what happens if Norgon is slain? Who has the sword, then?"

"Why, we can draw again," offered Hamilcar.

But Colchus objected vigorously.

"Not so. Let whoever first reaches the dead man's side take it. That is the fairest way to permit the sword to choose a master."

Hamilcar shrugged his massive shoulders.

"I am content; but it is my hope that we shall need no fresh master for the sword. Come, take it up, Norgon."

The sailor stooped and gently unfastened the dead fingers from the hilt. A great light shone in his face as he straightened himself, and swung the grey blade at arm's length.

"Gods, what a sword!" he exclaimed. "It is as if it were a part of me. It balances like a leaf in the air. And the edge! See!"

He dropped it flat across his arm, and razorwise, shaved the hairs off a patch above his wrist. Hamilcar pointed a trembling finger at the whorl-marked steel.

"There are marks on it. Other men have set their names to it, perhaps."

Colchus, craning closer, his envy momentarily forgotten, cried out at a certain symbol immediately under the hilt.

"That is Egyptian. By Hercules, it is a Pharaoh's mark! And beside it is the Egyptian Seft for sword. Ah, Norgon, great is your fortune! A king's sword should carve you a rich future."

The sailor grinned in embarrassment.

"For my future, I hope only that it will see me clear of Italy. I have had too intimate an acquaintance with oar-slaves to desire to spend my days rowing in a Roman trireme. But the morning wanes, friends, and we have to decide on our course. What are we to do?"

Nobody spoke for a considerable interval, and again through the silence sounded the stamping of the Numidians' horses outside and the buzzing of the bees.

"There are some few—drunkards—" Mago stressed the word faintly—"scattered about the town, who might be flogged to willingness to bear arms. Also, there is Baraka and his elephant."

"That elephant has taken sufficient toll," protested Colchus.

"Nevertheless, an elephant is feared by the Romans," said Hamilcar; "and if this one is out of his mad fit he is safe to employ. How if we go to Baraka, and learn his mind concerning our plight—which is no less his plight?"

And as nobody answered:

"But Norgon commands us. It is for him to say what we do."

"I asked for advice, old friend," quoth the sailor; "and I am free to admit to you that I am more accustomed to fighting afloat than ashore, and what is more, I know nothing of Italy, while you know it as I do the sea. So those who have advice, render it. Hamilcar has spoken. What say you, Colchus?"

"I say that it was a wise gamble for the sword which placed us under a leader who is ignorant how to conduct us to safety," rasped the Greek.

"Are you better-informed?" snapped Hamilcar.

"If he is ignorant of Italy, he is willing to ask advice—and to fight beside Numidians," spoke up Mago.

"That am I," declared Norgon heartily.

"My advice," continued Mago, "is to mount every man you can, take Baraka and his elephant, and strike over the hills into Lucania before the Roman legions close in. We shall have to fight, as it is; but from Lucania we can work into Apulia, and so, with some help from the countryfolk, northwards toward Etruria. That is as far as my mind sees today."

"And far enough," sneered the Greek. "For who ever heard of a Numidian who predicted the future! The man might be the Delphic Oracle!"

"What is your advice, then?" asked Norgon.

"Fight free of the Romans. What else is there to do?"

"And that is what Mago advised, although in more considered terms," remarked Hamilcar.

"It is all any man can advise," said the Numidian. "We are the spoil of luck, subject to the whims of that sword. It would be folly to plan far ahead. Talk to Baraka, Norgon, and if he agrees, then we can leave the town."

"And—this?"

Norgon pointed to the body of Hanno.

"Leave him," said Hamilcar. "It was his wish to receive the Romans when they enter."

"He mocks them as he lies," exclaimed Colchus in sudden awe.

A beam of sunlight from the roof trickled across the gaunt features, revealing the lips parted in a sinister grin of derision.

"They know more than we, the dead," murmured the Greek, awe turned to superstition. "Zeus guard us! Is it us he mocks, by any chance?"

No man answered him, but the four stole silently from the temple's echoing emptiness. It was as if a chill had fallen in the full tide of sunny noon.

VI

BARAKA WAS a wispy, leathery bit of a man, with a white kilt around his loins and a tangled mass of lank black hair through which his eyes smouldered like hot coals. He was half Indian, offspring of a Sidonian mother and a Hindu mahout, sullen and aloof as one of his own beasts. He received the four officers at the entrance to a courtyard wherein the slayer of Hanno was picketed, vast rump swaying rhythmically as the pliant trunk conveyed bunch after bunch of hay into the cavity of the mouth, little eyes squinting with sidewise cunning at the visitors.

"Why should I go with you?" he answered disagreeably. "The Captain of the Elephants is important no longer. Hannibal sails away without even a thought for me!"

"I might say as much," returned Mago. "My Numidians were forgotten."

"Who would have expected you to hide yourself with a beast that had gone *must?*" demanded Colchus. "It serves you right."

The hot eyes sparked at the Greek.

"Nobody interfered when I calmed the Big One, and led him off before he might trumpet his way down the quay," retorted Baraka. "But that is the old story: a man is given respect while he is needed. Hannibal returns to Carthage, and the Captain of the Elephants is no longer necessary."

Hamilcar made a gesture of dissent.

"You have served under Hannibal as long as I, Baraka," he said. "You know as well as I that Hannibal never abandoned any faithful officer, if he could help himself. There was an alarm in the night. Roman galleys off the capes! 'The Roman fleet off Targentum!' By the wrath of Moloch, who could stop to figure what each man did? 'Cast off,' ordered Hannibal, for what was left of the army was more valuable than you or I or that great idiot of a beast that waggles his tail like a Nubian dancing-girl."

"Was there no summons through the streets?" asked Mago.

"Oh, yes," Baraka admitted. "The quay-guards ran from door to door, and the trumpets blew twice. But nought was said of the Big One here—and was I to abandon him?"

"We are not suggesting that you abandon him," said Colchus.

"I am finished with the Army," replied the Captain of the Elephants. "Hannibal left me here—and here will I stay, and the Big One with me."

"And bide the coming of the Romans?" inquired Hamilcar.

"Why not? I have faced Romans before today. They will have little sport out of me."

"But the Big One," said Norgon slily. "He will fare ill at the Romans hands."

A look of uncertainty clouded Baraka's face; the smouldering eyes lost some of their fire.

"I had not thought of that," he answered. "But the Big One can take care of himself. A whole cohort of Romans would not be able to harm him when he has on his armor."

"They would not try to harm him," said Hamilcar. "They would capture him and learn from him the use of elephants in war, so that they might readily resist our elephants in the future. And that would mean the death of many elephants, Baraka."

The Captain of the Elephants shuffled his feet in the dust, more uncertain than ever.

"True," he conceded. "And you? What can you do for the Big One?"

"Why, if we succeed," replied Norgon, "we will break out of Italy into Gaul—"

"Across those snow-mountains?" Baraka was aghast. "Ah, my Big One's feet were cut to the quick by the ice! Take him through there again? Never!"

"Then will he become a chance for the Romans to learn how to master his brethren," insisted Hamilcar. "And afterward, probably, they will poison him."

Baraka's face became livid.

"Not while I live! First I will venture the snow-mountains with him. Yes, I will wrap his feet in hides. Some way I will get him through."

"But before we get him through the snow-mountains we must pass the length of Italy," Norgon reminded him. "And if that is to be done, we have no time to lose."

"It will not be I who delay you," shrilled Baraka. "Gather your men, and see if I am behind them when your trumpets sound!"

"So you will come with us?"

"Come with you! What would you have me do? Stay, and assist these cursed Romans to slay elephants as they do Carthaginians? Bah! And though Hannibal left me, I may yet surprise him by guiding the Big One up the road to Byrsa one of these days. Let us escape from Italy, and it will be because the gods owe us no favor if we do not find a path into Spain or pick up a ship that can ferry us oversea."

Norgon hesitated.

"We have all taken pledge of loyalty to this sword," he said finally, exhibiting the lean grey blade. "It was Hanno's, and—"

Baraka cackled.

"I have heard of it! A wizard sword—which could not preserve its owner from the Big One's feet. Heh-heh! He tramples hard. Well, if you will follow it, I have nothing to say. Myself, I ride the Big One's back. The rest is for you to manage."

"We have agreed," explained Hamilcar, "that he who carries the sword shall be leader."

"Let him be," assented Baraka. "What have I to do with a sword? It is not my weapon. If I can not ride from Italy behind the Big One's ears, no sword will hew me a path."

Colchus exhaled a deep sigh of relief.

"Then it is still between the three of us!"

"You are not anxious for me to live long, my friend?" observed Norgon drily.

Hamilcar shook his head, annoyed.

"This is a bad spirit for men in our position," he declared. "By Tanit, Colchus, our lot will not be improved if Norgon is slain. Forget the sword!"

Mago, the little, bow-legged Numidian, wagged his black face at the others.

"Who can forget the sword?" he reminded them. "It is like a god, for we trust in it and fear it—and my experience is that the gods are as likely to deal harm as good. That is the trouble with them: they do not act like men, so you can never be sure of them. But you have set up the sword to lead us, and therefore, I say you must respect it, you three. You cannot forget it, any more than you can forget the gods."

VII

FROM THE shelter of the cedars they had an unobstructed view of the valley below them, the deep, turgid brown of the river distinct between bands of greenery. The bridge at the foot of the hill on which they stood was barred by a mass of fallen trees on the farther side, and steel sparkled frequently in the opposite copses.

"I have marked two vexilia," said Mago dolefully. "That would mean six hundred legionary cavalry, and there must be four hundred or more auxiliaries."

"And we are a scant four hundred men," grunted Norgon.

"And an elephant," added Colchus with his wonted cynicism.

Hamilcar tugged savagely at his beard.

"A crossing we must make or else turn about and set our backs to the sea and slay as many Romans as we may," growled the Captain of Gaulish infantry.

"The legions are not up yet." Mago attempted encouragement. "And if we could once get an arrow-shot beyond those fellows over there we would be sure of gaining Lucania. I'd cross to the Tyrrhenian shore, and—"

"You might as well talk of crossing to the Punic shore," sneered Colchus.

But Norgon shook himself from the contemplative mood which had possessed him, and broke in upon the Greek.

"I have a thought, friends. At sea when we sight an enemy we close him to ram or board, unless he be too numerous. In that case, we endeavor to divide his ships, so that we may contrive to fall upon one division with a chance of conquering it. Now, here before us, as Mago has said, the Romans are twice as strong as we, and every moment that passes brings their supports nearer. If we are to pass the river we must pass at once."

"Hannibal, himself, could not be more inspired!" exclaimed Colchus sarcastically. "But I could have said as much in six words."

The sailor went on without noticing the interruption:

"And to pass the river we must trick the Romans into one place—and then come upon them unawares from another direction."

"That is a wise thought," endorsed Hamilcar.

"Colchus spoke more truly than he intended, perhaps," observed Mago, with a sour look at the Greek. "That is the kind of plan Hannibal used again and again. He would trick the Romans to mass their strength in one position, and after he had succeeded, outflank them and throw us of the horse upon their rear. Whoo! Many a legion have I broken that way."

"Yes, yes," agreed Hamilcar, "on a level plain, all else being equal, I would back your Numidians, Mago, against twice, yes, and thrice, their number of Roman horse."

"But we are on one side of a river and the Romans on the other," pointed out Colchus. "Also, I see no level plain."

"If we can beat the Romans on the level we can beat them on the hillsides," declared Norgon. "How if we divided our forces thus? I will take Mago and his Numidians and the bulk of the Iberians, and ride downstream around the next bend. In the meantime, Hamilcar and the rest, with Baraka and his elephant, must attack the bridge. And while they are occupying the Romans attention, we will surprise a crossing and come down upon the Romans in flank and rear."

"It will be a pretty task for Hamilcar and his men," commented Colchus. "I am disposed to accompany Norgon."

"You are not necessary to me," answered Hamilcar brusquely. "Leave me a score of your slingers, and I will be content."

But Mago looked worried.

"You will have only some six score men, Hamilcar," objected the little cavalry officer.

"What of the elephant?" gibed Colchus.

"The elephant will be worth more in this affair than all the rest of us," replied Hamilcar. "Go on, Norgon. You need have no fears for us. We will develop an attack that will draw every Roman within five stadia of the bridge. To horse, Mago."

"Perhaps I should stay here," said Norgon uncertainly. "On my ship I always knew where I should stand in a fight, but ashore—"

"You should stay where you will be safest," advised Colchus. "But I was forgetting the sword. You have no occasion to be concerned."

Mago snorted contemptuously, and Hamilcar answered the sailor:

"We who remain here cannot clinch the victory, old friend. That is for Mago's column, and the commander's place is where the victory is to be won."

Norgon stared down at the tumbling brown water, and shivered slightly.

"After all, I am to fight in my own element," he said. "But I could never abide fresh water. There is no kindliness to it."

"Trust to the sword," said Hamilcar lightly. "It will lead you safe."

VIII

HAMILCAR ALLOWED an ample time for Norgon to reach the cart-track which paralleled the river, and then sent forward his slingers and a half-dozen Cretan archers he had dug from the wineshops of Crotone along with a few score mingled spearmen and sworders, Carthaginian heavy infantry, Gauls, Iberians, Libyans. The slingers, from the river bank, employed their long-range slings, casting leaden balls at the enemy on the hill-slopes, while the archers raked the approaches to the bridge. Few as the missile-troops were, the viciousness of their attack and the boldness with which they descended to the river bank completely distracted the attention of the Romans, who rapidly concentrated at the bridgehead, even dismounting a portion of their Legionary cavalry in preparation to meet the anticipated attempt to force a passage.

Several bow-shot distant, in the shelter of a clump of trees, Hamilcar formed up his handful of dismounted infantry, less than a hundred in all, but hardened soldiers to a man, typical of the disciplined mercenaries who were dreaded by the most veteran Roman legions. In advance of them he stationed the elephant, with Baraka mounted on the beast's back. And a fearsome sight was the Big One, arrayed in his battle-armor, frontlet of plate mail covering skull and trunk, padded saddle-cloth hanging from his flanks, with sheets of chain mail pendant from the howdah on his back, and sheltering his vitals. Baraka, perched on the beast's neck, wore a light shirt of chain mail and a peaked helmet; but the only weapon he carried was the ankus with which he guided his charge. In the howdah were four of the Cretan bowmen.

Hamilcar waited until he judged his missile-troops were likely to reveal their weakness, and shouted to Baraka to rush the bridge with the elephant. The ankus tickled the beast's tough hide, his master's voice urged him on, and the Big One lumbered down the road in the midst of a cloud of dust that might have been stirred by a thousand men. Simultaneously, the slingers abandoned their long-range weapons, and took to the clumsier slings they employed for short-range work, casting stones the size of a clinched fist with a drive that knocked armored men completely off their feet.

The Romans, dazed by the cloud of dust and the hail of missiles falling on the bridge-head, closed the gaps in their ranks, and formed closely across the road, just in time to receive the terrible impact of the Big One's charge. A score of men were crushed under the immense feet or hurled to destruction by the flailing trunk; the Cretan archers aimed their shafts right and left. But the Romans refused to re treat. They saw their comrades ground to red paste, and stepped resolutely into the ranks to meet a similar fate.

In the midst of this boiling uproar Hamilcar launched his infantry across the shattered barricade at the bridge end. He crossed the structure unopposed, but notwithstanding their terror of the elephant, the Romans came at him resolutely on horseback and afoot, so that he was obliged to shift his formation to a compact circle, which wheeled slowly from right to left, with the effect of presenting the attacking troops with a constantly varied succession of opponents.

The Carthaginians' weapons were soon red to shaft and hilt, their shields were hacked and marred, their numbers were reduced a third. Baraka succored them twice, charging through and through their attackers and giving them a momentary interval of rest. But presently he was obliged to protect himself, for the Romans leaped from their horses and ran at the Big One's legs, reckless of death if they might hamstring a leg or thrust a spear up under the protecting drapery of the saddlecloth and the flaps of chain mail. And Hamilcar knew that he had exhausted his opportunity. A frenzied howl from Baraka sent the Big One crashing into the woods out of reach of pricks and slashes, and the little band of mercenaries were left to hold their own.

The dismounted Romans drew back, and a column of heavy Legionary cavalry was formed to ride down the Carthaginians. The Roman trumpeter had his instrument to his lips when another trumpet blew in the woods above the bridge. Baraka's howl became a yell of exultation. Hoofs thundered in the tree-aisles, and the Numidian horse burst into the open, riding compactly in squadrons, behind them Colchus's Iberians, casting middle-size pebbles from the waist-slings, which they used for ordinary work. The Big One rushed into view again, trumpeting madly in response to the blasts of the Numidians.

"Forward," cried Hamilcar, and his infantry trudged out from the bridge-head, shields braced and chins up, doing their share anew to break the Roman array.

At the edge of the trees presently, where the road wound away out of sight into the purple hills, Hamilcar caught up with Colchus, who was wiping his sword on a handful of grass.

"Mago has ridden on after them," said the Greek casually. "It was best to disperse them while we had the chance."

"But Norgon?" panted Hamilcar. "Where—"

Colchus held out the sword in his hand at arm's length and surveyed it critically, and Hamilcar recognized the familiar grey sheen of the steel.

"It was too bad about Norgon," answered Colchus. "Too bad! He couldn't swim."

"Not swim!"

"It was the river, you see. We had to cross where it was deep and swift, and he—"

Hamilcar's hand fastened on his own sword.

"Did *you* try to save him?" he demanded.

"Try?" The Greek's eyebrows rose. "Why not? Only think, my friend! Mago was there, and several hundred others. It would have looked well, would it not, had I seemed loath to haul Norgon out? The truth is that I and one of my Iberians and three Numidians went after him, but he slipped from his horse's back, and when we finally reached him he was dead."

Hamilcar's hand opened and shut spasmodically on the hilt of his red blade.

"You were—first?"

"I was, as witness this sword." And with satisfaction he proceeded: "It is evident that I was destined to possess it. Why, Norgon had it scarcely a day, eh? Ah, yes, it was intended for me."

"Take care, lest it leave you as swiftly as it left Norgon," snarled Hamilcar.

"No, no," retorted Colchus cheerfully. "I intend to be careful. It is all very well to have a wizard sword, but I don't mean to place too heavy a burden on it. The gods will do much for a man, but they expect him to do something to save his own head. Now, Norgon was a good cupmate and a fine companion, but—"

"He was my friend," warned Hamilcar. "Let that suffice."

"And a shipman. Therefore he could not swim," added the Greek mockingly. "But he is dead, so— Zeus be his friend! We live. I hold the sword. Do you recall our compact?"

Hamilcar tugged hard at his beard.

"I do," he answered slowly. "I am one to keep a compact. You are chief. What will you have of me?"

Colchus slapped the grey sword into its sheath.

"First, a disposition to believe well of a fortunate friend who could not have helped his fortune had he wished to, which I am bound to say— But my topic is not congenial to you. Very good! I suggest, then, that we collect our men and as many Roman horses as possible, and press on after Mago. The road is open to Lucania, but the man who does not seize his opportunity when it comes— Ah, the forbidden topic again! Suppose that we agree simply to continue after Mago? It was his recommendation."

IX

THE GIRL fled from the gate in a flutter of ragged brown garments, white limbs glancing in the sunshine. They had a brief glimpse of her traversing the vineyard, but the olive trees beyond swallowed her completely. The same drowsy stillness settled again upon the white farm buildings and dusty fields.

Colchus caressed his chin and straightened in his saddle.

"A fat place," he observed. "It would be well if we halted here. There should be meat for the men and grain for the horses—yes, even hay in plenty for Baraka's pet."

But Mago offered a decided negative.

"Hascar's troop that I sent ahead report the road clear. It would be foolish to delay. By tomorrow we shall be in the Etrurian foothills."

"Why hurry so?" complained Colchus petulantly.

He peered back along the jogging ranks of the Numidians, thinned by weeks of marching and fighting, privation and illness, to where the Big One ambled sedately like a mound in motion under his thick coating of dust. And behind the Big One lay the quiet farmstead and the orchards in which the girl had vanished so soon as they had noticed her. Not a human soul was in sight of the column. Above on either hand rose the Sabine hills, lush-green foliage streaked with the brown bars of the tilled fields or the petalled loveliness of orchards. But nowhere was there sign of man, woman, or child; no, not so much as the smoke of a deserted hearth. The fertile country was vacant, abandoned, although the sudden discovery of the girl lurking under cover of the farmgate might be taken to prove the contrary.

"That cohort we whipped by Tiber must be a long day's march rearward. There's not a Roman nearer than they."

"Ah, but these Sabine folk are unfriendly," answered Hamilcar, who had ridden up from his motley company of mounted infantry. "This is very different from Apulia, where the villages clamored to feed us."

"Perhaps," Colchus agreed reluctantly. "But that girl— A Hamadryad, by Aphrodite! She gave me a look."

"How often have we urged you to leave women alone?" growled Hamilcar.

Mago, being a Numidian half-breed, rumbled a comment into his woolly beard that was less polite.

Colchus only grinned at both of them, and deliberately shortened his reins.

"It is not I, my friends, but they! There is something about a Greek—"

Hamilcar smothered a curse.

"I beseech you to use your wits, for your own sake, if not for the rest of us. That is all. Remember, you are chief."

"And it is a pity if a chief can not have a few privileges," retorted the Greek.

"For example, turning aside from the road to try the knife of some chance-met Sabine girl," remarked Mago.

"Why not?" Colchus grinned broader than ever. "By Hercules, this is a dull life! Ride, fight, ride, fight! Now, I caught a glint in that wench's eye that augured—"

"Are you going after her?" demanded Hamilcar.

"I am, my Hamilcar. And before you have travelled another four stadia I shall be up with you again, richer in experience and happier in spirit."

"Let him go," advised Mago. "It is his own responsibility."

"But he is chief," persisted Hamilcar. "And I, for one, have felt eyes watching us all day from the hillsides."

"What Sabine farmer can harm me?" laughed Colchus.

He touched the hilt of the grey sword.

"Have I been behindhand when the steel was singing, friends? Say, who led in every bicker since we broke out of Bruttium?

Whose blade has been the most merciless? Whose head has been oftenest imperilled? Eh?"

"It is true," Hamilcar admitted unwillingly. "By the anger of Moloch, I never saw a man pass through such onfalls as he, Mago! And no steel could touch him."

"Humph," grunted Mago. "Hanno died, and so did Norgon."

"I shall not encounter an elephant on a Sabine farm nor attempt to swim a river," replied Colchus, reining out of the column. "Continue, friends. I shall be with you again before you have tired of discussing my recklessness."

He touched spurs to his horse, and cantered down the long line of Numidians and mounted infantry, waved to Baraka high up behind the Big One's flopping ears, and rounded a curve in the white track of the road.

"Talk to a jackdaw, talk to a Greek," commented Mago.

"He is a good fool," answered Hamilcar. "Let us be fair. We have had brave leadership from him."

"No man is a good leader who turns aside from his comrades to pursue an enemy's woman," denied Mago.

They rode on then in silence, the trees beside the way whispering gently in the breeze, the sun striking warm on the ribbon of the road, the country becoming wilder and more mountainous as they advanced, for they were heading into the ridge of the Apennines which separated Sabinia from Etruria. No longer were there cultivated fields and orchards on either hand, and the few habitations they saw were herd's cottages high up in the hills. Hamilcar lost the sense of being under the constant observation of unseen eyes, but his uneasiness increased, and at a crossroads where the track they followed forked in different directions he came to an abrupt halt.

"It may be that I am as much of a fool as Colchus," he announced; "but I cannot continue without him. Suffer me to take a troop of your men, Mago, and I will fetch him back."

The little Numidian squinted his yellow eyes toward the tail of the column.

"We have gone a good four stadia," he returned. "He should be up with us. But if aught has happened to him it is his own fault. Let him go, Hamilcar."

"You forget the sword," the Carthaginian reminded him.

"It would be well for you if you forgot the sword," snapped Mago. "You do not require a sword to be chief."

"Hanno said the sword should lead us safe from Italy," insisted Hamilcar. "And it is a good blade. You have seen it flash in the thick of the slaughter."

"And I saw Colchus take it from the hand of a drowned man," replied Mago. "Oh, well, have your way! You are as crazy as Colchus. I will wait here for you. It is as good a place as any—and if we are delayed we must make a night march."

"I will not delay you long," promised Hamilcar.

The Carthaginian ordered the rear troop of Numidians to wheel out of the column, and led the way back along the road at a gallop; but as he reached the Big One he moderated his pace, and hailed Baraka, sitting astride the thick neck, disgruntled and sullen.

"Did you mark what became of Colchus after he left us?"

"I looked back once," answered Baraka. "He was riding into the yard of that farm we passed."

"Then he was not trapped on the road," Hamilcar muttered to himself, and spurred his horse on.

Two score men, riding with loose reins, made short work of the distance the column had travelled so slowly. The white buildings of the farm loomed through the roadside trees, and at the entrance gate the hoofmarks of the Greek's horse were plainly cut on a plot of turf. Hamilcar followed the hoofmarks to the house door, where Colchus appeared to have dismounted; but the hoofmarks continued on around the house into a rear yard rimmed by barns and sheds. The door of one barn stood open, and a Numidian officer, who rode beside Hamilcar, pointed to the print of sandals on the earthen sill—and close by was the unmistakable imprint of a naked foot, a woman's foot, slender in the heel.

"Ho, Colchus!" called Hamilcar.

No answer.

"Colchus! It is we, your comrades!"

And again:

"Colchus! Hamilcar calls."

The Numidians stirred restlessly, and Hamilcar vaulted down from his saddle.

"It is strange," he muttered, and peered into the barn's shadowy interior.

The sunlight dappled the earth floor a spear's length inside the door; beyond that was darkness, a vista of wooden-wheeled wains, ox-yokes, tools, heaps of fodder, and over head a tangle of beams. From one of the beams dangled a dark object, which swayed and turned continually—a sack? Hamilcar asked himself. A slab of salt meat? No, too large.

The Carthaginian stepped across the sill, and started violently. The hanging object was a man.

"A file of troopers hither!" he called harshly. "Quick!"

The Numidians scrambled from their horses, and pelted in after him, bows bent, javelins poised. But all they saw was a dead man, swaying and turning at the end of a rope that hung from a roof beam.

"Make a light," ordered Hamilcar.

An underofficer took touchwood from a brass firebox, blew it alight and kindled a wisp of hay, and as the flame torched it was reflected dully on a grey shaft embedded in the dead man's chest.

"Higher," commanded Hamilcar. "Lift the flame higher. Yes, it is he."

For the light fell on the face of Colchus, a face distorted and askew, black with congested blood, dragged over to one side by the loop cast around his neck, the knot tight under one livid ear. Deep in the Greek's chest was buried the grey sword of Hanno.

"Slain by his own sword!" exclaimed Hamilcar. "But no, that is not possible. He came in—with the girl—" The Carthaginian stooped to the floor—"yes, here is her footprint again—he came in with her—they dropped a loop from above—she guided him into it. Gods! What an end. To be strangled to death in a Sabine barn for a farm wench! A wench who lured him to his death. And they buried his own sword in his breast as he kicked at the rope! Buried it in mockery."

Hamilcar put his hand to the hilt and sought to draw it forth, but the blade was caught between the ribs and it resisted him. He desisted for a moment and stepped back.

"Sword, sword," he said, "you have much to answer for. Three men who have carried you are dead—and the Gods only know how many owners died before them! Good luck, they call you. I wonder! Yes, I think I will leave you."

One of the Numidians nudged his elbow, suggesting that they set the farmstead alight, but Hamilcar shook his head.

"It would be a signal to every Roman officer in these hills. No, no, Colchus deserves no vengeance, for if ever a man was his own Nemesis it was he."

The Carthaginian started to leave the barn, but in the door he turned for a last look at the sword. Its grey blade stood out a span from the Greek's body, and it seemed to shiver and throb with life in the twilit gloom as the dead man twisted and swayed. A mighty itch to possess it, to feel the cool strength of its hilt in his palm, assailed him.

"Why should I fear it?" he whispered to himself. "I am not a fool like Colchus. Moreover, Hanno said that it should lead us—some of us—out of Italy. We swore that he who carried it should be chief—and I alone am left of the three who took the oath! By Tanit, this is fate! Sword, you are mine."

He retraced his steps, gripped the edge of the Greek's corselet in his left hand and with this leverage drew the dripping blade from the corpse's chest. Free of the dead man, it swung feather-light in his grasp, keen, trenchant, dully threatening.

Hamilcar wiped it on a fold of Colchus's kilt, then slashed through the rope that had hung the Greek.

"Bury him in the yard," he ordered the Numidians as what had been Colchus sagged to the floor. "Not deep, for we have far to ride tonight. There is death in these hills."

X

THE WIND that swept the pass was edged with the freezing breath of the glaciers that scarred the Alpine peaks. The Iberians shivered as they took their stance, and mechanically slung their missiles at the dwarfed figures of the Romans bobbing amongst the boulders a bowshot distant. Hamilcar shivered, too, for all the plundered cloak of fur which wrapped his shoulders; and he felt the quivers which wrenched the bony frame of his horse whenever the icy blast yelled off the mountains and funneled through the depression of the pass.

A short cast above the line his men had strung from cliff to cliff, Baraka's Big One teetered monotonously in the lee of a rock, more clumsy than ever in full war panoply and the huge bullshide boots which Baraka had fashioned so laboriously to protect the elephant's corns from the sharp rocks and icy stretches of the mountains that shut off Italy from Gaul.

Around an elbow of the pass hoofs rattled, and Mago galloped into view, his black features grey with the cold.

"Brrrrr, what a land!" he chattered, reining in beside the Carthaginian. "If we might only have found a ship!"

"What use to weep for the unattainable?" answered Hamilcar. "If we had made for the coast the legions would have gathered us in long ago. How do you progress up ahead?"

"Ill. There is a walled village in a bowl beneath the crest of the pass. I must have the Big One to crack it open for us."

Hamilcar frowned at the Romans edging steadily forward upon the tenuous line of Iberians.

"These border legions are stout fellows," he said. "I cannot hold them unaided."

"True, oh, Hamilcar," assented the Numidian; "but if we do not carry this village we are hemmed between it and these Romans—and my people report it is stuffed with light troops."

"It is the truth," agreed Hamilcar. "Take Baraka with you. I will retire slowly as far as that elbow in front of us. There I will leave a dozen to keep the legionaries in check, and with the rest hasten after you. We take the village or we perish. And it will be hard if after all the perils we have survived some of us do not escape."

"There are not so many of us even to perish," replied Mago grimly, eyeing the wide intervals in the ranks of the slingers. "Well, may the gods have their will of us!"

And he rode away to accost Baraka, and lead the Big One up the rough slope of the pass, while Hamilcar turned his attention to the withdrawal of the Iberians as unostentatiously as possible.

Two stadia beyond the elbow the pass widened into a valley, and in the midst of this the village was situated, a huddle of stone huts, the roof timbers anchored with boulders against the fury of the mountain gales, a crude stone wall surrounding it that would have crumbled at a blow from a catapult, but a formidable obstacle to a handful of troops without siege equipment. Mago was an experienced campaigner, however, and he had grappled with the situation before his chief arrived.

The Big One, rumbling and grumbling, was backed off a couple of bowshots from the village gate; Baraka touched him with the ankus, shrilled in his grotesque ear; and the immense beast lowered his armored head and lumbered into a run which was amazingly fast. The Roman auxiliaries on the walls showered the elephant with darts, but his armature protected him from all save surface scratches, and these only stimulated his rage. Squealing viciously, he thundered into the gate, burst its leaves asunder and pranced along the village street, trunk brandished against all who stood in his way. After him poured the Numidians, with the survivors of the column's infantry, and Hamilcar and the Iberians bringing up the rear.

The garrison took to the houses, defending themselves desperately, but whenever Mago or Hamilcar had difficulty in forcing an entrance they called the Big One from his parading and bade him shove in a wall, usually with the result that the inmates were buried beneath a heap of the loosely mortared stones and the heavy roof. The auxiliaries lacked the dare-all spirit of legionaries, and soon crumbled into flight, until the valley was covered with men struggling in groups and individually.

One company of the auxiliaries made for the upper mouth of the pass, a precipitous gut in the cliffs, and Baraka sent the Big One careering after them. The elephant by now was in a fiendish temper. He had been on short rations for several days; he disliked the cold of high altitudes; he objected violently to the boots which Baraka had put on his feet; and he had slain enough men to have a craving for bloodshed. So he kept after the fugitives relentlessly, trampling on them or throwing them against the rocks whenever he overtook them.

As he neared the entrance of the pass Baraka perceived the difficulty of managing the great beast in its constricted space, and endeavored to turn him from his prey. But the Big One refused to be amenable. Despite the goading of the ankus and his master's shrill adjurations he lumbered on into the gut. An arrow found a crack in the scales which protected his trunk, and the pain of the wound drove him frantic. His squeals resounded between the beetling cliffs. He caught a man in his trunk and beat him to a pulp against a boulder, then lurched on, eyes flaming, entirely heedless of the narrowing path, intent on destroying the enemies in front of him. One after another, he trampled them; but two men reached a section of the pass where the walls were so close that they could scarcely squeeze through shoulder to shoulder as they ran.

"Stop, my Big One," bleated Baraka. "Here is no path for you. Turn back, Great Baby of my heart! Turn before—"

But the elephant plunged into the straitened gut at a gallop. His tough hide chafed against the rock walls, tearing down a succession of loosened boulders and icicles that redoubled his rage. Heaving and straining, he wedged himself farther in the narrow way, and when Baraka prodded him with the ankus, begging him to back he trumpeted savagely, tossed up his trunk and caught the Captain of the Elephants in its supple grasp. A moment he dangled his master before his little red eyes as if gloating over the murder of one he held responsible for his plight. Then he hurled the unfortunate man after the two auxiliaries who had eluded him, and Baraka became a red splotch against the cliffs.

Hamilcar and Mago, called into the pass by the first of the Numidians to respond to the Big One's frenzied trumpetings, realized the danger to the whole column if the way continued blocked.

"We must slay him," decreed the Carthaginian.

"Easy to say," retorted Mago, cautiously investigating the elephant's restless hind feet. "But his vitals are at the other end."

"Hew him apart, if necessary," replied Hamilcar impatiently. "I care not how many men we lose. He stands between us and Gaul, no less than did your village."

Five men died or were mauled before the spears of Numidians and the swords of Carthaginians, Iberians and Gauls finally severed the spine of the Big One's mighty bulk, and it was possible, as Hamilcar had said, to hew him apart and so make room for the column to pass. But even when this had been done there was trouble with the horses, which shied at the bloody rocks and monstrous chunks of flesh and limbs. The pursuing legionary infantry were at the mouth of the defile by the time the column was moving again, and in its winding, precipitous depths there was scant opportunity for the accurate, long-range slinging of the Iberians which had been the most effective resistance the fugitives could offer against superior numbers. The rearguard of the Carthaginian troops and the van of the pursuers were crossing swords as the last of the Numidians passed the scattered remnants of the Big One.

Mago came to Hamilcar with a worried look on his face.

"I would try to ride the Romans down if the footing was better and our horses were not so worn," he said. "But my men feel the cold too much to be on their mettle."

"This is work for the Iberians and Gauls," replied Hamilcar. "Rest easy. I will see to it."

The Numidian tarried, his pride hurt because the situation was beyond him.

"If it was a field for horse—" he began, and Hamilcar clapped him on the shoulder.

"This is a field for infantry. You have done your part. Now we shall do ours. Push on over the crest, and we will overtake you as soon as we have given the Romans a bellyful."

"But you?" protested Mago. "You are chief, Hamilcar. You must not risk yourself."

"Each to his destiny," retorted Hamilcar. "Cheer up, man. In this defile the Romans can never overtake us. We will hold them until nightfall, then slip away and rejoin you. Tomorrow we shall be looking down on the plains of Gaul."

"May Tanit guide it so!" exclaimed the Numidian.

Hamilcar laughed, balancing the grey sword in his hand.

"*This* guides us!" he answered. "From end to end of Italy it has carried us. Will it fail us now? I think not!"

But Mago called back over his shoulder:

"I trust in you, not the sword! It is an evil friend, that sword, too thirsty, too changeable. All it seeks is the slaughter."

"So that it slays our enemies, why should we care?" replied Hamilcar. "It is like a woman, a lustful maid, ever hungry, never content. Feed its wants, and it will be faithful to you."

But as he picked his way amongst the weary Gauls and Iberians of the rearguard he found himself thinking otherwise.

Hamilcar made the grey sword hiss in air, and
strode out in front of the Carthaginians.

"So Colchus talked—yes, and Norgon said much the same. But neither of them did it serve so long as me. Phaugh, I am an old woman from the cold and hunger and toil of the fighting! A sword is a stout friend to the man who wields it with skill, no more. When my arm falters, my head will fall. Yet no steel has touched me since I drew it from the Greek's breast— and today I require its help more than ever."

He circled it around his head, and the keen purr of the blade became a hiss, strident, menacing.

"That is not a happy song you sing, sword," he muttered. "It bodes ill—for some one. Ho, men, let me through! Way for Hamilcar! Grey Maiden will make good the rear."

They stood aside readily enough, courage spurred afresh by the presence of the commander they believed invincible and the sword whose fabulous powers were debated at every campfire. Hamilcar took his place in the rear rank of four men, stepping over the body of a dead Carthaginian infantryman who had been impaled by a Roman pilum. On his right hand an Iberian and a Gaul fought with long, straight swords similar to his own; on his left a Carthaginian cut and thrust with a shorter broadsword not unlike the weapons of the Roman legionaries, who crowded into the pass behind their convex shields. The Romans pikes were gone; the fighting was hand-to-hand, sword to sword, the individual skill and strength of the Carthaginian mercenaries against the disciplined effort of the legionaries.

And if the numbers were unequal, Hamilcar, himself, was equal to a century. He was not content to meet the Roman advance. At times, when the pressure of the cohort jamming the mouth of the pass became so severe as to threaten to burst the fragile opposing line like a stream in freshet, he would spring forward alone, the grey sword darting and leaping, swooping and hovering, agleam with dreadful life and hunger, slashing gaps in the Roman ranks that slowed the steady tread of the legionaries and gave his men time to regain their wind.

Step by step he contested the pass while the sun sank lower and the bitter cold made the fighters shiver in their sweat. The Romans reached the narrowest section, where the Big One had stuck, just short of twilight, and here for some reason they seemed inclined to rest, nor was Hamilcar loath to seize the chance to ease his aching sword arm. Beyond this point the pass widened again, so that a dozen men might tramp it abreast, and he knew that on such ground the Romans, with their un-drained reserves, would plow ahead almost regardless of the resistance his battered fighters might attempt. So he was pre-pared for the fiercest struggle of the day when the ordered "tramp-tramp-tramp-clank-clank-clank" of the legionaries echoed up the defile.

"To the last, men," he said sternly. "There will be horses for you above—and tomorrow, remember, the plains of Gaul!"

A tired cheer answered him, and they dressed their shields as the Romans loomed in the twilight, a brazen double file.

Hamilcar made the grey sword hiss in air, and strode out in front of the Carthaginians.

"Two at a time!" he exclaimed. "This is a simple task for you, Grey Maiden. What are two Romans to you, who have slain them by cohorts?"

One of the two he cut in the neck below the helmet-strap; the other sank, pierced through the groin. He stepped forward to receive the next pair, sword raised to strike. But something swished overhead. He looked up, startled, as a net dropped around his shoulders. A roar burst from his lips, and he drove the sword into the armpit of a Roman in the second rank ; but when he strove to lift his arm the heavy cloth-strips of the net entangled the blade, one of his own men stumbled against him in the confusion and he plunged to his knees. The next moment he was down on the rocks, and the Romans rolled over him. The hobnailed sandals stamped into his flesh, the press of bodies suffocated him. He could feel the life ebbing from him under the cruel battering of human mallets, but he had no sense of resentment, only an amused wonder.

"No steel could touch me! Ho, Norgon, I—"

XI

THE TRIBUNE Paulus Sulpicius looked up from his seat by the campfire and dropped the stylus with which he was scratching his brief report.

"What success, Valentius?" he asked the Centurion.

"The Numidians escaped. They had too long a start for us. But most of the others we slew."

"That is well," said the Tribune approvingly. "Your name goes with this to the Consul, my Valentius. I am pleased with you. Ha, you have a new sword!"

He pointed to the long, grey blade that the Centurion extended for inspection.

"I took it from the body of the officer who withstood us so long in the pass, him we overcame with the net you bade us knot out of the strips of our cloaks. It is a fine piece of steel."

"A soldier's weapon," agreed the Tribune, handling it lovingly. "You have earned it, and if I have my way you shall swing it next at the head of your cohort. He was a gallant enemy, that Carthaginian. His sword should be a lucky one. May it carve you a path to command of a legion!"

The Centurion received back the sword.

"We took some prisoners," he answered. "For information. They say it is a magic sword. Who carries it cannot be slain by steel."

"Such superstition is Punic, my Valentius," the Tribune returned indulgently. "Bethink you, he who carried it last is dead, and how he came by his death matters little. Man lives while the gods indulge him. When they will he dies."

THE LAST LEGION

To the Senator Anicius Manlius Severinus Boetim, Consular, at Rome, from G. Flavins Domitianus, Count of the Bononian Shore, these by favor of the holy Modius:

I T I S a voice from the outer darkness which speaks to you by this pen, oh, Anicius. One encompassed by the myriads of the Barbarians, his humble talents devoted to the crude policies of a savage King, may well hesitate to address you who have sat in the curule chair and borne the highest dignity beneath the purple. Yet I am emboldened by two facts: the one the memories, always treasured, of those early days on the slopes of the Pincian when we stole moments from the Lives of the Saints to sample the splendors of the Mantuan, the other, my recollection of your curiosity concerning all events applying to the philosophy of life. You have been kind enough to express gratitude for my comments on the Christianizing of my Prankish employers—no, then, I will put pride aside, be honest and call them masters—and so it may be that you will discover profit in this narrative of an experience which has racked my soul to its foundations and stirred me to doubt the very basis of the faith the priests would bid us believe shall mould the world anew.

I know that you will not judge me hastily, friend of my youth, who have refused to forget our pagan forefathers simply because they were pagan. Must Cicero and Lucretius be condemned, to Hell fire for the crime of having lived before the revelation of Christ? No, no! Or if it be so, then, I'll choose to go with them. Rather the Old Gods of our ancestors, my Anicius, than a Christian God of injustice. And who shall say that Rome has had justice of Christ? Calamity after calamity, until a Barbarian sits in the Palace of the Cæsars, and the Conscript Fathers are become the puppets of his will! We are scourged for the sins of our ancestors, say the priests. Oh, God of any faith, what mockery! What virtues do these Barbarian converts possess that our forefathers lacked? What claim upon divine assistance have the heathen Saxons, who ravage today what once was Roman—and Christian—Britain? And this brings me belatedly to the subject of my tale, a truly marvellous tale, my Anicius, stimulating to Roman pride, crying aloud for Roman pity. But be yourself the judge. I will tell it as it happened, thus:

Two days since the *optio* commanding the Julius Tower by the quay summoned me by messenger, saying a ship of the Sea-wolves was heading into port. It is seldom, indeed, that any ship puts into Bononia,[1] which, in former times, even after it had lost the name of Gesoriacum, was thronged with traders, but is now, as it were, a *castra mare* on the far edge of the world. Here even the Barbarians stay their feet, for beyond is only the restless desert of the Western Ocean. But at intervals these Sea-wolves, wildest of all the Barbarians, appear along the neighboring shores and inspire with terror the ruthless Franks, who, to say truth, are as agitated by such visitations as are your peasants of Latium or Etruria by the raids of the Lombards against whom the Goths protect them. My task, as you know, is to safeguard this coast, and to conciliate my pride the Franks permit me to retain the old title which was established when the evacuation of Britain did away with the Count of the Saxon Shore, who had been charged with the prevention of piracy. Yes, and not alone do they yield me my traditional office, but the troops under my command, in name at least, are the same

---

1 *Boulogne.*

The strangers rowed into the port
very awkwardly and in silence.

bodies that Honorius stationed here, if we are to credit the *Notitia* of his reign, in which are inscribed the garrisons of the several frontiers.

So I ordered out the Ninth Alan Cohort, in which, I do assure you, oh, Anicius, there are no less than a score and a half of Alans and two Roman Centurions, not to speak of one who is Roman on the mother's side, and the rank and file stout Franks, who worship God very fervently because King Clovis bade them to. And with my "Alans" I marched down to the quay to receive the Sea-wolves as became them. But imagine my amazement when these strangers, instead of showering us with arrows from a distance and saluting us with indecent cries and gestures, rowed into the port very awkwardly and in silence, quite as though their doing so was a natural thing to be expected. I was so dumbfounded that they were within javelin-throw and inside the range of the tower catapult before I took thought to my responsibility and hailed them to yield to us. I did not think it likely they would understand me, so in the same breath I shouted to my archers to bend their bows and had the catapult discharged. Of course, the stone flew over their heads, but it made a mighty splash which rocked their vessel near to swamping it, whereupon arose one amongst them dressed like myself, and replied to me in our Latin tongue! Yes, as good Latin as you shall hear any day in the Forum, albeit with something of a throaty accent, and a slurring of final syllables.

"Are you Barbarians here?" he hailed. "Is this the way to receive a Roman officer in a Roman port?"

"Roman officer!" I gasped. "Who ever heard of a Roman officer in a longship of the Sea-wolves?"

He threw back his ragged, old brown cloak very haughtily, and he might have been Cæsar when he answered:

"I asked a question."

"So you did," I agreed sarcastically. "And I will answer it. I am Domitianus, Count of the Bonanian Shore. You are within my jurisdiction, and all men, save King Clovis, himself, must hold obedience to me therein. Now, do you answer *me!*"

But he shook his head, puzzled.

"King Clovis—who is he?"

I gaped at him.

"Whence do you come who can ask such a question?" I stammered. "Who are you?"

He signed to his men to pull up by the quay, and they managed it with the strong awkwardness I had observed before. As they drew alongside, I saw, too, that they were a mixed lot: some of them dressed like my own legionaries in tattered leather jerkins and rusty lorica, others hairy and clad in skins and bright-colored woollen cloths. The armored men had the look of drilled troops; the hairy fellows were as wild a set of untamed Barbarians as you can find anywhere north of Gaul. Their leader stepped ashore without a word from me, and not until then did he answer my last questions.

"I am Quintus Arrius Marbonius, Senator of Viroconion[2] and legate of the Sixth Legion, *Victrix*."

He said it, my Anicius, as you might say: "At what hour do we dine?" I stared at him a long time. It was one of my two Roman Centurions who replied to him.

"But—but there is no Sixth Legion!"

"Why, no," I assented. "The Sixth was struck off ages ago. It is not on the rolls. It was destroyed—that is, it disappeared nigh a century of years past."

The stranger smiled quietly. He was a man of middle height, a true Roman in face and build, stocky, with a huge chest and broad shoulders, and a nose and chin like those on the busts of the old Cæsars in the Capitol. He was young, compared to us; but his hair was flecked with grey, and there were deep lines in his cheeks, which were decently shaven. His armor was clean and polished, but he had no sword, only a light staff in his hand. I know men, O Anicius, and this man, I perceived at once, was

---

2   *Wroxeter.*

one to be depended on. So much, to be sure, any one must have seen from the way his crew kept their eyes on his face, and jumped to obey his slightest gesture. Yes, a soldier.

"The Sixth may not be on your rolls," he said, "yet I can assure you it—" a spasm wrenched his features—"it is here."

He waved one hand toward the longship nuzzling the shattered platform of the quay—these Franks keep nothing in repair; a stone the frost works loose is always left to fall.

"For all that century of years," he went on, "it fought honorably to maintain the repute it brought into Britain. Victorious it was called, and victorious it died—except the few of us you see here. Viroconion was its tomb."

"Where is this Viroconion?" I asked, striving to collect my wits.

Now, at mention of this name one of the crew of the longship leaped ashore beside his leader, and burst into a torrent of words in a tongue which sounded to me like rain spitting in the chimney, strutting back and forth and waving his arms in the fashion of a third-rate actor. He was an absurd person, short in stature, bandy-legged, with a large head and a tangled red beard and long, tangled red hair.

"Is this man crazed with suffering?" I appealed to Marbonius.

He smiled again.

"Oh, no, he is a poet. That is a song he has made: The Death-Song of the White Town in the Valley. It is the song of the end of Viroconion, the fairest of the cities of Britain."

"Of Britain!" he gasped.

But he had not heeded me. Turning to the bandy-legged man, he spoke to him gently, touched him on the arm—and the flow of words was stopped. The poet bowed his head, and dropped back into the longship.

"Llywarch Hen mourns the death of his master, Prince Kyndylan," continued Marbonius. "To him it is not so much the end of the White Town, but the passing of Kyndylan the Fair, which must be sung." His lips crinkled in a satirical grimace. "But his poet's mind can not resist the overwhelming tragedy of the death of a town. A city is greater than a man, even though that man be a Prince."

I discovered my wits at last.

"These are strange words that you speak," I said sternly. "First, it is of a Legion long forgotten—which you say is newly destroyed. Then it is of the end of a city. Next, it is of a Prince's death. You have much to render account for. You claim to be a Roman?"

He favored me a second time with his satirical grimace.

"All freeborn men in the Empire are citizens of Rome," he answered. "But I am descended from a family that earned the privilege under the Republic!"

"There are older families," I retorted, no less sternly; "and the title is not so honorable as it once was."

His hand went to where his swordhilt should have been.

"No true Roman would say that," he said.

"There is no such thing as a true Roman," I replied. "Whence do you come, stranger from the sea, that you should be as ignorant of the world as though you were not of it?"

There came upon his face a smile most piteously mournful.

"Count of the Bononian Shore, I begin to believe that Britain must be a different world," he said.

"Do you mean to claim that you are come hither from Britain?" I exclaimed.

"I do," he declared proudly. "I am a Roman Briton, a Senator of Viroconion—or of what was Viroconion, for all is gone, Cenric the West Saxon has levelled the walls, the house roofs gap to the sky, the churches are dens for the wolf. Yes, it is as Llynwarch Hen has sung: Its halls are without life, without fire, without song."

"But man, you speak madness," I cried. "No one has come out of Britain since my grandfather's time! It is a waste inhabited by the Northern pirates. For three generations the Saxons have desolated it."

"Not all of it," he corrected me. "I grant you they have ravished the fairest sections of the land, but in the West a line of cities have kept the Roman tradition, and behind them the Silurian[3] Mountains and the rough moors of Damnonia[4] have provided shelter for many more folk of the British tribes that never took kindly to Roman ways. We are ill-assorted, we of the cities and the mountains, but we have one interest in common in the enmity of the Saxons and their allies. Until now we have kept our freedom, but the fall of Viroconion means the end of all else—unless the Emperor send us aid."

It was incredible, my Anicius, but I believed him implicitly. And around us had collected a knot of my centurions and *optios* who could understand Latin, and I saw on their faces the same expression of awe mingled with consternation. Even the Barbarians, Alans and Franks, comprehended the dramaturgy of the moment.

"There is no Emperor," I said.

"No Emperor?" he repeated.

"Not in the West," I amended. "In Constantinople, yes. But he has no interest in Britain. All he asks is to be able to hold his own against the Persians and the Scythians."

"But you? You are Roman! And I see other Roman faces. Your soldiers have Roman discipline, wear Roman dress. This town—" His eye caught the broken coping of the quay, and he shook his head slightly—"No, that is not Roman, not what we Romans of Britain call Roman."

His glance roved to the cohort's standard, and his features lighted eagerly.

"But you carry an Eagle!" he protested.

"Yes, we carry an Eagle," I assented sadly, "and it is true, O man from another world, that certain of us, myself, a few others,

---

3   *Welsh really South Welsh.*
4   *Cornwall.*

may claim Roman citizenship. It is true that Rome still exists, true that the Senate meets in the Capitol, true that each year Consuls are elected for Western as well as Eastern Empire. It is true that this cohort, and others, some, not many, keep up the Roman discipline. It is true that the Prankish King, Clovis, gives employment to many of us Romans who served in Gaul before he conquered it. True, also, that Christ is worshipped in the temples of Gaul as He was before the last Emperor died in Rome. It is true, as I said, that Rome still exists—but Rome is dead. Theodoric the Goth is King of Italy. Clovis the Frank is King of Gaul. We Romans are their men. They rule, not we."

"I do not understand," he said dumbly. "Surely, the Legions—"

I cut him short. This was dangerous ground. Already, we had discussed openly in presence of the Barbarians subjects best kept for such intimate communications as this, my Anicius.

"There is much you do not understand," I answered. "Yet if you will be guided by my advice all shall be made plain to you."

He sensed a hidden meaning in my interruption, and his glance shifted keenly from my face to the others surrounding us: a couple of dark, thick-browed Romans, the rest towering, bearded Barbarians.

"You are wise," he conceded. "This place is public for discussion. If my men might have food and wine—"

"They shall have full rations," I promised. "And if you will be my guest I will endeavor to prove that however unworthy may be our station we Romans are still capable of appreciating a brave man, especially when he happens to be a Roman."

He bowed as became a Senator, draping his cloak togawise across his armor.

"I am honored, Count of the Bononian Shore. I had been cast down, but you—"

"There is no reason for you to be aught but cast down," I interposed hastily. "Your plight is a disgrace to all Romans, and there is little enough I can do for you. But come."

We posted sentries on the quay to keep the rabble from the

longship, and after I had given orders for food to be provided
the Britons and Marbonius had instructed them briefly, he rode
with me up to my quarters in the *Prætorium* above the town.
We said little on the way. My own thoughts were bitter, and
my companion seemed to be occupied in studying the sights
of the town. I have described it all to you before, O Anicius,
and you tell me it is much like your Rome of today: grass
sprouting betwixt the paving for lack of cart-wheels, two people
where once were three; priests, priests, priests, monks, monks,
monks, our Gauls—or your Romans—scurrying meekly about
such business as fortune affords them, and the Barbarians in
the background, sucking up the taxes. Somewhat of this I explained to Marbonius, and he heard me, tight-lipped.

"I begin to understand," he said as we dismounted in the
court of the *Prætorium*. "Your Franks are in some ways the same
as our Saxons. Both are Barbarians. But there is this differ-
ence—and it is a wide one: your Franks are Christians like the
rest of you, they ask only the right to rule and deal gently with
Gaul and Roman—"

"Oh, they are kind masters!" I admitted. "Kinder than we
deserve, if the truth be known. But what irks, and must ever
irk, is that *they* are masters, in *our* place."

There was a guard of Gaulish cavalry, *cataphracti*, the best
ala in my command, and they turned out for me as I rode into
the Prætorium, gigantic mailed riders on tall mailed horses, a
spectacle to move a soldier's heart. I glimpsed the flash in the
Briton's eye, and asked him if he would inspect the guard.

"Gladly," he said, then hesitated. "But no, I have no sword."

"You do not require a sword," I replied.

But he would not cross the courtyard with me.

"I can not inspect soldiers," he insisted. "For I sold my sword.
It is not fitting that your men should be paraded for me."

"By all the Saints, you are a queer fellow!" I protested. "And
they are paraded for me, not for you. But I am more interested

in hearing your story than in arguing with you. We will dismiss the guard, if you please, and try a skin of Coan wine."

It was that you sent me, O Anicius, beautiful, vibrant stuff, vastly different from the muddy juice they call wine in Gaul. With a drink or two of it under my belt I feel myself expanding, gliding back across the years. I hear the old Legions stamping by, the whine of the catapults at Jerusalem, the thundering hoofs across the Catalaunian Plain the day Attila's Huns were hammered to defeat! Mars knows, it is no Christian feeling! And much the same was the influence it exerted on this waif from another world, this chip from the rim of the whirlpool where Roman and Barbarian, Christian and heathen, struggle for God knows what.

Marbonius quaffed his goblet with an echo of my sigh of satisfaction.

"This is what Horace sang of, eh? I turn to him when my ears grow weary of the mouthings and posturings of Llywarch Hen. But I suppose all poets are the same if you must meet them in the flesh. Q. Flaccus drank beyond his due, you know."

"What do you know of Horace?" I queried, amused.

He quoted promptly:

> *What have the fatal years not brought of ill?*
> *Our father's age, than their sires' not so good,*
> *Bred us ev'n worse than they; a brood*
> *We'll leave that's viler still.*

"Is that apt to the times? By what you say, it should be. St. Alban be my witness, it's the pith and whole of Britain's plight!"

I ignored the pathos of his last remark in my astonishment at the sonorous ease with which he had fitted in that quotation—you remember it, my Anicius? The Sixth Ode of the Third Book, "Of Rome's Degeneracy." Five hundred years ago Horace wrote it to chide a Rome that was just embarking upon her last climb to greatness. And today it is more apposite than ever! After all, what is Time?

"But where do you learn Horace in Britain, you who, by your own story, must battle with the heathen?"

"We are not savages," he returned, with a hint of mockery. "At Corinium[5] there is a good Academy—and some of the priests refuse to despise true learning. But I forgot, I doubt if Corinium lasts much longer, and in any case, there will be no pupils for the Academy. Yes, the day draws near when the Britons must subsist upon the poetry and learning of Llywarch Hen and his kind. We have shot our bolt. And if you can give me no hope of aid from Rome, why, I am a fool for my pains, and might better have used the chance I bought to escape to Deva[6] or Isca Silurum.[7] They will need soldiers in either place. Here you have plenty—of a sort."

"They are not Roman soldiers, remember that," I answered without losing my temper. "Rome is a name, nothing more. Roman citizenship is an honor so empty the Barbarians do not envy it."

He fixed me with glowing eyes. They were not Roman eyes. Somewhere in his past there must have been a fair Barbarian mother, for they shone brightly blue against the tanned swarthiness of his skin.

"Yet you say there is an Emperor in Constantinople? And the Senate still meets? And each year you have a new Consul?"

"For the Emperor in Constantinople," I replied, shrugging my shoulders, "take my advice and forget him. He pretends, and Theodoric in Rome, and Clovis here in Gaul, permit him to pretend—yes, pretend with him—that he is Roman Emperor of the world. There is naught said of it, no homage asked or given. It is simply that some of the old forms are kept up, because the Barbarians like them. Rome dies, but there is a majesty in the name. It is like a great man's statue, cold to the touch, warm to the imagination. Some day the Barbarians will weary of Roman forms and ceremonies, or perhaps other Bar-

---

5   Cirencester.
6   Chester.
7   Caerleon-on-Usk.

barians will come in and conquer the Goths and the Franks as they conquered us, and then the last vestige of Rome will vanish. It may be the Capitol will be torn stone from stone, and Rome be come like that city—what was it you called it?—the White City—"

"Viroconion!"

The name was music on his lips.

"Ah, no! God in heaven, no! You do not realize what you say. You have not seen all that your fathers had labored for for four hundred years hacked and battered into shapeless ruin by Barbarians beside whom these Franks of yours are cultured philosophers. What have you, here in Gaul, suffered compared with us? Nothing! With us it is freedom or slavery, victory or extirpation. With you it is no more than new masters, rude, perhaps, but kindly, and Christians who reverence the Blessed Jesus. I tell you there is no comparison. You may bemoan a loss in trade, hurt pride that the Roman name has only the echo of its former potence. But we—we have seen two-thirds of our land, our finest cities, harried and wrecked, so that where a hundred families might find food the Saxons themselves cannot live without stealing from our settlements or harrying the mainland."

I could not gainsay the man, my Anicius. Indeed, he inspired me with a humbleness I am unaccustomed to.

"Tell me," I asked, "how it is that Britain is so shut off from intercourse? It has been a common saying for two men's lives that it was become no more than the haunt of the Saxon pirates."

"You have answered your own question, Count of the Bononian Shore," he said, with his wry smile. "We have been driven off the sea, and our harbors sealed by the swarms of pirate craft. Hemmed in ashore by the waves of Barbarians that have pushed us farther and farther into the West, we have had no opportunity to pass oversea. Twice in my day it was tried, but each time the men who attempted it were captured by the pirates who blockade the coasts."

"And this side of the water there has been no fleet to check them in so long a time that I doubt if there are shipwrights living who could contrive the framework of a trireme!" I growled.

"The Barbarians!" exclaimed Marbonius. "The world goes to pieces because of them. I was taught in school that they poured out of some unknown reservoir of men in the dim recesses of the East, one tribe jostling the other, fighting and brawling their way toward a more comfortable homeland."

"You were taught correctly," I assented sourly. "It is so. I think it will always be so. In the long run, no doubt, they will possess the earth. But here is no occasion to discuss philosophy, my friend—No, I must hear from you some explanation of the extraordinary claims you make. You are Legate, you said, of the Sixth Legion, and—"

"And that is the truth," he cut me off stiffly.

"But think, man! The Sixth, *Victrix!*"

I reached over and snapped open the chest in which I keep my scrolls of records and accounts, amongst others a fair copy of that *Notitia,* which some Emperor—I fancy Honorius—had prepared in imitation of the Antonines to show the distribution of the Empire's defenses. And I unrolled it to the sheet which noted the defenses of Britain.

"See," I urged him. "This list is a century old. It concerns the last days of the Empire, as an Empire. And here you have the Sixth, *Victrix*—at Eburacum[8] and on the Wall."

"Precisely," replied Marbonius smoothly. "At Eburacum and on the Wall. Mostly, it was on the Wall. The Sixth and a few cohorts of auxiliaries held the Wall long enough to give our people in the South a chance to stand off the Saxons before the Picts broke through from the North, and made things worse. That was in my great-grandfather's time."

"But to get back to the Sixth," I reminded him. "You will note, it is shown here. And that is its last showing in the records. It disappears."

8 *York.*

"What of the other Legions that were then in Britain?" he asked.

"The Second (*Augusta*) was brought back to Gaul; and I think it broke up in one of the civil wars, oh, a generation past. The Twentieth (*Valeria Victrix*) was brought over by Stilicho more than a hundred years ago to help against Alaric; old men have told me it was cut to pieces in some battle in Pannonia. Most of the old Legions are gone. You'll find one here and there, generally in the East, but it's not usual. Most of the old *Numeri* and auxiliary cohorts and *alæ* have disappeared, too. Everything is different. The world is different—so why should soldiers expect that there should be no change in an Army, which really is no longer an Army, but a band of Barbarian mercenaries?"

He let me rant to a finish.

"You are bitter," he said quietly. "It will be easier, then, for you to appreciate my bitterness. The Sixth was *not* destroyed. It was used up over and over again, its ranks filled, first, with our North Britains, afterwards with men of every tribe and city of those that professed to follow Roman ways. My grandfather became a Tribune in it; my father was Legate, appointed by the Senates of the Border Cities, which bore the brunt of its upkeep; I was appointed to succeed him after he died."

His armor clashed as he straightened involuntarily.

"It was not such a Legion as it was when it came to Britain. The year the storm broke, I have been told, it numbered scarce a thousand men—"

"All the Legions were under-strength in those days," I struck in. "It was one of Constantine's cursed policies."

"That I do not know," replied Marbonius: "but I do know that we filled its ranks in the beginning to five thousand men, and in my time of command it could muster three thousand with the Eagles. Men, mind you! Soldiers! As good heavy infantry as ever stepped. Not mountaineers like Llywarch Hen and his friends. *They* are good light troops, unsteady under pressure, but savage fighters and stout bowmen and fleet of foot. But when it came to the shock, to meeting the heathens Shield-wall, my legionaries and the *cataphracti* of the Icenian Horse always bore the brunt. To the very last! The very last! They—they are under the stones of Viroconion. Cenric won no slaves of us. He admitted it to me. Not a bad man, that heathen, a fighter. He offered to adopt me, but I—I preferred to buy my liberty after I learned his ambition, thinking that I might gain succor for our folk from Rome."

I poured more wine. A man always talks better with a wet tongue.

"Tell me," I invited him. "I am interested in your position, Briton. I have told you, and I tell you again, that I doubt if I can serve you at all—or any other man! But tell me, and if I can see my way to further your mission be sure I will. Only—tell all, as one soldier tells another. Otherwise, I cannot judge fairly of the matter."

"You mean: tell the truth," he retorted in his quiet way, almost jeering. "But what is truth to one man is a lie to another. If you find cause to doubt anything I say, ask me more of it. I will explain. For I am honest with you in that I must win help for our people in Britain. I *must!* Else the end is in view. And I cannot believe that Rome will let us come to that. When the Emperor Anthemius was beset by the Barbarians, long after Honorius had bidden us shift for ourselves, we sent twelve thousand men to help him, two strong Legions, although we could ill spare them. Give us those twelve thousand back, and we will fling the Barbarians into the sea!"

He drained his replenished cup.

"Well, that is boasting, and pushes me nowhere. I will tell my story."

"Wait," I said. "Before you begin your story instruct me further how matters stand in Britain. What is the division betwixt you and the Barbarians?"

"A soldier's question," he approved, and dipped a finger in the wine-lees. "Here is the island's shape. It is much longer than it is wide, you see, and broadest in the south. The eastern and southern parts, where were our richest cities, facing towards Gaul and the Saxon Shore, are low-lying and fertile. Here it is that the Saxons, and other Barbarians, who sometimes fight with them and sometimes assist them, have settled. The midlands are forests and fens. Today they are a debatable ground, the best barrier we have against the Barbarians, who must travel their wastes to reach our borders.

"We who hold true to Rome are forced back into this block of mountainous country, which is thrust out into the sea betwixt Britain and Ireland—"

"And what of Ireland?" I asked. "A monk I met lately told me it was the richest land in the world."

Marbonius laughed shortly.

"He was Irish? He would. It is a land of strong men and lovely dark women and the best breed of horses I know; but except for piety it has no riches—nor ever had. It is so poor that the heathen avoid it, for all it affords them is hard blows. Yet I would not seem to decry it unduly, for the Irish send us many fine soldiers and horses which are better mounts for the *catabracti* than the ponies of our hill country, although in recent years the fleets of the Barbarians have interfered to curtail the traffic to and fro.

"They are akin, the Irish, to Llywarch Hen's folk, the true Britons, and much like them, quarrelsome and forever falling apart. That is the reason why the Barbarians have had the better of us. If it were not for the cities all Britain would have been conquered long ago. It is we Romans—"his shoulders squared; his chin lifted aggressively—"who make resistance possible, for we keep up the Roman walls and Roman discipline.

"You see, here, in this map I have made, how a river—it is called Sabrina[9]—runs across more than half of the eastern face of our mountainous country. But South of it, across its estuary, is the land of Damnonia, not so mountainous, but very rugged,

---

9   *The Severn.*

and the dwellers therein are little squat men, who fight clev-erly from ambush. When they are not fighting they are mining tin. There are no cities worth mention in Damnonia, only the bare moors and the little miners who never strike a foe, except from cover. But alone with us of the Border Cities and the Britons of the Silurian mountains they have kept free of the Barbarian yoke."

"What of these Border Cities?" I asked.

"I was coming to them. First, below Sabrina, is Aquæ Sulis,[10] which once was famous through the Empire for its baths. Ah, I see you have heard of it! Great woods interpose betwixt it and the South coasts, where the Saxons are established. These, its walls and the valor of our legionaries have maintained it, but it must fall very soon, for it is isolated from the other cities of the border and is not sufficiently close to Damnonia to draw strength from the Little Folk of the Tin. Beyond it, and West of Sabrina, lies Isca Silurum, which in the beginning was called Castra Legionum, because it was the fortress of the Second Legion in the old days when the mountain Britons were as untamed as the Saxons who now oppress them. It is the might-iest fortress in Britain. When it falls, Rome has fallen."

"Rome has fallen," I gibed.

His head snapped back.

"Not in Britain," he retorted. "So long as a Roman city is free the Roman spirit shall endure."

"I am well rebuked," I acknowledged. "Proceed—last of the Romans."

He signed himself with the Cross.

"The Blessed Virgin avert so dire a consequence! Let me but have twelve thousand men, trained troops, heavy infantry and *catapbracti,* and we will clear Britain of the Barbarians—and make a new Rome."

"Constantine made a new Rome—in the East," I returned. "When he did that he threw the West away."

---

10   *Bath.*

"It is in the West that *we* hold out," exclaimed Marbonius. "In the westernmost corner of the westernmost Roman land. Perhaps that is a symbol, Count of the Bononian Shore."

"We talk of military matters, not of symbols," I reminded him.

For, indeed, my Anicius, he made me ashamed, with his steadfastness of belief. What is life without faith? Yet how regain a faith which has fled? Tell me, have I put my finger on the canker-worm which rotted the fibre of Rome's greatness? I wonder!

"True," he agreed. "But the symbols Rome left us are the backbone of our defense, for they remind us daily of the heritage of our fathers."

"We talk a different language, here," I said roughly. "Get on with your cities. Isca Silurum was the last. And the next?"

He sighed.

"Yes, yes, Rome is not the same," he admitted sadly. "A broken coping to the quay, and a Roman officer no longer believes in Roman destiny!"

"Now you talk sense," I growled. "Rome is no more."

For a while he said nothing, dabbling his finger in the wine spilt on the table.

"When I found the sword I thought it was a sign from God," he muttered finally; "my men all said it would bring a happy turn to our fortune. And but for it I should not be here."

"What sword is this?" I asked him. "Of what do you speak?"

Marbonius roused himself.

"The sword? The sword is my story. But let me finish what I began. I told you of Isca Silurum. Well, we cross Sabrina again and come to Corinium, and north a way, also on the east bank, lies Glevum.[11] They are stately cities, as Roman as Rome, our fathers claimed. After Glevum the country northward becomes marshy along Sabrina's course, and there are no more cities on

---

11   *Gloucester.*

the Border until you reach Viroconion. But I forget." His face clouded. "Viroconion is a ruin. But while it stood it was the middle bulwark of the Border, like the handle of a door. Southward, Isca Silurum was one hinge; northward, Deva was the other."

"And those are all your cities?"

"All those on the Border. And they are the fairest we have left. Deva, like Isca Silurum, was a legionary fortress. The Fourteenth, *Gemina Martia*, built it. Only Isca is stronger today. As for those beyond the Border, from Regnum[12] on the South coast to Eburacum under the shadow of the wall, they are heaps of stone."

"This wall," I said. "Is it—"

He shuddered.

"I saw it once. We had driven a foray far North to teach the Barbarians a lesson; if you strike at them vigorously they respect you the more. And one day at sunset we rode out of a forest onto a bare hillside, and across a valley was a line of towers that rose and dipped, lifted and sank, with a grey thread of wall between, from horizon's end to horizon's end. And nowhere a sign of life, not so much as a plume of smoke! Blessed Saints, what desolation! We camped by one of the mile-castles that night, and I poked this out of a heap of rubbish in the guardroom." He pointed to his belt-buckle of tarnished silver, with the worn inscription: "LegVI." "My own Legion, you see. The castle was in astonishingly good condition. Oh, the ramp was over-grown with lichen, and bushes and even small trees sprouted in the parapets; but it was defensible, as it stood. So was most of the wall. My men found a shallow breach a mile or two east, but we could have repaired it in a day. On one tower was the wreckage of a catapult, the long casting-arm propped above the battlements. All the Wall lacked, all it ever lacked, was men to hold it. It—it made us very sad, discouraged. We lost interest in our foray, after that. The work seemed futile. Do

---

12   *Chichester.*

you understand? Here was the wall which Hadrian had built for all time, and it had endured for all time; but as Horace said in that verse I quoted you, our fathers had bred a vile brood of sons. Yes, Rome's sons had failed her, not the brick and stone she had shaped for her purpose."

"I understand," I assured him. "You are not the first to nourish that thought."

He stared at me, half-disapproving.

"But it does not stir you to resentment!"

"Resentment!" I jeered. "What could I accomplish by it? What have *you* accomplished by it?"

"I don't know," he acknowledged. "It is in God's providence. When I had the sword—"

"God's providence! Briton, you talk like a priest. And what properties had this sword, which, as I remember, you said you sold? Why did you sell it, if it was so valuable?"

He smiled gently, seeming to penetrate the pettiness of my spleen.

"I sold it to come hither," he answered. "If my coming secures help for my people the sword will have saved Britain. Also, it bought—albeit without pledge—a truce for the balance of the year, seeing that Viroconion cost Cenric so many lives that he cannot afford to resume the war until he has received reinforcements of Barbarians from overseas."

"A good price," I admitted. "If there was an Emperor to turn the advantage to account for you. But we are stumbling in the dark. Go on with your story."

His smile became melancholy.

"You give me scant encouragement. Well, for that you are not to blame. And perhaps the sword has achieved all it can for us. Surely, if it fights for Cenric as it fought for me— But I talk at random. We will go back to the beginning of things.

"In the spring word came to us from the Fen Folk, who dwell in the woodlands betwixt us and the Saxons, that Cenric would launch a great stroke against the Border Cities. I was at Isca

Silurum with the Sixth and several alae of horse, and we had detachments of light troops out on the roads by which the Barbarians might advance. Usually they come by one of two ways: the old Middle Road up from what was Londinium,[13] direct toward Viroconion, or the South Road which skirts the vast Wood of Anderida and strikes the Border at Glevum, with byways toward Aquse Sulis and the Damnonian Marches. The Middle Road is the most direct, but they have more chance of surprising us when they come from the South, so I was not surprised by a message from Aquæ that the Barbarians were reported landing under Vectis.[14]

"There was a Council of Nobles, one of the curses of Britain, legates from the cities and the different Kings and Princes of the free tribes. The cities were for making me Consul, with absolute powers; the Kings and Princes, as always, were jealous of the cities and one another. The compromise reached was the one employed on every similar occasion: I was named to command the cities troops, and Kyndylan, Prince of the Cornovians, was put forward by the free tribes to command their contingents. 'There are more of our men than of yours,' they said. And that is true— But all their men are not worth two cohorts of Legionaries when the Saxon Shield-wall must be broken.

"Again, I was for waiting before we went out to meet the Barbarians, so that we might fight them on our own ground. But Kyndylan and his friends cried that it would be cowardly to permit the invaders to wreak more harm to the Border. It was strong talk, and they won over with it the legates of Aquæ and Corinium, who were most exposed to attack from the South. And the consequence was that I was directed to march South at once, seek the enemy and pursue them to the sea. I had the Sixth, an *ala* of the Icenian Cataphracti, a few troops of light-horse, Damnonians and Silurians, and Kyndylan's Britons, javelin-men and archers, a valiant, disorderly mob."

---

13   *London.*
14   *Isle of Wight.*

"What did you do with them?" I asked as he paused.

"Sent them on ahead. That was the safest use for them. They were hungry to close with the Barbarians, and I knew that if they met any considerable force of Saxons they would be routed. In that case I expected to catch the enemy in the confusion of pursuit, and smash them with my armored troops. But matters fell out very differently.

"We marched by way of Aquæ Sulis, and took the road east over the hills to Cunetio,[15] and then southeast through very rough country to what used to be Calleva Atrebatum.[16] The walls were standing; most of the houses were intact. A city of ghosts. Just beyond it we encountered our first Barbarians, a shipload or two, perhaps ten score men, plundering tombs along the wayside. I thought for a while they must be the bait for an ambush, and I sent my mounted men after them to spring whatever trap might have been laid for us. But they were unsupported. We harried them unmercifully, and then retired at evening to a ruined villa on the Calleva road, where we might rest behind walls. You can never be too wary of these Barbarians; they are always cunning and resourceful—as I was soon to discover.

"Near this villa was a group of tombs in a little glade, with a battered altar to the *Genius Loci*. The Barbarians had tumbled the stone cap off one tomb, and I ordered a squad of my Legionaries to lift it back into place. After all, it was a Roman grave. An *optio* called to me that within the stone casing was a leaden coffin, and I walked across the glade to examine it. One of the Barbarians had sunk his axe into the metal, and through the gash there was a grey gleam, almost as if an eye winked up at us in the twilight. I was curious. Who lies here? I inquired. A centurion pointed his *vitis* at the inscription on the capstone: 'Decius Maximus, Prefect of Britannia Prima, and the Sword of his Destiny.' 'Ha,' said I, 'let us have a look at this sword of Decius!'

---

15   *Folly Farm, near Marlborough.*
16   *Silchester.*

"The Legionaries pried off the leaden lid with their broad-swords, and there before us lay the dried fabric of a man in extreme old age, white-haired, his armor scrolled and enamelled, his helmet the work of a goldsmith. In his skeleton-fingers was clutched a long, grey sword of a steel I have never seen in any other weapon. I suppose the coffin was sealed against dampness, which would account for the blade's being rustless; but that was not the only peculiar characteristic it had. Its surface was marked with a multitude of convoluted lines and whorls, and graven in the metal were a series of letters and symbols. There was a writing made of little pictures; I do not know what that could be."

"Egyptian, very likely," I said.

"Very likely," he agreed. "I made out also several inscriptions in Greek; one was 'The Grey Maid,' meaning the sword, I think. Others were men's names or initials. There was a Latin inscription: 'The Tribune Valentius Martius won me from the Carthaginian,' And there were still more writings strange to me. Many men had owned this sword. It had a personal identity like a man or a woman. You could feel it, potent, sinister, a disturbing aliveness. 'Take me,' it seemed to say. I reached down and detached it from the dead hand of Decius Maximus, and it swung up with a lithe, balanced grace, feather-light, as much a part of me as the arm that wielded it.

" 'Blessed Saints, what a sword!' I exclaimed.

" 'It is a sign from God,' cried the centurion who had showed me the inscription.

" 'Yes, yes, shouted the soldiers. 'The Legate has a sign from God! St. Alban sends him a sword of destiny!'

"It is not my custom to rob the dead, Count Domitianus; but a voice outside myself bade me put to use what Decius Maximus had long since ceased to need. A good sword is a good sword—and it is never well to lose an opportunity to encourage your men. There was a hard campaign in front of us. The sword was a favorable omen."

"What did your priests say to it?"

He grinned.

"The holy Bishop Rufinus cleansed the steel of any heathen taint after we came to— But I am running too fast. I told the soldiers I would take the sword, and they were closing up the tomb again, when there was a thudding of hoofs in the road, and a vexillation of the Batavians galloped up, escorting a centurion from the Prefect of the garrison of Aquas. He was a stout, puffy fellow, and commenced shouting to me while he was dismounting.

" 'Cenric is on the Middle Road—Uaxacona[17] has fallen—at the gates of Viroconion—the Border is in flames!'

"He and his Batavians—of course, there wasn't a Batavian in the lot! I told him to be quiet, but the mischief was done. My Legionaries went straight to their posts in the ranks, but Kyndylan and his Britons were swirling around us like wild men, yes, like the cattle the Barbarians drive with torches. 'We are betrayed!' 'Oh, our wives and children!' 'Back to the Border!' And more nonsense of the same kind.

"Kyndylan struggled through the press to where I stood beside the tomb with the grey sword in my hand. He was a handsome man, with wavy hair, ruddy gold, and eyes as blue as the summer sea, big of his body, too. He wore armor like any Legionary, and because of that imagined he had done all that was necessary in order to fight as we did. I could never make him understand that without discipline and training his men were helpless before the Saxon Shield-wall. They were brave, they had weapons! What more could they want? Armor? It was all right for some, perhaps, but his mountaineers would lose their fleetness of foot if they must carry heavy *loricæ* and helmets and the Legionary's big shield.

" 'What are you going to do?' he shouted.

" 'Send on some light-horse to make certain the rascals we

---

17   *Oaken Gates.*

just cut up do not tarry hereabouts, and with the remainder of the column march back to Glevum.'

"The coolness of my voice disconcerted him, but he pointed to a group of Legionaries kindling a fire.

" 'Have we time for that?'

" 'To eat?' I said. 'The men have marched for five days, and some of them have fought hard this afternoon. They will be fitter for food and rest.'

" 'You will not march at once?' he shrieked.

" 'I will march in the morning.'

" 'But the Saxons are on the Border! While we wait the villages will fall to the torch.'

" 'Viroconion will hold Cenric from the back-country. We could not stop the Barbarians from burning and slaying in every place if we were camped tonight in the Middle Road. In any case, tired troops must sleep.'

"He threw up his hands in anger.

" 'It is easily seen you have no folk outside the walls! You men of the Cities are all alike. You think only of yourselves.'

" 'I think only of Britain,' I answered him. 'We shall gain nothing by wearing ourselves out. Let us take what rest we require, and march as hard as we can. That way we will make better time than if we fling ourselves at the road.'

" 'My people are not under your orders,' he fumed. 'They will march with me tonight.'

"I did not argue with him. It is never worth while to argue with an angry Briton. But I was not so sure as I had been that my new sword was a sign from God or a beneficent omen as I watched Kyndylan's yelping pack huddle off on the back-track, ponies slipping their loads, chiefs shouting and gesticulating, Llywarch Hen and his brother-poets chanting in the dust, and the common men eating whatever they could lay their hands on.

"In the morning we followed them, and by noon their stragglers were cumbering our column. We turned northwest by the road which leads to Corinium and Glevum, and so crosses Sabrina for Magna[18] and the other cities in the mountains. At Corinium Kyndylan was awaiting us, blustery and self-confident. He had marched the feet off most of his men, but refused to admit he was wrong. With three thousand of the stoutest he set forth again that night by the river-path, boasting he would be in position to strike the first band of Barbarians he encountered. The local Senate had begged him to wait for me and the reinforcements I had sent for, but he answered them as he had me. 'You have your walls. My folks must rely upon our bodies to protect them.' And it was true that every unwalled house on the east bank of Sabrina was given to the torch. The forum of Corinium was surrendered to the refugees; they slept in the churches and the Basilica; and the same conditions prevailed in Glevum and Aquæ Sulis. A stream of fugitives poured West by every road and foot-path. The old men said it was the worst visitation of the heathen since Ratae[19] and Lactodarum[20] and Bannaventa[21] and the other cities of the Midlands were destroyed.

"But I was very hopeful that Cenric had played into our hands. Instead of having to fight him on ground of his choosing, out of touch with our bases, as the Council of Notables had decided we should, his successful ruse to throw our strength to the South actually had placed us in position to give him battle on terms favorable to us. We had only to select the proper moment, and then hurl him back into the wilderness he had traversed, with the certainty that victory would enable us to slay or capture three-fourths of his men.

"I had no doubt of the ability of my disciplined men to withstand the Saxon Shield-wall, and to destroy it, if they had any assistance from the Britons. The way to meet these Barbarians when they are fighting in a large host is to involve them

---

18   Kenchester.
19   Leicester.
20   Towcester.
21   Norton.

first with masses of light troops, and after they are completely engaged attack them with heavy infantry, and finally, send a substantial column of *cataphracti* against them. By such tactics they can be shaken apart, and they are like any troops after that happens: chopping-blocks for an intelligent enemy.

"So I turned hopeful once more. The sword helped me. The slim weight of the blade, its worn hilt so easy in the hand, its balance so deft on the wrist, inspired me with confidence. When I drew it from the sheath a current of energy surged up my arm. The grey steel glinted with a soft fire that seemed to murmur for the coolness of the blood-bath. Even the soldiers noticed it. They called it 'Marbonius's grey maiden,' and made up rude sayings about it. And afterwards they never hesitated to take the bloodiest path it carved for them. It was as if it had a heart in it, almost, a cruel and lustful heart, but yet a heart. Yes, and a keen brain. Oh, very keen!"

"Did you follow after Kyndylan?" I queried as he paused for a draught of wine.

"That was what the Senators in Corinium wanted me to do. If Kyndylan runs into trouble you can support him, they said, and moreover, you will be a shield between the Barbarians and the river villages.

" 'Quite true,' I assented. 'And also, the Barbarians will be sure to hear of my coming. No, Kyndylan must shift for himself a while. Unless he is a very great fool he can not come to serious harm. I intend to attack Cenric at my pleasure, not his.'"

"You ran a certain risk in suffering your forces to be divided," I pointed out.

"Ah, but they were not *my* forces! That was the difficulty. And I was determined to come down on the Barbarians before they had any knowledge of my presence so far North. You see, Cenric would naturally expect me to have gone South in response to the lure he had set for that very purpose. Of course, he would likewise expect me to return as soon as I discovered the size of the band that had landed under Vectius; but he could not be

sure when that would be. I had tidings at Corinium that already
he had invested Viroconion, wasting all the land east and north
of it toward Deva. His attention would be diverted South by
the approach of Kyndylan's Britons, and my plan was to cross
Sabrina and march to Viroconion by the mountain road which
connects Isca Silurum with Deva. On this road I would be
wholly out of reach of the invaders; they could not possibly
hear of me; and when I came within striking distance I would
send word to Kyndylan, arrange to have him launch his attack
upon Cenric and throw in my troops the moment the Barbarians were completely involved with the Britons. As I have said,
such tactics are the best to employ against the Saxons."

"Your numbers were limited, then?" I asked. "You could not
procure additional troops?"

"Legionaries? No. There were a few cohorts in garrison in
the Border Cities, but the Barbarians move with celerity, and
there was always the chance that they might withdraw from
before Viroconion. All I could do was to call for another *ala* of
cataphracti from Isca; there were two more at Deva, but Deva
covers an immense stretch of the Border, and its garrison requires a considerable force of horse to make it good. Suppose
the Barbarians from the North had descended upon us when
we were engaged with Cenric? That is always our nightmare,
to be attacked upon two fronts. No, no, I dare not take a man
from any point except Isca, and there they could spare but the
one *ala*—and that meant stripping the South to the danger-
point. I had to rely on what men were with me."

His face worked.

"If only Kyndylan had acted a man's part, instead of a fretful
boy's!"

"Ah, he failed you?"

"I am coming to that. I marched West by way of Glevum,
crossed Sabrina, headed on West to Magna, and there turned
into the North Road to Deva. At Bravonium,[22] half way to

---

22   *Leintwardine.*

Viroconion, fugitives from East of the river told us of a victory Kyndylan had won in the swampy lands on that bank. He had trapped a large raiding party, and killed them to a man. The Britons were mad with joy. 'King Arthur is come again!' they shouted. 'Kyndylan is Arthur reborn!' One poet in the forum was singing a genealogical song to prove that Arthur's blood ran in Kyndylan's veins. I daresay it was true."

"Who was this King?" I inquired curiously.

"The only King the Britons ever had whom you would call a soldier. While he lived he held the heathen at bay. But he did it by our—by Roman—methods. He was more Roman than Briton, at that. My father told me he won his battles with our Legionaries and *catapbracti*. Anyway, the Britons in Bravonium were howling themselves hoarse in the delusion that Kyndylan was Arthur—or Arthur was Kyndylan—whichever you please. And frankly, I was worried. I knew what a hot-head Kyndylan was. Give him a taste of victory, and there might be no stopping him. So I did what otherwise I should not have done. I left word for the ala from Isca to push after me, and marched my men on from Bravonium as fast as they could travel. They never complained, and in twelve days of foot-pounding the physicians treated three—for bellyaches."

"A good record," I approved.

"I was proud of them. They—they— But you are a soldier. You know. I shall never command such men again. Humph! This wine is good, but it stings the throat. Humph! Well, my worst forebodings were realized. We made a night-march, but I called a halt after midnight, for the leader who enters battle with tired men is beaten before the first pilum is cast. We took the road again at dawn, and I sent forward the light horse to feel the country and establish communication with Kyndylan. At the second miliary southwest of Viroconion a patrol intercepted us with news that Kyndylan had attacked Cenric, and was stiffly engaged on the east bank of Sabrina.

"My heart sank, but I ordered the Legion to accelerate their

pace and galloped on myself with the *cataphracti*. As we rode
out of the hills above the ford the spectacle of the battle was
unfolded beneath us, the valley slopes green with trees and
crops, the city a white oval in the midst of its belt of gardens,
and just across the brown stream an immense swirl of men,
creeping closer and closer toward the South Gate. It was plain
the Barbarians had the upper hand. I could trace the great
wedge of Saxon shields, the tall figures of thanes and churls
looming above the squat Britons; Kyndylan's folk were fighting
in the disarray they seemed unable to forget, and a fringe of
wounded and poltroons extended as far as the city gate, which
stood open.

"A centurion of the Damnonians joined me at the ford. He
said that Kyndylan had crossed the river earlier in the morning,
intending to fight his way into town. That fox, Cenric, had
thrust out a small body to oppose the crossing; the Saxons had
been driven back, and with that their entire host had feigned
panic. Of course, it was too much for Kyndylan's Britons. They
had broken their ranks, and poured after the fleeing invaders,
who had promptly reformed a Shield-wall and faced around to
annihilate the pursuit. A trick older than my sword! While I
watched, the defense of the Britons disintegrated, and they fled
like so many sheep for the open gate.

"St. Alban assail me if there was ever such foolishness! In
the gateway a few of the garrison strove to pull the leaves together and raise the drawbridge over the moat, but the first of
Kyndylan's folk to arrive chased them away. And the boiling
throng eddied nearer with every slash of the Saxon swords. The
Britons were so demoralized that the Saxons abandoned their
formation, and the Shield-wall split up into innumerable companies, each fighting on its own account, but all driving headlong for that open gate beyond which lay the loot of Viroconion.

"Blessed Saviour, it was disaster! Disaster such as I had anticipated for Cenric. Here were my Briton allies destroyed, and
Viroconion all but taken. And if Viroconion fell like this how
should we be able to maintain the Border? Which City would

fall next? I surveyed the thousands of the Barbarians, looked at the few hundred horse I had available and calculated the effectiveness of the Sixth, tramping through the dust a mile or more in the rear. I might not even wait for the Legionaries. If the city was to be saved, it must be saved immediately. Its one hope was the flexible might of my mailed horsemen.

"We trotted down to the river, and were in the ford before we were spied by a handful of loitering Saxon churls who had been plundering Kyndylan's dead. They screamed a warning, but those open gates were so close now that the main attack of the Barbarians plunged ahead until the blasts of our trumpets gave warning of the charge. Then the rearmost Saxons turned and framed a ragged Shield-wall, while midway of their mass men milled in sudden confusion, some addressing themselves toward the routed Britons, others disposed to confront us. Clean through them we drove, and the troopers of the light horse supported us with a hail of arrows that staggered them further.

"But they were warriors, those Barbarians. Cenric cried on a band to continue for the gate, and hastily rallied the rest to face us when we returned to the charge. It was not so easy the second time. They were ready for us, their dense ranks heedless of the blinding drift of arrows from our bowmen. We struck them as powerfully as before, but the head of our column crumpled up, and the Saxons swarmed around us as they had around the Britons, flinging themselves at the *cataphracti* from every side, hacking with their axes, hewing with their swords, hauling troopers from the saddles with their bare hands. It was my sword put us through. Its grey blade was like a lightning-flash in the summer sky. It seemed to fight of its own accord. I swung it, guarded with it; but its sureness was uncanny, yes, more than human. Thane after thane clashed to earth under its strokes. Cenric, himself, I cut through his shoulder-plates. And so we reeled out of the enemy's ranks, leaving a tenth of our number behind us, and spurred after the Barbarians who assailed the gate.

"These fellows saw us coming, and decided to go elsewhere.

Nor did I seek to stay them. I was content with our achievement, and reined in my horse at the edge of the moat.

" 'Lift drawbridge, fools,' I hailed the warders. 'Close your gates. Heaven will not always be so kindly to you.'

" 'Do you come in, Legate,' they babbled. 'We are weakly garrisoned. We—'

" 'What of Kyndylan?' I called back.

"A howl of rage answered me, and Llywarch Hen—the poet who sought to entertain you on the quay, Count Domitianus—stepped into the gateway.

" 'The shapeliest sapling of Powys has been lopped by Saxon axes,' he wailed. 'Eagles of the North have drunk the heart's blood of him who was the pride of poets, the delight of maidens, the joy of his people, the—'

" 'Is he dead?'

" 'The choir of Saints stooped to catch his head, and the trees of the mountains soughed in unison when he—'

" 'Who commands there?' I demanded.

"A lean, hard-faced officer stepped on the battlements of the gate-tower. I knew him for a Tribune of the Third Cohort of Brigantes; his name was Marcus; a capable man.

" 'Are you coming with us, Legate?' he asked. 'If not—'

" 'Bar your gates,' I returned. 'And stand prepared to unbar them if I decide to come in. All my troops are not up yet. Also, I am not clear in my mind how best to safeguard the city.

" 'You can safeguard it best by joining its garrison,' he replied coolly. 'I haven't five hundred trained men to hold three miles of walls. As for these—' he waved a hand down at the Britons still clustered in the gateway—'they'll do for archers, but I can't put them in a breach.'

"It was a good argument. But I couldn't commit myself while the Sixth was out of touch.

" 'Do what you can,' I told him. 'When the Legion has come up I will decide. You can manage until then, can't you?'

" 'I can manage as long as I can hold the walls,' he growled.

"I had observed a cloud of dust billowing over the road across the ford, and I knew that this must be my Legionaries. The Saxons had drawn off east a couple of bowshots, carrying most of their wounded with them, and were standing in a sullen ring, with shields dressed to meet an attack from any direction. Apparently, they were not eager to push matters at the moment. Kyndylan's Britons had taken some toll, and my charges had been expensive. But east among the trees I saw the glimmer of steel, and south and north bodies of armed men were moving toward the slopes above the ford. There were more of the Saxons than I had expected. It was the largest host they had ever mustered against us. We were outnumbered two or three to one—and my men were weary and my horses heads drooped.

"I thought hard. Should I risk battle in the open? No, it was too dangerous. Should I withdraw to the west bank of the river and remain in observation? There was much to be said for this. I could menace Cenric's position at will, interfere with his plundering parties. But in the meantime what would happen in Viroconion? The Tribune Marcus had told me all he dared in so public a manner, and that was enough to warn me the people were faint-hearted. For which there was a reason. It had been accepted along the Border that when the Barbarians attacked again their blow would be directed at Aquas Sulis, which was most exposed. The citizens of Viroconion were doubly dismayed to find that Cenric's rage struck first at them. The defeat of Kyndylan must have shaken their confidence further.

"The city's fall meant the devastation of the Border. My mission was to save it from capture. And whether rightly or wrongly, I decided I might protect it most effectively from within its walls. Perhaps I— But what do you think, Count of the Bononian Shore?"

"I do not know what to think," I admitted. "I am very glad the decision was not for me to make. Did Cenric oppose your entry?"

"Not he! And it is recollection of his willingness to permit me to reinforce the garrison that prompts my doubts. You can see how his mind worked? Outside the walls he could never be sure what I was doing. Inside, he knew where to account for me every day and all day."

"A shrewd strategy," I agreed. "It amounts to this: he was playing for all or nothing, even as you were."

"You are right," answered Marbonius. "I have thought that, myself. But it is easier to look backwards than forwards. If only Kyndylan had— But the man is dead, and he could never have been other than he was. It was God's Providence, as Bishop Rufinius said when he blessed my sword, lest there be some deviltry connected with it—that was after it had become famous through the city. Yes, God's providence. God's Providence that the heathen should possess Britain. But why?"

"I have never found priest to answer me similar questions, my friend," I said.

"There are some things beyond priestly wisdom," he re marked shrewdly. "The Bishop said it was a blessing on the city when the Sixth marched in through the South Gate, baggage and gear, under cover of my *cataphracti* and some *tormentæ* Marcus erected on the neighboring curtains of the walls. But I can not see the blessing for anyone of us concerned therein."

I refilled the wine-cups.

"You strain my curiosity unbearably, man from another world," I urged. "What happened to your city after you entered?"

"Nothing for several days," he replied. "I had sent away the *alæ* of light horse with instructions to join the *cataphracti* from Isca, and finally, a week after I entered Viroconion I concerted an enterprise with these troops across the river by means of which we introduced a small train of provisions. And it was good that we did. In another week Cenric had secured additional men, determined his own plan and sealed us effectively within the walls. The days were not far off when we should have to kill the horses of the *cataphracti* for food."

"But this magic sword?"

"Ah, but was it magic? That is another question I have never had answered. Sometimes I thought it was. And Cenric did. Surely, it was the most potent defense we had. You see, toward the end of that second week the Barbarians began to attack the walls, not blindly and stupidly, so that we could shoot them down with arrows or crush them by ranks with the catapults, but quick, hard-thrust surprise assaults, two or three at once at widely separated spots. They had no siege-engines, but they rigged rams and worked them very ably, with hurdles protected by green hides to shelter their men. And after another week or so they began night-attacks, which were the most trying of all. We could never tell at which point in a circuit of three miles their ladders would be heard scraping under the battlements, and in consequence we were obliged to keep our men on the walls in full shifts at night as well as by day.

"In the third week, too, they found a weak place in the east wall, and set to pounding a breach. The wall was old, and once the rubble core crumbled we were helpless to stay their ravages. All I could do was to build an inner rampart of levelled houses. They made their first assault on the fourth night after the breach was started, and we lost five hundred men between midnight and dawn. Once they were over the inner rampart. And the following afternoon they opened an attack at the South Gate. By dusk they had bridged the moat and burst in the gate, and again we stayed them by erection of a makeshift parapet of earth and building-stones.

"From that night on we never knew an hour's peace. Cenric sent to all the Barbarians in Britain, the Jutes and the Angles, who hold the East Coast north of the Saxon territories, and the remnants of the Picts in the far North. 'This is the time to bury our own quarrels,' he said. 'Help me to take Viroconion, and the Britons' lands will be bare to us. Here is more loot than we have won since our fathers time.' They flocked to him, all save the Picts, who helped him by a diversion such as I had dreaded when I forebore to call for the *cataphracti* at Deva, drenching the Northern Border in a whirlwind of blood and fire. The Angles and Jutes, however, marched to Viroconion, and in the fourth week of the siege they battered a second breach in the west wall next the river.

"There was rivalry betwixt them and the Saxons as there was betwixt my men and the Britons, yes, and betwixt the citizens and the garrison. Several Senators wanted to ask Cenric for terms. All they thought of was saving their fat necks. One I hanged in his toga, and that shut the mouths of the rest. We also had a number of frays, in which men were slain. And I could never depend on the Britons. Oh, they were brave enough, but unstable. One day they would fight like Legionaries; and then they would become as frightened as children who had seen a spirit in the dark. But my real trouble was with the citizens. You would think that because of their families they would fight more desperately than any of us. But not at all. The town-life had softened them, and they were too accustomed to leaving all military duty to the soldiers. With the Barbarians, on the other hand, whatever their differences might be, they all forgot their animosities the instant the war-horns blew. Amongst them, as you doubtless know, every man is a soldier; his first wealth goes into his arms and armor. It is their pride to be well-equipped, as it is their pleasure to fight, and he amongst them who dies in battle is assured of salvation.

"When our provisions ran short, and we had to eat horse meat there were loud protests because I favored the fighting men in distributing the rations. I said the strength of the fighting men must come first, it was all that stood between the women and children and slavery or death. But the citizens charged me with cruelty and a policy of starvation. It was Bishop Rufinius who quelled them. He was a fussy old man I had never had much use for, but he developed new qualities in the siege. The night toward the end of the fifth week when the Barbarians burst simultaneously through the South Gate and the west breach, Rufinius marched in the midst of my *cata-phracti* to stem the assault, mitre on head and crozier in hand.

'Christ with us, my sons,' he said. He died in the breach, a Saxon arrow in his eye.

"The Tribune Marcus led the reserves we dispatched to regain the South Gate, and he succeeded after very severe fighting—we had to pay a life for every two we took. I had expelled the Jutes and Angles from the west wall, and stood leaning on Grey Maiden, listening to a report by one of his officers, when a tumult broke out behind us, and Llywarch Hen ran from an alley to say the Saxons had forced the east breach. I mustered my dismounted *cataphracti* and a cohort of Legionaries, and we tramped wearily across the city. St. Alban, how tired we were! In the Via Triumphalis, which runs from the South Gate to the forum, Marcus encountered me. 'You know the Britons have yielded the east breach?' he asked. 'By St. Paul, Legate, we are at the end of our tether. There is a fresh attack forming against the South Gate.' As he spoke the howling of the Jutes and Angles rose again at the foot of the west breach, and I heard our trumpets calling up the Legionaries, whom I had left prostrate amongst the dead, snatching the sleep that was as welcome to them as wine.

"Once more, I knew the worst. We could no longer maintain the circuit of the walls. 'Henceforth we fight from house to house,' I said. 'Pass the word to all your officers. The forum shall be our citadel.' 'And the citizens?' What could I answer him? 'We have done all we can for them. Now they must care for themselves. Our task is to hold the city so long as we can lift our swords.' He nodded grimly. 'That is common sense, Legate,' he agreed. 'If all must die, does it matter that some shall die sooner than others?' He sped off, and for a breath I would have recalled him. Who was I to pass sentence on the feeble thousands whose wan faces showed in every door and window? But then I chanced to look down at my sword, its grey glint burning hungrily through the red drops that trickled from hilt to point. It seemed to flash a message back to me: Fight! Fight on! And I remembered that I was not a man, but the custodian of a cause. Yet the shrieks of the women appall my ears as I sit here.

"Heavenly Father, those were bloody days! Have you ever defended a city from house to house, from street to street? Ha, you do not know war! The ruddy sweep of the flames, the hoarse barking of the death grapple, the sobs of the wounded, the thunder of falling walls, smoke of fire and dust of combat clouding the sun, so that at noon the streets are shadowed. Both sides were obsessed by the passion of conflict. For us it was the last stand to keep the Border inviolate. Viroconion became more than a city, more than the scene of our agony. It was Britain—Rome! All that Rome ever meant in that outermost province of the Empire. To the Barbarians the struggle was the final test of their prowess. They ceased to reckon the slaughter in overcoming our defense. Valorous always, they were now spendthrift of life. Any little spot that we clung to was essential to them, no matter what it cost. What if as many died as lived? The plundered countryside provided meat and wine for the living; they had hordes of women plucked from the ruins; we sold them day by day at the highest price we could wring from ready spenders.

"Back, we were driven, back, back. We fought hungry; we fought thirsty; we fought in our sleep. We slew until our arms hung limp. But however exhausted I was, the sword never failed me. I should have died a score of times but for the strange power which seemed to render it invincible. Again and again I was beaten down, isolated, trapped in a circle of heathen, my helmet knocked off, my shield in splinters—and the sword would find me a path of escape. 'Follow the Grey Maid!' the Legionaries would cry. 'Up *Victrix!* The Legate's Maid is lustful again.'

"By the tenth day after the Barbarians passed the walls we were hemmed in the block of buildings surrounding the forum, a scant cohort of the Legionaries, a troop or so of the *catapbracti* and a handful of Britons and townsfolk. We barricaded the street entrances with stones and pillars from the arcades, uniting the Senate House, the Basilica, the Church of St. Alban and the Baths into one massive fortress. But we lacked the men to make our resistance effective. Cenric battered a way through the rear wall of St. Alban's, and we retired into the Baths and the Basilica. Marcus and a score or so of the citizens maintained themselves in the Senate House for two days more. We in the Baths and the Basilica were almost impregnable. The two structures were built in Trajan's time, as solidly as this *Prætorium*, forming a right angle around two sides of the forum. Our principal defect was that each time we were attacked, despite our strong walls, we must lose men. And men we could not afford to lose.

"The Barbarians refused to be discouraged. They tried every device that ingenuity could suggest. Day after day they hurled themselves at us, three times forcing an entrance in the double-doorway of the Basilica which led to the Law Courts, as undeterred the third time as the second, although every man who crossed the threshold perished. They brought up a catapult from the walls, and endeavored to work it against the Baths, thinking to make a breach; but they had no experience with *tormentæ* and did us little harm. They tried to burn or smoke us out, heaping our walls with fagots, and under cover of the smoke, Cenric headed a fourth attempt on the Basilica. I slashed him in the thigh, and should have slain him when he fell if two of his thanes had not offered their bodies to protect him while others drew him clear of the ruck. They lowered men to the roof of the Baths from the porch of St. Alban's, thinking to fight their way down to the street floor; but we accounted for all who attempted the venture.

"It was the next day that Cenric limped into the midst of the forum, a thane bearing a peace-shield in front of him.

" 'I will speak with the Briton who wields the grey sword,' he called.

"These Barbarians have no cognizance of Rome, Count Domitianus. To them all who dwell in Britain are Britons. So I set him right.

" 'I am the Legate Marbonius,' I answered, climbing onto the barricade in the doorway of the Basilica. 'I command the

Romans in Viroconion. Who are you who assault the Roman power?'

" 'I am Cenric, King of the West Saxons,' he said, grinning. 'And Roman or Briton, you will not be able to withstand me much longer.'

" 'You have not succeeded very well against us this far,' I said.

" 'Why, that is true,' he admitted candidly. 'We have taken the city, and I suppose we shall kill you, if we can not come to terms; but I would never have climbed the walls had I known how many of my people should pass to Woden's halls. You are a good servant of your gods. It is a rich sacrifice you have offered them.'

" 'I do not sacrifice to my God, but to my country.'

" 'It is all one,' he returned impatiently. 'Will you talk terms?'

" 'What terms?' I parried.

" 'Join me, and fight for me, and I will adopt you for my son,' he proffered.

" 'Do I appear like a man who would sell himself to his people's enemies?' I demanded.

"He looked abashed.

" 'I am a plain-spoken man,' he apologized, 'and I say what is in my mind. I have thought often in the last month that I would be proud to call you son, though my blood is not your blood. You are the only man who can say that he has struck down Cenric twice—and lived.'

" 'There are a few more of us who still live,' I answered.

" 'You have made a brave fight,' he said, 'but I am willing to offer Woden another ten score warriors, if I must.'

" 'We do not sell cheap,' I taunted him.

" 'You do not. You are the best men I have ever crossed blades with. I have not taken one of you alive.'

" 'And you shall not.'

" 'I am content,' he retorted, 'if you will pay me a price to let you go free.'

"Now, this was an idea which had never occurred to me. I wondered if he would require some act of treachery from me.

" 'That must depend upon what price you ask,' I replied.

" 'I will give you and all who still live with you your freedom if you will give me your grey sword,' he said.

" 'It is a Roman's sword,' I objected. 'It has been blessed by our priests. What service could it render you?'

" 'A good sword will always serve a master who does not stint its thirst,' he answered. 'And I will chance the blessings of your priests. If the old one, who died in the west breach, had any part in it Woden could ask no fitter sponsor for a blade.'

" 'But what do you mean by freedom?' I asked, bewildered.

" 'I mean what I say.' He tugged savagely at his long yellow mustaches. 'You may be my enemy, but did you ever know a man of any race who could prove that Cenric the West Saxon had flouted his own word?'

"That was the truth, Count of the Bononian Shore. This Cenric was a man of his word. And his suggestion inspired me with the plan which brought me hither.

" 'Will you supply me and my men with a ship, and grant us safe conduct oversea to Gaul?' I challenged him.

"He was plainly puzzled.

" 'So you will not join your brethren—over there?'

"He waved a hand westward.

" 'I will give you the grey sword only on the terms I have named,' I said curtly. 'A sizeable ship, and safe conduct to Gaul.'

" 'You are not quite the man I deemed you to be,' he growled. 'I expected to meet you some day again—when I carried the grey sword. But you shall have your way. I, myself, will go with you to the sea, and give you one of my own longships. It is a steep price to pay for a sword, but I pay it gladly, for I have seen what the sword can do. And if it can do so much in the hands of a Briton or Roman or whatever you choose to call yourself, what will it do when a Saxon stirs the red broth with it?' "

Marbonius fell silent a moment, my Anicius, and I— But it is needless for me to describe my feelings.

"That is my story," he added presently, and sighed. "If it has wearied you, I apologize. Has it suggested aught that we can do for Britain's plight?"

I stood up before him.

"There is only one thing I can do for Britain," I said. "And that is to fight for her."

"Yourself?" he questioned eagerly. "Do you think many—"

"O, man from another world," I exclaimed, "how shall I make you comprehend that the Rome you expected to find is dead? Here nobody cares for Britain. Frank and Goth are concerned with their own conquests. The Romans left are degenerate and factious as your own British princes."

"But you—"

"Yes, I will fight for Britain, because I should like to sample the air of the island that could breed a Roman like you, Marbonius."

He was silent again for a while. Then he also rose.

"The dusk approaches," he said. "I must put forth."

"I can not go with you at such short notice," I protested. "I have responsibilities to fulfil."

"You must not leave them," he returned. "It warmed my heart when you offered to go with me, Count Domitianus. Despite what you say, it proved the Roman spirit still smoulders outside of Britain's tiny Roman corner. But I would have you remember that we who labor to carry on the tradition of Rome must each bend his back to the particular task God's providence has entrusted to him. You, I doubt not, implant some measure of discipline and courtesy in the administration of the Barbarians in Gaul. I, perhaps, accomplish an inscrutable purpose in striving to preserve our British heritage."

"We labor in vain!" I cried angrily.

His face twisted in that smile without mirth.

"Who shall say what is vain?" he asked softly. "Often I have known discouragement. Many times it has seemed impossible to reconcile the evils of life with an All-Wise Divinity. You have heard me chafe at the failures of my own people and their allies. But as I look back, now, as I adjust myself to the disappointment of all my hopes, I *know* that there is a reason for what we do and suffer. If Rome must die shall she leave no legacy behind her to enrich the earth?"

"She is dead!" I insisted.

"Then let us spread her legacy as broadcast as we may." His armor rattled in the movement of the salute. *"Ave, Cæsar! Morituri te salutamus!"*

And so he went. An hour later from the quay I saw his galley dwindling in the West.

Oh, my Anicius, tell me, you who are so much wiser, so much better in word and thought and deed than I, tell me: in very truth, have all our Roman centuries been in vain? Must the gathering night of barbarism obscure forever the learning and culture of the ages? What has Christianity done for us that the Old Gods did not do? Would Christ, if He were here, approve what Clovis and Theodoric do in His name? Does the world drift or is it spinning toward a definite goal? Is this Rome's end—or is there an hereafter?

Farewell! Farewell! Farewell!

ONE MOMENT the waste of sand and sun-scorched rocks stretched empty from horizon to horizon, the next the watchman on the gate-tower of Muta was shading his eyes to peer fixedly east and west at two spirals of dust sifting upward under the impulse of the hot wind. They were nearly half a day's journey apart, those two spirals, not likely that there was any connection between them. Still, every sign of life was worthy of suspicion on the desert march, and the watchman reached instinctively for his horn.

Below him the gateway arch resounded to the tramp of a column of infantry, drums tapping, cymbals clashing, armor rattling, as they marched in from the practice ground beyond the moat. By the end of the drawbridge stood a little group of officers, mounted and on foot, observing several *numeri* of horse, *cataphracti*, going through a series of complicated battle manoeuvres. The watchman on the tower glanced down at them. Huge Basilakes, who was called the Stammerer, the dux of the infantry, had stopped to speak to Crispus, the Deputy-governor. There was young Flavius Eutyches, too, tribune of the Tenth Thracians. The watchman resumed his inspection of the approaching dust spirals, prepared to bellow the alarm to his superiors. But he shook his head, puzzled.

The spiral in the east, whence came the fierce riders of the desert, was too small to be caused by more than a single rider. No harm there. And westward, the declining sun darted a ray of light into the heart of the more considerable dust cloud and produced an unmistakable glimmer of armor. There could be no armored enemies on the Jerusalem road, the watchman reflected; those riders must be the new Governor and his escort. Crispus would wish to know that.

He leaned over the battlements, and blew a single short blast on his horn. The group of officers across the moat broke off their conversation, and Eutyches, at a word from Crispus, spurred onto the drawbridge.

"What's your report, watchman?" he called.

"A cloud of dust on the Jerusalem road, Tribune, armored men."

"The new Governor," exclaimed Eutyches, and started to rein around.

"And another rider from the desert," the watchman cried after him.

The tribune of the Thracians nodded in sign that he had heard, and clattered back to Crispus.

"Stavrakios is in sight," he announced, grinning at the Deputy-governor. "So passes power, eh? You become dux of the cavalry again, and I must be content with my Thracians."

Crispus, a lean, restless man, tried not to look crestfallen.

"I don't think he can find cause to criticize us," he said.

Basilakes was more outspoken.

"S-s-ss-saint Demetrios," grunted the Stammerer—he was a black-browed Isaurian, gigantic in stature, slow-moving as his own clanking scutati. "To think that a l-lousy courtier is t-tto command soldiers!"

"Oh, Constantine Stavrakios is more than a courtier," exclaimed Crispus, with an effort at fairness. "You know him, Flavius?"

The younger man assented; he was small and compact, a fair Greek.

"Yes, yes! Don't under-value the Governor, Basilakes. I saw

him in the ruck at Nineveh. By the Forerunner, that was a fight! From sunrise until dark, and the Persians as thick as a pest of grasshoppers. After the Emperor, no man wrought more for us than Stavrakios. He had a moira of Obsequii, three thousand stalwarts. Heraclius led them in the last charge—when he killed Reza Khan. It was just short of sunset, and the dust was like smoke over the field. We'd hammered the Persians all day; our tongues were thick with thirst; our arms were tired from slaughtering. We couldn't break them—kill them, yes. I had a century of Macedonians, I remember. We were returning from a dash at a clump of spears, when we saw the Emperor on his white charger, Dorkon, like—like a streak of flame, Stavrakios at his elbow and the Obsequii thundering at their heels."

The group of officers gathered closer. If this was an old story, nonetheless it was unfailing in interest.

"Reza came out to meet them, and the Emperor rode straight at him. We could see the swords flickering over their helms, then Reza seemed to slip from his saddle, and Heraclius rode on. 'Christ for Rome!' he shouted. And he and Stavrakios and their Obsequii disappeared in the midst of the Persians. We all started forward, and almost before we knew it, the enemy were breaking up. If it hadn't been for the darkness we should have caught them all; but we were worn out, and the night—"

"Ah, that's all v-very well," interposed Basilakes, "but what does Stavrakios want out here on the desert march? It doesn't smell nice. He mu-must have d-done something pretty rotten to g-get b-banished here."

Crispus spoke up quickly with an obvious attempt at fairness.

"Not necessarily. Many good men lose the Emperor's favor. I have never been to Court, it's true, but Flavius will bear me out."

The tribune of the Thracians assented again, his brows knit in concentration.

"It's not a disgrace to be in disgrace at Court, the Bodyless

Ones know that! I was thinking, Crispus. There was a story about Stavrakios, a story of a sword he won at Nineveh."

"Many others won swords at Nineveh," scowled Basilakes. "And m-m-maybe w-we out here w-w-win—"

Eutyches waved his hand impatiently.

"Oh, this wasn't an ordinary sword. There were tales about it. The Persian who carried it had been knocked from his horse and crushed. Men said—let me think; it was several years ago, and I haven't thought much—ah, yes, men said that it was a magic sword, that whoever carried it might not be slain by steel."

Basilakes laughed contemptuously, and Crispus remarked:

"What has that to do with the appointment of Stavrakios to command here?"

"That's wh-what I want to kn-know," assented Basilakes. "Crispus did very well this last year. Y-y-you are a new man, Flavius, but w-we have been here years, and I don't see any lower military st-st-standards since the old days at Muta when Phocas was Governor. *H-he* was trained by Maurice, and if he drank n-now and then, he was a soldier. So is Crispus."

"You are good comrades," Eutyches answered simply.

He regarded them both, with a sudden effect of shyness.

"Perhaps," he went on, "Stavrakios feels as I did."

"And how did you feel?" queried Crispus, while Basilakes muttered sullenly:

"No fear! He's not your sort of Roman."

Eutyches hesitated.

"Well," he said slowly, "I came here because it seemed to be the place for a soldier, After we beat the Persians life was very slow in Constantinople, in the other big garrisons, too. I tried Dorylseum. But that isn't soldiering; it's just play. I wanted the same thrill we used to have, danger, the demand for vigilance. So I came here—where I knew a soldier must always be a soldier."

"And you think Stavrakios comes voluntarily, too?" asked Crispus.

"Why not?" returned Eutyches.

"But why?" insisted Basilakes. "H-he isn't you—or anything like you. H-he's another one of these b-back-scratching, b-bath-lounging pat-patricians, with a Senator and a Bishop for uncles, and farms all over the Empire."

"I wonder," remarked Crispus, gathering up his horse's bridle. "He sounds better than I expected. I don't mind being succeeded by a man who— Why didn't you tell us about him before, Eutyches?"

The Tribune of the Thracians flushed awkwardly.

"We're the same breed, Stavrakios and I," he said. "Didn't you ever wonder why a man as young as I had got ten my numerus? I'm—my family have farms 'all over the Empire,' Basilakes."

"I d-don't care how many farms you have," blustered the big Isaurian, patting his friend's mailed thigh. "Y-you're our kind. You re a soldier. And weren't you at Nineveh?"

"So was Stavrakios," Eutyches reminded him.

Crispus thin, intelligent features lighted with an understanding smile.

"You are a good advocate," he said. "Come, we must inspect the fortress. I want everything in shape for the merarch. Flavius, your Thracians will be the guard. Parade them here. Basilakes, we'll turn out one of your *numeri* in the fore-court. Which do you say, your own Isaurians?"

Basilakes shook his head.

"No, no, my friend. *I'm* not the one to start jealousy. G-give it to the Syrians. The Eighth are junior here."

"By all means," agreed the Deputy-governor.

"Oh, by the way," Eutyches called after Crispus, "the watchman reported a rider from the desert."

"Alone?"

"Alone."

Crispus shrugged carelessly.

"I'll see him when he comes in. There may have been a raid. I'm afraid we haven't much to offer Stavrakios in the way of action, as a matter of fact."

"All St-stavrakios will want w-will be a h-hot bath," grunted the Isaurian as he put foot to the drawbridge.

II

THE LONE rider on the desert track halted warily as the glittering centuries formed in double ranks on either side of the approach to the drawbridge. His eyes, burning, intense, flickered over the scene, taking in the orderly array of mailed cavalry, the knot of officers in gilded armor, with chased and befeathered helms, the bristling spears, the eagle-crested standards of pagan Rome topped by the cross of Christ, the military engines on the ramparts, the high towers. Muta rose from the desert floor as solid, as permanent, as endurable as a cliff. Beyond it, the horseman traced the beaten road which traversed the intervening wastes to the Dead Sea and came at last to Jerusalem.

A derisive smile twisted his gaunt face at sight of the cavalcade advancing from the west; white teeth shone behind the thicket of his black beard. He rode on, sitting his roan stallion very erect, a cloak wrapped around his tall form, his features obscured by a loose head-dress which was held in place by a circlet of woven camels-hair. Without swaggering, he contrived to be as much at ease as though he led a thousand men, ignoring the pomp and parade about him. He would have ridden directly into the fortress between the ranks of the guard, if Crispus had not hailed him in the dialect of the desert tribes.

"Ho, stranger, who are you?"

The lone rider reined in at once, and met the Deputy-governor with a level glance.

"I am called Khalid," he replied harshly. "I am of the Kore-isch."

"Of Mecca?" asked Crispus. And turning to Eutyches, the Deputy-governor added: "This is a far-travelled fellow, Flavius. He is from the South by the Arabian Sea."

"I was of Mecca," the Arab answered no less harshly. "I am of Medina. Who are you?"

"I am Crispus," said the Deputy-governor. "What do you wish?"

"I bear a message for the Emperor of Rome. Are you the sheik of this place?"

Crispus pointed his baton of office down the Jerusalem Road.

"Until that man comes, I rule in Muta."

"Then I wait for him," replied the Arab with decision.

"From whom is your message, Khalid?" put in Eutyches, more to test his hard-learned command of the dialect than to acquire information.

Two eyes blazed into his; high-arched nostrils quivered.

"From the Prophet of Allah."

The words fell with a sing-song intonation, indescribably curious.

"And what is Allah?" pressed Eutyches.

Crispus shook his bridle nervously.

"This is no time for gossip," he remonstrated in the Greek which was the normal speech of the garrison, outside of military exercises. "Stravrakios is almost here. Let the Arab go. He is no longer our concern. And he is crazy, anyway, by what I can make out."

"Your pardon, Crispus," apologized the tribune of the Thra-cians. "At your service."

The Deputy-governor motioned to Khalid, who would have followed them.

"Back! Stand back. Can't you see that the merarch is coming? You must wait. Here!" He beckoned a trooper from the rear rank of the Thracians. "Take care of this fellow. He has a message for the new Governor. Fetch him into the Castle after us."

There was no indication of humility in the desert rider's obedience. He backed his horse behind the ranks of the guard, and sat there, quietly watching the ceremony.

The horns of the cavalry echoed brazenly. From inside the gate responded the drums and cymbals of the Syrian infantry. The decurions muttered orders and directions from file to file. Crispus, Eutyches, and the other officers drew their swords and faced the oncoming troop in the Jerusalem road.

Stavrakios rode at the head of a decury. Evidently he travelled light for his baggage was limited to two pack-mules. His armor was coated with dust, his face was streaked with it; but the square sturdiness of his figure, the stern self-reliance of his face, were more impressive than the chased and gilded mail of the officers who received him. He was rather short, but tremendously thick in the barrel, dark in the old Roman way, with a beak of a nose, a black bar of eyebrows meeting above it, a jaw carved in almost straight lines.

As he came up with the guard of honor Crispus barked an order, the trumpets sounded again and lances were tossed in salute. Stavrakios' sword flashed out in a grey streak of light. The desert rider started and leaned forward, a hungry glow in his sombre eyes, his fingers twitching.

"Allah, what a blade!" he murmured.

The trooper beside him laid a hand on his rein.

"Keep your place, heathen dog," the cataphract ordered in bastard Arabic.

The cloaked rider tautened, then relaxed; but his right hand continued to open and shut, open and shut. It was as if he clutched at a sword-hilt, or, perhaps, throttled a man.

Stavrakios hailed Crispus with curt sincerity.

"You are the dux Crispus? Your men do you honor. Ha, I see my friend Eutyches. A tribune, now? And not afraid of heat and sand! Flavius, there are few like you in Constantinople—or elsewhere. Our young nobles are all for easy living. But perhaps we shall show them the Roman spirit is alive again, eh?

"Shall we ride in, Crispus? Humph! You keep your draw-bridge chains greased, I see. Is there difficulty in securing grease? We'll remedy that. I have the Emperor's leave to call for anything in the magazines at Antioch. That tower is well patched. A very defensive gateway. And here are your infantry! Syrians? Well drilled. Basilakes is dux of the infantry drungos? Ha, Basilakes, you are a man after my own heart. Always see to your men's boots. That was the Emperor's first rule in the Persian campaigns, and so we out-marched and out-fought every army that came against us."

Basilakes rumbled a half-hearted acknowledgment.

"M-more fighting th-than dressing here, merarch."

Stavrakios gave him a shrewd look.

"I am glad to hear it. St. George! That is why I am here."

Eutyches winked covertly at Crispus.

"What do you say to him?" the tribune whispered behind his hand.

"I like him," Crispus answered bluntly. "He is a man and a soldier."

"But Basilakes has made up his mind to dislike him!"

"We'll take care of that later."

Outside the fortress the trooper who had the desert rider in charge was urging his man toward the drawbridge.

"Make haste, you scabby dog," he growled. "By the Virgin, I think you are a beggarly Jew. Get on! Do you want us to be locked out?"

The Arab kneed his horse onto the bridge in a silence that was as much sinister as scornful.

III

S TAVRAKIOS GLANCED approvingly at the row of standards in the rack along the end wall of the sacellum. In front of them was an altar dedicated to St. George.

"I like that custom," he said. "If our ancestors were pagans, they were warriors. We Romans have a great heritage."

Basilakes sneered.

"Wh-what is a Roman, merarch?" he asked. "I'm an Is-Isaurian. Crispus is a Syr-Syrian. Flavius is a Greek. And you—"

"That is a bad spirit, Basilakes," Stavrakios interrupted coldly. "Rome was—Rome is—more than a city. It is an idea, a tradition. To be a Roman one need not have been born beside the Capitol. We—you, Crispus, Flavius, Eutyches, all of us, the least of us—are Romans because we carry on the Empire Rome founded."

"Well said," exclaimed Crispus.

"Basilakes must have the belly-ache this evening," said Eutyches, trying to cover the sour mood of the Stammerer.

"I can eat or d-d-drink any of you un-under the table," denied Basilakes, stammering the more in his irritation. "And I'm not a hyp-hyp-hypocrite. I don't believe in Rome. Who does? There isn't any Rome—just a b-b-big heap of ruins, with a lot of p-priests and Lombards wrangling tog-g-gether, and a Bishop who calls himself Pope and tries to tell us Easterns what we should believe. To hell with Rome, I say!"

Crispus and Eutyches murmured uncomfortably, but Stavrakios displayed no resentment. The merarch regarded Basilakes with a calm interest, poised, cool, unprejudiced.

"Your point of view is not new to me," he answered. "There are those in Constantinople, yes, at the Court, who hold it. I have heard men declaim against the retention of the Latin drill. But if we abandon our Roman heritage what shall we adopt in its place?"

"B-be ourselves," retorted the Isaurian. "Are you ashamed of being a p-pat-patrician of Constantinople, with more Greek blood, very likely, than Latin?"

"Not at all," replied Stavrakios collectedly. "But permit me to remind you that you sidestep my contention that to be a Roman is not necessarily to be Latin. Rome is an idea, a legend, a tradition. It is the Empire."

"Once it was," growled the Stammerer. "N-now the Empire is more Greek than Roman."

"What will Crispus say to that, who is Syrian?" inquired the merarch with a dry smile.

"It is true that many feel as Basilakes does," admitted Crispus. "We have little in common with Rome or the West, merarch. These days the West is a brawling ground for barbarians who batter down the monuments of the old Empire. Only here in the East are our fathers works maintained."

"Exactly," cried Stavrakios. "And our fathers were Romans, my friend. The Roman West is, indeed, Roman no more. Only the Eastern Empire persists in treasuring the memories of the past. So, I say, why should we refuse to call ourselves Roman? What other unifying force would hold our different races fused to the one purpose?"

There was an interval of silence. Basilakes, scowling, plainly hesitated to open wider the disagreement with his superior.

"Is not Christianity sufficient?" hazarded Eutyches.

Stavrakios rubbed his smooth-shaven chin, staring reflectively at the statuette of St. George.

"A difficult question, my Flavius," he answered finally. "Religion is a mighty force, yet— Bethink you, the Persians were able to capture Jerusalem and the True Cross—or what men call the True Cross," he added, frankly cynical.

"We won it back," objected Crispus.

"We won it back," repeated the merarch. "Heraclius won it back. And how? With Roman discipline. Flavius, you were at

Nineveh. Say, did cohorts of angels fight for us—or did we win with our own right arms?"

"I saw no divine aid," assented Eutyches. "We won by the sword."

The merarch's hand went involuntarily to the hilt of his weapon.

"By the sword," he repeated again. "Yes, if there was unearthly aid that day the Persians shared it with us."

He looked from one to the other of the three officers.

"I would not have the priests hear me say so, my friends, but this Christ of ours is not a warlike God. Christianity is a good religion, finer and better, no doubt, than any our pagan forefathers knew; but it does not spur men to con quest. No, no, for that we must rely upon our ancient Roman traditions, the spirit of the Legions."

"What is an idea?" growled the Stammerer. "O-on-only something in y-your head."

For the first time a hint of contempt appeared in Stavrakios voice as he answered:

"You are very much mistaken, Basilakes. An idea is the most powerful weapon in the world. One man with the right idea can overcome an Empire—if he believes in himself."

"If y-you believe in Christ I don't see how you c-can believe in Rome," said Basilakes stubbornly.

And Crispus thrust in:

"What you have said is true, merarch, but isn't it also true that the trouble with the Empire is that we have outgrown the Roman tradition, without finding a new one to take its place?"

"That would be to confess failure," protested Eutyches. "And the Empire has not failed. I am a young man, but I can remember when the Persians held all of Egypt and Orientem, from Alexandria to Chalcedon over against Constantinople, itself. Why, Stavrakios, when the Emperor took the field in 621, he had to go by water to reach his own dominions. Men said the Empire was dead. And what happened? In six years we had beaten the Persians, ravaged their lands, destroyed their chief cities. And the Empire's boundaries are restored."

"Roman discipline did it," Stavrakios replied steadily. "I do not agree with Crispus that we have outgrown our tradition of Empire. While the world lasts, Rome will last, not the ruined city that Basilakes is concerned with, but the spirit of organized endeavor which welded scores of different peoples into one whole. If that spirit died, then— Ah, but it cannot die!"

He turned squarely facing the row of standards, and his long, grey sword, a span longer than the regulation spatha, flared in the soft lamplight.

"I salute the Eagles," he exclaimed.

Even Basilakes was impressed, and Crispus inquired as the merarch sheathed his blade:

"Is that the sword you won at Nineveh?"

Stavrakios smiled sternly.

"Eutyches has been talking. Yes, this is the sword of Nineveh—and God knows how many other battles. It is as old as man. But I will speak of it another time. Now, I would have you tell me of the garrison. This is a post of two drungi?"

"Yes, Stavrakios," Crispus assented. "It is a small moira, strong enough for ordinary purposes, but too small for a great emergency."

"How?" questioned the merarch. "What is your strength?"

Crispus indicated the row of standards.

"I am dux of the horse," he explained. "Flavius, here, commanded the drungus while I was Deputy-governor. We have six *numeri*, the Seventh Paphlygonians, the Tenth Thracians—"

"What are Thracians doing here?" interjected Stavrakios.

"They were transferred from Adrianople as punishment for a mutiny in Justinian's time," replied Crispus.

"I see. Go on."

"Then there are the Twelfth Cappadocians, the Fourth Cilicians, and two centuries of the Fifth Syrians—the other century is at Rostra. These five *numeri* are *cataphracti*. Besides them we have the Twentieth Ghassanians, irregulars, for scouting work. But all the *numeri* are under strength. We couldn't put above 2,100 men in the field, and that is not allowing for sickness."

"And the infantry?" asked Stavrakios.

"Basilakes is dux of the infantry drungus," replied Crispus. "Let him tell you."

The Stammerer lumbered forward.

"My *n-numeri* are up to moderate strength," he reported sullenly. "I have the Fourteenth Is-Isaurians, and the Eighth, Ninth, and Thirteenth Syrians. They average five hundred men, two thousand in all. It is easier to get infantry recruits in this c-co-country; the Syrian *numeri* are always up to strength, and whenever my Isaurians fall below I send a message t-to my relatives."

"Your men are in excellent condition," Stavrakios complimented him as warmly as though they had not disagreed. "Humph! And we cover the frontier from the foot of the Dead Sea to Bostra?"

"That is correct, merarch," said Crispus.

"A long stretch for four thousand men. I could wish we had more cavalry, but we must do the best we can. The Emperor has laid a charge upon all his officers to economize. To finance the Persian War, as you doubtless know, he borrowed heavily from the Church, and the Church, my friends—" Stavrakios tight lips curved satirically—"must always have its debts repaid."

He moved toward the door.

"Is there food in the Principium?" he inquired.

"Surely," said Crispus.

"Then I could eat. Join me, I pray you, all three."

In the corridor outside, as they walked to the officers' refectory, Eutyches dropped back beside Basilakes.

"He hasn't had that hot bath yet, old Pepperpot," whispered the tribune of the Thracians.

Basilakes scowled with undiminished hostility.

"H-he's no good, little man. I never saw a man with one of these new p-pat-patrician double names who was any good."

"I have a double name," chuckled Eutyches. "All the Senatorial families have. It's part of the Roman idea."

"I-i-i-idea!" snorted Basilakes. "I'll take his sword instead of an i-i-idea."

"But you must have an idea to use a sword," jeered Eutyches.

"All I w-want is my arm and a head to cut at," rejoined the Stammerer.

I V

IN THE refectory Stavrakios shucked off his armor and placed his sword on the table within reach of his hand; it lay amongst the serving dishes, in its soiled and rusty scabbard, with an effect of hidden menace. Eutyches found his eyes returning to it again and again. Crispus, answering the merarch's stream of questions, still yielded attention to the subtle mystery which seemed to radiate from the sheathed blade. Basilakes, too, silent for the most part, stole an occasional glance at the plain hilt of electrum, modelled to fit the grip of straining fingers. Once Stavrakios touched it caressingly, absent-mindedly, as a man might touch the head of a woman beloved, continuing without interruption his shrewd interrogation of the others.

"What of the desert folk?" he asked finally. "Do they give you much trouble?"

"Nothing serious," replied Crispus. "They raid a caravan now and again, but they are an unstable race, jealous of each other, tribe fighting tribe. We use our Ghassanian irregulars against them usually. They are too swift for the *cataphracti*."

Eutyches remembered the desert rider.

"Perhaps the merarch will wish to see the Arab who arrived this evening," he remarked. And added to Stavrakios: "A strange fellow! He said he had a message from the Emperor from what in Constantine's name was it?—oh, yes, from the Prophet of Allah."

"The man is crazy," said Crispus.

Stavrakios nodded.

"Probably. But have him in. Any message for the Emperor—" He broke off as Eutyches rose to execute his order; Basilakes, likewise, pushed back his chair, stammering something about inspecting sentries—"I am selfishly disappointed you are so quiet, Crispus. I had hoped to offer a small sacrifice to Mars."

He laughed at his own quip.

"Denounce me not to the priests! They are all-powerful in Constantinople for having supplied the Emperor with his war funds. It was that as much as anything brought me here."

His fingers closed again on the hilt of the sword.

"Although I do not know," he went on. "Something seemed to draw me, to urge me. The Emperor grows old; his belly swells with disease. He is not the man he was. In Constantinople all the people think of is the latest gossip of the Court, who profited most from the African grain fleet, whether Blue or Green will win the next chariot race in the Hippodrome. So one day I took a map, spread it flat under an inkhorn and my dagger, shut my eyes and dropped the point of my sword upon it haphazard. The point rested in Syria, close to the desert march. 'An omen,' said I. And I made inquiry, and discovered there was a Governor to be appointed for Muta and besought the post of the Emperor."

A shadow on the face of Crispus attracted his attention, and he exclaimed contritely:

"By Hercules, I had no thought of cheating you out of promotion, man. Hold that not against me." His own face shadowed. "If it had not been I, it must have been some other favorite, perhaps less worthy. The curse of the Empire, my Crispus, is favor. It is not sufficient to be worthy. No, no, you must have wealth, family, friends. Not even the Emperor, great as he is, can resist intrigue."

"You shame me for my resentment," answered Crispus straightforwardly. "And it is as you say, Stavrakios, we are fortunate to have you to command us, instead of some cloak-preening younger son of a Senator, who hasn't a head for anything above racing. But I am afraid you will be disappointed here. There is little opportunity for action. Since we recovered the fortress from the Persians—"

The leather curtains of the doorway fluttered aside, and Eutyches led in the desert rider, Khalid.

"This is the messenger of whom we spoke, merarch," announced the tribune of the Thracians. "Do you know his speech?"

"Sufficiently," returned Stavrakios.

He rose from his chair, and bowed courteously to the Arab, whose glowing eyes scrutinized him with the fervor that had first attracted Eutyches attention.

"I am the merarch, Constantine Stavrakios," said the Governor in halting Arabic. "If you come in peace, you are welcome. If you come in war, you shall not be harmed."

"I come from Muhammad the Prophet, with a message bidding the Emperor of Rome seek salvation in the True Faith," the Arab answered curtly.

He reached into the breast of his camels-hair cloak, and drew out a small roll of parchment.

Stavrakios smiled.

"You are very sure of yourself," he said. "Who is your master, Muhammad, that he should presume to address the Emperor, who reigns in Christ, all-powerful and undefied?"

Khalid looked down at the merarch almost contemptuously. He was as tall as Basilakes, but where the Isaurian was thick and massive he was lean and rangy, with a suggestion of immense strength in his broad shoulders and loosely strung limbs.

"My master is the Prophet of God," he replied.

"What God?"

"The One God, Allah."

Stavrakios laughed.

"A new god, eh? Of the making of Gods there is no end."

He had spoken in Greek. The Arab offered him the scroll.

"Read," admonished Khalid.

And with an involuntary look of respect, Stavrakios unrolled the parchment and puzzled out the flowing script:

"Muhammad, the Prophet of Allah, the One God, Indivisible, the Compassionate, the Merciful, to the Emperor of Rome:

"Heed ye the warning while yet there is time. Repent of sin while salvation is promised. Accept the True Word. Say, after the manner of the Book:

> *He is God alone;*
> *God the eternal!*
> *He begetteth not, and He is not begotten;*
> *And there is none like unto him.*

"Infidels now are they who say, 'God is the Messiah, Son of Mary'; for the Messiah said, 'Oh, children of Israel! worship God, my Lord and your Lord.' Whoever shall join other gods with God, God shall forbid him the Garden, and his abode shall be the Fire; and the wicked shall have no helpers.

"They surely are Infidels who say, 'God is the third of three': for there is no God but One God: and if they refrain not from what they say, a grievous chastisement shall light on such of them as are Infidels.

"The Messiah, Son of Mary, is but an Apostle; other Apostles have flourished before him; and his mother was a just person; they both ate food. And when God shall say—'O Jesus, Son of Mary, hast thou said unto mankind: "Take me and my mother as two Gods, beside God?" ' He shall say: 'Glory be unto Thee! It is not for me to say that which I know to be not the truth. I spake not to them aught but that which thou didst bid me—"Worship God, my Lord and your Lord."'

"And this which is written here is the Word of God, revealed to Muhammad the Prophet. Therefore take heed, O Emperor, and submit, or thy power shall depart from thee, thy people shall be put to the sword and thy lands taken from thee."

Khalid seemed to grow in stature as the liquid phrases tripped from the merarch's tongue. Crispus and Eutyches looked at each other in mingled amusement and indignation. Stavrakios, alone, displayed no feeling. When he had finished he carefully rolled up the scroll and placed it on the table in front of him beside the sword.

"Who is Muhammad?" he inquired.

"The Proph—"

"Yes, yes, you have told me that. What else is he?"

"He is Lord of Mecca and Medina, master of Arabia," declared Khalid.

"Ah, the chief of a tribe!"

"God's Prophet," corrected the Arab. "Soon he and his seed shall rule the world."

"He would fight us Romans?" Stavrakios pressed gently.

The Arab's contempt was unconcealed.

"If you deny him he will rend you limb from limb. The birds of the air shall pick your bones. The jackals shall howl in the streets of your cities."

Eutyches interposed testily:

"The rascal deserves to be whipped, merarch. He is insolent."

"I think not," Stavrakios answered in Greek. "He believes in himself—in his master, which is the same thing."

The merarch addressed Khalid again.

"You understand that I must forward this letter to the Emperor in Constantinople? Very good! I do not think your master knows the might of Rome or he would think twice before he ventured to insult an Emperor who has humbled Persia in the dust."

"Persia, likewise, shall submit to the True Faith," asserted Khalid.

"So?" Stavrakios raised his eyebrows. "You will assail the world?"

"All the world must accept the Truth Faith," the Arab affirmed proudly. "There is but one God, and Muhammad is His Prophet!"

Crispus could no longer contain his wrath.

"The fellow is Antichrist, merarch! I agree with Eutyches, he should be whipped—or hanged."

"No, no," protested Stavrakios. "He is an envoy."

"Will you send that rot to the Emperor?" Eutyches cried hotly.

"Why not?" answered the merarch. "Recollect, my friends. It is addressed to Heraclius, in the first place. And in the second place, we have just concluded a war that drained our resources. The Empire requires a breathing space. If I consulted my own desires I should ask nothing better than an opportunity to march across the desert and punish this impudent chief of a tribe we never heard of. But small expeditions cost money as well as large. I shall advise the Emperor to make an answer, dignified, but conciliatory. Send this Muhammad some presents, and he will be content. Otherwise he may go to raiding caravans, and preaching heresy in the Syrian villages."

"Yes, you are right," Crispus agreed reluctantly.

But Eutyches objected:

"This Arab, here, is the kind to read weakness into such a policy. So will his master."

"Let them," retorted Stavrakios. "Then we can spend the Empire's money with clear consciences. For myself, I am moderately interested in a man with the ingenuity to set up a new god. We Christians have been so successful in upsetting religions that it may be a healthy thing for us to have a rival faith to match."

Crispus was visibly shocked.

"A ridiculous mess of words like that rival Christianity?" He jabbed a finger at the scroll by the sword. "Nonsense, Stavrakios! Divine revelation is one thing. Absurd pretense is another. Why, this petty sheik flouts the Son of God openly! He is mad."

"It may be." Stavrakios was unperturbed. "But my duty is to keep peace and bear down on expense. So by your leave, dux, we will speak the Arab fairly."

He turned to Khalid.

"This letter goes to the Emperor by post. I will beg him not to unleash his wrath upon a people who foolishly presume upon their ignorance. He is tender in his strength, and perhaps, will agree with me. In any case, return here in two months time, and I will have an answer for you."

The Arab's figure towered in the soft lamplight, tensed as a strung bowstave.

"I will return," he said haughtily. "See that the Emperor's answer be a plea for mercy. Otherwise you shall learn that the Persians are lambs compared with the sons of the desert."

He pointed at the sword on the table.

"You have a good blade, Roman. Show it to me."

Stavrakios hesitated, then decided to ignore the peremptoriness of the man's tone.

"It is a good blade, as you say," he agreed. "I took it from a Persian, but it must have served many men before him. You are a warrior?"

"I lead the Koreisch in battle."

Stavrakios slowly drew the sword from its sheath. His two officers regarded it as closely as Khalid. A grey blade, with odd flecks and whorls in the steel, forged differently from any weapon they had ever seen. It was very slender and shapely, tapering perfectly from hilt to point.

The Arab's right hand went out to grasp it, but Stavrakios shook his head.

"No, you may not touch it. Admire it, if you please. But a sword is like a wife; it should be for one man's use."

A gleam of appreciation showed in Khalid's eyes.

"You speak the truth, Roman. And the sword is like a woman—like a slim grey maid. But lustful. Yes, like a maid, but no maid. Ah, no! She has drunk deep of many men's blood. A maid, but—"

Crispus and Eutyches, leaning over the merarch's shoulders, peered curiously at the shimmering symmetry of the blade.

"It has marks on it," exclaimed Eutyches.

"Yes, there is a Greek word," cried Crispus. "And a Latin! And those marks—"

"Are Egyptian," declared Eutyches. "St. George, what a sword!"

"It is as old as man," said Stavrakios. "I showed it to an armorer in the Mesé. He knows steel, and he said he had never seen a blade of such balance and temper. It swings as light on the wrist as a centurion's vitis."

A feverish glare, covetous, threatening, supplanted the appreciation in Khalid's eyes.

"Will you sell the sword, Roman?" he demanded.

"At no price," Stavrakios replied shortly.

The Arab bowed mockingly.

"Very well," he said. "I will take it from you."

Stavrakios and his officers all stared at him incredulously.

"You will take it from me?" inquired the merarch.

"Yes."

Eutyches chuckled nervously.

"Surely, the man's mad," murmured the tribune of the Thracians.

But Stavrakios was aware of a budding sense of hostility.

"You are welcome to try," he said as shortly as he had spoken before. "Have you broken your fast?"

"I do not break the bread of the Nazarenes," the Arab rebuked him. "If you will open your gates for me I will return to my master—who shall be your master."

Stavrakios balanced the sword in his hand, struggling against the sudden, murderous craving that had assailed him. And as suddenly as it had risen the blood-lust succumbed to self-discipline.

"It's not too late to hang the dog," counseled Crispus.

But Stavrakios brushed the suggestion impatiently aside.

"Let him out the postern, Flavius," he instructed Eutyches. And to Khalid: "You deserve imprisonment for your insolence; but we Romans are so strong that we think no more of words from such as you than if they were uttered by children. Go, and learn respect. If you transgress another time I will have you whipped."

Khalid leaned forward across the table, his eyes shifting from the merarch to the grey sword, sparkling in the lamplight.

"When we meet again I will kill you," he said, and left the room without waiting for his escort.

"By the Forerunner, merarch, you do ill to let him go!" cried Crispus, as Eutyches hurried after the Arab.

"I liked his courage," answered Stavrakios, returning the grey sword to its sheath as lovingly as he had drawn it. "A firebrand, my Crispus. If there are more of his sort in Arabia we shall yet have a pleasant little border war, eh? A chance to win promotion, and train a few young officers. But we must not forget the Emperor's injunctions in the meantime. Peace, if it be possible with honor. And if it be not—why, then, my grey maiden shall not go thirsty."

Crispus frowned at the sheathed blade on the table.

"I believe that sword is a war breeder," he said.

"Crispus!" Stavrakios remonstrated jestingly. "Such superstition is unbecoming a Christian."

V

DUST BILLOWED across the exercise ground where the *cataphracti* charged and wheeled, and the infantry tramped and trotted, now extended in line, again arrayed in blocks of mailed scutati and light-armed missile troops. Eutyches, cantering up to the drawbridge where Stavrakios generally had his post, found only Basilakes, scowling upon the busy spectacle.

"What, Stammerer? You aren't working with your flat-footed legionaries?" cried the tribune of the Thracians.

"Don't t-talk to me about legionaries!" growled the dux. "That's what he is fo-forever prattling about."

Eutyches grinned boyishly.

"You refuse to like the merarch, eh? Well, by the Bodyless Ones, my friend, you can't truthfully say that we have slipped backward in these weeks. He keeps us up to discipline."

"Discipline!" rumbled Basilakes. "We always had discipline. All he does is to th-think up new ways to m-make us work."

"And very good for us, too," amended Eutyches.

"Yes, like posting a p-p-picket on the desert track during drill," jeered Basilakes. "A lot of good th-that does!"

"That's where you are wrong, my Basilakes," rejoined the cavalryman imperturbably. "The order has justified itself. I have to report to the merarch that a considerable body of men is in sight."

Basilakes's eyes widened somewhat, but he recovered his pessimism without difficulty.

"A caravan," he said doggedly. "And if it wasn't, wh-what harm could anybody from the desert do to us?"

"I don't know," confessed Eutyches. "But tell me: where is Stavrakios?"

The dux pointed toward his infantry out in the middle of the exercise ground.

"Th-there, curse him! Move deliberately, he says. Don't be in a hurry. The legions never hurried. S-S-St. George! Whoever thinks of the legions now? We re just foot-troops to garrison castles and help the c-c-avalry win battles."

His scorn was so exaggerated that Eutyches was nonplussed.

"At least, Stavrakios doesn't think so," said the tribune of the Thracian.

"N-no. All he thinks of is talk. The legions! My men are as good soldiers as he ever s-saw."

"Doubtless, Basilakes," chuckled Eutyches; "but I have no time to stroke the nap of your vanity. I ride to the merarch. Do you come, too—perhaps he will give you back your command."

Basilakes cursed with an efficiency that drew respect from the younger man.

"I'll c-come. He'll ruin my men, if he stays very long with them. T-talking about not hurrying! All battles are won in a hurry n-nowadays."

"I see what he means, though," Eutyches answered thoughtfully. "He's no fool, our merarch. All of us who were in Persia noticed how Heraclius used the infantry to good account. Men said it hadn't been done that way in battle since Adrianople, when the Emperor Valens and 40,000 men were killed by the Goths—and that was two hundred and fifty years ago. Personally, as a cavalryman, Basilakes, I don't see why good infantry in solid formation shouldn't be able to stand up to cavalry."

"D-don't you?" sneered the dux. "You have never fought on foot, Flavius. You don't know what it is to have three or four thou-thousand armored men on armored horses come crashing into you. We have our p-part, but we aren't supposed to fight cavalry in the open. In a line, m-maybe, where our archers and slingers can come into play, but—"

Stavrakios had seen the two approaching, and broke off a conversation he was holding with a group of infantry officers.

"You wanted to see me, Flavius?" Then over his shoulder, as he reined around: "Remember, the main thing is to keep your men in hand. Don't be afraid of having your flanks turned. We place too much emphasis on that in our tactics. A well-trained force should be able to bend back its flanks without falling into disorder. Gather into a square, dress shields closely and stand quiet while your missile troops volley over the scutati. Then if the enemy horse push home their charge you can meet them on your spear points. The cavalry aren't made who can break good heavy infantry."

Basilakes snorted into his beard. The merarch eyed him keenly.

"You don't believe me, dux? Prejudice, my friend. The dead weight of tradition on your imagination. In the old days the legions never feared cavalry. Why should we, who are as well armed, if we are as well trained, and possess the same confidence in ourselves and our leaders?"

"W-we aren't legionaries," Basilakes answered as disagreeably as he dared. "And the legions didn't face horse-archers in armor."

Stavrakios jaw tightened. He started to speak, then thought better of it.

"Put your men at ease," he said coldly. "Well, Flavius?"

"Riders on the desert track, merarch." Eutyches saluted. "It may be that messenger—you recall him? We sent his letter on to the Emperor."

"Oh, yes." Stavrakios rubbed his smooth-shaven chin, a trick he had when he was thinking. "An answer came for him, and some presents. The Emperor said to avoid trouble, if possible. Yes, yes! You say he is not alone?"

"It is a large body, by the dust they raise."

"Humph! We had better withdraw the troops inside the walls. There will be less risk of an accident. Tell Crispus, please. I will go on ahead." He called to Basilakes, who had joined the senior officers of the infantry drungus: "Take your men into the castle, dux. As speedily as you can."

Riding past Basilakes on his way to communicate with Crispus, Eutyches was hailed in a subdued voice by the Stammerer:

"He's a f-fine fellow to t-talk about the legions! Running behind stone walls when a parcel of Arabs show in the desert."

Eutyches regarded Basilakes soberly.

"You are talking foolishly," the cavalryman rebuked his friend. "It is not right to say such things of a man of proven courage. If you disagree with Stavrakios on military points, go to him frankly and—"

"Oh, you p-p-pat-patricians are all alike," fumed the infantry dux. "It's easy for a horseman to talk of footmen meeting cavalry wi-with spears. T-try it!"

The animosity of the gibe made Eutyches vaguely uneasy. He expressed himself so to Crispus, as they waited while the trumpeters summoned the *cataphracti* from their manoeuvres, but the Syrian declined to take the incident seriously.

"You know Basilakes as well as I, my Flavius. He must always be resentful of something or some one. For two months, now, it has been the merarch, and one of these days Stavrakios will send him to Jerusalem or Antioch to cool his heels drilling recruits for a while. But he is not a bad fellow. I'll talk with him later, and see if I can't put some sense in his thick skull."

"I know he's a good fellow," answered Eutyches. "That's why I don't like him to be so silly."

"He'll come around," reiterated Crispus. "Leave him to me."

VI

THE ARAB, Khalid, stalked into the Governor's audience chamber with Eutyches, who perceived that Stavrakios had made some attempt to impress the desert envoy. The merarch sat in a handsome chair of state, inlaid with ivory, on a low dais. The principal officers of the fortress were ranged behind him, glittering in armor, their shields and helmet crests gorgeous with the several regimental colors. Stavrakios, himself, however, was as simply clad as the Arab. His armor was clean, but unembellished. He sat, ruggedly erect, in his chair, his sword across his knees, leaning his chin on one hand, studying the strange man who had ridden twice to Muta on the fantastic errand of an unknown petty chief.

Eutyches placed Khalid beside the table at the foot of the

dais, upon which were spread the Emperor's gifts, and stepped closer to the merarch.

"The watchman on the gate-tower reports there are thousands of men behind the sandhills—foot and horse," he said in Greek. "Khalid rode to the gate alone."

A bleak look appeared in Stavrakios' rock-hewn face.

"Man from the desert," he said directly to Khalid, "why do you, who come as an envoy, bring with you an army, as though you came in war?"

He had employed the Arab dialect, and Khalid replied in the same medium, no less directly.

"It is to be seen whether I come in peace or war. What answer sends the Emperor of Rome to my master, the Prophet of Allah?"

"An answer dignified and kind," returned Stavrakios sternly. "The answer of an indulgent parent to a wilful child. He—"

The Arab interrupted as the merarch lifted a roll of parchment from his knee.

"If he has answered in that tone your Emperor is lost," he exclaimed, equally stern. "And so are you. Do you think we, who have the spirit of Allah breathed into our veins, will tolerate the insolence of an infidel Nazarene? Emperor or no, he must accept the True Faith!"

Stavrakios frowned.

"Is it your wish to hear what the Emperor says?" he inquired. "If not—"

"I will hear," said Khalid, and his words were a command.

The frown of the merarch became more pronounced, but he unrolled the parchment, and translated the courtly Latin into Arabic, stumbling now and then in his choice of words:

"Heraclius, Christ-loving Emperor of the Romans, to Muhammad, called the Prophet of Allah, in Arabia beyond the desert march:

"We have read the letter which you sent us by the favor of

the merarch Constantine Stavrakios, who governs for us in Muta. You speak boldly, but we feel loath to believe that you are sincere in professing doctrines which must destine your soul to the everlasting Hell. Think well, oh, Muhammad, before you assail those who worship the One God, whose Blessed Son, Jesus, was sacrificed for the sins of the world. Blasphemy is like the ignorant words spoken by a little child. It sounds aloud, echoing in a man's ears. But it means nothing. It recoils upon the utterer.

"We urge that you take counsel with our servant the merarch Stavrakios. He has our permission to send you priests, holy men, who will expound to you the Word of God, as Jesus revealed It upon earth. We urge you, likewise, to beware of vain threats, lest our patience be brought to an end, and we level against you the power of the Empire, which reaches from sea to sea and endures from the beginning of time to the ages of ages. In the meantime, as a sign of our indulgence and desire to show favor, we dispatch with this certain gifts. Yet heed well this admonition: the trouble-seeker receives not gifts, but blows."

Stavrakios rerolled the parchment, fastened the sealed ribbons which bound it and extended it to the Arab.

"The Emperor's favor is great," said the merarch. "Will you examine the presents he offers your master?"

Khalid accepted the parchment, but his face was like a thundercloud. He brushed aside the suggestion that he examine the presents, with a contempt as violent as a blow.

"Baubles," he snarled. "Why should I look at what I can take? Roman, this letter is not an answer. It is words. It is nothing. It is as empty as the wind. In Allah's Name, then, take what you deserve—war!"

Stavrakios sprang to his feet, and in his features, too, wrath kindled to fiery heat.

"Ho, wanderer," he cried. "Do you think to insult the Emperor, who has shown pity for your ignorance? Why, fool, with no more than the men I have here in Muta I can march to the miserable city that houses your lunatic master. And I will, if you do not humble yourself on your knees, and give pledge to fetch this Muhammad hither to render allegiance to the Emperor!"

But Khalid stared at him with an icy scorn that communicated itself to every man in the chamber.

"You will march no farther than the desert's edge, Roman," answered the Arab. "There I will kill you—and take your sword," he added, as an afterthought, pointing to the long blade, its hilt of electrum dimly gleaming on the merarch's knees.

Basilakes surged out of the front rank of officers on the dais.

"This is t-too much, merarch," he shouted. "Let us crucify him on the gate-tower for a warning to his rabble."

Other officers echoed the Stammerer's plea.

"Crucify him, merarch!" "The desert thief!" "Give him to the tormentors!" "Let horses tear him apart!"

Crispus said nothing, as did Eutyches; but the dux of the horse showed plainly that he was restrained solely by his sense of respect for his commander. As for the tribune of the Thracians, he was conscious of a renewed feeling of admiration for Khalid. The Arab never moved a muscle, standing with arms folded, his eyes haughtily intent on those who clamored for his life.

Stavrakios waved the officers to silence. His anger, now, was transferred from Khalid to them.

"You have forgotten that you are Romans," he said. "Also, it is to be supposed, Christians. This man, whatever his impertinence, is an envoy. He is entitled to go from Muta in safety. It shall be for Flavius Eutyches to see him forth of the gates."

The merarch pointed his forefinger at Khalid.

"I shall wait until the morning," he continued. "Then I shall march forth, and harry you until you make amends for this insane defiance. By Hercules, man, the Empire has too much work to do, too many tasks for its attention, to waste time with such as you and your master, mouthing of gods born of wine dreams, I doubt not; but if you compel us to action, we will take up the sword."

A sudden fury of spiritual rage vibrated through Khalid's tall frame.

"Infidel, you have mocked Allah, made light of the Prophet," he threatened. "For your men there will be choice of the True Faith or the sword. For you—"

He raised his arm in a gesture of denunciation, and stalked from the room, as regardless of Eutyches as when he left the first time. Hurrying after him, the tribune of the Thracians was oddly disturbed, tingling under the impact of a willpower he sensed to be utterly unchecked, malignant, over weening, blasting all opposition from its path. Behind them resounded a babble of voices in the audience chamber, where a score of officers besought Stavrakios to lead them to battle. But the Arab ignored it as completely as he did his escort or the stone walls surrounding him. He might have been out in the desert, alone with the faith which made him fearless of innumerable enemies.

He spoke once to Eutyches as the gate was opened for him.

"I shall be here in the morning. Bid your sheik carry his sword."

A short while afterward the sentries on the walls heard shouts of exultation behind the nearer sandhills, and as evening drew on myriad campfires pricked the dusk with their flames.

VII

MUTA SEETHED and hummed. Trampling of hoofs on the cobbles of the stable court; braying of trumpets in the infantry barracks; whining of engines under test on the walls; clanging of weapons in the salute as the standards were carried down from the sacellum. Inner court and outer court were aboil, and in the open gate Stavrakios stood with his officers, issuing final orders for the battle, while from the sandhills on the desert's edge the Arab raiders watched and raised at intervals their shrill, triumphant invocation to Allah.

"One numerus of foot to be left in garrison," the merarch was saying. "Which is it to be, Basilakes?"

"Th-thirteenth Syrians," scowled the Stammerer.

"Very good." Stavrakios was briskly confident. "That leaves you three *numeri*. You will march out after the horse, and take position in line, with intervals between each numerus. Your left flank will be protected by the fortress—you will be near enough for the engines to command the intervening space. Your right is to rest on that dry watercourse, which slices the southeast corner of the exercise ground; a few archers will prevent the enemy from getting across it. You should be able to hold that line very easily, until we—"

"You m-mean we are to stay back, and not get into the f-fight, merarch?" complained Basilakes.

Stavrakios bent hard eyes upon the Isaurian.

"You are to hold your position, unless I order you up. Your part in the battle is to provide a defense for the horse to rally behind, in case we are unduly pressed. There must be five or six thousand Arabs out there, as many mounted as afoot. They will outnumber us considerably."

"I th-thought you wanted us to fight like the legions," sneered Basilakes.

"Yes," Stavrakios answered steadily, "I want you to fight like legionaries—and to obey orders like legionaries. When the right moment comes, I will give the order for you to advance. That will be when the enemy commence to break. Until they have broken it would be madness for us to commit our entire force to the attack. Am I clear?"

Basilakes nodded sourly.

"And if you are attacked in earnest, you are to form square, not hold your line."

"Old tactics and n-new tactics," commented the Isaurian. "It ought t-to be interesting."

"It will be successful, if you obey orders." Stavrakios concealed his impatience. "I expect the Arabs will be shattered by our first real push. After that your *numeri* shall have their chance. Now, Crispus!" He turned to the dux of the cavalry. "Your Ghassanians to the fore as skirmishers. Let them try out the enemy. Main formation according to established tactics. Sound trumpets!"

The hoarse blasts of the tubae re-echoed between the walls; a racket of orders from centurions and decurions mounted the *numeri* and shifted them into column of centuries. Then Crispus raised his sword in signal to march, and the Ghassanians clattered across the drawbridge, their cloaks of orange-and-green fluttering behind them, orange plumes waving from light steel headpieces, their brown faces wreathed with smiles, voices raised in the same shrill note that distinguished the enemy.

"Christ for the Emperor!"

Inner court and outer court roared response:

"Christ for the Emperor!"

And on the sandhills there was a restless swaying movement amongst the brown-cloaked masses of riders and footmen, and an answering shout reached faintly the walls of the fortress:

"La illah ilia Allah! Muhammad resoul Allah!"

Muta vomited men. The Ghassanians spread out across the ground, providing a screen under shelter of which the *cataphracti* manoeuvred smartly into the traditional battle order of the Eastern Empire. Eutyches Thracians and the Paphlygonians were the first line of the centre, ranked four deep. In rear of them the Cappadocians took position. On the left, and slightly advanced, were the Fifth Syrians; the Cilicians constituted the right flank. Stavrakios, with a guard of three decuries, had his post between the first and second lines of the centre. Crispus was with him.

And in the meantime, Basilakes had arranged his infantry in the order prescribed by the merarch. The scutati in the front line, archers and slingers in rear. It was an imposing spectacle.

Stavrakios, drawing his long, grey sword, contemplated it with a distinct glow of satisfaction. The sun shone brightly on the array, every century in place, each numerus marked by its distinctive colors, the Eagles lifting above the oblong blocks of spear points.

"Khalid is not so ready to make good his boasts," remarked the merarch. "Prick him to action, my Crispus. Loose the Ghassanians upon him."

"I'll ride with them, merarch," Crispus answered eagerly. "They are stout fellows. One stiff charge should tear that rabble to pieces."

Stavrakios nodded assent.

"Very likely. We'll support you."

The trumpets of the irregulars blew the summons for column of centuries, and they wheeled out of line with the same cheerful, light-hearted spirit that had carried them shouting over the drawbridge.

Eutyches, on the flank of his Thracians, waved enviously to Crispus, grumbling to himself that the Ghassanians should have the only real chance of the day.

"Christ for the Emperor!" shouted the centuries.

On the sandhills there was a definite surge forward, and the Arabs flooded out to meet the attack, the foot in the centre, the horse on each wing. And as they advanced, they yelped with hysterical fervor, brandishing swords and lances:

"La illah ilia Allah! Muhammad resoul Allah!"

"They will fight, after all," Eutyches called to the merarch.

"Yes, this is better," agreed Stavrakios, pushing his horse alongside the tribune. "We shall be able to cut them up to the barber's taste, eh? Be prepared to charge when— Ha, well struck!"

Crispus had torn into the Arab centre like an axe-blade sinking into a tree. The Romans murmured appreciation to one another, expecting to see the Ghassanians rip straight through the mob of footmen and emerge on the far side of the Arab array; but nothing like that happened. The Arab wings folded in upon the attack, there was a flurry of steel—and the Ghassanians were swallowed up. A lance point flickered here and there, a few swords whirled in air. Otherwise the numerus was gone, disposed of with a celerity that made the Romans gasp. It was as if a great flame had licked out of the desert and consumed the irregulars. But Stavrakios was not dismayed.

"We have soldiers to face," he observed. "Flavius, you are dux of the horse. Take forward the first line. I will support."

Eutyches saluted mechanically, his wits still staggered by the amazing fury of the onslaught that had devoured three hundred and fifty wild riders in a single bite. Poor Crispus! And he had envied the Syrian a few moments since. Well, the Ghassanians must have taken toll, at least. And the Arabs would learn that it was one thing to meet irregulars, and another task to be pounded by *cataphracti*, wave following wave.

His trumpets brayed the signal to trot, and he saw that the Arabs had restored their original formation, infantry in the centre, groups of cavalry on the wings. His Thracians and Paphlygonians were in line, instead of column. They would not thrust into the enemy, but hammer at his front, pounding, pounding. After them the second line would sweep into the fight, then the onslaughts of the two flanking *numeri*. A recurrent series of shocks. The troops did not exist that could support such tactics. Success was simply a question of leadership, and Stavrakios was a leader in a thousand.

The trumpets clanged again. A thunder of hoofs acknowledged the summons. Dust billowed overhead. He saw a windrow of bodies on the ground, Ghassanians and their Arab brethren of the desert, hundreds of bodies. His horse's hoofs squelched in human flesh. He saw an Eagle buried under a heap of corpses. He saw a line of fierce, brown faces, a rank of spearpoints, unwavering. He saw a storm of arrows, heard the shafts whisper by his ear. A green flag waved in front of him, and he hacked a path toward it, fending and slashing, guiding his horse with his knees, both hands occupied with sword and shield.

Enemies swarmed around him. He had never encountered foes like these Arabs. The Persians had been brave, but the desert men seemed to welcome death. They hurled themselves upon his point; they sprang up behind the *cataphracti*, and pulled the armored troopers down with themselves beneath the frenzied horses. He reached the green standard, and slew the greybearded warrior who held it; but before he could seize the staff another greybeard had caught it. Eutyches pursued relentlessly, and hewed one of the man's hands off at the wrist. The greybeard clutched the standard tighter with his remaining hand and when Eutyches slashed that off, too, the old warrior hugged the staff between his stumps, and a quavering cry—"La illah il—"—brought assistance, which harried the Roman until the standard could be saved.

The tribune was astonished to note that the Arabian horse had not come into action against him. He had been pinned down by the dauntless infantry, any two of whom were willing to die if they could take a Roman with them. And he was secretly relieved when thudding hoofs announced the arrival of Stavrakios with the second line. The Arabs swayed visibly under this impact; their centre yielded, and as their wings started to fold in about the main body of Roman *cataphracti* the two flanking detachments Stavrakios had posted, the Fifth Syrians and the Cilicians, delivered assaults upon the enemy horse.

The battle became a whirlpool, blind, baffling, temporarily incoherent, despite the leaders efforts, a vast huddle of horse and foot, revolving about the green standard which was the rallying-point of the Arabs. Then two things happened. Stavrakios, his grey sword a herald of death, slew the third bearer of the green standard; and simultaneously, Khalid, at the head of a body of Arab cavalry, destroyed the Fifth Syrians on the Roman left, and drove a frightful blow into the flank of Eutyches Thracians, heavily engaged with the Arab infantry.

The confusion was frightful, and Stavrakios, sensing the trouble, shouted to Eutyches for a trumpeter.

"Sound the retreat," ordered the merarch. "We must retire behind the infantry. Basilakes can give us a breathing-spell."

The tribune of the Thracians craned his neck for a trumpeter, and peering rearward, he saw the Roman infantry advancing in full battle panoply.

"Too late, Stavrakios," he said. "Basilakes is marching to join us."

Stavrakios paled.

"The fool," he grated. "The blind, heedless fool. Now, indeed are we committed, Flavius. We must forget tactics. This is a butchery. The side that can slay the most—"

But a torrent of Arab infantry poured between them, and Eutyches heard no more, put to it to extricate the wreckage of his *numeri* from the persistent onslaughts of Khalid's horse. What saved him was the diversion created by the arrival of Basilakes and the Roman infantry. The Arabian horse ceased the attack upon the *cataphracti*, leaving them entirely to their infantry, and launched a series of charges against Basilakes. At first, the Arabs were beaten off by the hail of arrows and stones discharged by the missile troops, and the unflinching advance of the scutati continued; but Basilakes had left his flanks exposed the instant he abandoned the position Stavrakios had assigned to him, and he had similarly ignored the mer arch's injunction to fight in mass formation. Consequently, Khalid worked around into his rear, and rode rough-shod over his left numerus, the Eighth Syrians. The Ninth Syrians and the Isaurians tried to close up and form square when this happened, but they were so hampered by their flying comrades that the best they could do was to face about, and retire backwards—or advance backwards—upon their own horse.

Within an hour from the joining of battle the two armies were locked in a staggering combat that oscillated in response to the varying fortunes of the moment. The Romans were packed into several partially disintegrated groups, surrounded by swirling hordes of Arabs, horse and foot. Better armed, better trained, they were now at a disadvantage in face of their opponents greater agility and numbers.

Stavrakios rode up to Basilakes, as the dux panted into the diminished circle of *cataphracti*, and the men in the merarch's path shrank away from the ferocity of his face.

"Fool," exclaimed Stavrakios. "Do you know that you have robbed us of victory, perhaps of every man's life?"

"I th-thought you couldn't disengage," Basilakes answered sulkily. "Y-you were all swallowed up like the—"

"I was on the point of disengaging when you advanced. And if you had to disobey my order and advance, why must you disobey my other order, and advance in line. Oh, you fool!"

"I d-didn't bungle this battle," retorted Basilakes. "Y-you mix tactics, and expect—"

"I am tired of your stubbornness," roared the merarch.

His grey sword flashed shoulder-high, humming expectantly—and Basilakes head toppled from its neck, lopped clean just under the helmet's chin-strap. Eutyches, forcing a path through the sweating, bewildered press of cavalry and infantry, was in time to see the startled expression mirrored in the Stammerer's eyes.

"A Roman officer must obey orders," cried Stavrakios. "Let this be a lesson to all. We should have nothing to fear from our foes, if men did as they were told."

Eutyches found himself expressing solemn dissent.

"He deserved your stroke, merarch; but—I'm not so sure we can blame Basilakes alone for this. These desert men are no ordinary fighters. St. George! What can you do against men who *want* to die?"

"Yes," Stavrakios admitted mournfully. "They have an idea. And as I told Basilakes: an idea is the most powerful weapon a man can wield. They believe in themselves."

"So do we," protested the tribune, almost frightened by the Governor's gloomy mood. "We can fight our way to the fortress."

"Beaten by a mob of desert raiders!" murmured Stavrakios.

An arrow droned out of the air, and lodged in a chink of his mail; he plucked it free, and seemed to regain a measure of confidence from the circumstance.

"Yes, yes, we can fight our way to the castle," he exclaimed. "That is best. You and I will hold the rear—you and I and Grey Maiden, here."

His voice swelled in a bellow of command.

"Close up, men! We'll lure the Arabs under the walls—give the engines some work to do. Close up! Slow does it. Remember! Rome's pace, Rome's race."

VIII

SYRIANS, ISAURIANS, Paphlygonians, Cappadocians, Cilicians, Thracians, labored frantically to free themselves of the remorseless concentric pressure Khalid was applying. They were regular troops, inured to discipline; but Eutyches could not help hearing the muttered complaints and oaths of disgust—"Romans! There's too much talk of Romans!" "What have we to do with Rome?" "Our officers got us into this." "Rome's race? It's your race, Michael—and mine!" "Christ with us, what a muddle!" "Hurry, there, you bow-legged Greeks. Give someone else a breath of life." "Well, brothers, we didn't enlist to fight a pack of maniacs." "No, nor to have our officers killing each other." "I tell you those old ones with the green flag were sorcerers." "What? No doubt of it, Simonides saw a Daemon when the—"

Gradually, the merarch organized the retirement. The infantry led, an oblong of scutati crammed with missile troops. After them came the cavalry, in two separate columns, *numeri* all jumbled together, men whose horses were killed running to fill the gaps in the infantry's Shield-wall. The footmen marched along steadily, while the horse made short, swift dashes to hinder the pursuit. They had caught the Arabs temporarily off-balance when the retreat began; Khalid's original dispositions had been planned to stop the attack of the Romans and pin them down. But he shifted his arrangements with a speed that dazzled the plodding Romans. His infantry pecked at the flanks of the oblong of footmen; and his riders assailed the dwindling columns of *cataphracti*.

Twice and again, Khalid flung himself at Stavrakios, but the merarch was fighting with consummate skill, careful to protect Eutyches column at need, covering the harrassed infantry, declining the openings the enemy offered to lure him away from his supports. The Romans were within reach of the drawbridge when the onslaughts of the Arabs abruptly ceased, and Khalid rode alone into the space that separated the two armies.

"Ho, Roman," he called to Stavrakios, "I have beaten you fairly. Will you not stand up to me, as one warrior to another, and suffer me to prove I did not boast idly when I said I should possess your sword?"

Stavrakios hesitated. His conscience, as a commander, bade him refuse to risk himself in such a personal combat; the day had been sufficiently disastrous. But his soldier's pride yearned for the satisfaction victory in the duel would assure him, and he told himself that it would hearten his men, who sadly needed encouragement. Moreover, he trusted not only in his own ability, but in the uncanny power of his sword. Grey Maiden had drunk deep that day, an elephant's draught. His right arm was red to the elbow; the sword dripped blood as he sat his horse pondering.

The whine of a catapult decided him. Whatever happened, the survivors of his garrison were safe. So he slowly wiped the sword's hilt and his right hand clean, and trotted out from the ranks of the *cataphracti*.

"Stand to it, Arab," he said. "You are a brave foe, but this Maid of mine will not be denied."

Khalid kept his eyes glued on the merarch's.

"Perhaps," he retorted, "but Allah is greater than any sword—

even that sword. *She* would never fail a man as eight blades have failed me this day, shivered on Roman armor."

"All swords shiver on Roman armor," answered Stavrakios.

He jumped his horse forward, and struck at Khalid's head; but the Arab was watchful, and parried the blow. The blades clattered again, rattling and clinking, hammering on armor, ringing clear on each other, whispering hateful messages as they circled and swung. Khalid fought manfully, yet his blows were avoided or fended, while Stavrakios drew blood twice: once, from a slash under the armpit, and again, from a cut in the arm. Then, so swiftly that no man saw how it happened, the merarch's sword slid off Khalid's blade and chopped down upon his horse's neck. The beast leaped convulsively, and fell, and Khalid rolled clear.

"Yield," cried Stavrakios.

But Khalid scrambled to his feet, and replied with a stroke which the Roman caught on Grey Maiden. A twist of Stavrakios arm, and the Arab's sword splintered into fragments.

"Now, yield or die," commanded Stavrakios.

A cheer burst from the Romans. A sob of anguish escaped the Arabs.

"No, *you* die, Roman," gasped Khalid.

He stooped, and snatched from the ground a stone as big as his fist, and in the one motion hurled it full in the merarch's face. It struck Stavrakios on the temple, beneath the helmet-brim, with a crunching sound like the breaking of a very thick egg shell. And Stavrakios swayed on his saddle, and pitched backwards, armor creaking and clanging, the same look of surprise in his staring eyes that Eutyches had seen in the decapitated head of Basilakes; and the sword, Grey Maiden, as if denying responsibility for his end, slipped from his nerveless fingers and flew through the air to tinkle in the coarse gravel at Khalid's feet.

Unhurried, lovingly, the Arab bent and fitted his fingers to the grooves of the hilt. A river of fire ran up his arm, reviving his tired body. He sprang erect.

"La illah ilia Allah," he screamed. "There is no God but God! And Muhammad is his Prophet!"

A howl of approval from his followers drowned the sough and whine of the wall-engines, until he flourished the sword in a gesture for silence.

"Ho, you, young Roman!" He pointed the blade at Eutyches, hurrying the *cataphracti* into the fortress. "Tell your Emperor that this is the first of many blows the Prophet will deal him. Tell him that Khalid, the Sword of Allah, will smite him with this sword of the Old Ones. And when I come again I will break down your castle, stone by stone, yes, and Jerusalem and Antioch and the other cities shall conform to Allah or be given to fire and the sack."

IX

THE MAGISTER Militum per Orientem had just come from the baths; he felt very pink and comfortable and easy-minded. But a frown, that was very nearly a frown of displeasure, settled upon his plump features as he looked up from his tablets to the young officer the secretary had ushered in.

"Flavius Eutyches? Oh, yes, tribune of the—humph—Your uncle is the Senator Manlius Junius Eutyches? Yes, yes, of course! You are the senior surviving officer from this regrettable affair at Muta? Yes, yes! Your uncle has written me. I have—ah—been favored with a communi cation from the Emperor's own hand. Most regrettable. The merarch—what's his name—Stavrakios?—Ah, yes, yes! Bishop Cyril's nephew. I served with his father in Africa. An opinionated man—the elder Stavrakios, that is. But I was about to say: he seems to have been unduly rash, eh? Had trouble with his officers? And it was quite unnecessary to embroil himself with a pack of passing caravan raiders. And having done so, then, to get himself killed and his garrison nearly exterminated! I don't understand it. Most peculiar, most peculiar! The Emperor had sent presents, too, for the desert people. It needs explaining. A bad business. The Empire's prestige is endangered."

Eutyches gritted his teeth, and blurted into the oily flow of words.

"More than the Empire's prestige is endangered. There is a new religion being preached in Arabia. It makes fighting men out of the worst desert-scum. I never saw such fighting-men! Why, the Persians—"

"Blessed Timothy, don't get excited," pleaded the Magister Militum. "You know, you are really talking nonsense. New religions are often preached, and schisms, I regret to say, raise their heads every year. Yes, yes, very regrettable, too! But who ever heard of a religion making fighting-men? Now, now! Religion makes priests."

Eutyches glared at him—the nephew of a Senator might, upon occasion, presume so far with a porky Magister Militum, who owed his job to a cabal of women in the Imperial Court.

"And there's a story sweeping the desert, now—my spies brought it to me. The Arabs say that this sword Khalid took from poor Stavrakios is a holy sword, and they call Khalid the Sword of Allah—the Sword of God. They say he can't be defeated while he carries that sword, that they will overrun all of Orientem and Egypt and Africa."

The Magister Militum studied his polished fingernails.

"Let them try, tribune. Let them try. If they *will* run their heads against our walls we can't be blamed, can we? It will be an excellent opportunity to show your mettle. I—ah—forgot to mention that I have been requested to appoint you Governor of Muta—a slight recognition of your efficiency in bringing off the survivors of that preposterous affair."

"But it wasn't preposterous," Eutyches objected desperately. "It was the hardest-fought battle I ever saw. If it hadn't been for Basilakes mistake, we might have won; and it was owing entirely to Stavrakios that we saved any fragments after that. I tell you, the merarch was absolutely justified in—"

"Yes, yes, you are very loyal," the Magister Militum soothed him. "A good quality in a young officer, I always say. But don't lose your head over a trifling border fight. And stick to the tactics. Always stick to the tactics. Men wiser than you and I devised them, and they have been tested for hundreds of years. You can't go wrong if you fight by the tactics. Oh, yes, and leave the desert people alone. Better keep your men under cover, I should say. We'll have to leave you pretty weak."

"Weak?" Eutyches almost shouted. "Do you mean you won't recruit the garrison up to strength?"

"Why—ah—no. We are paring expenses at all points, and it has been decided to strike off or consolidate all *numeri* considerably below authorized strength. The Empire is at peace—"

"It won't be, very long," said Eutyches grimly.

The Magister Militum permitted himself a moderate amount of disfavor.

"You are a young man to be so opinionated. Take an older man's advice, and curb a bad habit. Enthusiasm for your work is all very well, but when it becomes confirmed—Humph! Well, we'll say no more about it. Keep your men in hand, and don't get into trouble. As I was saying, the Empire is at peace. Trade is very brisk here in Antioch. The merchants are much encouraged. No one thought we should recover so quickly from the Persian War; and if you hotheads will manage to keep the border at peace we may reach a point where taxes won't consume a third of our income, eh? That's the great idea! No country can be happy with high taxes."

"No country can be happy in slavery," returned Eutyches. "But I won't keep you. I—I— Won't you consider what I've said?"

"Consider it?" repeated the Magister Militum, much relieved that his caller was going. "Why, I'll be glad to. And you consider what I've told you, eh? A fair exchange."

Outside the Prætorium the young tribune stood for a moment contemplating the enormous city, still showing traces of the Persian occupation which had wrought more harm than all the centuries that had passed since Seleucus founded it.

"They won't understand," he told himself unhappily. "They won't see! He talks of ideas! Ideas of money-chasing! Stavrakios was right. Those desert men have an idea that means something—and they believe in themselves. That fat jelly-fish in the Prætorium only believes that the world owes him a soft living. He would have kicked me out in short order, if I hadn't a Senatorial family behind me. Yes, there's something wrong with the Empire. Maybe it's because we don't believe in it—and some of us don't believe in Christianity—and we are jealous of each other.

"By the Forerunner! If the Persians could do *that*—" he surveyed a blackened area blocks in extent—"what could Khalid do? Ah, the one mistake Stavrakios made was in fighting him! The Arabs had an idea—and now they have a sword."

He walked disconsolately to the barracks where his escort awaited him, and to the chagrin of the decury ordered them at once into saddle. The least he could do in the circumstances was to return to his post. There might be a chance to give warning before the desert men launched their great attack. And if his superiors were heedless, there was the more reason for him to keep a lookout for them. He took hope from the reflection. If enough men believed in—in—the Empire—Christ—duty, say—anything—the disciples of Allah might be repelled. A thought worth clinging to.

Alas, Flavius Eutyches lived to see the Sword of Allah supreme from Alexandria, in Egypt, to the Taurus Mountains; and in his old age he who had warded the desert march defended the Cilician Gates.

"Believe in yourselves," he used to tell his men. "Ah, if we only had an idea, a symbol, if only we all believed in one thing! But believe in yourselves—if you can't believe in anything else."

THORD'S WOOING

THIS IS the story of the coming into Iceland of Elin, the Ireland woman, who was called the Wise; and Aslak Flatnose, the Baresark; and the sword Grey Maiden; and of what happened therefrom.

There was a man named Geir Bjarni's son, who dwelt in the Hornfirth dales and owned farms and had money out all the way east to Berufirth and west to Skeidara Sands and The Side. He was large-bodied and lusty, and men called him the Wealthy. He took to wife Rannveiga Kolbein's dotter, sister to Aud who married Herjolt the Hairy, who dwelt at Borgarhaven, close by the Hornfirth dales, and who was the only man in that part of the country who could match Geir's power. They were fast friends.

Rannveiga bore Geir a son, who was named Bjarni. She fell sick of a fever in his sixth winter and died. Aud bore Herjolt several sons, and also, a girlchild, whose name was Astrid. After Astrid was born Herjolt and Geir used to talk over the ale of wedding her in due time to young Bjarni.

"It might be said that she could not do better," Geir would remark, "since all my property will go to Bjarni."

"There will be some few marks in my girl's portion," Herjolt would answer. "But see her out of swaddling-clothes before we set the betrothal feast, and handfast on it."

Geir had his household managed by thralls and serving-women after Rannveiga died; the boy, Bjarni, was brought up by such folk, and they found him a handful. He was large like his father, but evil-tempered and spoiled, for none would say him nay, and his eyes were very small and bright and separated only by the jutting beak of his nose. His color was red, and for this reason he was usually called the Red, until in afterlife he won the name of the Grasping.

Now, as the Norns spun life's threads, the year following Rannveiga's death the Fall gales were unusually severe, and a ship was driven ashore between the skerries on the seaside of Geir's stead by Hornfirth. Men saw the wreck, and sent hastily to summon Geir; but when he reached the shore the ship was gone, and of its company but two gained the land, and they unconscious, more drowned than alive, battered by the fierce waves and the sharp edges of the rocks. One was a man and the other a woman.

Geir bade carry them up to the skalli, and when they were laid by the firelight it was seen that the woman was young and fair, with white skin and hair blue-black like the underside of a crow's wing. Her garments were of rich stuffs, and she wore a gold chain around her neck and on her wrists golden bracelets. The man was a rough-seeming carl, burly, thick-thewed, taller even than Geir; his nose had been broken, and was caved into the middle of his face. But what impressed the folk was the splendor of his weapons, a great axe of bluish steel, fastened by a thong to his wrist, and a sword tied into its sheath, and the fact that he wore neither helm nor body-armor, no more than leather breeches and shoon and a jerkin to his back.

"Strange shipmates," quoth Geir. "It is true this fellow may have shocked his mail to lighten him in the water, but I see no rust-stains or buckle-rips on his jerkin, and he has the look of a common carl, while she—"

He looked long at the woman, and wet and bedraggled though she was, her fairness kindled a sparkle in his eye and started a little pulse a-hammering in his temple.

"—she has the appearance of a chief's daughter," he concluded.

Then he ordered a serving-woman to fetch hot broth, and turned his attention again to the man. Curiosity prompted him to untie the sheath-thongs and bare the seafarer's blade; a gasp of admiration escaped his lips as the firelight flickered on the lean, grey steel.

"A maal-sword," he muttered. "It is covered with runes!"

Whether it was the heat of the fire or what, the stranger opened his eyes at this instant, and seeing his sword in Geir's hand, snatched it back and scrambled to his feet, glaring savagely about the circle of tenants and thralls. Axe in one hand, sword in the other, he tottered against one of the pillars that upheld the skalli roof.

"Who takes Grey Maiden, takes my life," he growled hoarsely. "Back, carls! Or come! I care not, mailed or unmailed, so you give me room for weapon-swinging."

There was a wild scramble to get out of the way. Geir, alone, held his ground.

"A Baresark?" the chief questioned coolly.

"And an outlaw," the stranger boasted.

"You are not an Icelander," said Geir. "And I do not think I have seen you in Norway."

The Baresark laughed shortly.

"I am an Orkneyman. My name is Aslak—Flatnose folk call me."

"What errand have you in Iceland?"

"None. I fled after a man-slaying. A Sudreyar ship was sailing, and I boarded her. She was Iceland-bound. That is all."

The thrall-woman re-entered with two bowls of broth, and Geir took one from her, and offered it to Aslak.

"You need not fear us," he said. "As for your sword, I admired it. It is a king's weapon."

"It is Aslak's weapon," retorted the Orkneyman. "You did

wrong to bare it. There is bad luck for some one when Grey Maiden is sheathed thirsty."

"Grey Maiden, you call it?" questioned Geir. And added impatiently: "But drink, carl, drink! Is your belly full that you refuse good broth?"

Aslak accepted the bowl rather suspiciously. Behind Geir the serving-folk were working over the shipwrecked woman, and as the Baresark raised the broth to his lips he regarded their efforts with no less suspicion.

"Gently, there, gently," he admonished.

"What is she to you?" Geir asked quickly.

The Orkneyman scowled.

"You are a great questioner. Well, I will take your questions in order. Yes, my sword is called Grey Maiden—ask me not why; he I had it from called it so, and he said the man who owned it before him gave it the same name.... No, my belly is not full—and I am suspicious of all who tamper with my weapons.... The wench, there? She is nothing to me, but a fair lass."

A low, dazed voice, stammering broken queries, announced her return to consciousness. Geir spun around, peered down at the flower-white face and re-addressed himself to Aslak, heedless of the Baresark's insolence.

"But you know who she is? Maid or wife? Free or thrall?"

Aslak shrugged his shoulders.

"Her name is Elin. She came from Ireland with her grandfather—in my case, I think. They were a kingly couple."

"Outlaws!" Geir's voice thickened. "Humph! And orphaned. She must have shelter."

Aslak tossed his empty bowl to one of the thralls.

"Shelter?" he repeated hardily. "Yes, and kindly treatment, becoming one freeborn."

"How do we know she is freeborn?" demanded Geir. "You say she is Irish. She may be an escaped thrall."

"Look at her," commanded the Baresark.

She had been propped in a sitting position, and a thrall-woman was feeding her broth from a horn-spoon. Her eyes, grey-blue, fringed by long, black lashes, flitted fearfully from face to face, resting at last with an expression of relief upon Aslak's.

"Where are we?" she asked, stumbling over the unfamiliar Norse speech.

Geir answered for the Orkneyman, naming himself.

"Have you friends in Iceland?" he inquired smoothly.

She shook her head.

"I fled with my grandfather from Dublin in the night. There was a Sudreyar ship, and the Sudreyar men told us that if we journeyed to Norway the heathen would make slaves of us. So we took their advice, and sailed on with them for Iceland. Here we thought we should be safe from our foes."

She shuddered, and Geir licked his lips.

"But in Iceland we are what you call heathen, too," he reminded her. "You are an outlander here, without the law. You cannot even prove that you are freeborn."

Aslak stooped, and lifted one of Elin's wrists.

"She is a gold-wearer," he pointed out. "Who has seen a thrall—"

"Here I am chief," Geir interrupted, with his first show of authority. "The maid is my prize, cast up on my property. I might enthrall her, but she is fair to look upon, and I am a just man. My bower is empty, I am lonely and she has the making of a good housekeeper. Come! What say you, Elin? You can go farther, and be granted poorer accommodations."

She stared at him, wide-eyed, and a second shudder wrenched her body.

"Look about you," Geir invited, waving his hand to embrace the contents of the skalli. "Here you shall order all under me. Where will you find better quarters, more consideration?"

"Nowhere," sneered Aslak. "For you are his, whether you will or no. By the Hammer, a thrall in a golden collar!"

"Is it so?" she appealed direct to Geir.

"It is not," he answered, righteously indignant. "I have said I will take you to wife, although I might enthrall you. Belike, that was what the Sudreyar men intended for you when they reached Iceland."

"What shall I do?" she cried to Aslak.

He fingered the hilt of the sword Grey Maiden, and swept the skalli with a speculative eye.

"Do?" he ruminated. "Why, one of two things. Accept his offer, or, if you like, come with me. I don't urge you either way, lass. If you stay, you'll lie soft and never hunger. If you come with me—"

"Where would she go?" mocked Geir.

"Oh, I have driven a wolf out of his den before this," Aslak asserted confidently. "But the choice is yours, Elin. I'm not urging you, remember. You'll bed rough with me, and travel far. I'm no handy man with a woman. Please yourself."

Geir frowned at the Baresark.

"You do ill to cross me, carl," he threatened. "The maid is mine."

"As to that, I helped her ashore," returned Aslak. "But for me she would have died in the waves. If she is anyone's prize in law, she is mine."

Elin leaped up like a hunted thing, exhaustion forgotten in the desperate issue which fronted her.

"Is it my fate to belong to a man who is strange to me?" she cried wildly. "Let me go, both of you, and I will work the nails off my fingers for whoever will give me a roof and bread."

"Ah, but you are a fair woman!" objected Aslak. "Your kind don't work in still-rooms and brew-vats and dairies."

"All women marry strange men," said Geir. "My first wife

scarcely knew me when her father brought me to her on the cross-bench at the betrothal feast."

"There is much to be said in that direction," Aslak agreed largely. "And a woman must always be tagged to a man."

She cast her eyes from one to the other of them. Geir kept his eyes glued on her face, but the Orkneyman followed her brooding gaze as it studied, first Geir, then himself. And when finally she glanced sideways at the high-seat and the cross-bench, beyond the long range of fires, he tossed his axe on his shoulder.

"Skoal to you, Elin," he exclaimed. "If you haven't chosen right for yourself, you have for me." He tapped his sword-hilt. "This maid keeps me busy. A second might cause disorders in the household. One man, one wife—a good rule."

Her eyes met his frankly, with a look of mingled shame and defiance.

"I am house-bred," she confessed. "If I must yield me to a man—"

She lifted her arms in a gesture of resignation, and turned to Geir.

"I cry your kindness, Geir Bjarni's son," she said proudly. "In Ireland I was a Princess."

Geir caught her hands with a fine, rough courtesy.

"Here you shall be my wife," he answered. "Ho, thralls, conduct your mistress to the bower."

And, expansive in victory, he hailed Aslak, who was striding towards the Men's Door:

"Stop a few days, Baresark. There will be betrothal ale to drink."

"Not for me," replied Aslak. "I suspect no good would come of keeping our two maids under the same roof—more especially, as they belong to different men. And mine spits angrily when she thinks a rude hand caressed her."

He walked out, chuckling, into the twilight. As he stood by

the porch, considering which way he should go, a small boy rushed up to him.

"Ho, carl," screamed the child. "What is this the thralls tell me: that my father has brought in a new wife?"

Aslak scrutinized the red, foxy face and little eyes with amused interest.

"If your father is Geir—"

"Who else, stupid?" the boy thrust in arrogantly.

"Ah, youngling, what good manners you have! Well, as I was about to say, if your father is Geir, he has brought in a new— wife, did you say? Well, perhaps, perhaps! Who can read the future? Not I!"

The boy bellowed aloud.

"An ill-deed, an ill-deed! The house runs well enough. And this woman, they say, will raise up a pack of brats to annoy me. Loki's curse on my father! But I'll hold them down. And if she seeks to hinder me—"

His lips contorted in an evil grin, and he skipped up the porch into the skalli.

"Ah, Grey Maiden," Aslak murmured to himself, "perhaps I was over loyal to you. In most soft beds there is a husk."

He squared his shoulders, surveying the dim outline of far-off jokulls, a white tracery of snow across the serrated ridge of peaks.

"A hard land! Now, to see what can be made out of it. Quarrels aplenty, that I see already! But what else? Ah, yes, what else?"

II

THE SEA Woman, Geir's folk called Elin, but soon they spoke of her as the Wise. She was beloved by all the household, except the boy Bjarni; and Geir, himself, she could twine around the shank of her spindle. There was none like her in those parts for gentleness or courtesy or wisdom. Be it housework or husbandry or needlecraft or nursing the sick, she had a deft hand and an agile wit. Simples and herbs she knew like an old wife. Also, much of tasty cooking. But her wisdom shone brightest in unravelling the tangled threads of life. No man or woman asked her advice in vain, and it was commonly said that Geir owed considerable profit to her counsels.

It was she who withheld him from joining Herjolf in an East venture the summer of the Great Harvest; and Herjolf, who was prejudiced against her because of young Bjarni's hatred—and for another reason, which shall be told—hated her as bitterly as Bjarni thereafter, for there was so much food and livestock in Iceland the next winter that the oversea traders could sell only lumber and weapons, and to make a bad matter worse, the Fall gales took heavy toll of shipping.

It irked Herjolf that while he suffered loss Geir had only profit to count. He said she was a witch and practiced sorcery; but in Geir's presence he was careful to guard his tongue. Geir would suffer no harm to be spoken of her; the Wealthy held a tight rein on Bjarni, too, and restrained his son's malice in the skalli—with the consequence that Bjarni rode frequently to Herjolf's stead to unburden his woes, and in the course of years became as intimate a friend of the Hairy as ever Geir had been.

So if Elin entered Geir's bower reluctantly, she was not slow in growing reconciled to her lot. He was a good husband to her, as she was a good wife to him. And when a son was born to her in the Fall after their mating there was no shadow of a barrier between the two. This boy was named Thord, and he was of his mother's breed. He had her blue-grey, steady eyes and white coloring, with very black hair; and, likewise her sweetness of temper. The stead folk loved him, and it was often remarked how different he was from his half-brother, who was sour, close-fisted, and overbearing.

Meanwhile, at Borgarhaven, Astrid bloomed to girlhood. She was a golden maid, her eyes a violet-blue, handsome in feature and her yellow locks so long that folk jested of them, saying it was easily to be credited that Herjolf the Hairy was her father. She was not more than a year or so older than Thord, so it came about that they frequently played together. Bjarni would eye them angrily when they did, and come and stand over them.

"Take heed, baseborn," he would growl at his brother. "She is intended for me."

"I shall wed where I choose," Astrid would answer, with a toss of her head. And Thord would say in a cool, off-hand fashion:

"He who wants must take."

Bjarni itched to knife him, but once, when Thord was eight, Bjarni had beaten him insensible, and for that Geir had all but slain his elder son.

"If brothers fight, skallis burn," rasped Geir. "Moreover, an honorable youth does not assail children. Another time, carl, I will hew your head off, instead of skinning you with a whip."

Thus twelve years passed. Red Bjarni was a stalwart youth, of his father's height. Thord was well-grown, but it was apparent, now, that he would never equal his brother in stature. Yet he was a lad of high spirit, lithe and limber-muscled, and quick-witted, as became his mother's son. Elin found much joy in him. Her life was easy and happy. Secure in Geir's love and the loyalty of her serving-folk, and possessing the friendship of her neighbors, she cared little for the cold welcome she received when she accompanied Geir on his visits to Borgarhaven, where Aud was as hostile to her as Herjolf. Of Bjarni she took more account, always counselling Thord that he should not need-lessly offend his brother, but she reckoned it useless to borrow trouble for a danger unavoidable, and looked to time either to heal the breach or provide a settlement of her stepson's animosity. Truth to tell, wise as she was, Elin could not comprehend the measure of Bjarni's hatred.

If she had ever regretted her choice—if choice it was—between Geir and Aslak, that regret was years since buried. The Orkneyman had journeyed West. They heard of him at intervals,

usually in connection with fighting or brawling, once as having
made the Greenland voyage. He was retained by several chiefs
who had feuds against them for the sake of his weapon skill,
and he became famous in the Rangriver Vales and the West
Firths country for his deeds as a double-handed slayer. For he
fought as no man ever had been known to fight, with axe in
one hand and sword in the other. Few cared to encounter him
after his reputation was established. All the more so, when he
was outlawed for hewing down Kol Mord's son of Grimsness
in a dispute over wages due him. The sentence was that he must
pass three years overseas, and he took ship with Oddi the Stout,
a Sogn man out of Norway, in the White River late in the
summer. And so fared eastward, and was no more seen for the
period of his outlawry.

III

GEIR WAS riding home from the Berufirth dales,
where he had been collecting rents, when one of his
tenants hailed him as he was crossing Stafafell.

"Ho, Geir," bawled the tenant. "Aslak the Baresark has stolen
my calf."

"Your wits have left you, carl," returned Geir. "Aslak is in
Norway—"

"No, no, he landed a week past. He was outlawed for a slaying
in The Bay. And he says he will live always an outlaw, now,
seeing that he has had sentence passed on him in three—"

"Peace, peace," ordered Geir, reining in. "You seem to know
something, after all. But are you certain it was Aslak stole your
calf?"

"Certain?" quoth the tenant indignantly. "Did I not see him
cut its throat with that maal-sword of his? And carry it off
under my eyes? He has just gone off toward Vatna Jokull. You
could catch him if you rode fast."

"I will," said Geir, and urged his horse forward along the
track.

On the edge of the fell, where it dipped up to the foothills of the Jokull, he sighted the figure of a man, covering the ground with great leaps and bounds, and slung over the runner's shoulder was what looked like a dead calf. Geir shouted several times, and galloped faster, so that presently the runner heard him, looked back, dropped the carcass on the grass and brandished axe and sword in defiance.

"That is Aslak," Geir told himself.

And Aslak it was, wilder and raggeder than when he was washed ashore from the Sudreyar ship; but still clutching the axe of blue steel and the sword Grey Maiden.

"Well met, Geir," he said, a twinkle in his eye. "I hear you made a good match of it. But you ride in haste. Don't let me interrupt you."

"It is I who must interrupt you," Geir replied testily. "Why did you not introduce yourself at my stead, if you were hungry? Elin would have fed you for old times sake. There was no need for you to steal from yon poor carl."

Aslak leaned on his axe, and considered this point.

"Ah, but I have no fond memories of your skalli," he answered. "And for the calf, why, I asked the fellow civilly for a bite and a sup, and he asked the weight of my silver. I told him I had none, and he bade me apply to you for charity. So I killed his calf. If he had spoken me fair, I would have killed yours rather than his. When I must rob, I prefer to rob the wealthy."

"Is that what you have returned to Iceland for?" demanded Geir, flushing.

"More or less," admitted the Orkneyman. "I am tired of being outlawed. It will be easier to live always outside the law. Then I shall at least know where I am."

"Thieves talk," fumed Geir. "If that is your intention, take yourself elsewhere. You will receive scant mercy here."

"It may be, it may be," owned Aslak; "but I shall try this country, at any rate. The flocks look fat and the folk are prosperous."

At this Geir lost his temper completely, and drove his horse full-tilt at the Orkneyman. Aslak tried to dodge, saw that he could not and struck a lightning blow with Grey Maiden at the horse's crupper.

"Let the nag pay the debt," he cried.

The keen edge bit deep, and the horse pitched forward so suddenly that Geir was thrown headlong from the saddle, sprawling some distance away in a huddle of limbs. Aslak looked grave.

"This is in no wise as I intended," murmured the Orkney-man.

He sheathed Grey Maiden and laid his axe beside the calf, then went and knelt by Geir. The Wealthy's head—helmless for a peaceful journey—had crashed against a boulder; it was smashed to a red pulp. Aslak tapped his sword-hilt regretfully.

"Ah, Grey Maiden, Grey Maiden, did I not say twelve years gone that it was bad luck for someone to sheath you thirsty? You have a long memory, lass. Too long!"

He stood up and reflected aloud:

"Trouble must flow from this deed, I think. But it can not be said that Aslak slays secretly. No, no! All shall be properly accounted for." He cast a regretful eye upon the calf. "Well, well, there should be more cattle where you came from."

He slung Geir's body over his shoulder, making as little difficulty of the man's weight as he had of the calf's, picked up his axe, and strode back along the track.

Later in the day, a frightened farmer entered the yard at Geir's stead leading a nervous pony, to the back of which was strapped a stiffening corpse.

"Aslak did it," he babbled to the outpouring of tenants, serving-folk and thralls. "Aslak the Baresark. He stole a calf from Kettle Freedman's son—over there by Black Water—and Kettle met Geir—and Geir rode after Aslak—and Aslak would not give up the calf. So they fought. He says—Aslak says—that he tried to kill Geir's horse, so as to spare him; but when the horse fell, Geir was hurled against a rock. There is not a brain in his head!"

"It looks like an axe-wound to me," howled a man.

"Yes, yes, an axe," echoed the crowd.

Elin appeared on the skalli porch.

"An axe?" she exclaimed. "Who is hurt? What—"

The ranks split in front of her, and she saw the poor shell of Geir, distorted across the skittish pony's back.

"Mary aid me!" she sighed. "I thought life was over-fair. But carry him in, carls, carry him into his hall. His hall! What will his property serve him, now, who died in heathen wrath?"

IV

THE CORNERS of the skalli were in darkness. Overhead the shadows pranced and swayed among the roof-beams in response to the leaping flames of the hearth-fires. The ropes that bound down the roof creaked and groaned as the east-wind howled under the gables and pushed and clawed at the building. Elin clutched Thord tighter to her, and stared across the dais-table at the lowering faces of her enemies.

"But I—" confused, she made as if to brush a veil from before her eyes—"I was his wife. Thord was his son."

Young Bjarni's fox-eyes glittered wickedly.

"His wife! You witch, you tricked yourself into my father's graces, but he never wived you. His bond-woman, yes, that you were—and the brat beside you baseborn."

"The truth," confirmed Herjolf. "There was no thought of marriage. By Rann, who washed you hither, where is your settlement? Who handfasted your betrothal?"

Aud, sitting between the two, laughed venomously.

"Well said, husband! The creature thinks only to purloin our nephew's heritage for her baseborn son."

Now, Elin drew herself up, seething with bitter anger; but

the boy Thord spoke for her, his voice uncanny in its even coldness.

"All this is thievery, you three do," he charged. "And so shall it be termed in Iceland, for it is well known how you have hated my mother and me."

Bjarni clutched at his sword, and started to rise; but Aud held him back.

"No, no," she said. "Let them not tempt you to do that which they wish. Slay one or both, and you risk outlawry. Send them out to starve, and who can question your right? For where shall they find folk to bear witness for them? Or funds to sue at the Allthing?"

"I'll not rest easy while that bower-rat lives," snarled Bjarni. "Here is as good a chance as any to make an end of him."

Elin's heart near stopped beating. She marked the look of calculation in Herjolf's eye, the wavering in Aud's expression. But Thord glared fearlessly at all three.

"A coward's threat," he exclaimed scornfully. "Give me sword or axe, and I'll fight you, here on the skalli floor. What? Shall I call the house-folk to hear me?"

He raised his voice, and Herjolf made up his mind, reaching over Aud's shoulders to clamp a hand upon Bjarni's sword-arm.

"He is a fool who over-reaches his advantage," growled the Hairy one. "We need no witnesses tonight. And your aunt gives good advice. They have no case. They must take what we give them, and if that is life, alone, how can they complain? Do not all men know Geir came to his death by the stroke of Aslak's axe? And is it not common gossip that Aslak and Elin were washed ashore together from the same ship?"

Aud tittered shrilly.

"Past doubt, husband, past doubt! She concerted with the Baresark. He was to slay Geir, she would smooth matters for him, and then they would set up housekeeping together in a nest Geir had feathered for them. It is likely they planned next to slay Bjarni, and so assure themselves of all Geir's property."

"Then who shall say we have not the right to slay them?" protested Bjarni.

"Ah, some folk are prejudiced," answered Herjolf.

"She has a way with her, this grey-eyed cat," endorsed Aud. "Is she not a Christian? A witch?"

"Suppose she puts a spell upon us?" suggested Bjarni.

Herjolf glanced uneasily at her white face, proudly contemptuous.

"That is an idea worth debating," he admitted. "I suspect she has spelled us before this—and she must have woven a strong spell over Geir to hold him so long in thrall."

Elin broke her silence.

"Yes," she cried, "I will cast a spell upon you, knaves. And my spell is this: Little good shall you have of that which you steal. All that you set your hands to shall go wrong. The folk shall turn from you, and your names will be a mockery on every tongue. Bjarni, there, shall come to a sorry death. Yes, and I give him a new name. From now on he shall be called the Grasping. And you, Herjolf, shall be no longer called the Hairy, but the False. And Aud shall be called the Treacherous."

"Stop her, stop her," clamored Aud, clasping hands upon her ears.

Herjolf winced. Bjarni started to draw his sword again.

"I'll hew off her head," he mumbled. "Thor knows what curse she may yet devise!"

Thord seized a stool from the floor and would have gone in front of his mother, but she put him away and lifted the gold chain which hung around her neck. From the chain depended a tiny cross, with strange, mystic characters graven on it, and this she held on a level with her enemies eyes.

"By the power of this I stay you," she commanded sternly. "Bide, Bjarni! Touch not your sword, lest your hand wither at the wrist. Herjolf, Aud, over both of you falls my spell."

"Oh, touch her not," moaned Aud.

"Let be, Bjarni, let be," babbled Herjolf. "It is ill threatening steel to a witch."

Bjarni's fingers unloosed his sword-hilt, and he wiped a clammy dew of sweat from his forehead. Aud tremblingly signed the Hammer in front of them.

"Go, witch," she quavered. "You may not harm us."

"A horse to Odin," muttered Herjolf. "I vow a horse! No skinny beast, but a plump stallion."

Thord laughed aloud.

"Cowards, the three of you," he derided. "Come, mother, let us go."

"And take nothing with you," shrilled Aud. "Witch or no, there is law in the land, and you may not rob us."

"Not a kirtle," echoed Bjarni. "Not so much as a knife from the weapon-chests."

"No, no, go in peace," stammered Herjolf. "Be content with your lives. If we ever spoke of this night's work—"

"Who would believe you?" demanded Elin. "But I am an outlander and a lone woman, and Thord is but a lad. You are rich and powerful. Well you know none in the district will venture your wrath to aid me in a suit at law. But I am content. There is a Power above yours, and to that Power I yield my case. Come, Thord!"

"Do we take nothing, then, mother?" he asked. "Hark to the wind. There is a storm. At least, a cloak to shield you from the wet!"

"A cloak from this house would chill me," she answered curtly. "I will not be beholden to heathen enemies, who cheat and steal."

She turned away, and released from the grip of her slate-blue eyes, Bjarni screamed after her:

" 'Tis you are heathen, sea-witch! Look to it, when I am unbound to your spell."

But Elin ignored him. Holding firmly to Thord's arm, she

walked down the skalli and out by the Men's Door into the driving scud of the rain. Thord shivered as the wind smote them on the porch-step.

"Where do we go, mother?" he murmured. "It will be cold tonight."

She hesitated, pondering.

"There is a shepherd's hut vacant over toward Stafafell," she decided. "That will serve for the night. Afterward— He who watches all will be our guide."

v

THERE WAS much talk all through the South country of Bjarni's treatment of Elin and Thord.

"Wedded or unwedded, she was a faithful wife to Geir," said the women.

"Settlement or no settlement, Geir had great profit out of her counsel," said the men.

It was generally believed that Aslak had slain Geir intentionally, but all laughed at the story Bjarni and Herjolf put about that Aslak and Elin had concerted it between them. Yet no one was willing to risk the enmity of the two richest men in the Hornfirth dales by coming out openly and sponsoring Elin's cause. The South country folk helped her privately, and gave her enemies the names she had spelled them with; but that was as far as any would go. And indeed, Elin asked no man's help. With the gold links of her chain and her bracelets, she purchased Rolf's Farm, a tiny patch of ground and a poor hut of lava rocks and ship-timbers, and stocked it with a few swine and sheep. Here she dwelt, and only Thord for company. They would have gone hungry often that winter but for the folk who came to her with heart-aches and body-ills and problems of conduct. These paid gladly for a slice of her wisdom, and their fees kept Rolf's Farm in food and fuel—these and one other.

The second night after Elin and Thord moved into the hut a knock sounded on the door.

"Who is that?" challenged Thord.

"Is Elin within?" countered a man's voice.

"I am," spoke up Elin.

"Good," said the voice. "Let me in, Elin. Do you remember Aslak, the Orkneyman?"

"To my sorrow, I do," she retorted, but she unfastened the door.

Aslak blinked in the firelight as he bent his head to clear the lintel.

"You are cosy and warm," he exclaimed admiringly.

"This is better fare than I have. But it is not my purpose to envy you." He perceived Thord glowering at him from the hearth, and grinned at the boy, then instantly sobered. "Do you believe these tales that I slew Geir?" he asked abruptly.

Elin regarded him dispassionately, until he became restless and shuffled his feet on the earthen floor.

"I do not," she answered as abruptly as he had spoken; "but there is no question that you were the means of his bane."

He nodded slowly.

"That I can not deny. But hear me, you and Thord, yonder. I had a kindness in my heart for Geir because he used you well. I would not have slain him, save to defend myself. I thought, rather, to kill his horse, and then run from him. But it was not to be. I care nothing for myself, and mighty little for Geir; but I will do anything I may for you."

He paused.

"There is nothing," she replied a trifle less frostily.

"But these two carls who have robbed you and the boy of your portions?" he persisted. "They have told foul stories about me, as well as you. How if I slew them for you, eh? They are still at Geir's stead, the folk say, roystering over their triumph. I could—"

"If you slay them, Aslak," she interrupted, "folk will believe the stories they set afoot. Then, in truth, may it be said that you and I wrought to be rid of Geir and all who stood between us and his property."

Thord jumped up from his stool on the hearth.

"What of that?" he exclaimed. "The property would be ours. We could afford a few tales. And it would be a proper vengeance."

Elin fixed him with her slate-blue eyes that held mysterious depths of knowledge.

"Is it for one who is no kin to us to avenge our wrong?" she asked softly. "When you come to man's estate, my son, will you be proud to have it said as you ride by: 'There goes Thord Geir's son, who is wealthy because Aslak the Baresark slew his half-brother, Bjarni, and Bjarni's uncle, Herjolf, and hoped thereby to obtain the hand of Thord's mother, having first slain Geir.' Will that make you feel like an honor able man?"

"No," the boy answered sullenly. "I will take my own vengeance."

"That is my thought," she agreed. "You see how matters stand, Aslak?" she turned to the Baresark. "Much harm, unwitting, you have done us. If you slay Bjarni and Herjolf you will put us in very evil case. It might be that Aud would bring suit against us to secure sentence of outlawry. She might claim all Bjarni's inheritance by virtue that her sister was his mother or because there was a betrothal agreement between the families to unite him with Astrid, her daughter. Even if neither of these things happened, we should cease to be victims of malice and would become wrongdoers, man-slayers in intent, if not in deed."

Aslak bowed his head with unaccustomed humility.

"You have schooled me as I deserved, Elin," he said. "What you say is not to be denied. Is there aught else I can do for you? I wot well," he added hastily, "the company of an outlaw would be as dangerous for you as the deed I suggested."

Elin thought a moment.

"There is naught you can do, at this time," she answered finally.

"If there ever is, summon me," he begged. "I shall stay in these parts."

He glanced at Thord, who eyed him now admiringly.

"That is a stout youngling. He has the making of a warrior. Send him to me when he is ready for weapon-training."

He shouldered his axe, and strode out of the hut, and Elin and Thord saw him no more; but occasionally when they rose in the morning, they would find a dead sheep or swine or a quarter of beef or a basket of fish, tucked up safe on the eaves. And they knew whence it came.

VI

NOW, SIX years pass. Most of this time Bjarni was overseas, viking-faring or at the court of the Norse king. He left Iceland by advice of Herjolf, who acted in some sort as his fosterer.

"A man who blinks the truth is a fool, and merits the trouble which comes to him," quoth Herjolf. "There is no gainsaying that we two have won little popularity, but my experience is that men have short memories, and all folk, poor and wealthy, are anxious to be at peace with a powerful chief. Therefore I counsel you to fare eastward, and acquire a warrior's reputation. It is only fitting that a young man of your position should travel, so that you may know something of different countries. Geir talked of sending you before he was slain. It would be fulfilling his wish for you to go, and we will make announcement that it is your purpose to honor him in the journey."

"I do not like to go while that witch is free to work spells against me," objected Bjarni.

"Hut, boy, I shall be here," replied Herjolf. "I shall not be asleep."

"And there is Astrid," continued Bjarni.

But Herjolf swept aside this excuse, too.

"By Freya, you can not wed her at her age," he boomed jovially. "It will be years yet before we hold the betrothal feast, but when you return next it would be fitting to set out the heirship ale. By then the folk will have become accustomed to Elin's plight, and many will attend who might now answer that they must go upon a journey."

Herjolf had his way, and in the following spring Bjarni sailed east. Harald Greyfell was King in Norway, and for his family's sake and because he was big-bodied and wealthy and a stout fighter for his years, he was made welcome at Court; and in the summer King Harald lent him two long-ships and a Jarl of experience to teach him, and Bjarni sailed on a viking-raid east into the Baltic. For three years he lived after this fashion, spending his winters at the King's Court, and viking-faring in the summer. He obtained reputation by his efforts, and was regarded as a chief of promise, although the King was heard once to say: "He was well-named the Grasping, this Icelander. Much he may do, but all he will take what he can."

The fourth spring after his departure from the Hornfirth dales Bjarni obtained leave from King Harald to fare westward, and he made a swift passage and beached his dragon on his own stead. Herjolf rode over from Borgarhaven, with Aud and Astrid and their two sons, Half the Little and Starkad, to welcome him. Many other men of property came, too, for as Herjolf had predicted, the years had dulled the first burst of indignation over his selfishness toward Elin and Thord. And it was noted by all who saw him that Bjarni had learned the manners of a traveller and warrior of experience. The old men, who had wandered far, were glad to talk to him of the countries they knew which he had visited.

The maid Astrid was grown slim and tall. Her eyes were very serious, and her speech was slow, and she was shy in men's company—especially, in Bjarni's company. He spoke of this to Herjolf, but Herjolf laughed at him.

"What will you have of a maid?" gibed his uncle. "She thinks of you—and because she thinks, she fears. But she will grow accustomed to the thought in time, and from that the rest is a short step and a sure."

So Bjarni summoned his friends and neighbors to the skalli at Geir's stead to drink the heirship ale, and a great host of them attended, albeit not a few were shamefaced and jeered at him behind his back. Then, having assured himself that his property was in order, under Herjolf's supervision, Bjarni took ship again for Norway and was gone for the space of two more winters. As it chanced, during this visit, he saw none of the three people whose lives were inextricably tangled with his own; Elin, because she was at pains not to cross his path; Thord, because Elin had sent her son on a Greenland voyage to keep him from meeting Bjarni; and Aslak, because the Baresark never came near the dwelling-places of men, except when he needed food or drink, and that would be at night or by stealth.

The lives of these three were very different from his. Poverty they knew, day by day; cold in winter, and heat in summer. Aslak, to be sure, seldom raised his hand to work, unless it was to help some farmer who had fed him in the harvest season; but Elin and Thord had never an end to their labor. Mother and son planted and reaped scanty crops, toiled to rear their live-stock, and sought employment eagerly from all their neighbors. They knew no luxuries; their clothing was of the simplest; they were glad for sufficient food to stay their hunger; Elin must send Thord on the Greenland voyage for that she could not equip him with a sword to stand his ground, boy though he was, if he encountered Bjarni in the road. But all three had this comfort: that they lived their lives as pleased them best. Aslak was an outlaw, and took what he wished from those he disliked. Elin and Thord upheld their pride, and strove for a certain purpose.

Of the three Elin was happiest, for she might watch her son waxing splendidly toward manhood, a rangy, lean-hipped, deep-chested youth, his muscles supple, his limbs tireless, sharpened and hardened like a steel blade in the fire of adversity. She was never downcast, but had always a song or a bright saying on her lips; and she bred up this spirit in Thord—Smiling Thord, the folk called him. And every farmer who needed extra labor, every fisherman who could use one more hand, gladly accepted his services. When he had done his mother's stint he roamed the length and breadth of the South country, from Berufirth to Floi, many days journey, seeking to earn a penny or a slab of meat or a bag of grain or a jug of ale; and if eventide often found him near Borgarhaven, who would question him— supposing the steadfolk saw him not?

"He grows old young," said Elin, seeing the light in his eyes after these excursions, and it is not to be wondered at that there was sorrow blended with the joy in her heart.

VII

ON A certain day in spring Elin had occasion to go down to the strand to administer to a sick child in one of the fishermen's huts, and while she was there a woman cried at the door that a longship was pulling up the firth. And a little after came by a man, who shouted:

"Here is Bjarni Geir's son, and with him a notable company of Easterlings. Much booty has the Grasping."

But Elin gave no thought to this because she was wrestling with death for the child's life, and little it meant to her that there was a great scurrying of messengers to Geir's stead for horses and to Borgarhaven to acquaint Herjolf with Bjarni's return. She wrought on by the bedside until the child's fever was abated, and then took her way home, very weary and forgetful of what had passed. Under her arm she carried a mackerel the fisherman had given her, and she was hoping that Thord would be at the farm for supper to enjoy the treat.

Where the strand way crossed the Geir's stead road she heard a brisk trampling of hoofs and the voices of many men talking. The long column turned a clump of rocks while she stood, hesitating, and she found herself face to face with Bjarni. But a very different Bjarni from the raw youth who had cringed under her spell. He was grown larger than his father had been, three and a quarter ells tall and thick in proportion. He wore the red cloak of one of the Norse King's Guard, on his head was a gilded helm, and a fine shirt of linked mail, silvered, twinkled as the cloak fluttered in the wind. His face was ruddy and weathered, and his hair and beard flashed the same color as his cloak. And his eyes were the cold blue of the northern waters, hard and cruel, even when he laughed.

He saw her, standing by the track, in her old, worn kirtle and ragged cloak, the fish clutched under her arm in its wrapping of seaweed, and for a breath his jaw dropped. Then his lips met in a tight line, and hatred blazed up in his eyes, making their cruelty seem more alive.

"Ho, witch, you still live!" he exclaimed.

"I shall live to bury you for the sake of the father you dishonored," she retorted.

His hand stole to his sword-hilt.

"A threat?" he challenged.

"A promise," she answered steadily.

The column perforce had halted, and Herjolf, by his nephew's side, whispered that he should ride on, aware of the angry looks of the Hornfirth folk, who had accepted Bjarni's invitation to feast his return.

"What?" men were saying. "Does Bjarni come home to flout Wise Elin?" "This is an ill-deed, to assail his father's widow." "She was no—" "Ah, what of that? Elin the Wise is above the Grasping."

But Bjarni shook his head at Herjolf, and scowled over his shoulder at the muttering of his neighbors. He bent from the saddle to bring his eyes nearer to Elin, and all the time his fingers played with his sword-hilt.

"Of what account is threat or promise from you, Elin?" he sneered. "You are old and thin, where you were young and sleek. I see wrinkles in your cheeks, and is it my imagination or did you use to have hands so cracked and soiled?"

She lifted her hands, and examined them.

"Yes," she said calmly. "I am an old woman before my time. I was a Princess when your father wed me. He took me against my will, but he atoned for that. As men go, he was kind. It was you, Bjarni the Grasping, who put me to toil and hunger—as all the folk know."

She raised her voice.

"Ho, Hornfirth folk, behold Bjarni the Grasping, who has been over-seas to prove his mettle, and would show it to you by hewing down a woman—and that one his father's widow!"

The muttering was louder at the tail of the column, and Herjolf snatched at Bjarni's bridle.

"On, boy, on," he snarled. "There is naught to be gained here."

Bjarni's beard bristled in the excess of his passion.

"Not here, perhaps," he admitted. "But that misbegotten brat of hers shall pay for the witch's insolence. There is not room in Iceland for two of my father's sons."

"That is the truth," said Elin, and her eyes sought his.

He stared at her, but quickly averted his gaze.

"She seeks to spell me," he complained. "By the Hammer, I feel her magic in my veins."

He made the Sign in protection, and Herjolf and those near him reined hastily aside. Elin laughed, a terrible laugh, for she was trying to mask the fear which oppressed her, not fear for herself but for Thord—young, carefree, weaponless Smiling Thord. She wondered if Thord was paying one of his surreptitious visits to the copse behind the stead-yard at Borgarhaven that afternoon.

She drew the little gold cross from her bosom and raised it in front of Bjarni as she had done once before.

"This is the only magic I know," she said. "And it is the magic of love, not hate. Yes, I spell you by the love the folk bear me, Bjarni, and by the love they bear my son. Touch us, if you dare!"

She walked on across the track, under his horse's nose, and

all that could be heard was the stamping of hoofs and the clink of mail as men restlessly shifted position. Bjarni winged a curse after her stooped shoulders. But Herjolf turned in his saddle, and shouted jovially:

"Well, we have won a passage, carls! On to the ale-horns!"

And he murmured angrily to Bjarni:

"Smile, fool, smile! Will you let them think she curbed you? Make a jest! Be merry! Pretend you were but baiting her! Would you lose all you have gained in six years?"

So Bjarni roused himself from the sour rage that convulsed him, and strove to belittle the sorry scene.

"So much for a witch! When they talk of spells give them little heed. It is what they do in secret that nips a man's marrow, eh?"

But one of the small land-holders of the district spoke out boldly in answer.

"She is a good woman, Elin. The folk call her the Wise. She helps all who ask her. You will not establish yourself, Bjarni, by abusing her or Thord—who minds his own affairs, and works harder than any youth in the Quarter."

Bjarni scowled at this man, his patience at the bursting point.

"I am not come hither from the King's court to be lessoned by you, carl. Give us peace of your chatter! This Elin may be wise, but she cozened my father, and would have cozened Herjolf and me, had we allowed her. As to Thord, let him look to himself. I'll have no one befouling my rights. It would be better for all concerned if Elin and Thord were sent out of Iceland."

"No doubt, no doubt," Herjolf agreed hastily. "But here is no reason for quarrel, friends. It is a family matter."

But the man who had rebuked Bjarni and several more withdrew from the column, and of those who rode on to Geir's stead many held to the same opinion, but for sake of policy or interest, feared to give Bjarni open offence. Men said Bjarni had

made an ill beginning in Iceland, and all looked to see what
would happen when he and Thord met.

V I I I

FEAR STABBED at Elin's heart as she climbed the
path to Rolf's Farm, comparing in her mind the giant
figure of Bjarni, splendid in his war-gear, surrounded by friends
and house-carls, with Thord's youthful stature, naked and un-
protected. Thord was no weakling, but he lacked seven years of
Bjarni's age and better than a span of his half-brother's height.
And Bjarni, she knew, was trained to weapon-work, a redoubt-
able warrior, who had held his own with Kings and Jarls and
famous champions. Thord was more accustomed to tugging at
an oar or guiding a plough across the furrows; what little practice he had with sword and spear was due to the kindness of
old farmers, who had been viking-farers in past days and could
not resist an opportunity to school a likely lad.

She shivered, remembering the cruel look in Bjarni's close-
set eyes. Whatever Herjolf counselled, whatever the Hornfirth
folk might say, she was convinced Bjarni intended to slay Thord
the first time their ways crossed. From boyhood red brother
had hated dark brother. That hatred had been spontaneous,
inevitable. And now it must be emphasized by the Grasping's
dread lest Thord be able to assert a legitimate claim to their
father's property. Ah, and what if Bjarni learned of those visits
to Borgarhaven? What if Astrid rebelled against his wooing?

Elin stayed her feet, aghast at the thought. Why, of course,
Astrid must rebel! She recalled her own plight, forced to wed,
unwilling. How much worse the fate of Astrid, flung into
Bjarni's arms, loving another. That was something she, Elin,
had been spared. To wed, unloving, was bad enough. But to
wed, loving another—ah, that was unspeakable! And that other,
Thord, her Thord, Smiling Thord! Thord, who had been denied

so much, who had never complained. Thord, who stood this day in the shadow of death by his red brother's hand.

She walked on, thinking deeply. The time had come to act, she decided. It was useless to count the risks—rather she and Thord should perish than suffer love to be filched from them as well as land and money. But what should she do? Always, she recognized, she had looked to find a way to recover her son's inheritance. But how? What tools, what weapons, might they obtain, under the handicap of their poverty?

It was dusk when she reached her hut, with her questions unanswered. She was entering the low doorway, when she noticed an object wedged in the roof-thatch, and putting up her hand, drew down a swine's ham. She recognized it as one of Aslak's gifts, and it reminded her of the Baresark's offer of aid. The one fightingman she could call upon! But what could an outlaw do to help her in this situation? Slay Bjarni? She revolted at the idea of assassination. It would be one thing for Thord to slay his evil brother, but an unmanly act to allow Aslak to do the deed for him. Nor would it benefit Thord, she sur-mised.

Then a plan occurred to her, and she crouched upon the doorstep, hugging her knees, eyes fixed on the shadowy loom of the jokulls, thinking, thinking, thinking. When dragging footsteps sounded on the path, her plan was fully formed.

"You walk as if you carried a heavy load, my son," she called into the darkness.

"A load of sorrow, mother," Thord answered dolefully. "Bjarni is home."

"I have seen him," she replied. "Did you—"

"No." He emerged from the night, and sat on the ground at her feet. "I—I was at Borgarhaven—in the morning."

"So I guessed," she said.

"Astrid—she—we are of one mind, mother—of one heart. She—while we talked together one came running from the stead, crying for her—that Herjolf and Aud rode for Geir's stead—that Bjarni was returned."

Elin waited silently for him to continue, as he did presently:

"So she went. That was a doegr's[23] time since. I followed, and waited—behind the ricks in the yard at Geir's stead. Do you remember?"

"Yes," she answered. "It was I had them changed there, so that they might have better protection from the wet."

He nodded slowly.

"What the stead is I think you made it, mother. Well, I heard the sound of feasting. Bjarni was boasting of his deeds—how he slew two Englishmen by himself, and cleared a Daneman's longship, and fared east to Gardariki[24]—he had a gold band on his head the King of that country gave him. So I whistled the seabird's call that is the signal between Astrid and me—and—and after a while—she came. Her kirtle was blue—and she slipped into my arms almost before I saw her."

He groaned.

"Oh, mother! Oh, mother!"

Elin dropped her hand on the black head at her knee.

"Yes, my son?"

"Herjolf—Bjarni—the betrothal feast is set for the week before the Thing-faring. She—she is to ride with Bjarni when he goes to Almannagjaa."

Now, Elin said naught for another while, listening to Thord's steady breathing, her fingers caressing the heavy locks of his hair.

"Would you venture death for her?" she asked finally.

He looked up, surprised.

"Death? What is death that I should fear it? All we had Bjarni has taken from us. Whatever betides, I will not sit patient under this. But—but—without weapon—"

---

23   *Twelve hours.*
24   *Russia.*

"There is a way," she said. "It is a hard way, and a dangerous. But it is my thought that you are man enough to follow it, despite your youth. Yet tarry a moment, my son, and study yourself. Life is long. If you let Astrid go, another maid may—"

"No, no," he cried.

"She is older than you. Think! You are scarce more than a boy."

"Men have worn crowns and fought battles before my age," he returned proudly. "Yes, and begotten sons. It is not the years, but the will, that makes the man."

Elin bent and kissed his brow.

"Well-spoken, Thord," she said. "You must win yourself another name than the Smiling. That was sufficient for a boy, but you shall be a warrior, with a reputation becoming your race, or—or—die with honor."

He sprang up excitedly.

"That is my wish, mother. But what is this way you spoke of? I care not how hard it is or how dangerous. Give me a sword, that is all I ask. Show me how I may punish Bjarni!"

"You have not forgotten Aslak the Baresark?" she asked.

She sensed, rather than saw, how his face fell.

"Yes, but he is an outlaw. And one man—"

"He is not an ordinary man. And he has a sword, Grey Maiden, which has great powers. He told me once that it is reputed whoever wields it may not be slain by steel. Also, he is more skilled in weapon-craft than any man in Iceland. Go to him, and say you come from me. Ask him to lend you Grey Maiden."

"But he will not," expostulated Thord. "No man would. It would break his luck."

"I do not think that he will do so willingly," she replied calmly. "But I will show you how you may win it from him without doing him any hurt. For I would not hurt Aslak, since he has been kind to me, and likewise, because I have need for his testimony. You will require a man to guard your back on the venture I have in mind, and that is another reason for sparing him."

Thord regarded her in bewilderment.

"You speak with a confidence I do not feel, albeit I have no fear, mother," he said.

"Heed me, and you will understand," she replied. "Your one chance of securing justice against Bjarni and of staying him from wedding Astrid is to slay him lawfully in single combat— in holmgang. And you shall do it in this wise."

It was late in the night when she ceased speaking, and Thord assisted her to rise. He stood before her very humbly.

"Whatever name I may win, mother, it will not be as honor-able as yours," he said. "You are rightly named the Wise."

She kissed him, her heart too full for speech. For her thought was this: if I send him to defeat I shall be his bane, and if I send him to victory I thrust him into Astrid's arms. In either case I lose him. Woe is my lot!

IX

THORD SET out in the morning, a bag of food on his shoulder and gladness in his heart. He felt that he was at last a man and by way of becoming a warrior, of whom scalds should recite rhymes and tales by the hearthfires for years to come. Elin saw him go with a smiling face and bright words, but when he passed the lip of the fell she turned back into her hut and sat by the fire and let down her hair and wept, with the quiet grief of a woman whose life has turned the corner into the lonely dales of age. So we leave her.

Thord's path lay over Stafafell. On his left hand towered the gigantic mass of the Vatna Jokull, its rocky wastes stretching away as far as could be seen. Some said that Aslak's hiding-place was in one of the ravines which projected like finger-tips from the mountain's immensity, but Elin had been sure that the Baresark would not den so close to the haunts of men. She advised Thord to inquire of the shepherds and wayfarers he encountered whether they had seen Aslak or had knowledge of his resort; it might take time, but soon or late either he would find Aslak or Aslak would hear of his inquiries and seek him out.

So Thord strode sturdily along, greeting all he chanced to meet, and never failing in his question:

"Have you seen Aslak Flatnose in these dales, carl?"

And shepherd or farmer or traveller—passing, belike, from Berarstead, on Lagarfleet, to Hornfirth—would answer in much the same words:

"What? The Baresark? You are like to have a warm welcome, Thord. No, we have not seen him. As well chase a shadow in the night!"

That evening Thord slept with a shepherd on Oxenlava, who admitted he had seen Aslak faring toward Hornfirth several days past, but had not noticed the Baresark's return. He recommended Thord to several friends in Fleetdale, and from these folk Thord receive much the same change during his second day's search. All knew Aslak, but professed ignorance of his whereabouts. One expressed the opinion that the Baresark dwelt in the neighborhood of Snaefell, beyond the Fleetwater, and with this to go upon, Thord headed inland the third day.

The country was the most desolate he had ever seen. A spur of the Vatna Jokull intervened, now, betwixt him and the Hornfirth dales; and a man might wander the whole day and never see a human face—although the shepherds were agreed that the wilderness maintained a sinister population of trolls and other evil spirits. They were full of tales of men and maidens who had disappeared, and several claimed there was reason to suppose Aslak in league with the demons. How else was the Baresark immune from the perils which befell ordinary folk?

So that night, when Thord bedded beneath an overhanging rock, he repeated a prayer Elin had taught him and arranged a number of pebbles in the form of a cross by his side. It was very still, high up there on Snaefell, the jokull peaks hulking like

*Aslak appeared, a wild figure, dressed in
sheepskins, hairy as Herjolf's self.*

half-seen, grotesque monsters across the pale northern sky, and he listened for the scream of demon voices; but all he heard was the chatter of a branch of the headwaters of the Heradsfloi, clinking over its boulderstrewn bed, on the first stage of its descent through the Jokull dales. Then he slept, and in the morning awoke unharmed.

This day, again, he saw no one until close to evening, when he encountered a shepherd, a very old, withered man, who looked at him with suspicion when he propounded his usual question.

"And what will you seek of Aslak?" demanded the shepherd.

"I have a message for him."

"Who sends it?"

"I see that you do not know me," Thord replied patiently. "I am Thord Geir's son, and my mother is Elin, whom the Horn-firth folk call the Wise. I bear her message."

The shepherd stared hard at him.

"Elin! She was the maid cast ashore with Aslak. Humph! Yes, the maid Geir wedded against her will. You are brother to Bjarni Geir's son, who is called the Grasping."

"Half-brother," corrected Thord.

The shepherd stroked his long beard, and deliberated further.

"Humph! It is to be seen that you are unarmed. Bide here two days."

"But I am seeking Aslak—"

"Bide here two days."

"You know where the Baresark—"

"Bide here two days."

And not a word more would the old carl say. So Thord sat himself down in that spot on desolate Snaefell, and waited the night, the next day and night and a part of the ensuing day. It was past noon when a voice hailed him from the mouth of a ravine, and Aslak appeared, a wild figure, dressed in sheepskins, hairy as Herjolf's self, the sword Grey Maiden at his belt and the axe of blue steel resting on his shoulder. He was no longer a young man, but he walked with the quick, firm tread of one who does not tire easily. He had a chest as round as a barrel, and if he was not so huge as Bjarni, yet he was a thought stouter than Thord, massive as the jokulls amongst which he dwelt. A champion.

"So you are Thord," he cried in a voice that boomed like the wind in a sail. "I have seen you from afar, youngling; but never close enough to judge how you have grown."

"I am not so large as some," replied Thord, gathering his wits for what must follow.

"No, you are of your father's build, and that means you are bitling to me—and to Bjarni, too, eh?"

"Bjarni is as much bigger than you as you are bigger than I," said Thord. "He returned to Geir's stead a few days ago—the day you left the ham for my mother."

"Ho, did he?" exclaimed Aslak. "Ill tidings! I wish I had tarried. I might have put sword or axe to that red head of his."

"That is for me to do," declared Thord.

"For you, bantling? And how will you come by it? For I guess you to be no warrior, as yet—which is no fault of your own."

"It was for that reason my mother sent me to you."

"To be taught weapon-craft?" Aslak nodded sagely. "I remember I made such an offer to her—six years back, after Geir and I had that unlucky bicker. Well, well! That is best forgotten. Will you begin with sword or axe?"

Thord cleared his throat, resolved to plunge without delay into the true intent of his mission.

"There is not time for much of that, Aslak," he answered. "It was the thought of my mother that you would lend me your sword."

"Grey Maiden?" Aslak gaped in amazement. "Boy, you are mad! No hand but mine touches Grey Maiden, until Odin sends the Valkyrs for me. Hut! It is unlucky for another hand to draw it. See what befell Geir!"

"Nevertheless, I must have it," Thord persisted doggedly. "I must challenge Bjarni to fight in holmgang, and to win against him I require Grey Maiden."

"Come, come," remonstrated the Baresark, "I'll fight him for you."

"That can not be, for the reasons my mother gave you once before. Also, in this case, I must fight Bjarni, not only for my rights and my mother's vindication, but to save Astrid Herjolf's dotter—he seeks to wed her, and the betrothal feast is set."

"Hutatut!" growled Aslak. "Here is a mad youngling! And cause enough for a lifetime of feuds and bloodlettings. I am for you, Thord, and for Elin; but not for you or Elin would I let Grey Maiden pass out of my hands."

"So my mother said," replied Thord. "I will do as she bid me, and fight you for the sword."

Aslak sat down on a rock, and wiped a mighty hand across his brow.

"Fight me?" he asked weakly. "You?"

"If you are larger than I, I am younger," asserted Thord.

"For less than that, boy, I have slain men." And Aslak's scowl was as ferocious as Bjarni's. "But have done. I will not harm your mother's son—or any boastful bitling, who finds satisfaction in raising his first crow. So think of an other plan."

"There is no other plan," insisted Thord. "I must fight you for the sword. You cannot refuse me in honor, seeing that you are armed, while I—"

Aslak bounded up, with a bellow of rage.

"Who are you to talk to me of honor? Honor—because I will not slay you out of hand, and save Bjarni the effort! Do not try me too far."

"I do not seek to try you, but to fight you," Thord explained reasonably. "Bethink you, Aslak, if I do not procure the means to thwart Bjarni in wedding Astrid and win me my father's property, I might as well be dead. And if it be at your hands, why, that is of small account to me. So I pray you, have at me, and give me the chance to win the sword."

Now, the Baresark surveyed him grimly.

"With what do you propose to fight me?" Aslak inquired.

Thord unslung the bag in which he carried his store of food, and removed from it a length of hide-rope, very strong and supple, to either end of which was fastened a cow's hoof. And then he proceeded to discard his jerkin and breeches, so that he stood only in his shoon and drawers. Meantime Aslak stared as if his eyes would pop out of his head.

"You—you mean to fight me with that rope?" demanded the Baresark.

"Yes."

"What can you do with it?" scoffed Aslak. "Do you think to strangle me?"

"No, for my mother charged me not to injure you."

The Baresark made the Sign of the Hammer. He was dazed, no longer scornful, a little resentful.

"It is an ill-deed, boy, to mock an older man, a proven warrior."

"Here is no mockery," quoth Thord. "It is my necessity urges me—and my mother's. If you will lend me your sword—"

"That would serve neither of us," retorted the Baresark. "It would mean only bad-luck, I tell you. Grey Maiden is true to one man at a time. Well, I will try not to injure you. But the sword is a thirsty wench."

He shook his head sorrowfully, and started to lay his axe on a boulder.

"Here," he offered, suddenly changing his mind. "Take Skullshaver. It won't help you against Grey Maiden, but I can't bring myself to hew at a defenseless man."

"That is a generous offer," replied Thord. "But I will fight as I had planned. I should be no match for you with the axe."

The Baresark bellowed his exasperation.

"And that is the truth. With the axe or any weapon! This

fight neither of us will find pleasure in remembering. Look to yourself. If I can stop Grey Maiden in time, I will save you; but—"

He rushed abruptly at Thord, the sword wheeling in an arc of grey steel; and Thord retreated, swinging the length of rope by its middle, so that the weighted ends were revolving over his head. Youth against experience! Cow's hoofs against steel!

"Stand still," cried Aslak.

"That is not the way to fight in this manner," Thord answered and continued retreating warily out of the long sword's deadly sweep, his rope twirling ceaselessly.

The Baresark pulled up, snorting disgustedly.

"A poor business, youngling! Come, take the axe, and fight, or—"

Thord struck with appalling swiftness. Leaping in to close quarters, he whirled the weighted ends of his rope around Aslak's sword-arm; the Baresark instinctively jumped back; Thord pulled on the rope, gave it a twist—and Aslak's fingers opened. Grey Maiden clanked on the rocks between them and in the one motion Thord stooped and seized it, released the rope and sprang clear.

"I have it," he said, trying not to seem as proud as he was. "But it shall be yours again. So why should we fight?"

The Baresark peered down at the contrivance which had snared him, and the startled look in his face became imbued with superstitious awe.

"No, no, Thord," he answered. "We will not fight. And as for Grey Maiden, she is yours. She would not have left me so, if she had not wearied of me. I suppose I did not give her the drink she craved. So it is! A man is young—and waxes old. In your hands she will fare better, for I see that you are not without guile, and that is to the credit of any warrior."

Thord looked shamefaced.

"It was my mother's trick—"

"Ah, yes, but you wrought it. A keen eye and a sure hand,

youngling. You will make a fightingman of note, even as I predicted."

"If you will help me," said Thord awkwardly. "I have but begun my endeavor."

Aslak extended his hand.

"By the steel that fathered me, I am your dog! Outlaw or inlaw, I stand by him who wrenched Grey Maiden from me, without holding weapon in his hand. Come, Thord, we will arrange it so, with Elin's wit to aid us, that Bjarni's wealth and strength shall yield him little good. I perceive a task after my own heart. Ha, this is fate! It is doom, boy! The Gods willed this. Not for nothing was I cast ashore in Elin's company, and Grey Maiden bound fast in her sheath at my belt. It was not accident that you were born—or that Grey Maiden sped by my arm should be Geir's bane. I tell you the sword came into Iceland for a purpose—as Elin and I came safe ashore, alone of four score souls."

X

ALL THE Hornfirth folk rode to the betrothal feast. Herjolf's skalli resounded with the din of the feasting, for here was more good feeling shown than at any time since Bjarni's return—and this because Astrid was well-liked and men said the Grasping would be more amenable when tied to a wife. So there was shouting of songs, and boasting of exploits and comparing of heroes, all up and down the lines of benches; clicking of ale-horns in salutation, rapping of marrow-bones on the board-tables, shuffling of feet of the serving-folk as they sped hither and yon, satisfying the needs of the guests. And on the cross-benches at the east end of the hall the buzz of women's voices was scarce lower than the men's; but here the talk was not of trade and fighting, but of the bride's woebegone face, and the hard look in Aud's eyes.

"The maid has been weeping!" "Who? Astrid?" "Who else?" "Why should she, gossips? Bjarni is a stout champion, and a wealthy." "What is wealth without heart's craving?" "What right has a woman to judge her man before she has known him?" "True! Well-spoken! It is ill-done, if maids begin to hunger for love before wedding." "Ah, no! Freya knows we women are hard put to it by fathers who think first of the husband's property and last of his kindliness." "Yes, there is reason in that. And Bjarni has little kindliness." "As much as Aud. It took Elin's wit to name her the Treacherous." "What of Elin in this? And Thord?" " 'Tis no concern of theirs. The men say Thord has fled the country." "Well, he might, poor lad, and no dishonor to him."

On the high seat, midway of the south wall where ran the upper bench, Bjarni sat by Herjolf, his red face twisted in a sullen scowl, his ale-horn never full. Herjolf, too, beneath his hearty manner, was puzzled and perturbed.

"I tell you, I like it not, foster-father," growled Bjarni.

"Loki snatch me, if I understand," defended Herjolf. "She never showed this feeling before you came home."

"Better push to a finish," urged the Grasping. "Pay over the bride-money, and let we two ride for Geir's stead."

"Bide, bide," counselled Herjolf. "If there is undue haste, the folk will remark it. Already, there is whispering and head-nodding on the cross-benches."

"The more reason to be through with this." Bjarni waved a hand toward the smoky turmoil of the skalli. "Let us go, and there will be less occasion for talk."

"No," resisted Herjolf. "Belike, she will weep. Wait until dark, and—"

There was a sudden swirl in front of the Men's Door at the west end of the hall, and steel flashed over the heads of guests and serving-folk. Men tumbled right and left, a thrall-woman shrieked; a bench was upset; voices exclaimed and protested.

"Way," shouted a gruff voice. "Gangway, there! Out of the way, fools. We will not harm you."

Both Herjolf and Bjarni started to their feet. In the high seat on the cross-bench Astrid leaned forward, the color rising in her wan cheeks, an expression of unbelief, tinged by fear, in her eyes. Aud was equally startled, but her face mirrored anger and annoyance.

"Who comes?" called Herjolf. "Name yourselves. Is it necessary for you to bare steel at the betrothal feast?"

A riot of voices answered as the strangers slowly forced a passage.

"It is Thord!" "Aslak the Baresark!" "They have Elin with them!"

And now all the folk might see the little group, Thord in front, a long, grey sword flashing in his right hand, his left guiding his mother up the hall, and Aslak striding behind them, the axe Skullshaver a blue flame on his shoulder. Elin looked proudly, almost haughtily, at those she passed. She held herself very erect, and her eyes shone with a light no man might face.

"The witch!" cried Bjarni. "What do you seek, witch?"

"My son is come to demand justice," she answered curtly.

"With an outlaw to aid him," amended Herjolf. "I see Aslak at your back, and it is known to all that he has stolen and slain from one end of Iceland to the other."

"As to the slaying," rumbled Aslak before Elin could speak, "it is true I have cropped a few heads that deserved it, whatever the law-men might say; and I have lifted a sheep now and then from those who could afford it by way of punishing them for the thieving they did upon folk who were not so powerful." He eyed Herjolf tolerantly. "Yes, I have taken many a sheep from your folds, False One."

There was a faint bubbling of laughter in the back-benches, for every man present had had dealings at some time with Herjolf, and knew how hard he was in compelling the terms his wealth made it possible for him to secure. But Elin stopped Aslak, when the Baresark would have continued.

"Aslak is come hither as my witness," she said.

"A witness to what?" asked Herjolf angrily. "What has that

to do with Thord's demanding justice? I think you have come seeking manslaughter."

"And little good shall it do you," Bjarni added grimly. "For none of you leaves this hall alive."

He made to vault over the table, and there was a scattering of men from his path; but he paused as Thord spoke.

"Hear me, all you people," announced Thord. "I am come to demand of Bjarni Geir's son the half of our father's property, which he has wrongfully withheld from me."

"To what purpose?" scoffed Bjarni. "It has been established that you are base-born. Elin, your mother, entered this house as a thrall, in the clothes she wore, and possessing naught else."

Now, Elin spoke again.

"I am, and was born, a free woman," she said calmly. "And Geir took me to wife, as Aslak shall testify. Not otherwise would I have gone to him, nor would Aslak have suffered it."

Bjarni laughed sneeringly.

"A likely tale! And a known thief and outlaw to bolster it!"

"Touching Aslak's outlawry," replied Thord, "I make myself responsible for it. When I have obtained justice from Bjarni I will pay any fines assessed against Aslak, and the complainant shall set his own price."

"A fair promise," mocked Herjolf, "seeing that you are penniless as you stand here, Thord, and shall be lifeless a few moments hence."

"That is to be proven," Thord answered steadily. "I appeal to the folk here to see justice done. I have dwelt among them my life long, and I ask any man to say if my mother or I have wrought injury to a soul in Iceland."

Several men cried out, affirming this statement, and their boldness encouraged others to give similar testimony.

"It is well known, Thord!" "They are good folk, Thord and Elin." "Give the boy justice."

And then a great roar from every corner of the skalli, women's voices shrilling through the men's, and Astrid, on the cross-bench, staring starry-eyed at the sturdy showing her champion made:

"Justice! Justice for Thord! Justice for Thord and Elin! Justice!"

Bjarni ripped his sword from its sheath, and he swept the hall with a ferocious glance that marked those who shouted loudest:

"It is in this spirit you come to my betrothal feast! I shall remember it, Hornfirth folk. When the harvest fails, when your cattle die, when the fever-blight assails your children—then come to me, and ask aid. Come, and hear my answer!"

The shouting dwindled to a frightened silence, for there was no doubt in the minds of the Hornfirth folk that Bjarni had the power to cause suffering in every stead. So they sat back, and eyed one another uneasily, half of a mind to believe they had made fools of themselves.

Aud spoke acidly from the cross-bench, holding tightly one of Astrid's wrists—so tight her grip that the girl winced:

"Here is much neighborly feeling, husband! It has been said that those who confer favor may look first for ingratitude, so we need not be surprised. But at the same time we should not permit Thord to ride rough-shod over the legal rights of our son-in-law. You and I had speech with Elin after Geir was slain by Aslak, the very witness she now brings forward in proof that Geir took her to wife, and we know that she had no proof to offer, then. I do not see what profit will come of this business, yet if Thord is so foolish as to meet Bjarni in the open Bjarni would be equally foolish not to accept the challenge and slay him."

Thord took a step toward her, and the fire in his eyes dimmed only when his gaze slipped from Aud's cold features to Astrid, pinned down in her seat by her mother's cruel grasp.

"I remember how Aud persecuted my mother that day after Geir was laid in hough," he answered, boyishly stern. "The three of them hated us for the one reason: Bjarni wished all Geir's property for himself, and Aud and Herjolf desired the same thing because they would have Bjarni wed Astrid—" he paused—"against her will."

Aud leaned across the table, her eyes glittering snakily; Bjarni and Herjolf frowned, dumbfounded.

"So!" hissed Aud. "It is to you we look, Thord, for Astrid's tears and protests!"

And she twisted Astrid's wrist until the maid wept. But Thord might not see this because Bjarni had vaulted the table from the high seat and alighted on the floor rushes near where he stood. Once more men tumbled over each other in their haste to get from under the feet of the champions. Aslak, axe poised to strike at need, took position at Thord's back, and cast a keen eye around the nearby benches. Elin stood to one side. But Thord raised his sword in a gesture for attention.

"Hear me, Hornfirth folk! I, Thord Geir's son, being deprived of my just inheritance by Bjarni Geir's son, who has also cast dishonor upon my mother, Elin, who was Geir's wife, do challenge Bjarni Geir's son to fight me on this issue in holmgang. It is my right to challenge, and so I do challenge and if he does not fight me on these terms, he is niddering, and thereby forfeits the rights I challenge."

"I fight you, now, base-born," snarled Bjarni, and he would have rushed at Thord, but that Herjolf called to him, and there were still folk in his path.

"Bide, Bjarni," advised Herjolf. "I say naught against the slaying of these folk, and if you will wait I will have in my housecarls, and we will finish them; but there is no occasion for you to meet Thord in holmgang. If he wished to challenge you he should have done so six years past when Geir died, and we settled the inheritance."

Thord laughed aloud, with a savage mirth that sat ill on his young face.

"Six years ago," he answered, "I was a boy, not half-grown. Bjarni was a man older than I am today. Could I have challenged him? Ho, Hornfirth folk, you are freemen, Icelanders, who deal justice evenly, man to man! I ask you: is not a man who argues so putting himself in the wrong? Could a boy of twelve years challenge a youth of nineteen to holmgang? And would Bjarni and Herjolf and Aud have plotted against us as they did if I had been able to defend our rights?"

For the second time a roar of approval broke from the crowded skalli. The Hornfirth folk might fear the wealth and power of Bjarni and Herjolf, but their elemental sense of justice triumphed over the temptation to stand aside from Thord's quarrel. Likewise, here was a case which might set a precedent in future years. Every man saw that if the right of trial in holmgang was limited they could never be certain of obtaining justice. Cravens, especially, all cunning fellows, would exploit such an advantage.

"Holmgang," was the shout. "Let Bjarni take up Thord's challenge. Justice for Smiling Thord!"

Herjolf, never willing to venture against odds, sank back in his seat, biting his fingers, pulling at his beard. Bjarni thought only of slaying Thord.

"Bah," he shouted. "Too long have I suffered the witch and her brat to live. Why wait for holmgang? I can slay him as well here."

And he leaped at Thord, but both Elin and Aslak came between them, and when he would have cut at Elin the Baresark's axe struck up his blade.

"Have a care," rasped Aslak. "I would save you for Thord, carl, but—"

Bjarni gave ground, not liking the red glare in Aslak's eye. He was as brave as most men—but few men cared to do battle with a Baresark, and they unmailed.

"The challenge was to fight in holmgang," Elin appealed to the bystanders. "This is not holmgang. There is little room for footwork."

"True," agreed Aslak, "and the lighter man requires the room.

But I do not think we need worry." He grinned—derisively at Bjarni, with confidential amusement at the serried ranks of men standing back against the walls on tables and benches. "Thord has a sword that— Well, carls, it is a sword."

"He has the right," Elin corrected gently. "But there must be no reason for Herjolf or another to claim the fight was unfair."

"All I seek is the fight," snapped Bjarni. "Have done with talk."

"No, no, one thing more," cried Thord. "I ask the folk to protect my mother and Aslak. If I should fall—which I will not—"

A shout answered him.

"Well-said, Thord!" "Hew, and fear not." "Elin shall go free." "We'll guard the Baresark."

"The Baresark guards himself," retorted Aslak.

He let his axe hang loose from its wrist-thong, caught Elin under the arm-pits and swung her off the floor onto one of the tables, where men readily made a space for her. But she still persisted in asserting her point.

"This is a fight in holmgang," she cried. "It is a fight to prove Thord's cause."

"Holmgang," agreed the spectators. "It is a fight in holm-gang."

Even the women on the cross-benches leaned over their tables, wrapt in the clash of the two champions; but of them all none watched more closely than Astrid. And as Bjarni sprang at Thord, and Thord met him foot to foot, with a clatter and clang of steel that sent the sparks flying to the rafters, she wrenched her hand loose from her mother and gained her feet, eyes ashine, cheeks crimson.

"Hew on, Thord," she called. "Astrid for Thord! Hew, lad, hew!"

And the skalli echoed her, discretion forgotten.

"Hew, Thord, hew! Justice for Thord! Justice!"

Aud clawed at Astrid, and sought to pull her down, but the girl repelled her mother, and other women spoke so sharply that Aud cowered, dazed by the turn of events. On the high seat Herjolf was in like case, chewing at his fingers, mumbling in his beard. For what did he see, but Thord darting and striking with a speed and sureness that roused the enthusiasm of every fightingman present, the grey sword a flicker of lightning, his strong young limbs carrying him here and there, now inside the sweep of Bjarni's blade, now far out of its range!

Bjarni was in a rage, fuming at the lack of instant success he had anticipated. He cursed and howled as Thord clipped him in the thigh, and then danced away.

"Hold still, jumping-jack! Do you fear the steel?"

"Do you?" countered Thord, and nicked his shoulder.

Panting and foaming, for he had drunk deep and his belly was soggy, Bjarni forced himself to a speed approaching Thord's, and tried to exploit his superior height for one of those terrible strokes which there is no parrying; but always the sword Grey Maiden flickered beneath his steel, and Thord's lithe muscles resisted his battering strength.

The skalli went wild, and the blood-lust was kindled, so that if the guests had not been of practically the same mind there must have been such a folk-slaying as the sagamen had never recited.

"Hew, Thord, hew!" "At his head, youngling!" "Well-struck!" "Under his arm-pit!"

There were but two who kept silence. Aslak leaned on his axe, eyes intent on the flying figures. Elin stood, with hands clasped in front of her, and in them the little gold cross. Her eyes, too, were on the pair who leaped and whirled and charged and retreated in a flickering maze of steel—yet she seemed to see something else, beyond them, something that was beyond time and space.

Thord now was confident he had Bjarni's measure. No longer did he dart away before his half-brother's bull rushes. He countered Bjarni's strokes by might of arm and weapon-skill, and the shouts of applause threatened to lift the roof-beams. Grey Maiden heaved and swung, thrust and parried, as though the blade was a part of him. Bjarni was bleeding from several cuts, and the folk commenced to realize that Thord was playing with him. Laughter spiced the applause. And Bjarni became insane. He abandoned all caution, heedless of his own fate, if he might slay Thord, who ignored this recklessness, warding every attack with mocking ease.

"Be merciful, my son!"

Elin's voice carried distinct in all the hubbub, and Bjarni faltered, his sword poised overhead.

"The witch spells me," he muttered.

Then Thord struck, a low, sweeping stroke that caught Bjarni in mid-thigh and hewed his legs from under him, and Bjarni crashed down on the floor-rushes, his stumps spouting blood, but he clutched at an overturned bench and pulled himself erect for a moment, his sword yet poised for the blow he had not dealt.

His eyes fixed Elin's, malignant, hateful, defiant.

"Your doing, witch," he gasped. "Come with me!"

And he hurled his sword straight at her breast. It turned once in air, hilt over point, a flash of light in the dimness, sped by the last strength of his body even as he collapsed in death. But Grey Maiden flew faster. Thord cast the long blade like an axe, and once more it parried Bjarni's blow. The two swords clattered at Elin's feet.

Aslak sprang to pick them up.

"What said I, Thord?" exclaimed the Baresark, tendering Grey Maiden. "It was not for nothing this sword and I and Elin came into Iceland together. There was fate in it! The Norns spun our skeins with the one bobbin."

But none heeded Aslak. The folk in the skalli were shouting: "Hewing Thord!" "Well-struck, Thord!" "Well-hewed!"

And the women on the cross-benches were helping Astrid

to climb to the floor, and Thord was trying to make his way to meet her, Grey Maiden dripping in his hand.

Aslak was quick to perceive the situation.

"Way for Thord," he commanded lustily, brandishing Skullshaver aloft. "Gangway for Hewing Thord!"

And the folk parted before them, so that Thord took Astrid in his arms under the high seat where Herjolf gloomed. Aud had fled, tears of rage in her cold eyes.

From the north side of the hall Elin watched what passed, and if her heart ached, she curbed her feelings with resolute courage. Youth to youth! It was as it should be.

"Herjolf!" she called.

The folk turned toward her. Herjolf ceased chewing his fingers, and eyed her shiftily, conscious the tide of opinion flooded against him, fearful of Bjarni's fate.

"This was a betrothal feast," she went on when she had attention. "It was ill-planned, but that has been remedied. It would be discourteous of us to slight your hospitality, so I counsel you that we continue the feast. I seem to see a blither look in Astrid's face, and—"

The laughter of the Hornfirth folk drowned out her voice.

"Well-wooed, Thord," they cried. "Ho, what a wooing!"

"I suppose it must be," said Herjolf sulkily.

"Yes," agreed Aslak in the same tone. "It must be."

"Ho, ho, ho," shouted the Hornfirthers. "A rare jest! Thord's wooing! Ho, ho, ho! Pay down the maid's portion, Herjolf. More ale! More ale!"

XI

AFTER THIS Thord was known as Hewing Thord, and he became one of the most famous men in Iceland. He kept the sword Grey Maiden until his death, and much glory he won with it, both in outfaring and infaring. So highly was he regarded that when Olaf Tryggvi's son became King in

Norway he sent word to Iceland that he wished Thord to visit him that he might do proper honor to one whose deeds had carried across the Western Ocean; and the skalds tell how Thord assisted King Olaf in many exploits.

He lived to a considerable age, and he and Astrid had many children. From them descended several lines of worthy folk, warriors, skalds, seafarers, and priests, who were settled in the south of Iceland. The most noted of these was Snorre Sturla's son, who collected the Heimskringla Sagas, which tell of the deeds of the Kings of Norway.

When King Olaf, of blessed memory, dispatched Thangbrand Willibald's son to preach the White Christ in Iceland none helped Thangbrand more than Thord, and Elin was not behind her son in bringing the people to accept the new faith. It was she who set Aslak to slay Arne Dag's son, of the White River dales, when he told the folk at the Allthing that it would not profit them to turn from Odin's worship and the Old Gods. Aslak earned much sanctity by this and other slayings in behalf of the new faith, and the end of it all was that he became a monk. He hung up his axe Skullshaver in the chapel of his monastery, and the folk called it God's Axe because it had been the bane of so many heathen.

Close by, on Oxenlava, Elin dwelt in a convent Thord built for her, and here she died, and it is said that feeble-minded folk who were brought to her tomb had their wits restored to them. Whether this is so or not, it is certain that she was a very wise woman.

This is all of the tale of Thord's Wooing.

LITTLE MAN in jester's motley looked down from
the top of Neri's Tower upon the hulking mass of Castello Gritti, crouched on its promontory like a great stone
monster ready to leap from the shadow of the Apennines into
the dancing blue waters of the Adriatic. Opposite him, and on
a level with his eyes, rose the round bulk of the Gate Tower,
where watchmen moved restlessly in the hot Spring sunshine.
Below, the life of the fortress droned its normal course: hoofs
thudded in the tilt-yard, and curses bellowed upward as old
Gianni schooled a batch of green men-at-arms; a leisurely
clanking and clanging marked the location of forge and smithy;
in the forecourt crossbow-bolts whizzed at target-practice; a
few sentinels lounged on the walls—and from the green bower
of the garden that nestled in their seaward tip came a shrill
clamor of woman's laughter.

The jester skipped lightly to an arrowslit commanding that
side of the castle, an expression of whimsical amusement on
his ugly, brown face. When he moved, the muscles rippled and
bulged under his tight garments, with an effect of power in
startling contrast to his diminutive stature.

"Per Bacco!" he muttered. "You are no sluggard, Madonna
Lisa."

A man's laugh, hoarse, perhaps a trifle tipsy, echoed from the
garden.

"Ho, ho, Old One," grinned the jester. "And you—you are as

fat in your mind as of your person. They are wily folk in Venice. Trust to the Signoria!"

The woman's voice rose again in a snatch of song, lilting and amorous; but the jester's attention was distracted by a stir amongst the watchmen on the Gate Tower. They pointed south-ward along the white ribbon of the Coast Road, which looped and coiled between the foothills and the shore, and the jester had no difficulty in identifying the object of their curiosity: a sparkling clump of lance-points, poised momentarily on one of the elevations in the road.

The jester pursed his lips in a soundless whistle.

"Home rides Guido—and halts to look to sea! Can Young Nicolo be on the way, as well?"

He shaded his eyes, and peered keenly southeast across the sapphire-blue expanse of the Adriatic. Yes, far, far off, on the utmost horizon, the sunlight was reflected from the square sail of a galley. The vessel, itself, was yet invisible, but the little man in motley imagined how it skimmed the waves like a multi-legged dragon, oars swinging, whips cracking on the naked backs of the slaves. Always in a hurry, Young Nicolo, in his calm, imperturbable fashion.

A race, eh? Guido's men-at-arms galloping north on the road as Young Nicolo drove his galley for the landing-cove inside the fish-hook bend of the promontory, just beneath the garden where Madonna Lisa was now laughing again as if some tremendous sport was forward, and Old Nicolo was gurgling and grunting and apparently—if that waving of branches meant anything—pursuing her clumsily.

The little jester laughed, in his turn.

"A family reunion, signori! Per Bacco, what affection! All of us together—Madonna Lisa, the Old One, Young Nicolo, Black Guido—and me! Yes, forget not Ciutazzo, Magnificent Signori. The Gritti, the Signoria and the Emperor! Ho, ho, all but the Po— Now, may the devil fly off with me! Who is this?"

From the foothills inland a second road debouched to join

the Coast Road at the miserable village which huddled at the base of the promontory on which the castle stood. Down this road strode a single figure, bare-footed, bare-legged, dusty brown robe flapping at his heels, cowl thrown back to expose sunburned face and tonsure.

"A most purposeful monk," commented the jester. "How he strides! No wanton, wandering, pilfering shaveling, this fellow. Not he! He goes upon an errand—hitherward. Yes, hitherward, beyond a doubt. And that errand can be but the one. But it is too excellent a contrivance for credibility. It would round out the picture. We should have completeness. And why not? Why not, I ask, per Bacco? Shall the Holy Father be excluded from the board? Impiety! So shall Ciutazzo sharpen his wits, and win to—win to— Now, what in Mary's name *shall* I win to?"

He rubbed his clean-shaven chin, and pondered the question, then skipped with his peculiar airy ease of motion toward the trap which opened on the tower-stair.

"Time enough to think of that," he decided. "I'll consult the Gritti Luck. Yes, yes, that will be best. Let the Luck decide!"

I I

THE WARDERS in the gateway laughed uproariously as Ciutazzo turned a somersault into their midst, with a merry jingling of the tiny hawk's bells which edged his garments. A frown showed on the dour features of the friar, whose interrogation was so abruptly interrupted.

"How, now, brown brother?" exclaimed the jester. "There is dust on your feet, there is sweat on your brow. You have travelled far. Who are you? Whence come you? Whither go you? Are you for Pope or Emperor? Milan, Venice, Genoa, Padua, Pisa? Your own man or Abbot's man? Pilgrim or beggar?"

The friar's face hardened. It was a stern face, square-jawed, with close-set lips and eyes that burned steadily.

"I am called Fra Pietro," he said shortly. "I am of the Minorites. I travel upon God's business."

Ciutazzo peered vacuously at him. Gone the shrewdness, the alert intelligence, which had characterized him when alone. He seemed almost the natural, pertly ignorant.

"A Minorite," he babbled. "One of the flock of the blessed Francis, eh? But you haven't the look of your brethren, Fra Pietro. A scurvy lot—dirty, withal—forever whining and thirsty."

"You talk of your betters," Fra Pietro answered contemptuously. And turned to the warders: "Must I waste time with this jingle-jangle fool? I asked for your lord."

One of the warders bowed, humorously apologetic.

"If you would see Old Nicolo, let Dogface be your usher, good brother. He has our lord's ear. A mighty droll fellow."

The friar's hot eyes stabbed into Ciutazzo's.

"Ah, yes, there is none can make Old Nicolo laugh like me," the jester babbled on. "Come with Ciutazzo. I know where he takes his pleasure. I know how to approach him. Ah, yes, and I know what he plots and schemes. Who better than Ciutazzo? Ciutazzo, who makes him laugh when the black moods are on him, and who waves his bauble between Young Nicolo and Guido when their swords are half-drawn! Per Bacco, there is none in Castello Gritti knows more than I, brown brother."

"Christ's truth," swore a warder.

"Loose talk," reproved the friar. "Our Lord God's name in vain, and a heathen oath! You show no grace, you of the Gritti's folk."

The warders scowled, and Ciutazzo intervened quickly.

"Why, as to that, brown brother, no priest stays long with us, and those who have come wrought little good. What with the slayings and burnings and wenchings and stealings and—"

A warder coughed warningly. Fra Pietro crossed himself.

"Where the devil sows, I plough," he said. "Come, Ciutazzo. Show me to Lord Nicolo."

The jester turned a back-somersault, landing expertly on his feet.

"Follow, brown brother," he directed. "I'll take you to him. He's in the garden—with Madonna Lisa." A vacant grin distorted the gnarled features. "Perhaps there'll be work for you to do—a wedding, eh? But that's not his way. Not of late years. We take, but we wed not, we of Castello Gritti."

The warders chuckled covertly, but Fra Pietro kept silent until he and his guide were in the forecourt, behind the line of crossbowmen practicing at the butts ranged against the opposite stable wall.

"You have been here long?" the priest inquired then.

"I? Per Bacco— Oh, pardon, brother! I meant to say: no. I came last year about this time. They gave me food and clothes. I make them laugh, keep Old Nicolo from slaying his sons, his sons from cutting each other's throats. We are all content. So I stay."

"The devil's own, these Gritti," murmured the friar. "But who is Madonna Lisa?"

Ciutazzo stole a glance at the iron face of the man beside him.

"She whom the Signoria sent," he prattled. "Did you not know? Everybody—"

"The Signoria?" broke in Fra Pietro. "You mean Venice? The Doge's Council?"

"Who else? Old Nicolo was there a month since, selling some of the plunder, and a great lord— Oh, belike it was the Doge, himself!—gave her to him. A fine, sleek wench, brown brother. Red-haired, but a thought too plump for my fancy, and—"

"And what do his sons say to this?" pressed the friar.

"Oh, they curse and quarrel and tell him he is old and worthless. But if he gives them the chance—ho, ho, ho! hee, hee, hee!—watch them, brown brother! Just watch them! Per Bacco, Young Nicolo has looked at her more than once. He has an eye for her kind. And Guido, he fears her because—because—"

He appeared to flounder awkwardly, in doubt whether he should continue what he had been about to say.

"Yes, yes," Fra Pietro prompted him. "Go on! Go on! Why should Guido fear her?"

The pair had reached the top of the ascent from the forecourt to the upper range of buildings. Over the landward walls might be seen the hazy skyline of the Apennines.

Fra Pietro's hand, a large, calloused, powerful hand, clutched the jester's arm.

"You hurt me, brown brother," Ciutazzo reproved him gravely, and the friar relaxed his grip, in his preoccupation failing to note that his fingers had been able scarcely to dent the jester's mesh of muscles.

"But you have not answered me," chided Fra Pietro. "Why should Guido fear Madonna Lisa?"

The jester glanced cautiously around them.

"Why, you see," he confided, "she is for Venice, eh? And Guido, he—he is for—"

"Who? The Emperor?"

Ciutazzo shook his head.

"Not he! He leans toward the Holy Father."

Something that might have been a sigh escaped the friar's lips.

"And Young Nicolo?" he asked. "Is he, too, for our Holy Father?"

Ciutazzo snickered.

"You know not the Gritti, brown brother. No, no! What one is for the other is against."

"Ah, then, Young Nicolo is for the Emperor?"

"I said it not, for I know it not." The jester swelled out his chest with a comic travesty of pride. "He keeps his own counsel, does Young Nicolo."

"But he is not for Venice?"

Ciutazzo considered this.

"Most likely, not. For then he must agree with his father—and he would almost as soon agree with Guido as with Old Nicolo. Oh, a brave den of wolves! Hands always on sword-hilts, teeth always bared, a curse on every tongue."

He started to enter a wide, arched doorway, but Fra Pietro restrained him, gazing out across the forecourt and the land walls at the vista of the hills.

"It is a fair place, jester."

"And a strong," agreed Ciutazzo, his puckered eyes intent on the friar's. "The old Romans built it, men say, and this I know: that all men crave it today. Young Nicole's galley levies tribute at sea, and Black Guido's men-at-arms take toll of all who travel on the Coast Road. Ah, nobody can pass by Castello Gritti. In Venice they call it the key to the Adriatic. The Emperor says who sits here might pour troops as he would into the South. And the Pope—"

"Never mind the Pope," Fra Pietro rebuked harshly. "It is not for vermin such as you to speak lightly of him who holds Peter's Keys, who sits as God's Viceregent on earth."

"An uncommon warm seat he has, brown brother," quoth the jester.

And when the priest glowered at him gave back a step and added innocently:

"But that is what all say! He and the Emperor are forever at each other—like Young Nicolo and Black Guido. And the Venetians flout him, and the other cities ignore him and in Rome the nobles brawl on his doorstep. Why, many's the Pope has been in fear of his life in Rome!"

He waxed confidential.

"Now, you have the look of a great man to me, brown brother. Yes, yes, per Bacco, you might be a Lord Cardinal. You might be Pope, yourself! But if I were you—"

"I have not asked your advice," exclaimed Fra Pietro. "You are to lead me to Lord Nicolo."

"At once, at once," the jester fawned eagerly. "This way. Through the hall, and then—"

His tongue clacking on, he secretly hugged himself with satisfaction.

"Touch, that time!" he recorded. "You are not what you seem, Fra Pietro. Nor are you concerned for our souls. Tonsured you may be, but you would not be the first churchman who could survey the strong points of a hold. What's toward? Is this the day I've waited for? Shall we scatter the pieces on the board, and play at chess like the Emperor and his knights? A brave pastime! But be wary, Dogface. Be humble."

III

THE HALL was a wide and lofty chamber, two rows of pillars down the middle and at the end a dais of stone, backed by a fireplace and carven chimneypiece, in front of which were placed a long table and half a dozen chairs of state. But what caught the friar's eye—and held it—was a mystical grey shimmer of steel, slanting across the chimneypiece.

"The Gritti Luck," he murmured.

"You have heard of it?" the jester queried softly.

"Who has not?" countered Fra Pietro, and swiftly traversed the empty chamber, ascending the dais as one accustomed to his own way.

"Ha," commented Ciutazzo, "you sit above the salt, brown brother!"

Fra Pietro checked himself, and a mask of humility settled upon his features.

"A poor friar, without wealth or ambition, may walk without fear of temptation, jester," he answered in a tone of mild rebuke. "Surely, there is none here my curiosity may harm."

"None," Ciutazzo agreed whimsically. "But you will not accuse me of curiosity if I say you are the first friar I ever saw interested in a sword."

"There is much you have not seen," retorted the friar.

"There you have me," admitted Ciutazzo, executing a little prancing step. "And what do you make of it, brown brother?"

Fra Pietro peered up at the long, straight blade, with its plain steel hilt. The light from several narrow windows, high up in the west wall, bathed the chimneypiece in radiance and showed clearly the strange series of letters, signs, and symbols etched and bitten and scratched in the sword's flat surface.

"There is more writing on the other side—against the stones," remarked the jester.

But the friar paid no attention to him, spelling slowly the lowermost of the visible inscriptions:

> *Li demoyzel griz*
> *Ma vengance je priz.*

"It is a French blade, then," he muttered to himself.

Ciutazzo goggled at him comically.

"A friar who reads!" wondered the jester. "A very monk! But you are wrong, brown brother. That may be French, that writing; but the sword is older than France or Italy. There is Latin on it. There is Greek on it. There is Arabic—or so said the Saracen hakim from Palermo, who bled Old Nicolo the last time he over-ate himself. Yes, and there are tongues no man can put a name to."

The friar stared up at the lean, shimmering mystery of the sword—and presently looked away, as if the reflection of the sunlight in the grey whorls dazzled him.

"As old as evil," he growled.

"As old as death, more likely," replied the jester.

And the gravity of the tone drew a sudden, penetrating glance from Fra Pietro. Ciutazzo giggled inanely.

"And that would be as old as the Gritti, eh?" he ruminated aloud. "For they are lords of death—oh, very proper signori! At least, since Old Nicolo's grandfather won the sword at dice. He—the grandfather, old Annibaldo, you know—was expelled from Venice—killing a doge's son or some little trick of that kind and fled to France. He was down to his last byzant when he won Grey Maiden here from a Provencal knight in a main that ran all night in the Bishop's guardroom at Carcassonne. His luck changed from that day. He made a pile of ransom money; raised his own company; hired out to the Florentines; sold them to the Milanese; deserted to the Holy Father—who, they tell me, paid him in indulgences rather than coin—not that he didn't need them, per Bacco!—and took this place by treachery from the Chiessi, who probably had it by the same means from whoever sat here before them. And old Annibaldo bade his son consider Grey Maiden the luck of the Gritti. The luck of the Gritti she has been ever since; they won't even carry her in battle. Oh, no, she hangs there on the wall, and if they don't say mass to her it isn't for want of respect."

The friar crossed himself.

"Heathen superstition! It is sufficient to jeopardize the souls of all within these walls."

"Humph," commented Ciutazzo. "I know not as to their souls, but I am certain their bodies would be jeopardized if aught happened to the sword. The Gritti would be as fearful as any man-at-arms. They, who, with it, are arrogant as princes!"

"Yet they seek alliance with the Venetians," objected Fra Pietro, his eyes darting sidewise at the jester.

"Not Young Nicolo—or Guido, either! Young Nicolo says the Gritti need no alliance with folk who must pay tribute to them in any case. Trust to the Luck, says he. Guido—saving your presence, brown brother—says to hell with Venice! If we traffic with any overlord, let it be the Pope."

"He speaks wisely," the friar said warmly.

"Wisely? In sooth, yes!" Ciutazzo's homely visage was entirely vacant. "The Pope, says Guido, is an old woman, who can not compel us to anything we dislike; but we might always have occasion to wring favors from him—for which we need pay little. So he plumps for the Pope."

Fra Pietro crossed himself again.

"The brood of Satan! And the Emperor? Does none speak for him?"

The jester pondered the question.

"Why, there is Young Nicolo. He is not for the Emperor. He is for Young Nicolo. But I suppose he would sooner be for the Emperor than for his father's Venice or Guido's Pope."

"Infidel that he is!" cried the friar. "All infidels! Such as they are no better than the sons of Mahound. Hell gapes wide for them."

"That is as may be," Ciutazzo observed impartially. "We hear sorry tales of your churchman. And the Gritti are not likely to come to harm while they have the Luck. After all, they are no worse than Ruggieri, who bred Old Nicolo, or Annibaldo, who bred Ruggieri."

Fra Pietro studied the jester's hazel eyes that held a peculiar hidden glow, buried deep beneath their childish twinkle.

"Strange, no man has stolen the Luck," he remarked. "It might be thought—"

"Many have tried," chuckled Ciutazzo. "And all have died."

And added inconsequentially:

"There are serving-folk watching us this moment."

"St. Paul!" the friar exclaimed involuntarily. "You distort my meaning, Dogface. Guard your tongue."

"Ah, but my tongue is privileged," chuckled Ciutazzo. "None so privileged as I in Castello Gritti. I jest with Old Nicolo. Come, I'll take you to him—in the garden, where he toys with Madonna Lisa. Hee, hee, hee! They were clever, the Venetians. The Madonna, she has a surer grip on Old Nicolo than much gold would have bought them. But wait until Guido rides in! Wait until Young Nicolo is up from the cove! Wait until the supper wine is served! Ho, ho, ho!"

He leaped his own height in air with a jingling of bells, and danced a few steps, preening himself like a peacock on a lawn.

"Only wait, brown brother! Ciutazzo is a rare showman. And first, I will show you Old Nicolo at his ease. Speak him gently. He is quick, for all his fat—and what is a friar to him? Ho, ho, ho! What, indeed?"

Fra Pietro shuddered, despite himself.

"You have a foul tongue, Dogface," he rebuked. "Privileged or no. Lead on."

I V

OLD NICOLO'S enormous body bulged out of a creaking armchair, placed in front of a green tangle of olive trees in a shady corner of the garden where the seawind blew through an opening in the walls. His little squinty eyes were veiled by the fat buttresses of his cheeks and a thick mat of beard, scarcely shot with grey. His mouth was a red slash, studded with stubby white teeth. A beaked nose, netted over with crimson veins, jutted from his swollen face. On one velvet-clad knee he poised a golden flagon of wine. A great square hand, its strength concealed under layers of fat, stroked the red curls of Madonna Lisa, who sat on a stool against his knees, twanging at a gitern.

"So it is to have strong sons," he was saying. "Why should I work, who have reared them these many years? No, no, this is my time of ease. Work them, Madonna, work them so that they sweat! So I'll keep them from conspiring against me. Make them hate each other always, favor one, then the other, whisper tales, eh? Tell one the other says— But what's this, Ciutazzo? You come unannounced, with a stranger?"

Ciutazzo executed a caper, and made pretense of kissing one of Madonna Lisa's hands.

"No stranger, Lord Nicolo," denied the jester. "A brother in God, yes, a brown brother. The holy Fra Pietro, who was faring past, and thought he would tarry to inquire for the state of your Magnificence's soul and pass a mite of gossip, withal. I met him at the gate, and plucked him hither. Was I not kind? Was I not thoughtful?"

Fra Pietro bowed stiffly, folding his hands on his chest. Madonna Lisa pouted. She was, as Ciutazzo had described her, buxom of person, languorous, moulded in ample curves, her skin a perfect blend of pink and white hues, her hair tortured by chemicals to an unnaturally vivid red. The true type of Venetian beauty.

"Only a priest, Dogface!" she protested. "From all your pother I had expected entertainment."

"I am content," spoke up Old Nicolo, with a sly gleam in his pig-eyes. "And you must be content with me, Madonna. God wot, there is enough of me!"

His paunch waggled to the rhythm of his laughter.

"Whither go you, priest?" he challenged curtly.

"On God's business," Fra Pietro responded in the same phrase he had employed with the jester.

"That means nothing." Old Nicolo's voice was peremptory. "Whence come you?"

"From Rome."

"So! You travel for your Order?"

"In part, Lord."

"Ah! And in part—"

"I bear messages for the Holy Father to those of his supporters on my way," returned the friar, seeming to conquer a certain reluctance.

"By my Luck, I do not question that!" proclaimed Old Nicolo. "And I doubt not, too, that you make report of what you see on the way."

"A traveller's tales always find hearers," evaded Fra Pietro.

"I have known it to be so," the fat man agreed ironically. "How were matters in Rome when you left?"

The friar twisted his hands in the cord bound about his waist, choosing his words carefully, speaking deliberately.

"The Holy Father is still in health, not so hale as some might wish—"

"Nor so pindling as many of my Lord Cardinals could desire," burst in Old Nicolo, contorting his huge face in a satyr's grin.

Madonna Lisa laughed shrilly. Ciutazzo pranced and jangled his bells.

"How if Fra Pietro be a Lord Cardinal?" he demanded. "Look to the sternness of him, Lord Nicolo! Look to the air with which he comports himself!"

Old Nicolo squinted malevolently at the friar, who denied hastily:

"May Christ forgive the wastrel his loose talk! I a Cardinal? Lord, a Cardinal does not walk the highways in brown robe and bare feet. I am a humble brother of the Minorites—the rule of St. Francis."

"So!" grunted Old Nicolo. "Perhaps you speak truth—albeit, if so, you are the first friar of that stamp ever I saw. Well, well! And what of Rome? The Holy Father is in health. Hath neither over-eaten nor over-drunken, eh? And how go his affairs with the Emperor?"

The friar's face darkened appreciably.

"That tool of the Evil One!" he barked. "God pity one so distraught. There can be no pity on earth. He labors still in the mire of confusion, heedless of God's commands, selfish, wilful, ignoring the needs of Christendom."

"He'll not go on the Crusade?" Old Nicolo prompted drily.

"He evades, Lord."

"And the cities? The Princes?"

Fra Pietro shrugged his shoulders.

"It is as always. They consult their own ends."

"And rightly," approved Old Nicolo.

"There are more ends than one for each of us," the friar said slowly. "Bethink you, Lord, he who scorns the Holy Father merits ill of God."

Madonna Lisa smote a chord upon her gitern, a jolly, mocking chord.

"He prates like Black Guido," she cried.

"So he does," assented Old Nicolo. "You waste breath upon me, priest."

Fra Pietro drew a step nearer.

"Lord Nicolo," he began earnestly, "there is more than heavenly vantage for those who aid the Holy Father. What prince of Christendom is greater? Year by year, the power of Rome increases, and the day shall dawn when all the world owns the sway of the one ruler—him who rules in the name of God, who holds Peter's keys!"

Old Nicolo yawned.

"I am for amusement, friar. You were not bidden to preach."

"Perhaps I buy and sell," Fra Pietro answered significantly.

Again Madonna Lisa smote her gitern, and the plump fingers of one hand fastened upon Old Nicole's mighty fist.

"A friar to speak of buying and selling with the Gritti!" she scorned.

"The fellow merits flogging," boomed her master. "What, knave? Have you a message for me? If so, speak it. If not, begone!"

Ciutazzo heard the clank of armor behind them. So did the friar, who stiffened appreciably.

"Here is Guido," cried the jester.

Fra Pietro relaxed.

"Lord Nicolo," quoth he, in proud humility, "I am a poor friar, and of no account by myself; but it is true that I travel upon the Holy Father's affairs, which are God's affairs—"

"With that some of us beg leave to differ," interjected Old Nicolo.

A gigantic figure, all shining in black mail, a black torrent of beard pouring from the opened visor, strode into the garden. Black eyes blazed ferociously in a swart face; a cruel mouth was pressed close. Huge, like his father, but with none of his father's fat, Guido was both similar and dissimilar to Old Nicolo. He walked slowly, ponderously, trampling a flower in his path rather than turn aside; Ciutazzo skipped out of his way, jingling merrily, laughing into Madonna Lisa's startled eyes.

"My brother is not returned?" he asked harshly.

"Not yet," answered his father.

Guido stared from one to the other of them.

"Who is this priest?" he demanded.

The friar named himself, preserving the appearance of self-sufficiency which had impressed Ciutazzo.

"He is from Rome," amended Old Nicolo a thought sourly. "A messenger. The Pope would buy us. That was what he said, eh, Dogface? He buys and sells."

"I will talk to him," said Guido.

Old Nicole's eyes gleamed savagely.

"I am the chief of the Gritti," he warned. "It is my word which carries."

Guido glanced sneeringly at the woman at his father's feet.

"If I sell the Gritti, I sell them for a decent price," he replied.

"By my Luck!" Old Nicolo started up, hurling Madonna Lisa aside as brutally as Guido might have done it. "You'll not talk so to me, boy. Not while my word runs."

Ciutazzo danced airily between them.

"Peace, peace, signori," he commanded. "Shall we brawl? Must we mishandle lovesome ladies? And in face of Holy Church? Per Bacco, signori, all Italy is rent with war! In Castello Gritti, alone, is peace. And what do I hear? Hark! Who comes next?"

He halted, and as his bells jingled into silence all heard the rattling of oars below in the cove, the cracking of whips, the harsh, panting grunts of the galley-slaves— "Ha! Hoo-oo! Huh!"—veering the craft in to its moorings. An order was shouted, repeated, and men's feet pattered on planks.

"Young Nicolo," said the jester. "Soon the party will be complete, signori."

Old Nicolo extended a massive arm to Madonna Lisa, cowering on the ground by his empty chair.

"Up with you, sweeting," he ordered gruffly. "I'll not quarrel with these devils I begot unthinking."

He dropped into the chair, and she sank beside him in her former position, darting a single stab of hatred from under her heavy lashes at Guido's lowering form.

Old Nicolo pointed a menacing forefinger at his son.

"Mark you, boy," he thundered. "You are no lamb and I am no ram—but there are marches to my patience. You to your diversions, I to mine. And the policies of the Gritti are my concern. I do not push my head between the shields of Pope and Emperor—let other fools be crushed to cream cheese, if they will. I sit back, and pluck what comes under my nose. And while I live I rule here."

Guido's jaw squared angrily.

"Yes—while you live," he answered. "Come, friar, I have somewhat to say to you."

Fra Pietro hesitated, with more of nervousness than he had yet revealed. Old Nicolo grinned wickedly.

"Go with him, fellow. Tell him all you know. Offer him all you can pay. It will serve you ill, and harm me none."

"But what of Ciutazzo?" cried the jester. "Who will serve Ciutazzo? Belike, signori, you will all serve him—all serve Dogface, who makes you laugh!"

He waved his hand to Madonna Lisa, who smiled at him without mirth, and danced away amongst the bushes. Tinkletinkle, rang his bells. Jingle-jangle! Fainter—fainter. But he was not gone. Esconced behind the trunk of a centuries-old olive-tree, he spied upon the grassplot where Old Nicolo sat, head bent to Madonna Lisa's ear, while both eyed intently the disappearing backs of Guido and Fra Pietro.

"There was poison in her look," whispered the jester to

himself. "Yes, and there is poison in the cock of the Old One's head. Lords of death! They are like serpents, twining and twisting, striking their venom into each other. Hatred is the one emotion they know—hatred and lust. Walk warily, Dogface. Be humble."

He stole quietly from the garden, planting his feet deliberately, clutching his bell-hung garments, lest their silvery voices betray him. At a door behind the dais in the hall he peered around a curtain's edge to where Fra Pietro sat at the high table close by Guide's elbow, above them the shimmering mystery of the Gritti Luck.

"What is a single fief?" the friar was saying. "What is it to be a simple baron, lord of one castle, however strong? The Holy Father is generous, Lord Guido. He can afford to be, for he holds all Christendom in fee, and those he favors—"

Ciutazzo chuckled.

"Poison," he whispered. "I smell it. It is in the air. Men speak it—and breathe it. Even I! But who dies last, Dogface? Ha, that is the question! Who dies last?"

v

A T T H E water-gate the jester encountered Young Nicolo, breathing easily despite the steep ascent from the cove. A splendid figure, Young Nicolo, sinewy limbs clothed in green velvet, a green cap with a yellow feather on his blue-black hair that was cut at the line of his clean-shaven jaw. Splendid, yet sinister. Yellow cat's-eyes that met every scrutiny with a blank glare, face that mirrored cruelty, for all its grace of contour. Tall and lithe and shapely, men feared Young Nicolo most of the Gritti; they could never be sure of him. He was reserved where his father and Guido were loud-mouthed, kept a grip on his temper and killed without so much as a curse by way of warning.

"What sport, Ser Nicolo?" hailed the jester.

Young Nicolo ignored the question.

"My brother?" he asked shortly.

"He rode in an hour since," replied Ciutazzo. And added casually: "Hard on the friar's heels."

A flicker of interest showed in Young Nicole's stony gaze. "What friar?"

"From Rome, Lord. He talks of the Pope and the war."

"With my brother?"

"They sit at the high table."

There was no sign of interest, now, in Young Nicolo's features; but the atmosphere was charged with a psychic tension which warned the jester of the rising storm of hatred in his heart.

"My father?" he asked.

"The Lord Nicolo is in the garden," Ciutazzo answered charily.

"With—her?"

The jester nodded, fascinated by the conflict he sensed in the other's breast.

Young Nicolo looked out to sea, not a nerve or muscle quivering. When he spoke again he affected to be immersed in the view.

"You see everything, Ciutazzo. You are privy to all that goes on in Castello Gritti. Why do you stay here?"

"I was hungry, Lord. I have a roof—and food and drink."

"You could earn as much elsewhere."

"I do not think the Old One would let me go," said Ciutazzo simply. "But I am content."

"Where did you come from?"

Young Nicolo directed the full force of his yellow eyes upon the jester's, and Ciutazzo made no attempt to evade the inspection.

"But that is known to you, Lord," he protested. "I am a stroller. All Italy is my home."

"You have a Saracen look to you," charged the other.

Ciutazzo spread out his hands; his features settled into lines of friendly stupidity.

"I can remember, Palermo, Ser Nicolo. But that was when I was very young."

"And you have never seen the Emperor?"

Almost the jester smiled, but twisted his lips in time into a grotesque grimace.

"Ah, yes! On his horse once, ahawking. And again, when he rode with his knights to the North."

Young Nicolo's manner became subtly threatening.

"And do you suppose you could find a means of approaching so august a person, Dogface?" he inquired.

For two or three breaths Ciutazzo locked his eyes with that menacing stare. Then he nodded blandly.

"But yes, Lord. A jester may go anywhere."

"Even to the Emperor?"

"Well, Lord, you should know better than I, who am only a poor fellow," the jester answered reasonably. "But I have heard the Emperor's Court is a fine place for entertainments, so I make no doubt all folk of my persuasion are received there."

"If I could trust you!" muttered Young Nicolo.

"Why not, Lord?"

"And why?" returned Young Nicolo. "I trust no man. If I use you, Dogface, it will be because you fear me. Remember!"

"And when do I go?" questioned Ciutazzo, capering joyfully.

But he froze into servility at the first glare from the yellow eyes.

"I have not said you shall go anywhere," snapped Young Nicolo. "I have no occasion for curious servants. Put a buckle on your tongue or I'll have it out and send you to an oar in the galley."

He paused.

"Be within call this evening," he went on. "Near the dais—within the crook of my finger. And keep silence."

"Yes, Lord! Oh, yes, Ser Nicolo. Ciutazzo—"

"I said: Silence! " cautioned Young Nicolo, and faded into the passage leading to the living-quarters, his foot-steps falling as delicately as a cat's, his head bent in thought.

Ciutazzo hugged himself.

"Silence, quoth he! There'll not long be silence, signori! The Old One playing for Venice, Guido harkening to the Pope, and Young Nicolo conning his profits with the Emperor. And Dogface? What of Dogface? A brave condottiere you d make, per Bacco! There's two can run your course, Ser Nicolo. But watch the Madonna, lad. She'll set the tune. Always a woman to set the tune!"

V I

LIGHT STREAMED down upon the dais from a dozen lamps, Byzantine and Saracen work, and to the shocked amazement of Fra Pietro tall altar-candles burned at intervals in the depths of the hall, where myriad shadows played hide-and-seek across the stolen tapestries that draped the walls. Ciutazzo, crouched on the dais floor in a dark corner, his arms clasped around his knees, kept his ears attentive to the snarling debate at the high table, but his eyes were concerned with the flooding shadow play and the mystic radiance of the grey sword that hung above the fireplace.

Sometimes, the sword would seem to disappear, swallowed up in darkness as a draft sent the light eddying roofward or hurled a wave of shadows to submerge it. Again, it would dominate the room, shining out upon the wall, with an evil lustre as uncanny as the spiritual wickedness which radiated from the Gritti, who brawled beneath it. And another time Ciutazzo thought it flared amongst the shadows, half-seen, half-hidden, like a shy maid, averse to over-much attention. But even as he watched the light smote it once more, and it flared hardily, a streak of power, lean as Young Nicolo, brutal as Black Guido, sly as their father—but more, much more, instinct with a strength that was timeless, limitless, inhuman.

The jester blinked up at it.

"What is life to you, Grey Maiden?" he ruminated. "Ha! What is flesh to steel? Something to hack, eh? And men think you are but a tool. I wonder! How often have you urged the blow? How often did you prompt the deed? Per Bacco, as I watch you, you lure me—to—what?"

He cocked an ear toward the table.

"Patience, Dogface. This is a matter that can not be hurried. Yes, yes, he who lets sword or greed or wench give him the spur, he strives for him who waits. Who dies last? That's the question."

The argument waxed louder. Madonna Lisa long since had fled. Fra Pietro, in no wise embarrassed by the seat at the high-table Guido had allotted him, was yet disturbed at the yelling and bellowing of Old Nicolo and his patron—Young Nicolo spoke seldom, and then in measured accents; occasionally, the friar sought to mediate, and inevitably, the conflict became the more bitter thereby, Young Nicolo grinning tigerishly and prodding both to renewed assaults whenever they revealed signs of flagging animosity.

"Bah, you are a wineskin, not a man," fumed Guido. "What have you ever done—"

"Ever done?" roared his father. "I reared a viper in you, boy! And I maintained the Gritti in the fear of all Italy. You'll never do the same."

"You sold yourself to the Venetians—for what? A woman, a—"

Old Nicolo pounded his dagger-hilt on the table.

"There are limits my own son may not pass," he cried. "And it is not true I sold aught to the Signoria."

Young Nicolo struck in.

"You had naught of them, Old One?"

"Not a ducat."

"Only that red-haired—"

Young Nicolo interrupted Guido.

"Why do you think Lisa was given you?" he asked, mildly venomous. "Because your friends in the Signoria admire you? Would serve you? Because you are a fine figure of a man? Because she demanded to come?"

"You talk foolishly," swaggered Old Nicolo. "She was a bribe—and not the first I've accepted, with my tongue pouched where it belongs: in my cheek."

"A bribe," repeated Young Nicolo. "Yes, a bribe! And what do you think she does here? Besides cozening you? How much do you think the Signoria know of our garrison and stores, of the way we operate, of the castle approaches? She is no innocent! She could bribe a guard, open a gate—"

"I was not born yesterday, boy," fussed his father. "By my Luck, you talk like a child! Is it amusement you begrudge me? Are you jealous?"

Laughter dripped coldly from Young Nicolo's lips.

"Jealous? Yes, of being sold to a master I despise."

"The Venetians are masters," exclaimed Guido. "They would own us, body and soul. We should be pandered to for a while. Then—Zut! Some day there'd be treachery, and the Gritti—"

He drew an expressive finger across his throat.

"But the Pope! Ah, there is an ally for you, easy to serve, generous—"

"You have learned your lesson well, Guido," mocked his brother, with a meaning eye upon Fra Pietro.

The friar accepted the challenge.

"Call the Pope master, Lord," he said boldly. "Why run from the truth? The Holy Father is master, not only of Italy, but all Christendom. But he is a kindly master, and appreciative."

"And forever bleating that the Emperor disdains him or is disrespectful," gibed Young Nicolo. "He can not compel even the Romans to respect him. And you would have the Gritti become his men! Not I! If I took a master he should be strong enough to make me fear him."

"What of the Signoria, then?" demanded his father. "Venice is feared."

"A city of merchants," scoffed Young Nicolo. "And what is Venice compared with the Emperor?"

"Or the Pope?" exclaimed Guido. "Venice is out of it, I say. Italy is torn betwixt Guelph and Ghibelline, betwixt Pope and Emperor. The Emperor is a mighty prince; none mightier—save one. The Pope is more than prince. His dominion stretches into Heaven and Hell. His power is over souls as well as bodies."

Old Nicolo gaped scornfully.

"That a son of mine should prate like any shaveling!" he growled. "You are an apt scholar, Guido. If this is how you grow, lapping up priest's chatter, gabbling of souls and heaven and the devil knows what— By my Luck, it is well we have the sword there to hold up our fortunes! I can see you are not the man to further us."

All four at the table followed his forefinger to the slim blade of the sword over the fireplace. The light was rippling the length of the grey steel, ruddy as warm blood—and Fra Pietro, for one, crossed himself, as though he sensed the evil Ciutazzo also felt.

"If you trust in the Luck, why treat with any prince or power?" asked Young Nicolo.

His father's big, blunt finger came down like a lance in rest.

"I am older than you, boys. I can see that the days I have known are past. The cities are growing stronger; the nobles are joining one faction or another. But I would not commit myself any more than I must. The Emperor and the Pope are too big for me; they could bide their times, and at the right moment gobble us in one bite. But Venice would be different. The Signoria—"

"They'd treat us as you predict," rumbled Guido. "And what honor is there in acting as castellans for a crew of merchant-traders?"

"I am of the one mind with Guido, there," drawled Young Nicolo. "But what honor is there in buying titles from a dawdling old priest, who lacks the guts of a man-at-arms? We might be princes under the Pope. I'd rather be a count under the Emperor—if we must hoist another banner beside ours."

Fra Pietro's face flamed wrathfully, but Guido took up the cudgels for him.

"And what advantage would we win from allegiance to the Emperor? The Venetians are north of us, their galleys are always at sea. Across the Apennines is Rome, and the Holy Father has allies on every hand. The Emperor is south in Sicily, when he isn't beyond the Alps in Germany. Much good he'd do us! We'd earn a title, and the privilege of riding at his tail. And Fra Pietro says he must soon go on the Crusade, in which case he'd require one of us to attend him, with our best spears."

"The devil take Fra Pietro, and the Pope along with him," snorted Old Nicolo.

The friar lifted hands in horror. Black Guido looked solemnly angry.

"That trenches on blasphemy," he said slowly.

Old Nicolo's little pig-eyes sparked fire; he raised his hands in mimicry of Fra Pietro, and burlesqued Guido's tone.

"Our Guido fears blasphemy! Did you hear him, Nicolo?"

"I heard," Young Nicolo assented. "We are far apart, we three."

Ciutazzo, from his corner, marked the sinister note that underlay this interchange. He stiffened at the abrupt finality of Old Nicolo's manner.

"Guido, you are no man to turn religious. No, no, be quiet while I speak! Not the Pope, himself, if he labored day and night for a month could absolve you of your sins. Therein you are my son, and I am proud of you within reason. But do not make the mistake of thinking that because I am old and fat I must step aside and let you or your brother manage the affairs of the Gritti."

His chest boomed as he thumped it.

"*I* am the Gritti! It is I who decide policies. You—" he levelled that stumpy forefinger of his again, this time at Fra Pietro—"you, friar, I have suffered you to hear this discussion because there is no harm that you or any other can wreak upon me while I sit here in Castello Gritti, with the Luck over my head. Go from here, and tell all—all, I say! Tell the Pope I despise him. Tell the Emperor he is a time-waster, afraid of strong measures. Tell the Venetians I work with them so long as it suits my purpose. Tell any man anything. You can not harm Nicolo dei Gritti. And when I can not manage my own sons— Ah, why, then, he can have this castle who will take it."

He sank back in his chair, and Guido leaned across the table toward him, beard bristling, cheeks ensanguined, fingers opening and shutting—as if they reached for a dagger, Ciutazzo thought.

"You stretch my patience, Old One! What? You sit here, at your ease, toying with that red-haired spy, and we—my brother and I—we must take the toll that keeps our company together. We must take the risk of the road, venture the galleys of Venice, the Saracens, the Emperor—for you! For your lousy profit! Ho, Young One—"

But Young Nicolo shook his head gently, a mild gleam of amusement in his yellow eyes.

"This is your quarrel, Guido," he said. "It is on your head. We work better alone. A man must trust another to—"

Guido cursed him with an awful malice and earnestness that chased cold shivers up and down Ciutazzo's spine. But the jester forgot this as he noticed the friar's face. Fra Pietro had ceased acting a part; he was watching the Gritti with the level interest of one who gauges a quarrel which may conceivably work to his personal profit. Calm, a hint of disdain in the curve of his lips, he sat entirely aloof from the hateful atmosphere of his surroundings. It was he who finally curbed Guido's rage.

"Curses are ill weapons, Lord Guido," he remonstrated sternly.

Guido lapsed into silence.

"At least, there are others," he sputtered sullenly.

Ciutazzo, inching forward, saw the red glare Old Nicolo bent upon his son. And the jester was as nonplussed as the rest when the chief of the Gritti burst into raucous laughter.

"We are a rough brood, eh, friar?" he cried. "Minions of hell, you say. No doubt, no doubt! I say with pride I have shown mercy to none who could not enforce me to. But our tempers are stretched tonight, over-stretched. Our throats are dry. It is poor quarrelling, with a dry throat."

He clapped his hands, and the hangings of the door behind him were pushed aside to make way for Madonna Lisa.

"You called me, Lord?" she asked.

"No, no, the servants, Madonna."

"I sent them forth," she answered humbly. "They—voices were raised—"

She glanced apologetically from under her long lashes. Old Nicolo patted her shoulder approvingly.

"The servants in Castello Gritti are used to high words at the high-table, Madonna. But you shall serve us. Bid them fetch us wine—some of that Apulian vintage the Young One found in the Sicilian dromond. It is fiery enough to burn out our tempers."

She laughed softly, understandingly, and glided back through the hangings.

"Strange," commented Young Nicolo. "I do not find myself thirsty."

"My throat is a furnace," snarled Guido. "If I ordered the castle we should not have to send for wine."

"All in time, my Guido," rebuked his father. "You would not have the holy friar think you wished to hasten me to my grave?"

Old Nicolo's grating laughter brought the cold shivers again to Ciutazzo's spine.

"The devil comes for his own at last," grunted Guido.

But Fra Pietro intervened before the quarrel could be resumed.

"If wine quiets tempers, let us apply wine, signori," he said in his deep, resonant voice. "But in truth here is no reason for temper. Three several courses, it appears, are open to you, and of you one is sponsor for each. I, it is true, am prejudiced a certain way, yet am I able to perceive the reason which abides in other men's prejudices, and if you will suffer me to speak of the position of the Holy Father I am certain you will put your minds upon the problem with a clarity conformable with wisdom."

"You know not the Gritti," Young Nicolo murmured lazily. "But continue, friar. You make me think of waves thundering on the rocks—which are unfretted by all the pounding and wetting."

"Give the waves time," returned Fra Pietro. "There is no rock they will not annihilate."

"Ah, but I am not interested in time," objected Young Nicolo. "My little day suffices me."

"Let the friar talk," rasped Guido.

"Yes, yes, let him talk," agreed Old Nicolo, peering over his shoulder at the door through which Madonna Lisa had vanished.

It seemed to Ciutazzo that there was a hint of eagerness in his bearing.

VII

"SO KINGS and Emperors are but mortal, whatever be their pretense to majesty; but Holy Church is immortal. Pope follows Pope. Christ reigns eternal. And what are men-at-arms and crossbowmen compared with the winged words of innumerable preachers? Both forces the Holy Father controls. Force of flesh and force of spirit. Who can resist him—"

"Ha, the wine," exclaimed Guido. "Your pardon, Fra Pietro,

but this talking makes dry work. We shall all be the better for a sup of the Apulian."

The friar's brow had darkened at the interruption, but he made no comment, leaning back in his seat with his hands folded squarely on the table in front of him. The Gritti all leaned forward, hands outstretched for the goblets Madonna Lisa offered them—booty of many a raid and piracy, poised on a tray of handbeaten silver from Morocco. She stopped first by Guido, tendering him a golden chalice that once had held the sacramental wine in a Syrian cathedral.

"You were thirstiest, Lord Guido," she said prettily.

He accepted it with a grunt of thanks, and buried his mustache in the ruddy liquor it contained. Ciutazzo, bright-eyed in his corner, marked Old Nicolo incline farther forward, and simultaneously, Fra Pietro wave away the companion to Guide's chalice.

"You show no respect for my cloth, woman," the friar growled angrily. "That vessel was consecrated to the Blood of our Saviour."

"Surely, then, it will not harm you to drink from it," she answered, smiling. And Old Nicolo snarled:

"Take what is given you, shaveling."

"I fear you are abandoned to primitive superstitions, good friar," jeered Young Nicolo, his yellow eyes afire with derision.

But Fra Pietro pushed the chalice from him, doggedly persistent.

"I have broken bread with you," he said; "and I will drink with you, albeit from another—"

He extended his hand toward a slim goblet of hammered silver, but Madonna Lisa retired hastily.

"No, no," she stammered. "The chalice—"

And she looked uneasily at Old Nicolo. Ciutazzo hugged himself the closer, matching the feral gleam in the Old One's little eyes with the sudden tenseness in Young Nicolo's still face.

The jester was not surprised as Guido hurled his chalice from him, features drawn and anguished, hands plucking at the air.

"Poison," groaned Guido. "Poison, friar! The red-haired devil!"

She had watched him, fascinated, from behind Fra Pietro's chair, and now, with a clumsy readiness, he kicked his own chair back and stumbled toward her. She squealed and dropped her tray, so that the wine splashed on the friar's brown robe and the lovely goblets rolled upon the floor.

"Not I, Lord Guido," she clamored. "He told me—I was bid—"

She turned to flee, her foot slipped in a puddle of wine and Guido clamped one hand upon her shoulder; his dagger flashed from his belt—down—swift as summer-lightning the hilt clicked smartly on her collarbone—she screamed!

Ciutazzo, on his knees, clinging to a fold of tapestry, saw her swing limp from Guido's arm, then tumble in a heap of sodden finery. And Guido, the dagger dripping in his hand, caught at the friar's chair, steadied himself and reeled round the table's end.

"You, Old One!" he gasped. "Your doing. A thousand pains gnaw me. Curse you!"

Old Nicolo gained his feet, with the extraordinary agility of which his huge body was capable.

"Yes, I bade her do it," he said scornfully. "So perishes any son of mine who thinks to supplant me. I lead the Gritti, boy! You are food for worms as you stand."

And lightly as Ciutazzo, he leaped onto his chair and snatched the sword Grey Maiden from its place above the mantle.

"While I have strength to swing the Gritti Luck, I am the Gritti," he boasted.

The sword circled his head, lambent, alive, terrible in its menace, hissing faintly as it split the air.

"For so long, Old One," agreed Young Nicolo, lounging

"Too bad," old Nicolo deplored. "This
needn't have happened for years, lad."

comfortably as if nothing had happened. "But I am not so stupid as Guido."

Fra Pietro started up, aghast, but unafraid.

"This is mortal sin you do," he cried. "Lord Guido, I command you—"

"Let the boy die as he pleases!" roared Old Nicolo. "I'll give you my blessing later."

He jumped from the chair, and waddled to meet his son; and Guido, mastering the agony of the poison, staggered erect and reeled on.

"Too bad," Old Nicolo deplored. "This needn't have happened for years, lad. But I couldn't let you flout me to my face. It's true what the Young One says. He's not so stupid as you."

"May every torment of hell be yours," sobbed Guido. "If my mother—"

He lurched, and falling, lunged forward with his dagger. Old Nicolo stepped to one side, and ran him through, taking an obvious satisfaction in the precision of the thrust.

"His mother," reflected the chief of the Gritti. "Humph! She it was who would have run off with the Frenchman from Naxos—the year after you were born, Young One. I remember! We—ah—entertained her very passably. I had a Greek in the kitchen, then, who made a delectable dish of sheep's hearts."

"Give heed to the friar," Young Nicolo advised him impartially.

Old Nicolo smiled at the fury of detestation in Fra Pietro's face. And again Ciutazzo, huddled in his corner, sensed one of those tempestuous outbursts of psychic energy which are loosed by strong characters in moments of deep feeling—"Ha, brown brother," thought the jester. "Are you one will face the devil in his lair?"

"You must acquit me of any desire to be unpleasant, shaveling," remarked Old Nicolo pleasantly enough. "But you *would* try to make trouble in Castello Gritti. So it must be a lesson to you. Sad, eh? Two folk slain, and your fault— Or shall we lay the blame to the Holy Father?"

"You are possessed by the Evil One," the friar exclaimed hoarsely. "Satan leers through your eyes. Yes, there is a devil in you! Behind me! Behind me, I say! Get thee behind me, Satan!"

He flourished his crucifix, and Old Nicolo nodded cynically.

"You *would* say that, friar. A man always seeks refuge in superstition when he encounters an evil stronger than his own. Now, I am generous and broadminded. I recognize my own evil—and yours, too. You came here to trick me into your master's course, and you did not scruple to endeavor to set my son against me. But you are startled because I slew that disobedient son—yes, that traitorous son. I believe I have grounds for my action in Holy Writ, but once more, I am not disposed to share the responsibility. I did it because I deemed it to my own interest to make away with a son who would have fought with his brother, if not with me. Now—"

"Now," drawled Young Nicolo, "you and I may poison and wrangle, undisturbed. Well, we are better matched, Old One."

"Better," admitted his father. "You see how it is, friar? You tried and failed. And having plotted murder, you must bear punishment."

Fra Pietro did not quail.

"Perhaps it is I who shall punish," he answered. "But it is fruitless to talk of punishing such as you in this world. Only the hell your son wished you can avail."

Old Nicolo's pig-eyes twinkled amusedly.

"Ah, yes, I have heard much of that hell! I assure you, if there is such a place Guido is tapping on the door. And I regret to seem to hurry you, but I must send you the same road."

Fra Pietro regarded him steadily, then looked down at the pitiful heap that had been Madonna Lisa—and from that to the inert clay of Black Guido, whence trickled a dark-brown stream to mingle with the stains of poisoned wine and trollop's gore.

Ciutazzo chuckled noiselessly, clasping boney knees. A man, this friar! Per Bacco, what a scene! Fat Old Nicolo, Grey Maiden's slim shape pendant from his hand, and across the table the squat, heavy-set figure of Fra Pietro, with only a crucifix for weapon. And Young Nicolo, lolling back and enjoying it all.

Fra Pietro moved; his fingers fumbled at the cord around his waist. Old Nicolo nodded approvingly.

"That's right. Get ready. Say your prayers, friar."

"Per Bacco," cried Ciutazzo, and Young Nicolo half-rose.

So swiftly that none of the three who watched comprehended his intent, Fra Pietro ripped off his brown robe, and cast it like a net over Old Nicolo's head and shoulder. The coarse cloth draped down about the fat man's sword-arm, binding and hampering him. He could not see; he could only wave his sword and yammer curses. And while he struggled, the friar vaulted the table, and tripped him.

Young Nicolo was on his feet, at last, yellow eyes expanded, a tinge of color in his olive cheeks; but Ciutazzo saw that he moved deliberately, in no apparent haste.

"What are you doing, friar?" he inquired coolly.

Panting and wrestling, fighting for a grip on Old Nicolo's sword-arm, Fra Pietro ignored the question, until he had contrived to loop his waist-cord around his enemy's throat. Then he gave a great tug, and as Old Nicolo gagged he turned a flushed face and answered:

"It is forbidden us to draw blood. Therefore I strangle the wretch."

"So? You strangle the—wretch," Young Nicolo repeated. "But he is my father, good friar."

"He is Satan," retorted Fra Pietro, and tugged the harder.

A single whistling cry escaped his victim; the huge body leaped in a convulsive spasm, and lay still.

Fra Pietro detached the fingers that clasped the sword, and

stood up in his shirt, sweat beading his forehead and thick neck, blood oozing from a small cut in one of his hairy, brown legs.

"It is not fitting that I should be an executioner," he said composedly; "but the man was a murderer, and moreover, would have slain me. I will make due report to my superiors."

"Indeed?" asked Young Nicolo. "You will have much to tell your superiors."

The friar gave him a keen look.

"That is so, Lord."

Young Nicolo's eyes expanded and contracted, staring unwinkingly the while.

"That sword you have is the symbol of my family's power," he remarked curtly. "Hand it to me."

But Fra Pietro shook his head.

"This is a den of sin," declared the friar. "Perhaps I shall require a weapon."

A deadly note rang in Young Nicolo's voice.

"I ask the last time," he threatened. "That sword is the Gritti Luck."

Fra Pietro laughed contemptuously.

"The Gritti Luck? When it suffered your father to be slain by an unarmed man? You speak of a foolish and godless superstition. No, no, Lord Nicolo, I will take the sword and presently throw it in the sea. And do you lead a decent life hereafter or the Holy Father will—"

Young Nicolo's dagger glinted from its sheath; his right arm crooked forward. Fra Pietro ducked and retreated; Nicolo pursued, cheeks pinched and chalky, lips bubbling curses. Slow-moving, the friar, yet firm on his feet and vigilant, wielding the sword with a strength that atoned for his awkwardness: an odd figure in flapping shirt-tails, contrasting weirdly with Nicolo's supple, coiling form in green velvet that shone golden under the lamps.

Nicolo pressed the fight. He cared little that the friar had a sword, while he had but a dagger. The friar was a friar. He was Nicolo dei Gritti. So round and round they stamped, feinting, foining, blades rattling, breath hissing, tripping on the corpses, slipping in the runlets of blood, eyes intent on each other, heedless of Ciutazzo, flattening himself against the hangings—Per Bacco, what a night! One, two, three dead folk, and—

Young Nicolo snatched one of the chalices from the floor and flung it in Fra Pietro's face. The friar stumbled blindly, and Nicolo closed, hacking and stabbing in a frenzy of hatred; but Grey Maiden flashed up like a living thing, a dazzling, shifting web of steel, and Nicolo yielded ground, panting from his efforts.

Fra Pietro, too, retired a pace, unhurried, cautious. And the pair stood motionless in the glow of the lamps—stood motionless so long that Ciutazzo blinked his eyes in the strain of watching them. And as he blinked, Nicolo leaped to the attack, a very tiger's leap, sure and ferocious, the dagger hooked like a great claw to disembowel the friar. Ah, but the friar had not blinked! Grey Maiden whistled ominously, a flat arc of cold light—Nicolo collapsed in mid air. He lay, outstretched as he had leaped, his feet by his dead father, one balled fist touching the clay of the brother he had hated.

"So pass the Gritti," Ciutazzo exclaimed aloud.

The friar peered stupidly at the jester's motley, then down at Nicolo's headless body and the red-gemmed blade of the sword that winked at the two living with a kind of savage mirth—almost as if it knew what had been wrought with its aid, Ciutazzo thought.

"This is mortal sin," said Fra Pietro. "I have shed a man's blood. I must have absolution."

"If you will," assented the jester amicably. "And I will have the sword."

"You, jester? Nonsense! What will you do with a sword?"

"Use it, at need," returned Ciutazzo. "The castle must have a master."

"A jester rule in Castello Gritti?" Fra Pietro frowned suspiciously. "Who are you?"

"I am called Ciutazzo," the jester answered straitly.

"Whose man are you?" persisted the friar.

"This night? Per Bacco, my own!"

Ciutazzo took a step toward the other, lithely, easily. Fra Pietro presented the sword.

"No, no, stand fast. I suspect you, Dogface. And I have won this castle for the Holy Father."

Ciutazzo seemed to consider this, sliding one foot forward, turning sideways, a hand resting upon the chair in which Old Nicolo had sat.

"For the Holy Father, eh? Why, that is to be seen, brown brother. Suppose, now—"

He paused, aggravatingly, and rubbed his chin. Fra Pietro eyed him askance.

"Suppose what?" snapped the friar. "If you think to stir up the castle folk against me I will have you banned, yes, and imprisoned. Be off, and summon men to clean up this shambles."

"Bide, bide," protested Ciutazzo. "Here is much to be decided. Suppose, as I was about to say, we declared for the Emperor?"

Fra Pietro made an impatient gesture.

"You are a pestilent animal, Dogface. Go, and call the servants."

"All in good time," answered the jester.

He picked up Old Nicolo's chair as casually as though it had been a foot-stool, and with no more warning than Fra Pietro had given Old Nicolo in casting his robe, he threw it half the width of the dais. The friar was swept over the edge, his head snapping back with a hollow crack against the stone step; the chair shattered to pieces; and the sword Grey Maiden leaped free of Fra Pietro's lifeless grasp, soared up to the roof and clattered on the table within arm's reach of Ciutazzo.

The jester lifted the long, slim blade, fitting his hand lovingly to the plain, fluted steel grip of the cross-hilt, balancing the weight upon his wrist.

"Ah, you beauty," he murmured. "What other sweetheart would a man have than you! Per Bacco, you have slashed many a road to fortune, I'll wager! Why not mine? Birth—what is that? Name—what is that? I have a sword—and a castle for the taking. Many a condottiere has started with less."

Feet shuffled down the hall's shadowy aisles; he had a glimpse of pale faces, hovering, prying; a whisper echoed in the silence.

"Ho," he cried, "enter, my people. You have had a change of masters. See, the Gritti are dead! Madonna Lisa, too. And this friar. Now, Ciutazzo rules in Castello Gritti."

They poured up the hall, men of the garrison in the lead, under-officers, crossbowmen, men-at-arms, a scattering of upper servants.

"Who has done this, Dogface?" quavered old Gianni, who had been with the Gritti, men said, since the Luck came into the family.

Ciutazzo waved an airy hand about him.

"You see the dead, Gianni. You see me. And you see in my hand—"

"The Luck," rose a whispered chorus. "He has the Luck!" "The jester has slain them all." "Was ever the like?" "Dogface has the Luck."

"Lord Dogface, if it please you," Ciutazzo corrected them merrily.

"But you are a jester, Dogface—I mean Lord—I mean—" Gianni floundered desperately. "You—perhaps we should slay him," he appealed to the others.

Ciutazzo raised Grey Maiden significantly, and the mob of retainers swayed away from him.

"I am come from the Emperor," he announced. "I hold Castello Gritti for him, as his man. And you owe me allegiance because I have won the Luck."

He glanced down at the proud, sinister features of Young Nicolo, whose head had rolled toward the dais edge.

"Who dies last?" he murmured, chuckling faintly. "Eh, Grey Maiden, who dies last? That is the question, per Bacco!"

The castle folk receded from the hall, muttering and crossing themselves.

"He talks to the dead," they whispered. "Yes, and to the sword." "Was there ever the like? A jester to be Lord!" "But no ordinary jester." "And he has the Luck." "The Gritti Luck!" "Ah, but it was no luck for them." "There is magic in this." "Yes, yes, black magic."

But old Gianni wagged his head disapprovingly, safe in the outer corridor.

"A man does not use magic to break people's heads and stab them," he declared bluntly. "Ciutazzo—" He bowed hastily in the direction of the hall—"Lord Ciutazzo is a great man in disguise. Perhaps one of the Emperor's knights. We must serve him well. Now, if it had not been for me, some of you foolish fellows would have gone in there, and said more than you should—and whisk!—"

A woman whispered from the hall door.

"He stays there—with *them*—the Lord Jester. He sits on the table. His chin is in his hand. He is looking at *them*. He speaks— See, his lips move."

She fled, and all the folk with her.

On the dais, Ciutazzo continued to sit, alone with the slain. The fire had burned out of him, and the exaltation.

"I shall always wear motley," he was thinking. "Life is a jest. To succeed one must be a jester. Eh, Grey Maiden? You should know—who have pointed so many jests. Ha, lass, we'll jest together. Let the humor out of men's bodies! What say you, Fra Pietro? And you, Madonna Lisa, who were so fair? And the Gritti, so strong, so treacherous, so cruel, so certain? What did you have of your religion and your lusts and your power and your cunning? A jest, only a jest! A breath of life—and death.

That I might profit from you! The sword was mightier than all of you, mightier than I, who live longest. So walk warily, Dogface, be humble! Some day the jest must be on you."

A STATEMENT FOR
THE QUEENES MAJESTIE

A statement prepared for the Queenes Majestie concerning the casting away of the galleon St. Jago de Compostella in the parish of Tinsham, in Dorsetshire, the night of All Hallowes in the yeere of our Lord 1588, and especially the strange relacioun of the Illustri- ous Señor Don Martin Alonzo de Viraflores, Maestre de Campo of the Terza of Arragon and sometime Master of the Horse to the famous Captain Hernando Cortes; here set down by M. Humphrey Dawkins, clerk, Rector of the said parish, at the direckcion of Sir Myles Conyers, Knight, of Friars Minton, in Dorsetshire, Deputy Lieutenant of the same.

IT BEING afternoon of the feast of All Hallowes, and the Westerly gales continueing to blow most prodigious (as hath been the case since the dispercioun of the late Invincible Armada, the invincibility whereof was put to the touch by your Grace's valliant subjects) there come a messenger from the fisher-folk by the shore, acrying they seed a tall ship drifting in under Portland Bill. Whereupon Sir Myles Conyers and the gentry his friends did do upon them their swords and cloaks, and sallied forth that they might endeavor what was needful and as seemed them best. And being come to the shore, we had clear sight of the ship, a stately vessel of three tier of ordnance, and above 500 tuns burthen, high-built in the Spaniards fashion; but fearfully ravaged in her spars and cordage by reason of the battering of the seas.

Of the gentry here gathered divers had fared westward ho! with Sir Myles in the venture of the *Gods Providence* of Poole, and M. Dawkins, Rector of the parish, who writes these lines, was tooken by the Spaniards out of the *Revelacioun* of Plimmouth, off La Vera Cruz, in the yeere '72, and was two yeeres in the dungeons of the Inquisition in the city of Mexico—and for the proof of the above statement hath to this day the marks of the Rack, but for a sure ointment to the said hurts the recolleflcioun that by God's favour he endured all torments and was faithful to Christ His Church.

The gentry, clapping their heads together, made no doubt the stranger was a Spaniard, and for preference one of those ships of the Armada which fled North after the fighting in the Narrowe Seas and circumnavigated these Islands. The which many of the Armada have attempted, as your Majestic must know, and being caught by the prevailaunce of the aforesaid Westerly gales (raging this year, as by God's mercy, with the awful might of Divine wrath) do be blown ashore and shattered utterly, as we do heere, both upon the coasts of Scotland and Ireland, and latterly hereabouts on the Southerly coasts of your Realm of England.

In the circumstaunces here recited, Sir Myles took heed that he should prepare a right hearty recepcioun for the Spaniards, did they come ashore, so he sent messengers in haste to summon the shire levies, and ere evening we were joined by a multitude of stout fellows, with rich store of long bows, arbalests, handguns, musquets, pikes, partisans and like tools of warre. But in the meantime the Spaniard was in such plight that we perceived we had no need to fear him, for the devil had catched a twist of his tail about his bowsprit, and was hauling thereon to fetch him to destrukcioun at our feet.

In the beginning, he having weathered the Bill, our mariners did acclaim it possible he might fetch eastward of our coast and wear around St. Albans Head into Studland Bay, or perchance, wafting onward, even contrive to reach Solent. There was likewise the chaunce, however slender, that by seamanship

The Spaniard drifted straight upon our shore.

and a slight shift in the wind, he might beat under the lee of the Bill. But all these prognosticaciouns were barren in the result. For lack of seamanship or sails to spread or more like because his tiller was amiss he could make no head at all and drifted straight upon our shore. And we gave thought rather to the salving of such poor wretches as were washed to our feet than to the array of our troop and the readiness of our weapons.

By now it drew toward evening. There was no rain, but the clouds hung low and the light was dull and sullen. Our shore was crowded with folk, and as the Spaniard drifted nearer we might see the desolacioun of his state, the huge waves which did oversweep him and the struggles of his crew to resist the suck of the waters. Man by man was carried away from his waist, until all who could find standing room were packed upon the fore and after castles or clung to what was left of the rigging. It was most piteous to beheld, albeit we knew them for Papists and enemies, who had voyaged hither in the intent to harry and enslave us; and by Sir Myles his favour I did venture a brief prayer in behalf of their sin-laden souls, in the midst of which they struck upon the shoal the fisherfolk call the Blind Pig.

We heered faintly the screeches of those shooken off by the shock of the ship's taking ground and the after-rush of the waves that pooped him, and we might see how the wreck of the masts went by the boord, the foremast in its fall crashing down upon the forecastle. Ten score souls perished in that first moment, for this was a great ship, a galleon of the first rate, and there were fifteen score in her company at her putting forth to sea. Verily, a judgment such as Heaven doth frequently vouchsafe in your Majesties behalf.

The darkness thickened apace, with a driving scud that blew in from seaward and blinded those at the water's edge. However, Sir Myles bade our people to put aside their weapons, and stand hand-in-hand as deep into the waves as was safe that they might pluck from the water the Spaniards that were borne inshore; and the people went to their task with a right goodwill, cheering one another and reckless of their own sakes. And by the suggestion of M. Dawkins there were two great fires lit, the which shed their rays afar across the waters. But for all the efforts we made there was not one soul saved. Bodies aplenty, but none that lived.

Sir Myles would have had the fishermen launch a boat to carry him beyond the surf, and four who had sailed with him westward ho! offered themselves, albeit they said freely they should row to their deaths, whereupon M. Dawkins did intervene, and calling Sir Myles to mind that it would not serve your Grace or prophet his honour to lose his life, Sir Myles was pleased to desist from his plan, the which was roundly endorsed by the gentry present, who said, as with one voice, that every Englishman must consider the Queenes Majesties service before his own ambicioun.

So passed the night, until near morning the wind dropped and shifted into the East. But the seas were running high, and since few bodies were coming ashore, the fisherfolk counseled Sir Myles that he should wait for daylight when they might better steer a course. Nay, they said, belike the Spaniard hath gone to pieces. But to this Sir Myles wagged his beard, and pointed to the slender wreckage which had drifted in.

And he was right, as the first streak of daylight proved. The Spaniard was broke in two, his forepart awash, the forecastle settling deeper with every wave that smote it; but the aftercastle thrust itself above the combers tops, and there was one man standing beneath the stern-lanthorn, nigh the trap through which the master of the mariners doth call down to the seamen who sway the tiller. He stood very still, by which the mariners amongst us determined he was tied to the lanthorn's foot, as how else might he have survived the fearful seas?

Howbeit, Sir Myles insisted again that he should put forth to the wreck, and the same four fishermen offering to ferry him, two of their brethren joined them, and M. Dawkins declared the venture would be the safer for a religious flavour, to which Sir Myles consented the more readily for knowing that M.

Dawkins was conversant with the Spanish tongue by reason of his yeeres in prison in the city of Mexico.

The fishermen's boat being launched, they rowed hardily through the waves until they come beyond the inner bar, when they steered around the flank of the Blind Pig and so come to the wreck from seaward, the which in that wind and sea was the more safe. And when we had come so far we marvelled for that we might see fairly the person of him who was lashed atop of the poop beneath the stern-lanthorn, him seeming the most anciount person we had ever seen in life: a mighty lean, tall, old man, with a long, white beard that reached to his waist and was tucked in his belt that the wind might not blow it into his face; and withal, very proud in his face, having a high, beaked nose, and brown eyes, bright and fierce. He was choice, too, in his garb and armature, wearing a suit of half-armor, handsomely enscrolled and but a little rusted, and on his head a morion chased with gold. He had Cordovan boots, laced to his thighs, and in his hand a long, straight sword of a peculiar grey steel, such a sword as the Spaniards are not wont to carry, for it was thicker in the blade than a rapier, flat, also, and two-edged.

As we rowed alongside, under the lee of the galleon, he stared down upon us with a kind of high disdain, most honourable to behold, and he made to fumble with his fingers at the ropes about his waist, as if he would cast him loose; but he staggered somewhat in the doing of it, and we could see the color drain from his face with the effort. So I called up to him without more ado: Surrender, Señor. A buena querra. Which is to say in English: at good quarters. He bowed very slightly, and answered in Castilian that lisped a trifle: I am not of those who surrender, Señor Englishman, while I have breath in me. I am a true Conquistador—and the most anciount of all.

Now, at the time the words meant little to me, and less, maybe, to Sir Myles, who likewise hath some Spanish; but we were vastly pleased with the old man's spirit, and I hailed again, acquainting him of Sir Myles his style and office, and that it was no disgrace to surrender to an officer of the Queenes Majestic. To the which he replied no less haughtily than before: Señors, I would not surrender to you, though you were the Lord God, Himself, so that you were enemies of Spain. And he added, in a savage voice, as he would spread it broadcast: Aye, there is one Castilian of the Old Breed left.

Here is a proper caballero, quoth Sir Myles. We must use him gently, parson. And he, that is, Sir Myles, would not suffer the fishermen to accompany us aboord the galleon, saying it was not fit that a gentleman of the Spaniard's quality should be tooken in the presence of common men. So only M. Dawkins accompanied Sir Myles to the poop, where the said Spaniard awaited us most despitefully as to countenance, leaning upon the ropes which bound him to the lanthorn's foot, his sword naked in his hand, his aged body so weak from exhaustion it was a sight to entice sympathy in an enemies breast.

Señor, saith Sir Myles then, will it please you to make yourself known to me, who am the Queenes Majesties Lieutenant for these coasts? The old Spaniard stiffened himself erect. I am not unknown in my own country and elsewhere, Englishman, saith he. I am Don Martin Alonzo de Viraflores, an Hidalgo of Old Castile, Maestre de Campo of the Terza of Arragon, a Commander of the Order of St. Jago. Sir Myles and I bowed low before him. And may it please you, Illustrious Señor, saith M. Dawkins, what is the name of this ship and how come you aboord her?

He made pretense to curl his mustache, albeit his fingers trembled so he scarce twisted a thread of hair, and saith he: She is the St. Jago de Compostella, a galleon of the squadron of Castile in the Armada which hath been punished for the craven conduct of men who did not deserve to be called Spaniards. I sailed in her as Captain of the soldiers because that she bore the name of my Order, and I thought she would be lucky, which she was not. We bowed again most respectfully, and Sir Myles spoke up in ragged Spanish: Since you are enemy to the Queenes Majestic, Don Martin, I must ask you to render yourself to me, and in sooth, Señor, this ship is no safe place. But Don Martin's face went white, and he advanced his sword, and saith he: Señors, I am a true Conquistador. It is not in me to surrender.

Nay, Señor but here is no dishonor, pleadeth Sir Myles. We would but save you from drowning. What is death to one as aged as I? saith Don Martin bitterly. All I have known are gone, and with those who supplant them I have no sympathy. We of the Conquistadors were the last of the true breed.

Of a sudden I took heed to his meaning, and cried out: But, Señor, you are not of those iron men who won Mexico and Peru for the Emperor Charles? He bowed slightly in his turn, and saith he proudly: Señors, I sailed with that most glorious company of caballeros who followed the great Cortes. But think, Señor, protests M. Dawkins, that was seventy years gone by. And your Grace should know that whilst M. Dawkins abode in prison in the city of Mexico the word came hither of the death in the city of Guatemala of one Bernal Diaz, who was of the captains under Cortes and commonly accounted the last of the Conquistadors.

Don Martin frowned eaglewise upon us, and saith he: It is not my custom to permit my word to be questioned. I marched with the Marquis of the Valley as a stripling, and I stand before you, Señors, in the eighty-ninth year the Blessed Jesus hath been pleased to graunt me, and as steadfast against all His enemies as I ever was. And this I will prove upon your bodies if you do not abandon my deck.

The words were yet on his tongue when a giant wave rolled down upon the galleon, and our fishermen in their boat beseeched us that we should come back to them speedily for that the galleon crumbled under the stress of the sea. Ha, by St. George, quoth Sir Myles, we must have an end to debate. Don Martin, come with us you shall, for I owe it to my manhood that you should not drown, as I owe it to my Queen that you become her prisoner. Never, Señors, saith Don Martin. With the which Sir Myles steps toward him, and when Don Martin lungeth feebly Sir Myles putteth aside the stroke with his arm, cometh to handgrips and taketh the sword from him. Here,

Parson, saith Sir Myles, make shift to handle this bodkin the while I unlash the gentleman.

M. Dawkins was the more inclined to obey for the furore of the curses emitted by Don Martin, which, even in the Spanish, were parlous heereing for clerkly ears. There was a stop to them only when the gallant anciount fainted from the turmoil of his rage and the excess of his weariness and hunger, for, as we did later learn, he had not eaten in the space of two days and for a day had not moistened his lips. We bundled him up in an old cloak and made shift to lower him over the galleon's side to our fishermen, and when we had rejoined them they thrust off from her and we rowed back to land, more than a little grateful for our salvacioun, the wind and waves arising again and the poor ship dissolving under their cruel strokes as she were a chemic soluble.

When we reached the land there was a great todo, which Sir Myles quieted, and he bade his serving-folk contrive a litter of pikes, into which we laid Don Martin and carried him kindly up to Friars Minton, Sir Myles his seat, wherein your Grace's royal father was once moved to visit to the continued joy and reverence of this parish, the which could not fail to be mightily stimulated anew did your Grace but deign to honor us by graunting the opportunity to demonstrate our overweening love and loyalty, as we do pray may yet be graunted us. And beside the litter walked Sir Myles, carrying Don Martin his sword, and M. Dawkins, bearing a flask of aqua vitae for administering to the prisoner-invalid did he reveal a disposicioun to consciousness. But what with his age and exceeding weariness, and a flux of evil humours deduced from the same, he remained in the stupour until after we had fetched him withindoors and bedded him; and to say truth, we deemed it likelie he would not awaken in this life, for he was but a skeleton in the body and bore upon him the scars of a ship's company for record of his diligaunce in the warres.

Being assured that we had performed all things possible for Don Martin his comfort, Sir Myles let summon a pair of varlets to furbish his armour and accoutrement, and eke haileth M. Dawkins to lift up the grey sword which stood by the bedfoot, the which M. Dawkins undertaking he did perceive the blade thereof to be scrawled and scratched with divers inscriptions, yea, from the hilt to the point, and lastways in the broader part, two lines of English. Exclaiming thereat, M. Dawkins bore the sword to the window, where, by the sun's light he deciphered these lines in a crude, antique script:

> Grey Maide men haile Mee
> Deathe does not faile Mee.

Above and belowe these was much other lettering in more tongues than M. Dawkins had wit to read: namely, French, Italian, Latin, Greek, Hebrew, and belike, Arabic, not to account those that were but gibberish to his eyes. Of the French lines, one ran somewhat in conformity with the English doggerel above cited, to wit:

> Li Demoyzel griz
> Ma vengence je priz.

And likewise a motto in the Italian dialect of the North, which, being roughly Englished, saith:

> Grey Maids bright Jest
> Giveth good Rest—
> Death Sirs is Best.

But I might quote your Grace a score more, rimes, boasts, signatures, assercriouns of ownership, which must become tedious in the recitacioun. Let this suffice, and it please you. What was most singular in the whole was the manner in which many men of several nations had bechristened the sword the Grey Maiden, a name which could not be surpassed for aptness and sufficiency, since there was that about the dumb steel which did infallibly suggest the clean shapeliness of a green lass. As Sir Myles did testify of his own will, when M. Dawkins drew the sword to his notice, and he decreed likewise that it should

not be sent from the chamber, since, above aught else, there was
the question how it had passed from an English hand to Don
Martin.

Impatient though we was to unravel the skein of the mystery,
we must bide until the morning, for by God's blessing Don
Martin was suffered to sleep so long, rousing a little by times
to accept a sup of aqua vitse and a moiety of broth, but anon
lapsing off into what was akin both to sleep and the stupour of
the phlegmatic ills. But for this I make certain he might never
have told us the tale of the sword, the which is the excuse for
this statement for your Graces eye, for it was the strength he
gained by the enforced rest which restored him to consciousness
in the noon warmth of the new day. And the first word he spake
when we approached his bedside was of the sword.

Señors, saith he, very stately, despite that he lay on his back,
with but a pillow to prop his head, you have not deprived me
in my weakness of that symbol of honour, without which a
caballero must go bare of pride?

If you mean your sword, Don Martin, saith Sir Myles, we
bore it for you because your illness overcame you.

Now, there come a tinge of colour into the old Spaniard's
cheeks, and saith he: I perceive that you are a gentleman of
excellent training, Señor. You will permit that I say this, who
am of an age to be your grandfather. It is not necessary for me
to remind you I did not yield my ship to you nor my sword, but
succumbed in my person to the forces of nature.

Don Martin, saith Sir Myles, bowing very prettily, we carried
you hither for the sake of your health, I trow, and for the ship,
she was demolished by the winds of God. But touching the
sword, which I have here, we do perceive it to be enscribed in
our English tongue, which would imply it came from an English
hand, and you being an enemy, we must make inquiry on that
score, to discover if perchaunce some countryman of ours had
his death by your endeavour and in what circumstaunce it befell.

The anciount shook his head, smiling. Nay, Señor, quoth he,

it may be I have slain Englishmen in fair fight, but this sword I had from him who was the heart's friend of my youth. *He* had it of his mother, who was English and wedded an Hidalgo of Arragon who visited your country in the affair of the marriage of the Princess Catherine to the Prince of Wales. My friend— he was Gonzalo de Almodovar, called el Pulido, for his foppish ways; but a good soldier, oh, yes, a valliant soldier—told me the sword came to him by reason that all the men of his mother's house had perished in your Warres of the Roses. It was hereditary in that house; a knight of the name—let me think, Señors—would it be Stourton of Ringham? Aye, saith Sir Myles, there was a family of that name in Kent. Don Martin nodded courteously. It must be as you say, Señor. Howbeit, a knight of this name fought in Italy with the great condottiere, Hawkwood, and there won the sword for them. They prized it highly; my friend parted with all else when poverty overtook him in Old Spain, but the sword he treasured as his honour. He was used to say it was the oldest sword in the world, that it had shed more blood than we in all our battles in Mexico and that he who wielded it might not die by steel. Nay, I know not if that be true, but he did not die by steel, nor shall I, who received it from him in death.

Sir Myles laid the sword upon the coverlet, and Don Martin's fingers folded eagerly around the worn grooves of the hilt. There, Señor, saith Sir Myles, do you win strength from the feel of it. There is naught like a sword in the hand to banish evil humours. But Don Martin smiled upon us very mournful, yet withal as one who hath no foreboding. Señors, saith he, I am a dying man as I lie here. The spark of the soul flickers low; and indeed, I am ready to go, who have outlived my time. For Spain is dying, even as I am. He shuddered, and lay still a moment, and M. Dawkins took thought to divert his mind, saying: You have hinted at a brave story, Illustrious Señor. Would it please you to recite for us such details as linger in your memory? If it doth not tire—

Don Martin broke in upon me, smiling again, this time with

a kind of pranksomeness, truly marvellous in one of his yeeres. Tush, Señors, saith he, you would turn me from the corridor that leads to death. It may not be. I am past-due for my stint in Purgatory. Yet I take your efforts in good part. You are noble enemies. Aye, you English are such a race as we Spaniards were a century gone. Pray to God that you will not burn out as have our people. His face clouded, but presently he continued: I never thought to see a Spanish Armada harried by a handful of Englishmen like a xiquipil of Zapotecans being flailed by a score of lances. Aye, that was how it looked, Señores. It was such a sea-battle as we Conquistadors often fought on land when we had to make head with hundreds against tens of thousands. There was honour for you in it, but for Spain there was only disgrace. And I am too good a Spaniard to wish to live in disgrace. Let me die unbeaten, for I can still say that I, Martin Alonzo de Vireflores, never lowered my colours or tendered my sword to any foeman, Christian or heathen.

That can you, Don Martin, quoth Sir Myles. And M. Dawkins, proffering a glass of aqua vitas, saith to him for diversion again: You lie here, sword in hand, Señor, Sir Myles your squire of the body and I ready to be steward, major domo or eke chaplain, and you can support the ministracions of a heretic. He laughed heartily thereat. Ha, Englishman, saith he, you are a priest for the field, such a one as Fra Olmedo, who went throught the warres with us. Christ's Splendour, our priests have gone the way of the laity—whiners and drivelers, fit for naught save the shriving of Indian converts. Pah, I need none of them. I have fought for the Lord God my life long, and if my soul is spotted I will trust to His justice, rather than any shaveling's mumbled prayers.

Now, at this both Sir Myles and M. Dawkins fell alaughing, for twas mighty comical, and M. Dawkins saith to Don Martin afresh: We be all three men who have adventured widely, albeit I am but a clerk. Prithee, Señor, if it likes you, tell us the story of your sword. Nay, that I can not do, answers he, for I know not the whole of it. But Sir Myles exclaims thereat: You know how it came to you, Don Martin. And Don Martin nodded his head very slowly, as one who hath a swift rush of memories. I do, saith he, I do.

For a spell we were all of us quiet, and the booming of the waves on the shore came in the windows and the wailing of the seabirds. So be it, saith he, of a sudden. I will tell you, Señors. Being honourable men, it will please you. And afterward— But we will speak of that later. Sit, I pray you. And you, priest, keep your flask handy. I hear the beating of death's wings, and I would finish what I undertake, so let me not pass until I am through.

This, then, your Grace, is his story, as told to Sir Myles and M. Dawkins the whole of the afternoon, being the day next following All Hallowes, as afore cited:

You must know, Señors, I was born a younger son of an honourable Hidalgo, resident in the district of Segovia, in Old Castile, whose estate was measureably curtailed by the terminacion of the warres with the Moors under the auspices of those glorious sovereignes, Ferdinand and Isabella. When I had attained the age of eighteen yeeres, my militarie education being complete, my father called me to him, and presenting me with a thousand crowns, notified me that must be the sum of his charitie towards me. In common with most youths in my situation at that period, I took thought to achieve my fortune in the Indies, and sailing from Palos about the beginning of the yeere 1518, landed at St. Jago, in Cuba, to find the Governor, Velasquez, and a distinguished Hidalgo, Hernando Cortes, a settler in the Island and son of a worthy family of Medellin in Estremadura, beating up for recruits for an expedicioun to the land of Mexico, beyond the great Gulph of that name, which was reputed to be the seat of a mighty nation of Indians, who dwelt in houses of stone and mined gold as we Spaniards mined iron.

It is not necessary for me to detail to you, Señors, the attraction of such an enterprise for a youth in my circumstaunces. Nor have I the breath to narrate to you the numerous details of our setting forth, of the earlier battles we fought, of our march through hostile nations numbering millions of savages and across stupendous mountains, traversing the extremes of heat and cold, to the splendid capital of the Emperor Montezuma, as kindly and wise a monarch, if his supersticious be put aside, as any that ever lived. This city, which we Spaniards now call Mexico, but which the Aztecs denominated Tenochtitlan, was of a bigness greater than Venice and situate in much the same manner, amidst the waters of a lake in a pleasant vale surrounded by mountains, capped with snow, as fair a site as the Lord God ever established for a peoples pride and wellbeing. And it was ornamented with innumerable palaces, and spacious and lofty temples, wherein were celebrated the bloody rites of those false gods the Blessed Jesus sent us to destroy.

For look you, Englishmen, it is not to be argued that we Conquistadors had the assistance of the Lord God, and His Son, our Lord Jesus, not to speak of the Blessed Virgin, the Intercessor, for valliant though we were, and tireless, not otherwise might we have wrought such deeds, who came ashore in this strange land but six hundred souls, counting the mariners who entered our ranks after we destroyed the fleet. Six hundred in all, and few of us armed in steel. For myself, I know, I was glad of a casque to my head; my body was protected by a quilted cotton coat; and for arms I had sword and shield. And most were in like case. Sixteen possessed horse and lance; thirteen had musquets, thirty-two crossbows. Of the remainder less than half carried pikes. Our artillery was ten brass guns and four falconets. And this was the force that marched into Mexico, took captive the Emperor Montezuma, held his capital in subjekcion, and wrung from the Aztecs in this very dawn and prelude of the Conquest treasures amounting to upwards of a million crowns in gold and precious jewels.

All this had we achieved, with the death of many of our comrades, in battle and by sickness, when word came from the coasts that the Governor Velasquez had been stirred by jealousy to dispatch from Cuba a second, and far mightier armament, under one Pamphilio Narvaez, of whom no more need be said than what the Italian Dante wrote of Ugolino in Hell, that we will pass him in silence and afar-off. Narvaez landed at our port of St. Juan de Ulua, with 1400 men, including no less than eighty cavalry and one hundred and sixty musqueteers and crossbowmen. They had twenty cannon, and more armoured soldiers than our entire company. Narvaez announced to all, Spaniards and Indians, that he was come to supplant Cortes, and declared war upon us, with fire, sword and free rope, aye, as though we were infidel Moors.

But we of the first Conquistadors were not men to be frightened like children by tales told in the dark. Cortes gave Pedro de Alvarado eighty-three men, with four cannon, to hold our quarters in Tenochtitlan, guard Montezuma and keep the city in awe, and with the remainder, two hundred and six in all, he marched out to baffle Narvaez. It is better to die at once than to die dishonoured, Señors, saith he, and we agreed with him. So we marched back over the mountains, with the beard always upon the shoulder, as the saying is, for we never knew when we might be attacked. But by God's grace we came unharmed to the coast, and were joined by Don Gonzalo de Sandoval, with seventy men of ours who had sufficed to keep the Indians of this vicinitie in subjekcion, so that now we numbered two hundred and seventy-six.

From Sandoval we learned that Narvaez had taken up his quarters in the town of Cempoal, and thither we marched, as secretly as we might contrive. I remember, Señors, the night was dark and rainy, such rain as is only to be encountered in those low coastlands, where the heat is as fierce as in Algiers. We had intelligaunce of our spies how that Narvaez was lodged in the quadrangle of the temple, his guns arrayed in a line along the temple's front; and Cortes set aside my company, under an active lad named Pizarro, a bastard cousin of his, as I have heard tell, who was then as little known as Peru, to seize upon these guns at the first rush. So we stepped off into the rain, each holding to the belt of the man before him, for we could not see one another. Our countersign was Spiritu Santo, Spiritu Santo.

That of Narvaez was Santa Maria, Santa Maria, which we knew from our aforesaid spies.

Our company was in the lead, and as we came through the street to the temple we heard the alarm being shouted. Pizarro bade us charge lances, and our drummer beat up, and we advanced so swiftly that the artillerymen could put the matches to but four of their guns, which slew three of us; the rest we seized and turned about to bear upon the temple, but we dared not fire them, lest we harm our own people. And Pizarro bade us march on to aid Sandoval's company, who were fighting to climb the steps of the Teocali, or pyramid, whereon were the altars at a great height above the ground, and where, likewise, Narvaez had his position.

This was as blind a struggle as ever I was in, betwixt the darkness, the rain and the confusion of the two parties. Sandoval had just been forced down the temple steps when we reached him, and now he charged a second time, swords rattling and pikes thrusting, our people shouting Spiritu Santo, Spiritu Santo, Victory for Cortes, the while our enemies cried Santa Maria for Narvaez, Santa Maria for Narvaez. It seemed that we might not make head against the weight of numbers opposed to us, but in the midst of the combat Narvaez screamed out, in agony: Santa Maria assist me. They have killed me. They have struck out my eye.

Señors, I am not one to boast; but I was neere by him in our front rank, and so soon as I heard him, I shouted in my turn: Victory for the Spiritu Santo. Narvaez is dead. Victory for Cortes. And at once the pressure of the foe weakened; they commenced to yield to us, and we pressed them upward, step by step, until we had attained the summit of the Teocali, where they sought refuge in the house of stone, which had been the adoratory of the idols. Here, again, they were in the stronger position, for the doors and windows were easily defensible, and it was difficult in the rain to distinguish comrade from foe. But we pressed our attack vigourously, and in the maindoor I crossed swords with him who was to be my friend.

We fought blind, as I have said, but I knew my antagonist for a master swordsman. His blade was uncanny in its percepcioun of my purpose. It was as if it had human eyes that pierced the blustery darkness. However I cut or thrust, it was ready for me, aye, more than ready. I slashed for my foeman's head in an unguarded moment, and his blade slipped under mine and ran me through the shoulder. I fell forward, and as I did so, one Martin Lopez, a shipman, who was of our party, and a very sturdy fellow, withal, climbed upon the roof of the building and set the thatch afire. The which inspired the people of Narvaez with a gross fear, so that they began to cast down their arms and cry for quarter; and our people, being able to see their way, ran in at them with a boldness which did the rest.

For myself, I got to my feet, sword in hand, and made a pass at the youth opposite me; but he laughed in my face, saying: Nay, Señor, you are in no case to push this bicker, if you would, and for that matter neither am I, seeing my friends are yielding themselves and Señor Narvaez is become a cock without spurs. Señor, saith I, then, tottering on my feet, for I was nigh as weary as I am lying here in death's presaunce, one of two things you must do: fight on or surrender to me. With that he carefully wiped his sword on a body at his feet, sheathed it and bowed most courteouslie. Why, Señor, saith he, I will even surrender. I leaned against the wall, heedless of what went on around me. You are my prisoner, I told him. Give me your sword. But he slapped his hand on its hilt, and answered quickly: Nay, nay, Señor, that I may not do. This sword is my honour. I yield it not while I have life. If you insist I will fight on, but by your leave with other foemen, seeing that you are wounded and unsteady.

Now, a rage possessed me, and I flourished my sword, and cried to him: It must be that you fear me. He flushed and named himself very quietly, and his parentage, and when he had done this, he added: And if, when you have recovered, Señor, you are still of a mind to question my courage I will fight you, but I must warn you that the man doth not live who may resist this sword with steel. For there is a property abiding in it, by virtue of which it can not be overcome by kindred metal.

I looked at him as well as I might, for the growing dimness of my sight, and saw him to be of about my own age, a dark stripling, with cool grey eyes, he had them from his English mother, I suppose; they were of the same hue as his sword, Señors, save that at times they warmed with affection. What I would have said to him, then, I do not know; but as we stood in the door Cortes brushed by us, the sweat streaming down his face, his armour streaked with mud, his sword bloody in his hand. And he called out in a high, thin voice, as of one fatigued: What is become of Narvaez? How is Narvaez? To which Sandoval answered from the temple's interior: Here he is, very safe. And Narvaez, himself, groaned from a corner: Prithee, Señor Cortes, in God's name, send me my surgeon, Master Juan, for my eye is beaten out.

Cortes stared at the corner in some surprise, for despite the flames from the dampened thatch the light was none too bright; and saith he presently: It shall be done. And added curtly: Son Sandoval, keep good watch upon him and his captains. This hath been a sore night's work. No man can know what I have gone through. And he turned with out more ado to pass out, but in the door he saw me, and paused a moment, for—and I say it without vanity, Señors—he had an affection for me, asking: What is this, Son Martin, (So he called all of us young lads, whatever our rank) are you wounded? I made endeavour to salute him, and would have fallen as I stood, but that my enemy caught me in his arms. He is wounded by my hand, Señor Cortes, saith Gonzalo. But I will make amends for that when next you lead us to battle. Cortes regarded the two of us, pulling at his beard, and quoth he: By my conscience (that was his one oath), if I can bring all of Narvaez his people to your mind, Señor, I will not despair of the future. Gonzalo bowed, and saith he: Most men would rather follow the lion than the jennet. Now, the groans of Narvaez, in his corner, were not unlike the braying of an ass, so a snicker arose from those who had been lately our enemies, and several cried out in approval of Gonzalo's speech. Cortes bowed to them shortly. He who is loyal to me I am loyal to, he answereth, and strode off to terminate the fighting in the inner courts.

That was the last of Narvaez. Him we imprisoned at Villa Rica, on the seacoast, and all his men we took into our army, so that Cortes had now such an armament we deemed ourselves competent to complete the conquest we had begun. Alas, Señors, how little doth a man comprehend of God's inscrutable purpose. It is well said that he who rides high falls far.

But I am diverting from my tale, the which I have but scant time to conclude for you. For I am no longer as I was in those days, able to be up and about the day after a sword had gone through my shoulder. Ha, what cared we for wounds, we Conquistadors? We counted him lucky who had no more than one in a single combat. But I will not seem to lack gratitude, so I must demolish my hardihood to the extent of admitting Gonzalo would not suffer me to undertake any endeavour which he might perform. Why do you serve me? I asked him, mighty annoyed after two days of his ministracions. You are no page, and I have marched my six leagues a day and fought a pitched battle, with a hole as big as this prick in me. He smiled in a light, whimiscal way, which was all his own. To say truth, Martin, quoth he, I have a kindness for you.

It was the first time he called me by name, the first time we spoke to each other, save as Señor. Ah, me. The ache in my heart. I remember I blushed like a nun. Señor, saith I, and then, thinking better of it, Gonzalo, there were certain words betwixt us the night— Put them from your mind, saith he. It is not for friends to poke steel into one another. What could I say? I swaggered a little, hinted my sword boasted no magic qualities, yet had let its share of blood. He smiled, and would not take offence. So I yielded to him, putting aside the false pride that bade me resent the wound he had dealt me. Many is the time I have been glad for that since.

Ah, those days, Señors. All too short. But while they lasted we dreamed brave dreams. We should win promotion together. We would take our shares of the gold and buy horses and harness. Cortes should be impressed by our valour, and assign us to conquer a kingdom for ourselves, and there we should rule as twin sovereigns, until we were rested for fresh conquests. Ay de mi, Señors, there is nothing like youth. Nothing like the first glory of youth, nothing like the first friendship of youth.

Everyone in Cempoal had his dreams, for the matter of that, from Cortes down to the pages. We made no doubt the land was as good as ours. But it is rightly said that the wheel of fortune maketh sudden turns, evil following closely upon good. We were still licking our wounds when a message came from Alvarado, in Tenochtitlan, notifying Cortes how the Indians had risen in insurreckcioun and besieged him in his quarters. Sad news for us, Señors. But Cortes was not one to temporize with fate. Allowing for the coast garrisons, he mustered thirteen hundred men, one hundred of them cavalry and one hundred and sixty musqueteers and crossbowmen, and so we returned to Mexico, who had quit it two hundred and six, reckoning the fifer and drummer.

In Tlascala we recruited a complement of 2,000 native auxiliaries, and then pushed on by forced marches, and on the day of San Juan in June of 1520 re-entered Tenochtitlan. They who had come with Narvaez were all agog over the beauty and stateliness of the city, but we veterans had eyes only for the sullen looks of the Indians. It was plain to us their earlier respect was become hatred, and we were not surprised that the insurreckcioun broke forth again, more virulent and bitter than before. Blessed Saints, Englishmen, was there ever such fighting? I heard men say, who had fought in the Low Countries, in Italy and with the Turks, that they had never seen the like.

In the commencement of the struggle we sallied out each day, and fought in the streets; but it did not seem to matter how many thousands we slew, and wherever we moved we were covered by sheets of arrows, lances, and stones. We fought our way one day to the Great Temple on the square they called the

Taltelulco; we slashed through the hordes that filled the courts and swarmed over the Teocali, and burned the shrine and over-turned certain of their idols. But to what purpose? It was all we could do to hew a path back to our quarters. Cortes swore it was not worth the price. He made Montezuma mount our battlements, and cry to his people to let us leave the city in peace, and they slew their Emperor for our friend.

By the Mass, Señors, if we were not afraid, yet we understood that this was no place for us. For we were short of provisions and water, our gun powder was exhausted, and we were ringed about in the heart of this hostile city, where almost every house was a fortress, and a web of canals shut off one quarter from another. Moreover, the only escape from the city to the main-land was over one of three causeways, each of which was broken at three or four intervals by bridges, and we knew that these bridges had been removed. Surely, never men were in more evil case than we.

But Cortes had a remedy for every ill. He directed our ship-wrights to construct a portable bridge, and he issued orders to the captains to have all the men ready to march at midnight of the next night. For as I have said he was not one to lose time. But when the news reached the soldiers they raised a clamour for the treasure we had acquired, which was in Cortes his keeping; and he, nothing loath, had it fetched into the great saloon of the palace which was our quarters—did I say that it had been the palace of Montezuma his father?—and there he bade, first, the King's fifth be set aside, after which he told the soldiers they might help themselves as they chose.

Ah, Señors, that treasure was the death of scores of our com-rades, notably of those foolish fellows who had come with Narvaez, and who could think of nothing but the joy of pos-sessing gold in bars. They loaded themselves down with the precious metal, where we veterans, who had some concepcioun of the night which was confronting us, either dipped spar-ingly into the heap or else took naught. I remember, Gonzalo came to me in the courtyard, where I sat mending the arrow-slits in my cotton coat, and saith he, very gayly: Come, Martin, and let us take that gold which will buy us the horses and harness we require. Nay, nay, amigo, I told him, that gold will be a weight upon your back, when the Indians are chopping at us with their two-handed swords. We will buy one of the Tlascalans to carry it, saith he. Not even that, quoth I. Cortes hath decreed that eighty of them, and the lame horses, shall be reserved to carry the King's fifth. Every other Indian and horse must bear his share of the fighting.

So Gonzalo was guided by me, and contented himself with a handful of calchihuas. I am glad that it was so. Otherwise— But I go too fast. What is the proverb? A lame goat takes no siesta.

A little before midnight all the preparations had been completed. Martin Lopez and his shipmen had built a bridge of stout timber, which was carried by four hundred of the Tlascalans; one hundred and fifty of our soldiers were detailed to guard it. Sandoval and a group of caballeros, with one hundred infantry, were the advance guard; Alvarado commanded the rear guard of one hundred and fifty, all picked men—and do not accuse me of vain-glory, Señors, when I say that Gonzalo and I were amongst them. Betwixt these two bodies was a long line of artillery, baggage, Tlascalan auxiliaries, prisoners, and foot-soldiers. Most of the cavalry rode with Cortes, who held himself in readiness to act as a reserve, lending his aid wherever it was required.

How silent was the great city as we mustered in the courtyard. We had difficulty in believing that at sunset the air had rung with shouts and whistles and the blasts of horns, that the sky had been clouded by the deluge of missiles hurled upon us. Now, it was as if we were alone in a wilderness. Not a cry nor a curse from the multitudes of our enemies. And to our considerable satisfaction, as we were about to open the gates, a gentle rain commenced to fall, obscuring the light of the stars and covering the city with a mist, which rendered the darkness denser than it had been the night of the attack upon Narvaez in Cempoal. Gonzalo reminded me of this, as we finally received the word for the rearguard to march. It is Cempoal over again, saith he, and no less Cortes his night. And so it seemed. We stole out the gate, and traversed a street littered with the corpses of that day's assaults. We turned into another street; we followed the embankment of a canal; almost we might see the approach to the causeway ahead of us. A messenger from Cortes rode up to acquaint Alvarado that Sandoval, the baggage, the King's treasure, the artillery and a portion of the infantry had passed the first breach in the causeway; we were bidden to stand fast, until the bridge was ready to be taken up.

What said I? quoth Gonzalo. I opened my mouth to answer him, and an Indian howled the alarm in the canal by which we stood. Señors, before a man might straighten his helmet the night became hideous with noises. Horns blew, men shouted and whistled, and of a sudden, from the Teocali of the Great Temple came the boom of the monster drum of serpents skins, which the priests were used to beat to announce their sacrifices. Never heard I aught like this drum; the sound of it carried two leagues, and it was so doleful, so threatening, so loud, that we shivered only to hear it. The bravest man could not help asking of himself: Ha, will it be beating soon for me?

The column surged forward by instinct, men treading fast on one anothers heels. Lights flared up in the rain; we had glimpses of savage faces, stones clanged on our morions, arrows and lances whistled through the ranks. A man sank wounded, sobbing a plea not to be left to have his heart torn out on the altar of their War God; we lifted him, and ran on for the bridge, jostling and tripping, in danger from our own weapons in the press. Faster, men called. Make way, comrades, let us get forward.

We were so close that we could see the blank space by the bridge where the buildings came to an end, and as a gust of rain blew over the lake we heard a brisk racket of hoofs, the squeal of a frightened horse. Shouts and cries drifted back to us. Men called warnings against the horses. Men who were trampled under the hoofs screamed with pain. And there was a crash like the breaking of a ship's mast. Señors, we knew what it meant. We knew without being told. The bridge had broken under the stress of the horses passage. But no man was willing to stop for that, and the pressure continued from the rear of the column, until Alvarado and a few of us forced a halt by useing cold steel on several of Narvaez his men.

Slow, lads, slow, shouted Alvarado. You drive your comrades into the water. Give them time. Face out, face rear. Here come the heathen devils. Ready, pikemen. Slow.

Ah, there was a gallant caballero, Englishmen. He and his cavalry charged back along the way we had come to scatter the first attack, and that gave us time to array the infantry in order. The Indians were coming on us from every side, from the houseroofs, from the streets, from the canals, from the lake. We dared not think of what was happening ahead. The screams, the moans, the clattering of steel, the thud of bodies falling, splashes in the water, horses crying almost like men. Afterward we saw for ourselves: a new bridge was being built, a bridge of dead men and horses, of cannon, of baggage packs and chests.

Some of us passed that bridge, but not many. The Indians struck us like tidal waves of human flesh. They rolled out of the mist in a flood that never diminished, and they cared naught for their own lives, if they might snatch a Spaniard alive for their altars. We slew, and slew. Our arms ached from slaying, our sword-hilts were slippery with blood. Gonzalo made himself captain over thirty or forty of us who fought in a group, and he was always in front to meet every rush. Use the point, lads, saith he. Stab through, and recover. Always the point. Shields up for Spain.

But it was all to no avail. Alvarado and his cavaliers had their horses slain under them, one by one. One by one, our company was reduced, as we retired, a step at a time, toward the gap in the causeway where the bridge had fallen. And Señors, the worst of our plight was that we knew retirement gained us no respite, for up ahead the column was beset no less viciously than were we of the rear-guard. All the way across the lake, the length of the causeway, we could hear the trumpets and whis-tles of the Indians, as their Princes rallied them to the attack. And if we passed this first bridgeless gap, how should we pass the next two?

Some men cried it was useless to fight, and leaped into the water or went mad, and ran amongst the enemy to wreak what harm they might. Alas, poor lads, most of them felt the yoke of the sacrificial-stone on their necks before the week was out. But all of the veterans, and the greater portion of Narvaez his men, fought like honourable caballeros, defiant of odds, refus-ing to despair. After a while, too, Alvarado and a few of his horsemen joined us, and their long lances and half-armour were a vast help.

But not Alvarado, himself, wrought braver deeds that night than my Gonzalo. Ho, Señors, the blood quickens in me as I think of him, his glance so cool, so watchful; his shield poised at an angle to catch the blows of the Indians two-handed swords, edged with keen obsidian that bit like steel; his grey blade flickering before him, tireless, unfailing. It was he who held us together, when all about we heard the groans of the dying, and men crying upon the Holy Virgin and San Jago as they were drowned or trampled upon or carried off in the Indians canoes to the sacrifice.

It was he bade us make haste slowly. Why hasten? saith he. He who runs may stumble. My sword is betwixt you and the savages, lads. She is thirsty, is my Grey Maiden. Give her chance to drink. And when Alvarado threw himself into our ranks, his horse having been killed, Gonzalo cried to us: See, the captain prefers walking to riding. And this, Señors, with the Indians clutching at him as he talked. Don Pedro, Alvarado, laughed, saying: Not many fight as well as they jest; but if I had this to do again the lad should be on my righthand.

Thanks to him, thanks to my Gonzalo, I say, eighty of us reached the bridge of the dead, a mound that writhed and wriggled the breadth of the canal, a man's height beneath the level of the causeway. We wondered how we should cross it.

The Indians canoes were crowded against it, bow to bow; they were running back and forth upon it, howling and dancing; and our people on the opposite brink were more intent upon fleeing than waiting to help us pass over.

Alvarado cast a swift glance about him. Down, all of you, saith he, save Viraflores and el Pulido. Sweep the passage clean, and climb the other side. And this time, haste.

They obeyed him with a right goodwill, for sooth to say, no man had thought ever to win this far. As for us three, who bided where we stood, we had no leasure for refleckcioun. We must cover a causeway eight ells wide, and that was one time I was glad I had no steel to my back. Gonzalo and I fought with the sword; Alvarado used his lance, thrusting with the point, reversing betimes to batter at his foes with the butt, and it becomes me to say that albeit he wore half-armour he was as lively as we two. A lusty captain, Don Pedro. God rest his soul.

In the midst of our play come a shout from our comrades, notifying us they were across, and Alvarado jerked an order from the corner of his mouth: Leap for it, you two. But Gonzalo shook his head. Nay, Captain, there are three of us, saith he. Leap, young fool, snarled Alvarado. I come after you. Gonzalo laughed. So be it, Martin, saith he, if it was not for the acolytes, the Bishop would have a poor train.

We turned together, and sprang down on the quaking mass that bridged the canal. Our comrades had swept it clean, but they were encompassed by fresh hordes of savages upon the far brink of the causeway, and seizing advantage of their predicament, canoes came paddling in from either side to cut us off, torches ruddying the night. We had gained the abutment of the causeway, which was as high as I could reach with my fingers, when a clamour of surprise burst from the Indians; and we looked back to see Alvarado running toward the brink of the canal, as if he would leap down to us, but instead, he dropped the point of his lance to the bridge and vaulted up and out, soaring high over our heads to alight easily on the causeway above us. That is what men called the Leap of Alvarado, and to this day, Señors, the bridge over that canal is named the Bridge of the Leap of Alvarado.

But we who witnessed the deed took no thought of fame. Alvarado drew the lance to him, propping it against the abutment, and cried that we should climb it. Gonzalo gave me a push. Up with you, Martin, saith he. Nay, you first, amigo, I denied. Alvarado cursed us both. Here is no occasion for punctilios, quoth he. Climb, or I leave you.

But Gonzalo turned his back upon us, flourishing his sword at the Indians who were jumping from the causeway we had quitted. Martin, you have a green wound in your shield-shoulder, saith he. What would you have done, Señors? I climbed the lance. If I waited longer to argue it seemed that we must be trapped. Up, Gonzalo, I cried. And Alvarado added his command. I am with you, Señors, said Gonzalo, very debonair. And he made a little charge at the savages, then spun on his heel and ran toward us. In his path was the snout of a cannon that projected above the wreckage; he leaped from it, sword in hand, and landed beside us, scarce out of breath.

Two ways of skipping a gutter, Don Pedro, saith he. Alvarado swore at him, and tossed a gold chain, what we called a fanfarona, around his neck. No more of that, springald, bade the Captain. This is not fun. Nay, it begets wealth, saith my Gonzalo, grinning.

We set off, without more ado, to rejoin the body of our people, who had gone on a matter of a ship's length; but of a sudden there was a din of horns, and hundreds of Indians rose out of canoes to right and left, their missiles as thick as the rain which smote us with the full force of the wind off the lake. We made attempt to run, but the savages gained the causeway before we could catch up our comrades, and we must slow to a walk, stabbing and thrusting desperately for dear life, Alvarado in front, Gonzalo and I guarding the rear, the red demons so close about us that we could smell them and the blood of their wounds spurted in our faces.

Help, comrades, shouted Alvarado. Will you let us perish, who held the bridge for you? The rearguard steadied, and men cried to us to bide their coming. But it was one thing to promise help, and another task to deliver it. Alvarado was known to many of the Indians, Tonatio they named him because of his handsomeness, and they kept shouting to one another: Let us take Tonatio, brothers. Here is Tonatio for the catching.

So they fought with a determinacion even beyond their wont, streaming in betwixt us and our relief. Yet, despite their effort, they might not resist the good swords of our comrades, and presently the clang of steel was in our ears, and hearty Spanish oaths and the stamping of booted feet. We deemed ourselves all but saved, but to the Indians this was a summons to a final endeavour, and they hurled themselves upon us, heedless how they died, aye, Señors, clutching at our swords that they might hinder us the while others strove with clubs to stun us. It was thus they brought me down, a man rushing upon my sword, taking the blade in his belly to the hilt, and one behind him beating at my shield, so that I lost my footing and fell prone.

Santa Maria, I sweat to remember it. They were dragging me away when Gonzalo came to my rescue, slashing and thrusting himself a path with all the cunning that lies in this blade beside me. You smile, perhaps, Señors, you think an old man wanders in his mind. Ah, you should see Grey Maiden in action. Never was there such a sword. Set me upon my feet, now, my back to a wall, the sword in my hand, and I will meet any six men you send against me, aye, old as I am, dying withal.

But this is not my story. Nay, nay, not my story—Gonzalo's. There we were, the savages ringing us, I on the ground, Gonzalo hacking a space to permit me to rise. Behind him Alvarado had joined the rearguard, and was leading them on to free us. But too slowly, alas, too slowly. He could only achieve so much, my Gonzalo. I staggered up to help him as a two-handed blade of obsidian flakes crashed under his raised sword-arm into his unguarded side.

He looked surprised in the flaring torchlight, peered down

a moment at the red tide that gushed from the hole in his cotton jack-coat and handed Grey Maiden to me. She is yours, Martin, saith he. God aid you to your kingdom. And in a breath he was lying on the causeway where I had lain, and I was standing over him as he had stood over me, a sword flashing in each hand—for I cast away my shield to accept Grey Maiden.

I remember Alvarado shouting in my ear, plucking at my arm. I remember a press of friendly bodies about me, Spanish voices argueing, urging me. They must have persuaded or compelled me away, for next I have a dim recolleckcioun of interminable fighting along the causeway, hurried flights, brief stands, charges which left us with constantly diminished ranks. There were Indians in front of us and behind us, and Indians scrambling out of canoes on either flank. I know the men on each side of me were snatched for the sacrifice as we passed the second gap in the causeway over another mound of dead men and animals and discarded artillery. Why I was not taken I do not know, Señors. I did not care. Life meant nothing to me. Mayhap it was the sword. For Alvarado told Cortes that but for me he might never have gone farther than the second canal. The lad fought like an angel, saith he, his sword was everywhere.

I do not remember the passage of the third canal at all, but men say that here again there was a heap of corpses and baggage to scramble across. The first thing I do remember is the light of a murky dawn under the walls of Tacuba at the causeway's end, and a little knot of horsemen, with Cortes at their head, coming to meet us. Sandoval was there, and De Oli, and Salcedo, and Lares, and De Morla, a few more. Sandoval's arms were red to the elbow, and the tears fell from Cortes his eyes.

Is this all of you, Son Pedro? saith he. I looked around stupidly when he spoke, and I saw that we who were with Alvarado were but seven, and eight of the Tlascalans, and all of us wounded sorely.

We are all who are left, Don Hernando, saith Alvarado sadly. There is not a Christian soul alive upon the causeway.

Ah, Blessed Jesus, what a sad night, cried Cortes. There are not five hundred of us, nor a thousand of the Tlascalans. We lack powder for the musquets and arrows for the crossbows. I know not what to do.

Perhaps I was mad, Señors, and whether or no, it was not like me to be forward, for I was a quiet-spoken lad; but I shoved myself to the front and waved the sword Grey Maiden in our captain's face. We have our swords, quoth I. My Gonzalo gave me this blade, dying that I might not be tooken for the sacrifice. Shall we betray such as he by weeping because the Lord God hath chastised us for our sins? And thereat Cortes smote his thigh so the cuisses rang, and saith he: Son Martin, Son Martin, I am well rebuked. The women in Castile have bred soldiers before this, and they will continue to breed soldiers for the King, though all of us perish on the altars of these heathen gods. If it be God's will, we shall return to bridle this wicked race.

All the others applauded him. We have achieved so much we must conquer, saith Alvarado. And Sandoval saith: Aye, so it shall be, Señors. But now let us march for Tlascala, and tend our wounds, and abide the coming of more companions from Cuba. Cortes said this should be done, and when we had rested somewhat and made arrows for the crossbows, we set forth again. But of what followed, and of how on the third day we did battle with all the hosts of Mexico and Tezcuco and Salto-can, hosts that covered the plains and the hills until the eye wearied with watching them, of all this, I say, and of our return to Mexico in December, and of the deeds we wrought then, I may not speak, Englishmen, for my strength ebbs with every breath.

I have told you how the sword came to me. More I cannot tell, save that it hath carved me whatever of fortune I won in a long life. In Mexico all the Conquistadors knew it as if it was one of themselves; they talked of it, and its properties, as they did of the brave horses with which our caballeros rode down the heathen ranks. It is more than cold steel, this blade, Señors.

Aye, there is life in it, if not a soul. I think sometimes the spirits of all the valliant men who used it in their seasons have entered into the fabrick of its metal, tautening it, hardening it, teaching it the craft and wiliness of battle. Cortes called it the Sword of the Conquest; he and a certain priest would have hung it over the altar of the Cathedral we built in Mexico where the Great Temple had stood on the Taltelulco. I was Master of the Horse to him in those days, the days of his greatness, when he was Marquis of the Valley, an uncrowned King. But I would not yield the sword to him and the priests.

Nay, nay, I told them, this is no trophy to hang in a church. She hath more work to do, hath my Grey Maiden. Let her follow her bent. There will be brave men after we are gone. What did you say, Don Hernando, that morn after the Sad Night when all seemed lost? He pulled at his beard, which was thin and grey, and saith he: Son Martin, you have me in the armpit. The women of Castile have bred soldiers in the past, and shall again. And later, after we had returned to Old Spain, we sailed to Algiers with the Kings Majestic, and being wrecked, lost all but what we stood in, yet my sword was unharmed; and Cortes spoke of this to many people as being singular and strange. By my conscience, Señors, saith he, this sword serves a purpose.

So it doth, Englishmen. But alas, no more for Spain. For the women in Castile no longer breed the same stock. We Spaniards have had our share of glory. Now other nations shall flourish their little while, as the Lord God directs. You English are heretics, and why He favours you I do not know; but one who has lived as I have for hard on ninety years learns that there is much in life not to be understood. So take the sword when I am sped, Señor Conyers, remembering Grey Maiden is worthy of all honour. She is no camp wench, but a virgin of battle, exceeding proud and undefiled. Aye, and her kiss is death.

MAY IT please your Grace, Don Martin being so far forward in his tale, did grow visibly weak, and M. Dawkins, proffering him a swallow of aqua vitae, he gulped a trifle of the licquor, strove mightily for speech, crying upon Christ His succour, and so died very hearteningly, about sunset. Sir Myles let bury him in a corner of the park, where the old friars of this house were wont to lay their dead, and for that he was a gentleman of a sweet courtesie and noble demeanour, albeit Spaniard and Papist, he was put in the grave decentlie clad, and his armour on, the gentry of these parts attending for mourners. The bodies of his crew were laid in a common grave at his foot.

MYLES CONYERS, *Kt.*

HUMPHREY DAWKINS, B.A.

Richmond, 21st Dec. 1588

For my Lord Burghley:

Let you look deep into this. An arrant, waggle-tongued knave. What hideth he? Conyers may keep this sword, but perchaunce there be treasure in the wreck, and of that I would have accompt in full.

Elizabeth R.

www.ingramcontent.com/pod-product-compliance
Lightning Source LLC
Chambersburg PA
CBHW061514020726
47502CB00006B/2065